LADY OF A THO

*I can remember the b
sirens...*

And how Jason three years before had said to me: "I am going to be killed. They are going to shoot me down in public some day."

"No," I said, "that's ridiculous."

"Is it? There must be a million people who would like to kill me, at least a hundred million more who would enjoy seeing it no matter what they tell you."

"Don't talk about it anymore."

He stared narrowly at me then. "It excites you, too. The widow in black, his living memory. People would never forget you. You'd be more famous than I am...."

Then three years later on that fatal afternoon, he'd fallen into my lap like a sad enormous doll, his head there like a big flower, blooming blood. And the roses, of course, blood and roses, and me wondering why I, too, had not died....

CONFESSIONS OF WESTCHESTER COUNTY

She asked me to kill her husband.

She placed in my left hand the most delicate of lady's revolvers...

"It needs to be done, believe me Luther," she said, "and I think that Harold would agree with this himself because you can't imagine how many times he's come home from that terrible office and said to me that he knows he'd be better off dead. He really wants to die, Luther; there's a lot of guilt mixed in with his cruelty and that's why I can't hate the man. I want to do him a favor. I want to give him this gift of death. But I just don't quite have the strength. Thank God that you do, Luther."

Lady of a Thousand Sorrows

■   ■   ■   ■   ■

Confessions of Westchester County

■   ■   ■   ■   ■

BARRY N. MALZBERG

Stark House Press • Eureka California

LADY OF A THOUSAND SORROWS /
CONFESSIONS OF WESTCHESTER COUNTY

Published by Stark House Press
1315 H Street
Eureka, CA 95501, USA
griffinskye3@sbcglobal.net
www.starkhousepress.com

ISBN: 978-1-944520-61-8

Layout by Mark Shepard, SHEPGRAPHICS.COM
Proofreading by Bill Kelly

First Stark House Press Edition: April 2018

FIRST EDITION

Contents

Lady of a Thousand Sorrows

**BARRY N. MALZBERG
WRITING AS LEE W. MASON**

PROLOGUE
VIVIEN IN SECLUSION AGAIN:
HER FRIENDS AREN'T TALKING
1978 — NEW YORK CITY

Tempestuous Vivien Sarris, recently dubbed by the press "The Lady of a Thousand Sorrows," is off the museum benefit, cocktail party, champagne reception circuit again, and this time, it is rumored, it may be for good. Her friends aren't talking, at least for the record, but this reporter has managed to stalk her way through the steel traps and gates of "no comments" to learn the following.

The lovely former First Lady is terribly shaken by the death of her second husband, multi-billionaire magnate Nicholas Sarris, who died six months ago under mysterious circumstances in Paris. At first, beautiful Vivien tried the "c'est la vie; life goes on" attitude which had served her so courageously and well when Jason Kelly was murdered in Texas, but her sadness and shock were so real that even acquaintances became alarmed at her depression. "Nicholas was her real love," one of them confided to us. "She loved the President, too, but Nicholas, all his money to the contrary, was the real thing, with bells on. She took his death awfully hard. She felt all the light had gone out of her life."

Since March, sensual Vivien has not been seen. Not at the Metropolitan Opera, not at Carnegie Hall, not at the Parke-Bernet galleries or any of the "exclusive" soirees in Manhattan which were once her spring stamping grounds. She even failed to appear at the Fresh Air Fund Ball at the Plaza last month, a favorite charity function which she had not missed even during the years of her marriage to Nicholas, since before the inauguration of the President. Her absence caused some of her friends to become alarmed, convinced that beautiful but brooding Vivien was indeed reacting to the latest tragedy in her stormy life in a way that she had reacted to no other, leading one of her friends to speculate that "she's had so much pain that she may not be able to bounce back."

Rumors of her current whereabouts abound, but no one is talking for the record. Some outside sources think that she may have had a genuine nervous breakdown, while others pooh-pooh this, reminding this reporter of Vivien's great strength during crises, speculating that she is merely in seclusion preparing for the next chapter in the stormiest and most dramatic woman's life of our time.

Adding spice to the rumors is the well-known fact of the falling-out between Carrie Sarris, only daughter of the multi-billionaire shipping magnate, and Vivien shortly after Nicholas' funeral, when a very public scene occurred to the embarrassment of both at the gravesite. The rivalry between these two attractive women, rooted in their battle for the heart of the deceased multi-billionaire, is well-known, but there was an open break at the time of the death and there are those who see some connection between Vivien's retirement from public life and the fact that Carrie herself has not been seen in the establishments which she used to patronize on the Continent.

Perhaps both of these glamorous women share a deep and terrible grief which, this reporter can speculate, they might even be sharing in privacy at this time.

But one thing is clear: the destiny of The Lady of a Thousand Sorrows remains as imponderable today as it ever was. Witnesses of her tragic burden, as well as fellow participants in her tempestuous and dramatic life, can only wish her well during her time of spiritual struggle, and they pray that she will emerge, as she always before emerged, beautiful and transcendent!

Josephine von Houten
THE NATIONAL INSIDER

PART I

1
1978 — NEW JERSEY

Blood and roses, yes. I will never forget the blood and roses and will get to them in time. But I must at least start off by being organized. Everything controlled. This is the last promise I made Jane and the only promise of all I made to her that I will keep.

2
1978 — NEW JERSEY

So here I am, here I am on this small estate, with my loyal staff of three, in the farmlands of Edison County just sixty miles from the great city of New York. No horses, thank God. Jane, on her last stay, had them all taken away. It was good for me, if not for her, because I could not bear to deal with them, to deal with my riderless horses. We, the three of us, have been here for months now in what they like to call "seclusion." Annie, Thomas, Mildred and my faithful self, all here. My friends of the press have even lost the trail.

3
1978 — NEW JERSEY

Had she indeed come all the way to New Jersey to kill me? Of course she had. Nothing would have been more in character, even the irony, after all of it, to kill me finally on this ranch surrounded for thirty miles in every direction by stinking swamp and refinery. I went back to my bed and lay there, thinking about this and many other topics of current interest for a long time, of how reasonable it was that at the end it would come down to this; it not only made the most compelling kind of sense, but there was a beauty in it. Looking at it from a distance, which, in a way I am, one could see the beauty in it, if beauty was what one sought: the bitch bringing death to New Jersey like some rare and precious gift. Annie must have led her to me.

I knew that it was Annie. It would have to have been. I have known from the moment that I hired her that Annie would keep my enemies in the closest touch with my whereabouts. But that tickled my sense of irony, just as New Jersey must have tickled the murderess; I did not mind Annie's spying because I had resigned myself to something like this even before she came into my life. How I must have sought death, right up until last night when I saw it! Now all is different of course. Now I will not even make fifty. Events have absolutely overtaken me, and they were closing in. Closing in. How could I not have thought that before one dies one has to be killed? How very silly of me. One cannot live forever in the web of abstraction.

They mean to kill me, I thought. *They mean to kill me*. The man was monstrous; his descendants would have no pity.

"Annie," I said when she came in with the coffee and the needle this morning, "Annie, someone was on the grounds last night." Why doesn't she load the needle with poison and get rid of me that way? I thought incuriously, and then the answer came: Of course they would not do it that way. There would be no satisfaction. *This* way was for pleasure. "Annie, there was someone outside at around midnight."

"I heard nothing," she said. "I would have awakened if there were any visitors. There was no one here at all."

"I saw them."

"Impossible, Vivien. The security, the surveillance, is absolute and Thomas keeps a *very* careful eye on all the alert devices. No one could get through here."

"Someone did. A woman."

"No," she said, competent, thirty-five years of the institution in her voice. She put the tray down with a crash, the coffee spilling in absent little surges over the edges of the cup, deftly turning over the needle, bringing it toward me. "Just relax for this now. You still get so tense."

"I don't want it this morning."

"Certainly you do," she said, "you know you do, dear." Which was true, there is no resisting her or her truths and I felt the thin penetration of that needle, the sense of fusion at the point of impact and then almost immediately the slow flowering, opening. Heroin: it has got to be heroin, although there are certain matters in polite society which are never discussed. Vitamin shots, then.

More calmly I said, "Why are you lying to me?"

"About what, dear?"

"About who was here last night?"

"There was no one here last night."

"Why can't you tell me the truth?"

"You are being told the truth."

"All right," I said. Heroin helps. Heroin helps a great deal. "Forget it then. There was no one. I must have dreamed it, in my sleep that is. There was no one and I imagined all of it."

"That is for sure, Vivien. If there were anyone who had indeed come here the police would have been summoned at once, automatically by the devices. You know that you are perfectly safe."

"Ah," I said, cunning. "Then let us call the police. Let them check."

"Not necessary. No one was here."

"Let them tell us that," I said shrewdly.

"Too much publicity. Once we inform the police, your whereabouts will become known. You know that, Vivien. You know what they'll do to you, once they find you're in Bristol County." She put the needle into a small glass whisked from some fold of her clothing, smiled at me. She is really, in her way, a rather humorous person, Annie, although one has to know her quite well to understand that. "What we're here for is a nice long rest."

"You're all so *elfin* about this. Doesn't anyone take me seriously?"

"Very much so."

"It's diabolical. Just diabolical."

"What is, dear?"

"All of it," I said. "Everything here."

Her face, her large congested face, became sharpened to a series of fine points about her mouth. "This is doing you no good, Vivien. You know that excitement is no good for you, not of this sort."

"I ought to call the police," I said. I had no intention, of course, of doing this. Who would want to call the police? Under the circumstances, matters could become only more disastrous. "Let them tell me there was no one."

"No."

"*You* call them."

"I will do nothing of the sort," she said. "I don't know what's got into you this morning but this is getting us absolutely nowhere. Perhaps you would feel better if you were left to yourself for a while," she said and did something that she had not done before, she must have been quite angry. She left the room, taking away her precious, now-empty vial, but leaving me the coffee. She did not lock the door, however. We have not discussed this subsequently, and of course there is no need to do so, no need whatsoever. One might say that Annie and I have reached a relative impasse.

4
1976 — NEW YORK

Lady of the thousand sorrows he said he did not sound pleased there was no affection in his voice, oh you lady of the thousand sorrows you play on a one-stringed instrument and the string is guilt. No, I said, no that was not it, I never wanted them to feel guilty no it was something else and he laughed, he was always laughing at that time, he had turned to laughter in those last years. You don't know, he said, you simply don't know and I cannot explain, cannot explain to you lady of the thousand sorrows. Is that all you think of me? I said. Yes, that is all I think of you he said but that is enough that is enough that is quite enough for now if not forever.

5
1963 — TEXAS

Give it to them though, give it and be done. This is the stuff they want and they are entitled to have it. Start at beginnings, or perhaps it is middles or ends of which I am speaking. All right, Lady Mac-Beth, let them have it then. Just as I turned and looked at him I could see a piece of his skull, and I remember that it was flesh-colored.

I remember thinking, he just looked as if he had a slight headache and then he sort of put his hand to his forehead and fell into my lap, his head there like a big flower, blooming blood. I remember also right away asking myself why I too had not been killed. Why had it not been both of us? It did not make sense, him dead, me not. I knew of course that he was dead. One can tell about things like this. The car seemed to hang there and only after a very long time did it seem to gather speed again.

And I remember thinking that he just looked as if he had a slight headache and then he began to slide away, slide past my lap too, the roses red in the car, the roses leaping blood. I cannot forget looking at the blood and thinking of the roses. All of us must remember that. If nothing else, we must hold it close; I will never, I will never, I say, permit them to forget this.

Lying in my lap he turned toward me, already dead, his head like that of a sad, enormous doll, pulsing pulpily beneath my hands, his eyes open. He was talking to me, already dead, talking to me on that private level in which his voice moved within me. This is a surprise, Vivien. Such a surprise. Who would have thought that it would have ended so suddenly just when things seemed to be going so well? And, by the way, not to give any offense or to get you angry, but how come you aren't dead too? I don't understand this. I simply do not understand why I am dead and you are alive; there has got to be some awful mistake here. It wasn't supposed to be this way and I cannot understand it at all.

But by that time the car was moving and the movement cut off his voice. I never heard it again. So sorry about that, but it was the last time. When you're dead you're dead, and that's all there is to it; it would be ridiculous for me to claim communication with the dead. That is for mystics. It was his last speech to me. There was a fair amount of pain and I shall never forget his words, so many words out of all the thousands, but it had already happened a long time ago and he had a tendency, unfortunately, he had a tendency to talk too much. Always did. It was something which had happened a long time ago the first time he died.

6
1963 — TEXAS

"Vivien," he said the last night, "Vivien, come here, come here now, I want to touch you, I want it now, want it fast, want it slow, want it hard." Soft. Reaching, touching, clinging, he was always ready for it. Even in our worst times this has to be made clear, he was always ready for it: sex never died between us. This is what I could not stand, more than everything else. It made me feel that somewhere at the center we existed in poison, because I was always able to take him. Even when I hated. Perhaps mostly when I hated. Obsessed with power he was, all of the time. This part of it is true, I would not want to mislead any of you; he was the same way with me as he was on television. He loved to talk, sometimes in bed, about standing them off, about his ability to use the ultimate weapon — not that he would want to of course not that he would ever want to create holocaust, but how about every now and then you had to show the enemy your willingness to do it only so that the fear always existed in the enemy's mind. Sixty million would die in the first strike, and that would be unfortunate but you had to live with the idea of those sixty million, had to face the abyss, he said, because only in that way if you were really willing to do it, only in that way could you be strong enough to make it sure, he thought, that it would never happen. From your willingness to face absolute death, he said, you were able to reaffirm life, and let's fuck. Let's fuck now. That kind of talk excited him.

Sometimes I thought that it was just Jason's sense of humor. It was easy enough to fall into that; you could not believe he was serious, and for a long time I did not but then I saw that he was. He was serious. He was absolutely serious. It must have been the death that excited me in him as well as the passion; to hold him was to hold death and it excited me, I can see this now. And it must have excited him too. He played upon it; he played upon death.

In the car, oh God, in the car I could feel as he fell, brushing against me, the slight wedge of his erection leaning there, comically poking me just after impact, and this seemed so appropriate. I could not keep out of mind the sheer appropriateness of the gesture. It was Jay, it was utterly Jay. He would go out of this world, I thought, as he had moved through it and me, filled with eagerness, my God, his brains were falling out and he wanted to fuck. (It was only later that I learned how common this was with mortal wounds, erection, that is to say, the last reflex of the body toward life before it goes tumbling through the last barrier forever.)

Is it necessary for me to go through this? Yes, yes I am afraid that it is. Eventually I will get to the stuff over which I have more control, but there is no getting away from this now; this is the essential, basic material which all of them will be looking for, and it is best to get it over at the beginning. It is pointless to try to put it off. Isn't it better this way? At least I am almost done with it now; there is little more that I have to say on this. I have given over my blood.

This is the last time I will go through it. I simply refuse to have to go through this again. But I will, I know it. Time and again it will be worked through, because this is not only what they wanted, all of them. But it must be what I want as well. Over and again, in and out of time, there is nothing else I will ever know as well, and it frames everything before or after, the killing shot, the frozen moment, nothing to be seen out of that perspective. Oh, how I hate him, hate them, hate what has happened to me, and yet this is all of life that I will ever know.

The roses, the blood, the sound of the sirens all around us, on my hands and knees, scrambling around the trunk. (I do not remember this but the films are definite, that must have been me out there, what did I want? Not to get away I am sure of this, otherwise I would have leapt from the car.) Vivien, he had said the other time, the last time, Vivien, come here. I want to get inside you, oh, that damned fool, the roses and the blood of the fool, I want to get inside you: he must have seen his death in that hotel room, I have thought later, some clear intimation of it blowing through him chill, and he reached toward me, grappling, just as he had told me of the dreams of assassination.

"I am going to be killed," he had said to me. "They are going to shoot me down in public some day."

"No, that's ridiculous."

"Is it?" he said. He ran his fingers through his excellent hair. "Too much pain, too much envy. There must be a million people who would like to kill me, at least a hundred million more who would enjoy seeing it, no matter what they tell you. It's a high-risk position."

"Don't talk to me about that anymore."

"But it *is*," he said, "of course it is. That's one of the penalties of the job. You don't expect that anything like this comes without its drawbacks, do you? Killing me would make someone ultimately famous."

"Do you like to talk this way? Does it excite you?"

"A lot of things excite me," he said. "Not being killed. That I can do without. Still, we have to be realistic. We might as well be prepared for it. I wouldn't be the first president murdered you know and surely not the last either. But there's just too much ambition, too much hatred, too much exposure. It could well happen."

"Please stop it," I said. "Please don't make me listen to this anymore."

"It excites you too. The widow in black, his living memory. People would never forget you. You'd be more famous that I am."

"I don't want to be famous."

"Everybody wants to be famous," he said. "This is my fundamental insight. If nothing else this is my contribution to the public dialog; everybody wants to be famous and the best thing you can do is to give them a piece of yourself at the beginning so that they can imagine themselves being you. Come on," he said, "cheer up. Everything's a high-risk performance nowadays. It's more interesting this way than dying in bed. They'll remember McKinley longer than Grant, and Grant had more to be remembered for and suffered more at the end too. Take the long view," he said, "cultivate some perspective, cheer up, and you'll see that this is the only way to do it."

I have no memory of coming out of the limousine. Clearly I did this; there is no way of denying the evidence of the films on this point, but it does not seem to be the kind of thing that I would have done. I did not even see the films until almost five years later, 1968, and then just that one time and never again, but once I saw them I simply could not deny what seemed to be clear: I had attempted to jump ship. But under the circumstances what could I have done? The riderless horse was my idea, no matter what anyone else says. I thought it was the nice touch necessary to bring everything into focus. No matter what anyone tells you, that was my idea alone, and certainly the right suggestion. I could see a piece of his skull in my lap and I remember that it was flesh-colored. He had touched his hand to his skull just as if he had had a slight headache and then he fell forward into my lap. I remember wondering why he was dead and I was still alive. The film is clear that I came out of the limousine, reached behind, trying to pick up that piece of his skull before being pushed back so maybe that's the answer: I wanted to put him back together again. Of course. I wanted to put him back together again.

7
1968 — WASHINGTON

His brother, Harold, arranged a private showing of the film in 1968. Until that time I had never seen it. Harold thought it was important that I do so. It was "emotional material," as he put it, and since he took his election for granted, the next step would be the opening up of the entire investigation. Which would mean sooner or later that they would have to take testimony, which in turn would mean that I would have to deal with the films, so better to get it out of the way now. A ruthless person, Harold; that much of what they said about him was certainly true. No fooling around. "Got to face it, Vivien, and it would be better for you to do it now," he said. "It's a kindness. Otherwise it will just be hanging over you."

A kindness indeed. He was lying. Of course he was lying: the real reason that he put me through the film in front of him is that he wanted to see my face when I watched, and learn from the expression whether I still cared and how much. He wanted to evaluate to the last degree exactly how much I still cared for Jay, how much I was still back there and how the remainder of my feeling for Jay could be funneled through Harold. That was Harold, that was Harold for you. I meant nothing to him (no one meant anything to him); his only concern was the use to which he could put my feelings. But I did not see this at the time, I was still listening to him, when he said that reopening the investigation was going to be his first priority. Not the war. The war was bad, very bad and it would have to be slowly dismantled, but it could not be done abruptly, it had been booked for a full five years, and to try to terminate it before 1970 would have thrown the military into a dither, caused extreme dislocations all the way down the line. Whereas the investigation could be plunged into right away. He would give the military the war, they would give him the investigation; that was pretty well the bargain that he thought they would agree to. But the investigation was personal, and he wasn't going to be deprived of that, even if they got tough.

So we sat in Alexandria one afternoon, just the two of us, and watched it in the darkened room. At the point of the film where I came out of the car I screamed but Harold was too transfixed by the screen to pay any attention other than to signal with a wave of his hand that I should shut up. He must have seen it hundreds of times by then but he was still transfixed. It was always new to him. "Shut up," he said when I began to cry. "Shut up, Vivien, and let me watch my brother die."

PART II

1
1978 — NEW JERSEY

Annie just came in unexpectedly with the pewter plate holding another serving of pills. "I don't want them," I said, pushing them away. "Why are you giving them to me? I only have them with breakfast. You never try to give them to me later on."

"I spoke with Dr. Richards. He feels that it would be better if you had an extra dosage, just for today."

"I don't want them," I said. "You just want to make me into a vegetable, you and Dr. Richards. I don't need any pills."

"Come on, dear," she said, "it's for the best." She held the tray before her steadily, unshakable, her gaze fixed on me.

"No," I said, "you just don't want me to be alert, you think that you can smother me in those drugs so that I won't know what's going on here."

"I'm getting tired of your accusations, dear," Annie said. "I've listened to too much of this, and I'm beginning to lose patience. If you want to continue to be a very sick person, that's your prerogative, but there are some of us who are charged with helping you, and we're going to do our jobs no matter what."

"If I take them now, will you leave me alone?"

"I came in here to give you these."

"So you'll leave if I take them?"

"Take them," she said.

"You give nothing, Annie. You won't give an inch. Do you get paid bonuses for not yielding?"

"Take them," she said, but it was not without humor. "You're just overwrought," she said, "but everything's coming along splendidly. Everyone's going to be so proud of us."

So I took the pills which seemed identical to those I had taken earlier and choked them down without help of water. Annie followed their passage intently. "No hiding them under your tongue now," she said. "I don't have to pull open our mouth and look behind our teeth, now do I?"

"Of course not," I said.

"Perhaps after lunch we can have a lovely game of cards," she said. "It's up to you, of course, but you might appreciate the diversion."

"I would appreciate your leaving."

"That's exactly what I'm doing, dear. You don't have to be hostile, you know. Aggression merely breeds aggression; unhappiness feeds on itself. All of us are trying to help you just as hard as we can. You have many friends. You cannot imagine how concerned Dr. Richards is. He said he might even want to come out here this week to look at you."

"I don't care about Leslie goddamned Richards."

"As you wish," Annie said and turned and left the room, pulling the door quickly, but the rubber padding along its edges denied her the hoped-for slam, as she should have known. The Thorazine, or at least I am pretty sure it is still Thorazine, did indeed have an immediate calming effect and it is with renewed concentration that I proceed with this record.

As much as I can project events, tonight will be the night of my death. If this is true, it is necessary to talk the more frantically. Eleven in the morning. It is not impossible that I could complete this record with necessary hidings and interruptions by midnight. When I started I projected a rather bucolic existence, using odd moments of the days for weeks on end to fill up these tapes, but now matters have assumed a grimmer cast. Can I possibly get it all down under this kind of time pressure?

Can I? After the matters which I have lived through, to be a little bit formal, I think that I can get through anything.

Nicholas, Nicholas, Nicholas, Nicholas, you should not have done it. You shouldn't have done it, it could have all been different, there were other ways. Oh you fool, don't you see that precisely because of what you were, you were granted all the options in the world? Why did you do it? Why, when he would have done it to himself anyway within less time than you can imagine?

2
1947 — CONNECTICUT

I have no distinct memory of the first time, but I distinctly remember the second. The first time is for poets or for the emotionally impoverished, who, in later times, build it up out of all proportion; for most of us, I believe, it is little more than a scramble in the dark. But the second I recall quite well, the second in that sense must have been the first; we lay together close side by side in the living room, all around me the even sides of the night. Daddy sleeping upstairs, Jane somewhere in her little bed on another level, which must have added to no small degree to my excitement. Risk is part of the adventure; there is no question about it. That is why Jason and Harold were so good in bed.

"Come here," he said to me. "Come here. I want to touch you." He was nineteen years old, which is to laugh, except that at this time I was eighteen and he appeared very mature and sophisticated. Later he became a certified public accountant, I understand, but at this stage of our lives he showed great promise. "I want you," he said. "I want you." His hand was on my breast, the breast naked, the breast filling all of his palm, and far below I could feel the absent tweak of his genitals, gathering energy. "Don't be afraid," he said. "It won't hurt."

"It won't hurt." That was his promise. As if it had hurt the first time: it had not, I had no memory of it at all, space, fissure, gathering and the muddling of liquids in the distance. It had been the absence of pain which had surprised me; all the books that I had read had made it quite clear that it would hurt the first time and it had not at all. But that had been over a year ago with a boy I hardly remembered, and now another was telling me that it would not hurt as if hopeful that it would. "Come on," he said. His hand was between my legs and I could feel the slow curvature of his strokes. He was very practiced, I later came to understand, for a nineteen-year old or, for that matter, for a thirty-nine-year-old. "Come on," he said. We were both naked. We had been there two hours to reach that point.

"I don't want to," I said.

"Yes, you do. You know you do."

"I don't," I said.

"Then I won't. I won't do it. I'll just rest against you," he said, and pivoted and then, shockingly, I could feel the full weight of him and then the slow collision of entrance. He went in so easily that it must have shocked him. I heard him gasp, an intake of breath that was not entirely sexual. I put my lips against his ear. "I never told you I was a virgin," I said.

"I thought you were."

"I'm not," I said, "but that doesn't mean that I'm easy."

"You're not," he said. "You're not easy at all." And then the slow rhythmic pulse of his gathering began. I let him do it. It was as if his finding out that I was not a virgin had removed from him the last obligation for even an assumed patience. "Oh my God," he said. "Oh my God." I put my hands on his shoulders and felt the slight pulse within them, realizing, not for the first time, how totally men were in the thrall of sex, chasing their one pitiful emission as far as it would take them, seeking that one spurt that would take them to nothingness. A sense of pity not unmixed with contempt. "Slowly," I said. "Slowly."

"Yes," he said, "yes, I won't rush." And his movements increased, became frantic. I felt his muscles beginning to loosen in the onset of orgasm. My own detachment was absolute. It was absolute. I cannot say that it was unpleasant to be fucking him, but it meant nothing either. Some deficiency in the anatomy, perhaps some more intricate failure. It had meant

nothing the first time, either. It would be many years until it meant anything at all, and then it would fill me in ways that I could not have imagined. "Oh my God," he said. He snaffled. I felt the final gathering and
then with a cry he was discharging into me.

At the moment of his release I thought I caught a glimpse of a white
face ballooning out of proportion, grotesque, misshapen, pained, but
when I opened my eyes to stare at him he was concentrated, squeezed
shut, diminished. Jason, then, seen sixteen years later. Jason in the limousine with the great open top. Sex as connection, as premonition. As
fusion.

3
1959 — WASHINGTON

It must have been in 1959, June of that year I think, hard to keep the
dates exactly straight what with all of the past jumbling together just as
they always said was the case when you got old but then again. Then
again it might merely be the effect of the Thorazine tablets on the
pewter plate.

June of 1959. It must have been a reception for the Vice President. Yes,
that is what I think it was, ceremonial reception held by the Vice President for the Greek ambassador and premier and of course Jason felt that
we'd better go, since he was keeping a very close eye on the Vice President at that time.

Nicholas was there when we came. Jason disappeared for three hours
as he always did, and there I was being pursued by this fat, determined
old Greek, finally pinned against a wall as he brought me first one drink
and then another. I knew his reputation of course but I knew nothing of
him personally, and it seemed impossible for me to match his manner and
appearance with what I had heard.

"Hello," he said, "I am Nicholas Angelo Sarris. I have heard so much
about you and have been so anxious to meet you. You are fully as beautiful as all your pictures and even more charming. The pictures cannot
possibly render as your appearance renders to me your soul."

I never wanted to meet him, never. I wanted him to go away. I hated
him from the beginning. Always. Forever. Couldn't you find someone
else? I thought. Please go away. That is what I wanted to say. This is what
I will always remember as my first reaction to Nicholas Angelo Sarris,
that I hated him and wanted him to go away. But one never said things
like that of course, not to anyone, least of all to one of the three or four
richest men in the world as Jason had reminded me. To say nothing of
what Jason would have said if he had had to confront that behavior.

"Well," I said, "I've heard so very much about you too. It's such a pleasure to meet you."

"The pleasure is mine," he said. "I am wholly *enchanté*."

"You speak French?"

"Oh no," he said, "not a word of it. In fact," he said, showing me for the first time that smile of his. "I can barely be said to speak Greek." I became aware of his respiration, which was regular, but very deep, like a man concentrating on breathing to stave off a heart attack or perhaps to remind himself of the fact that he is still simply alive. "Of course I manage rather well in my own peculiar amalgam of English."

"Would you like to meet my husband?"

"Not at all," he said, "I am a great admirer of the Senator and am sure that he will play an ever-increasing role in your nation's government in the near future, but in the hope that you and he will take no offense whatsoever I would much rather talk to you. He is not nearly half so charming as yourself and I suspect that you are the true motivating influence behind his career."

"Not so."

"Not so? Really. I thought it was a tradition of American politics that the woman was almost always the support of the famous husband and usually the sculptor of his career."

"Well, that is not the case here."

"Is Jason his own sculptor?"

"Not exactly. Not that either."

"Then what are you trying to tell me?"

I do not know what I was trying to tell him. I have no idea of what I was getting at but I found myself suddenly then talking to him as I had talked to no one else. Jason's family, all of the damned Kellys and their politics had blended into a sense of legacy, mysticism and blood together. You couldn't really talk to them on a personal level. They had a terrifying sense of themselves. Jason lived with his own nightmare vision for thirteen years. He was next in line for the Presidency. He had no choice but to want to be President even though he was not sure that it was for his own good, let alone the good of the country. Some twisted sense of fate, some macabre manifest destiny drove them — the way all of them worked together, the sense that you often got when you came into any room where Jason and Harold were sitting together or had recently sat together that you were invading some secret or sacred ground.

As I talked to Nicholas at that reception, I found all of this coming out in one choked, uninterrupted monologue, and through all of it he looked at me with those interested, weary eyes of his and said nothing. Once or twice waiters passed with trays of drinks, a few times someone came over and tried to join the conversation, until Nicholas with one gesture waved them away — I had never seen a man do that so well before, not even Jason, when he was courting me — but it could have been fifteen minutes or an hour which had passed when I realized that I had not stopped talking, not at all.

"What am I saying?" I said to him. "Why am I doing this?"

"I am very flattered that you will talk to me in this way."

"But I don't," I said. "I don't want to talk to you in this way, don't you understand that? This is none of your concern. And I must be boring you."

"You are not boring me at all. Do I look as if I am bored?"

I could not explain myself. I could not understand what had happened to me; all that seized me then was the desperate urge to escape him. "You must excuse me," I said. "I must look for Jason."

He stared at me a long minute, his eyes narrow and hard. "You do not want Jason. Jason, as you said, is quite capable of taking care of himself. Jason does not need to be found at this moment. When he is finished he will come back to you as he always has, and will undoubtedly tell you that it is time to leave."

"Yes."

"That is perfectly all right," Nicholas said. "I do not sit in judgment of the Senator. As you say, he wishes to be President."

"Not in an off-year," Jason said. He was at my right elbow, coming up quickly and silently, smiling ironically at the two of us. "That would be highly illegal."

Foolishly I started to introduce them and then realized that they had no need of me; they knew each other better than I could ever have known either of them. "Your wife is charming," Nicholas said. "She is even more charming than the press accounts or photographers would indicate. It has been a delight to have met her. You must be very proud of her."

"Of course I am," Jason said.

"You are truly a fortunate man, many times blessed, to have such a lady."

Jason smiled again. Wryly. "I think that we'll be leaving now, Vivien," Jason said. "Unless there's any reason you'd like to stay."

"That is perfectly all right," Nicholas said. "I was on the point of leaving myself many hours ago and would have long since if I had not met your wife. These parties are quite a trial, are they not?"

"I like them," Jason said.

"I know you like them," he said, "but it is a trial for you to like them, and you are simply making the best of it. Besides, they serve certain purposes for you, *n'est-ce pas?*"

"Everything serves purposes."

"That is what I mean," Nicholas said. "You are the ultimate utilitarian, you are a man utterly of circumstance. As one who is of the same stripe but not as excellently developed I can only extend my hand and my admiration." And he reached out, took Jason's hand so skillfully that it was obvious that Jason would realize only hours later that he had been appropriated. Then Nicholas leaned over, kissed me on the forehead. "I do hope that I will see you again," he said. "*Enchanté*. Absolutely *enchanté*."

"You say you are enchanted?" Jason said. "You are right, she is enchanting. But then it was the fate of your own Greek enchantress, one Circe, I believe, to live among swine."

Nicholas' eyebrows raised slightly.

"I do not speak French, I remind you," he said. "But I tell you in your own language that I trust I will meet you again. Perhaps at an inaugural ball, eh?" he said and with a wink he was gone. Jason looked after him and then took my hand.

"He is a remarkable person," he said. "Did you like him?"

"No," I said, "I did not like him at all."

Something in my tone even more than the words must have caught him. "My," he said lightly, "you sound very certain of yourself."

"I am," I said. "I did not like him at all."

4
1978 — NEW JERSEY

"I have called Dr. Richards again," Annie said when she came in. "He has agreed to come and see you. He feels as I do that you are coming along nicely but he would like to come in and check on you, and he'll be out in this area anyway. He is going to Monmouth Race Track so he can stop on the way."

"He is a truly dedicated physician."

"Yes, he is, and he really cares about you."

"I don't care about him," I said.

Dr. Richards is merely the latest and the least interesting in the succession of Feelgoods who by hook or crook I have been seeing for these past years. Richards is neither better than them or worse but lacks the sanctimony which makes so many of them offensive; when he has written out the drug prescriptions or administered the amphetamine shots, he has not, at least, done it in the context of upholding the Hippocratic oath.

He sees nothing spiritual in his calling. "Have you told Dr. Richards about your plans for disposing of my corpse after you're done with me tonight?"

"I'm sick of your paranoid reactions," she said. "I had a long talk with the doctor and he says that it's no longer necessary for me to pretend to be polite to you when you carry on like a fool. I don't like your paranoia and I'm getting tired of this. If there's one person in the world who cares for you, and is even responsible for the fact that you're alive right now, it's me and you had better not forget that."

"I'm so touchingly grateful."

"You had better get hold of yourself, Vivien. I understand you and can deal with this and Tom and Millie don't pay it any attention at all, but if you start to carry on with Dr. Richards like this, he's not going to be so understanding. He's going to hospitalize you, and that's all there is to it. And everything we've done to keep you *out* of the hospital."

"I'm even more grateful."

"You won't like the hospital. Most particularly you won't like the attention that you'll get there. Or do you want everyone in the world to know what's happened to you?"

"I've run out of patience with this," I said, which was at least partially true. "I'm sick of your threats."

"It's mutual. I've run out of patience too. I don't like your implying that I'm somehow involved in a plot to murder you."

"I'm not implying anything. I'm saying it to you directly."

"It's not worth being near you to listen to this. If I didn't have a deep feeling for you, Vivien, I would have left this assignment many weeks ago. I'm a skillful, competent nurse. I'm in a great deal of demand. I can have any one of a number of jobs any of which would be easier than this. I don't have to take this kind of abuse."

"You don't want any of those jobs. You're a celebrity-fucker, Annie."

Finally she said nothing. Hands on her enormous hips, she looked at me.

"Are you going to tell me that that's a disgusting thing to say? You have such a deeply developed sense of morality, after all."

"I don't think I want to say anything to you at this moment."

"Then why not get out of the room? Who asked you in?"

"How do I know what you're doing in here?"

"I won't kill myself, I promise. Besides, there's no need to. You're going to do the job yourself, I wouldn't disappoint you."

"You're a very sick woman, Vivien."

"And so are you."

"The doctor will be here in about an hour or so. I don't know how much of this to tell him. If I tell him everything he's going to recommend your hospitalization on the spot you know."

"So you won't tell him everything. How could you have your fun if I were hospitalized? You'll do exactly what you want to do which is to tell him nothing. But I've got a secret," I said, coming off the bed, "and I'm going to tell you that secret right now just so that you understand everything and can carry it back where it will do the most good. I don't give a damn," I said, "I don't give a damn if you kill me. I simply have no fear at all. In fact, I think that I'd be grateful. You're just saving me a lot of trouble. If you think that an arsenal of terror tactics or something is going to make me suffer before I die you're quite wrong. I'm prepared to go and there's nothing you can do to frighten me. You're just wasting your time and everyone else's. Get out of here," I said, looking up at her. "Get out of my room now. This is my room. This is my property. You are still only my employee, and you have no right to stay if I want you out. Get out."

"You'll regret this," she said and she left.

So much for that. Of course Richards is on the case, also. They are all on the case, but I do not think that it will be Richards himself who will administer the killing shot. No, that will come from a very special source. She feels that she has earned it and of course she has. All of those associated with Nicholas were insistent upon earning what they got. Which is one of the factors of course underlying his huge success.

5
1978 — NEW JERSEY

I lied of course, I lied to her. It was all that I could do: the lie is thin but it is my only chance; perhaps it will work. I am terrified of dying. I do not want to die, I have learned at last to value my life and when I saw her in the darkness last night the full extent of that commitment came upon me: I want to live, know that now, but what can I do? What can I do but try to preserve for them the fiction that I do not; perhaps if they believe this they will spare me for want of satisfaction. It is not much but it is all I have.

Oh my God, it is all I have except for this wretched taping machine and all of the material I am talking into it, coming over me, crowding me, and yet I cannot make sense of it. I cannot find the sense: it was merely a matter of day by day trying to live, and only far into it did I see that all of the others thought that there had to be a meaning. And that was the meaning that they then forced upon me. What is it? What is it? I must find it; somehow I must recapture my life and yet I do not know if at any point up until these last days I was living at all. I was reacting.

6
1963 — WASHINGTON

How do you think it feels to stand beside a coffin on worldwide television and know that more than half of the men who are watching and a good percentage of the women too are thinking about nothing so much as how they would like your own brains blown away and splattered across the back of that limo, too?

7
1964 — BOSTON

Harold always wanted what Jason was denied. They were crazy in that way, all of them, but they could not see it: it was simply the way they lived, it was simply their right. One of the things Jason had had was me, and that meant for Harold that he had to have me too, but I cannot say that there was anything beyond that. I was merely Jason's baggage, just like the Presidency was Jason's baggage too. The investigation was the only personal and private thing which Harold wanted absolutely. The first time that he took me to bed was also the last, but it could have gone on for a long time. It was his decision to stop it. I would have done anything that he wanted. It was a time of my life in which I was very anxious to please.

"No," he said, lying next to me, the stain of his completion not only draining from me but on the sheets, scattered around; he had come copiously, more than Jason ever had. "No, we can't do this anymore." His eyes were very abstracted, he never lost that containment, even at the moment of coming he was turned inward, controlled. "It isn't right."

"You wanted to."

"I know I did," he said, "and it was good, it was good that we did it, something that had to be done, but no more. No more of this."

"Who asked you to?"

"All right," he said. "Don't be that way."

"I'm not being any way at all. I'm asking you who started this?"

"That's true," Harold said. "That's true but you've got to finish things as well as start them." He put his fingers on my arm, ran them up and down the inner surfaces, starting to get me hot again. He always knew what would get me hot. It never took very much. "We shouldn't stay here," he said. "We should get dressed and leave." We were staying in a small apartment rented by a senior Senator which, Harold told me, had been taken for precisely things like this, even though the Senator himself never used it. Merely a courtesy to the party. "Stop looking at me that way," he said.

"I'm not looking at you."

"You were. You were looking at me before. I know you were."

"I wasn't," I said which was the truth but it was hopeless, obviously hopeless, there was no way to change Harold's mind or Jason's for that matter once that mind had gotten itself around to a certain perception. That perception became part of them so quickly that it was integrated into their personality; they could not conceive of not being always that way. "Oh, let's go," I said, "I'm not making you stay here. This was your idea."

"You said that," he said angrily, "you said that already, it's nothing that gives you any power over me, you understand. Or do you say that you were the helpless victim?"

"No," I said, "no, no, you've got it wrong." And this was true, he always had it wrong, never understood that I could care for him simply and without any of the baggage that he had to bring between us. But it was a bad time for Harold that year after the assassination. He was sorting through everything, and I was part of that context. I brought as much of this understanding to him as I could but he always made it very difficult. The Kellys would never make it easy. He was into his clothing even faster than he had gotten out of it, standing, pacing before me. With a few quick gestures he had brought himself back to focus.

"Aren't you going to get up?" he said, "or are you just going to lie there?"

"You've got to schedule things, don't you? You've got to rush things through, go from one to the next without anything in between. What are you afraid you might learn if you had time, Harold?"

"Come on," he said, "it's time to go."

"Did you schedule me for just once?"

"You're an impossible woman," he said and then something broke within him. I had never seen this happen to him before nor again until that moment on the kitchen floor. "Oh my God," he said, coming toward me, stumbling, falling on the bed, reaching to hold me, "oh my God, do you realize that I've done this thing? I shouldn't have; it was wrong — "

"I'm not in mourning anymore."

"It's not mourning, it's not that. I shouldn't — "

"It was my decision too," I said, stroking his forehead, feeling the little damp pulsing underneath. "You didn't make me do anything that I didn't want." His face went into my neck and I could feel that he was crying but there were no tears. "It's done," I said, "it's done, Harold, it's done, it doesn't matter, no one's hurt at all; it's just something that had to happen and it happened and that's all." And he was still shaking, shaking harder. I stroked his head. "It's all right," I said, "all right," and thought that it was remorse which was driving him. But when his face came away from my shoulder and he looked at me his expression was bleak and controlled once more and I could see that it was not remorse at all. I had utterly misunderstood.

"All right," he said, "that's enough of that. Get dressed, please."

"Yes," I said.

"It's one of those things which happens, but that isn't to say that it will ever happen again. It's as much your fault as mine."

"It's not a matter of fault."

"And don't you forget it. There are always two people involved in a situation like this."

"Of course," I said. "Who said otherwise?"

"So let's go," he said, "and let's hear no more of it," exactly as if I had been the one protesting, not he, and what I came to understand is that the sobs, the dry sobs, had not been for remorse at all but merely out of regret. He had done it once, in his disciplined way had permitted himself to tap Jason's legacy, but it would only be that once and never again. That was the way they were. Once for the impulses, but all of the future for their destiny.

8
1954 — NEW YORK

Oh, they were a wonderful family, it was a pleasure and a privilege but above all an obligation to marry into them, to become part of their destiny. That was what the old lady pointed out to me shortly before we were married. You realize that there are very special obligations, she said, obligations to being a Kelly. He's going to be very difficult in many ways but I know that you have the understanding to help him.

Oh, of course, I said, of course, I have the understanding. I was always saying yes to these people, that is the remarkable thing, I cannot recall more than once or twice in all the years ever saying no and then it was minor things. Otherwise I could not have been more agreeable about everything. Oh yes, your destiny. Oh yes, your responsibilities. Oh yes, of course we'll go to North Dakota for three days so that you can see the Governor. Yes and yes.

9
1953-BOSTON

"Lots of luck with those people," Jane said to me before the wedding. "You're going to need it."

"Well thank you very much."

"They're crazy people," she said. "I'm not saying that by reputation;

I've been around a lot who had to deal with them. Still," she said, "who am I to talk? I'm a two-time loser myself. Are you getting married just to please him?"

"What?"

"I'm asking an honest question. You don't have to answer if you don't want to, of course. Not that I care," she said. "Anything that makes you happy is all right with me. I'm really kind of fond of you, you know, whether you've been able to believe that or not. Having the same name and everything. Do you love him?"

"I guess so," I said.

"You could have said that's none of my business and I would have accepted it so I suppose that you really do. You poor thing, you really do love him."

"Yes, I think so."

"He's not a very lovable man but then you wouldn't want anybody easily lovable. This way it's to your credit. He's going to go a far distance too, you know. He's only thirty-seven and in the Senate. He has a good chance of being President someday."

"He doesn't think so."

"He'd tell you that. You don't think that he'd be courting you on the basis that you're into a twenty-year campaign for the Presidency, now do you? But you listen to me, he wants it and he's probably going to get it. You have a chance of being First Lady."

"That isn't why I'm marrying him."

"How well I know that," Jane said. "Don't you think that I understand you at all? Of all the things that the future could bring to you that would frighten you the most. You're really a very shy, private person as we both understand. I'm not but you won't exactly thrive on being a pol's wife. Ah, the hell with it," she said. "This is my little bachelorette party and all I'm doing is depressing you. Drink up. You've got three days left."

Three days later, however, and despite all the things which Jane said, and which turned out to be true and sensible projections, I did marry Jason Kelly in a lovely wedding attended by four hundred of our most intimate friends with a reception for six hundred and fifty in addition who were only slightly less close.

10
1968 — CALIFORNIA

"You can come to me," he said the day after Harold's assassination in L.A. as soon as he got on the phone in Jane's apartment. "Now you can come to me and I will take care of you," Nicholas said.

"That isn't why I called," I said. "I didn't want that. I only wanted to know — "

"Of course it's why you called. You wouldn't have for any other reason. You want to know that there is someplace where you can be safe.
I can understand your fright. It is a very normal reaction. It is a terrible
thing that it would only be through something like this that you would
know that I am always here, that I am here to give myself to you, offer
you anything you want, but if it is something only this awful which will
make you call, so be it. Come to me," Nicholas said. "You can come to
me right now."

"I'm so confused," I said. "I don't understand anything. I just don't
know what to do anymore. It seems that I don't know a thing."

"It is all right," he said. "There is nothing to understand. No one can
know things like these. Once in a lifetime is enough; no one can be expected to live through it twice, and you have done magnificently. Come
to me."

"Do you think that's why I called you? So that you would say you
would protect me?"

"I will protect you."

"I don't need a security force. There are hundreds of people here, any
one of whom would take care of me."

"Don't you think I know that?" he said. "Do you think I'm a fool? But
I'm the one you called."

"I'm so tired. I'm just so tired, Nicholas, I can't deal with it anymore.
I thought that I could. I thought that I was the strongest person I knew
but this is too much for me to deal with. I've gone beyond my limits. It's
just too much."

"It's all right," he said. "Stop talking. Don't apologize. Don't make ex-
cuses anymore. Just come to me. Come now."

"I can't," I said. "I have to stay for the funeral."

"Well, of course. The funeral. Then I will come to you. I will be there
by tomorrow, and I will stay with you, and we will return together."

"That isn't necessary. I don't want you there."

"But I knew Harold too. I had much feeling for him. It would be proper
of me to come."

"Then come," I said. "Come. I don't care anymore. If you feel that you
must do so, I won't stop you."

"And then you will return with me."

"I don't know. I don't know."

"Yes, you will."

"Is that the only reason you'd come here? To take me back with
you?"

"Be practical," he said after a long pause. "You have got to be practical in this world."

"I know all about your practicality. I see what it's gotten me. And what it's gotten Harold."

"Do not be bitter. I had nothing to do with Harold's murder. I knew from the beginning that all of this was doomed."

"Did you?"

"Of course," he said. "And so did he."

"You know everything," I said bitterly. "You're so practical. I'm so sick of practical people."

"I'll send a plane for you after the funeral," he said. "That would be the most practical. Coming now would only upset you and I do not want to do that."

"Why don't you leave me alone?" I said. "Why can't you just let me be?"

"You called me," he said. "Do I have to remind you of that? You were the one who initiated this contact, so you do not want me to leave you alone."

"I'm so sick of your practicality. I'm so sick of all you practical people."

"This conversation is leading us nowhere. I would talk to you for as long as you wanted if I thought that I was helping you, but it's pointless. You are clearly overwrought. Tell me where I can reach you, and I will be in touch with you tomorrow."

"I give up," I said. "You win. I can't deal with it anymore. I don't even want to."

"What are you talking about now?"

"I said I give up. Isn't that clear enough? I'll marry you. I can't fight anymore. Not after Harold. I'm afraid," I said. "I'm afraid, Nicholas, and I'm so tired of being afraid. This is no way to live. So I'll marry you. You can take care of me."

He said nothing. It was the first time, perhaps the only time, that I knew him that he did not immediately have something to say. I thought that the connection had broken. "Did you hear me?" I said. "I said I'm tired and I'm afraid and I can't fight anymore, so I'll marry you. I'll marry you if that's what you want."

"Yes. I heard you."

"You don't sound happy. Isn't that what you wanted all the time? Well now you have it."

"I did not want it this way. I did not want it to be the result of terrible tragedy."

"It is what it is."

"I wanted you, yes, but on different terms. For my own sake. Do you care for me?"

"Of course, I care for you."

"This is the most difficult thing I have ever asked any human being. You must be tolerant, you must understand. This is not easy for me; I do not know if I can deal with it yet I must. Do you really care for me? Would you have made this call, would you have given me this offer if what happened did not?"

"No," I said, "I wouldn't."

"At least you have told me the truth."

"You have to know that," I said. "I can't live a lie with you. I've lived enough lies. I would not have called otherwise. I am fond of you, but I do not think that any marriage would have worked, even the kind of marriage you are offering me. But now I am willing to try because I am frightened, and I see, after what has been done to Harold, that it could be done to anyone."

"All right," he said. "That I can understand, at least. You are talking a language which is mine and I respect you for it. There will be no deception between us, and that may be the start of happiness."

"I hope so."

"You can come to me after the funeral and we will work out all of the details. Yes, I will have you under those circumstances. I wish it were otherwise, but I will take it any way that I can. Does that mean that I love you the less?"

"No, of course not. It means that you love me the more."

"That is what I wanted to hear," he said. "So that there is a beginning, do you hear that? And maybe from this more feeling can grow. I will talk to you later," he said. "It is too overwhelming. I will talk to you later." And he disconnected.

I held the phone, a long, singing emptiness in my hand and then I replaced it. This is the true and real story of why and how Nicholas and I were betrothed. I wish it were otherwise.

11
1978 — NEW JERSEY

It is so hard to go on with this, so hard to be logical and controlled, to pick my way through this material carefully selecting only that which will lead to a nice, chronological summation, omitting other details which can come in only much later after all of the necessary background.

I am so tired of being a good girl, of making a conscientious effort to deliver a neat, well-organized account of myself, when what I really want to do is to scream it all out. The hell with progression, the hell with holding back this and telling that, just get it all down as it comes to me so that

the truth, or at least those portions of the truth which matter, will be on
these reels no matter what happens to me.

They may kill me before I finish this, you understand. I have no idea
of what Richards is going to do to me. In all likelihood he is here to monitor my life processes just before the killing blow is delivered; maybe they
want him on the spot to sign the death certificate. And yet even though
all of this is true, I am still being a good girl, still trying to deliver a neat,
organized report. I cannot stand it. But what would the point of it otherwise be?

Should I speak of the way Nicholas was in bed, should I talk of the look
on his face when at last he told me everything, when at last all of the truth
was out and nothing to be done but for him to take it? Should I speak
of what he said to me when I hit him again and again and again, hard
blows on the soft, dense meat of his face and then ran from that terrible
room? Shall I talk of the words he said in bed, the words Harold said in
bed, Jason's words, should I speak of ten other men?

No, I cannot do that, I cannot do it to myself or to any of them. The
only way I know is the straight and careful way, from beginning to end,
but I cannot stand this, the pain is too much, it is *too much*. Jane, do you
hear me? You once said that I did not feel pain, not the way that other
people did anyway, and that this explained more than anything else why
I had been able to go through all of this, not feeling pain, I mean. But
that was terribly unfair, Jane, terribly cruel, even though I felt that you
were the person who knew me best. I do feel pain, I feel it as intensely
as anyone alive: why do you think that I am in this condition? Because
I feel pain, that is why.

But the feeling is not enough. What else could I do? I had no choice, I
had to do it that way, the other way would have led to chaos.

Though in the end it will all work out the same. I will wind up like Jason, my brains blown out, scattered over these reels the way that his were
on the seat of the car. I will be another Harold, running out in blood and
little particles of gray on the shiny floor of this little room.

No, it had to be my way, I had to do it my way. All smiles and laughter and glitter and good cheer, glamour and romance and good form. People are not interested in you if you show a sad face to the world. Because
there is enough sadness already, and they know it so well, people want
to be entertained, they want to be cheered up. There is enough misery
and horror, they do not need any more. I must be forward-looking. It was
all of quality, it was all for the very best, everything works out for the
best, nothing for the worse. I do not know, I simply do not know.

Nicholas had turned toward me on his deathbed — after Jason's and
Harold's deaths, after our marriage — his face open as never before so

that I could see the engines of his person underneath and he said:

"Of course, of course it was done that way, Jason's, Harold's, their deaths were done that way, what else did you expect? How else could I have had you with those two brothers around?" he asked. "I thought that you knew it yourself, that you understood that? What kind of fool are you?"

I screamed, or I did not scream, as I struck and struck and struck him, it is so hard to remember, and I came from that room and I —

PART III

1
1978 — NEW JERSEY

"Well," Dr. Richards said, "how is our patient? I must say, you don't look bad at all, not bad at all. You've gained some weight. You look considerably better. In fact you look fine." He put solicitous hands on my shoulders, brought me close against him as if he were to deliver an intimate caress and looked into my eyes. "I don't even think that a full physical examination is necessary," he said. "We'll just do a superficial blood pressure, pulse and readout and I'll be on my way."

"That's up to you, Doctor," Annie said from the doorway. "We're completely in your hands."

"No one is completely in anyone's hands," Richards said. "This would be an even more imperfect world if we could not be responsible for ourselves."

"You can wait outside," he said to Annie. "I'll call you if I need you."

"As you wish."

"She's afraid to leave me alone," I said. "She doesn't know what I'd say to you."

"That's ridiculous," Annie said and left the room. Richards stood and went to the door, leaned against it to make the closure complete, then came back, crouched by the bed. "Is there anything you want to tell me?" he said in a whisper. "Everything between us is in absolute confidence. You know all about medical ethics."

"I don't know what you're talking about."

"It's really not necessary for me to do an examination," he said. "I'm quite familiar with your condition and there are obviously no radical changes. Perhaps you'd like to talk."

"About what?"

"I understand that you're very disturbed about something or other. Is it anything you'd like to talk about?"

"What did she tell you?"

"She told me nothing except that you seemed to be upset and that I might be needed here."

"You're all in this together. All of you are working together. But why do you have to pretend to be my friend? I know what you are."

He shook his head, a small man in his early fifties. "Unreasonable," he said. "Unreasonable and very sad. Maybe we'd better do a fast physical after all."

"Don't you even have the decency to admit the truth?"

"I'm sorry," Richards said, "I'm sorry that you don't trust me. Nothing can be gained from this, though, don't you agree? We're not getting anywhere."

"But I don't care," I said. "That's what she doesn't understand and what you don't, either. There's nothing you can do to me anymore because I have absolutely no fear. You're the people who ought to be frightened. You'll pay for this."

He sighed, leaned toward his bag on the floor, and, like an exhibitionist, unzipped it and emerged with a private part; a stethoscope and sphygmomanometer. "Just lean back and relax," he said, "and we'll do a superficial."

"Amphetamines lead to paranoia. Except that I'm not having a paranoid reaction. It's just a case of reacting to too much truth. But you can try decreasing the dosage if you'd like."

"Don't take medical terminology unto yourself. I'm the doctor."

"You're no doctor," I said. "You're an assistant. Annie's assistant, that's all."

"Come on, Vivien," he said, "come on, be reasonable, just sit back and relax now and we'll make this go quickly." And he began to work upon me. Skillful this most recent of the Feelgoods is; he has the medical hands, the medical detachment. What I said to him came out of spite rather than belief because if this latest of the Feelgoods is one thing, it is indeed a doctor. I felt the coolness of the stethoscope disc penetrating me, the pressure of the sphygmomanometer building on my arm, although all of this was as if from a distance and I not really that at all. I felt myself literally going out of my body, something which has happened to me on occasions in the past, most notably in Texas when someone else must have been trying to get out of that car.

And then I was back in there again, Richards looking at me with great compassion. I am not mistaken; it was compassion which I saw in him. An intolerable emotion for the Feelgoods — although of course it is the emotion which they can mime best. "You've got a rapid pulse," he said, "maybe a hundred at rest, which is a little high although nothing to worry about. Otherwise, blood pressure, respiration, superficial signs are all within normal limits. Clinically you're not in bad condition at all, but something is terrifying you." He put his tools away. "Wouldn't you like to talk to me about this?"

"I've talked to you. You know what I feel."

"This is up to you. I can't force you."

"Sure you can. Administer Scopolamine. You probably have some in that bag of yours."

"The things you are saying depict me as a man of no ethics. You're perfectly free to dismiss me from your case, if you desire, and seek another doctor. If you don't trust me, maybe you should find someone who you will."

"Don't be ridiculous. I have no control over you or anything else."

"I think that we'll keep you on the maintenance dosage. There's really no reason to change your treatment at this time. The important thing is a question which only you can answer: do you want to get better or not?"

"According to you, I've gotten much better."

"Do you want to go out into the world and resume a normal life or do you want to stay here a self-pitying invalid? That's a level of medicine with which I'm not qualified to deal, but I understand that you don't wish to seek a therapist."

"Do you think what I had was a normal life? Are you referring to it that way?"

"It was a normal life for you. Beyond that I wouldn't make any judgments." Richards picked up his bag, looked at me with his most intent, sympathetic expression. "Ultimately you've got to decide how you want to live," he said. "Nobody can make that decision for you, and no one can save you from that responsibility."

"I'm very moved by that, too."

"Paranoid withdrawal won't help."

"Now you're being a psychiatrist."

"Quite right, and I'm not qualified."

"Besides, paranoia is a very common side effect of amphetamine dosage."

"Your amphetamines have been very carefully controlled," Richards said. "They have been prescribed well within normal limits for a patient of your age and circumstances. There is no need to continue this conversation, I am afraid. We aren't getting anywhere, and I don't think that I have anything more to say to you."

"Now you're just acting offended."

"I respect you. I want to keep on respecting you," he said and left. Lacking Annie's neatness and sense of structure, he did not close the door behind him.

It was only midafternoon, with five or six hours to go until sunset, during this warm and difficult August. I knew that they would attempt nothing until nightfall. Otherwise they would not have gone to the trouble to invite Richards. His name on a presumptive death certificate would not have justified his presence immediately prior to the event, if they were going to do away with me immediately; the time lapse would have been much too short and consequently risky.

After a time, Annie came back into the room with her pewter tray. "Dr. Richards has left," she said.

"Oh? I thought that he might stay overnight. But then again he can get to the track in time for the second if he goes fast. He's such a horse-racing fanatic. Don't they have a 2:00 p.m. post-time at Monmouth? Just like Saratoga used to be; they're so leisurely in resort towns."

"I don't think you're being funny at all."

"I'm not trying to be funny."

"Your behavior is very offensive. Dr. Richards is most concerned about you. You hurt him very much, you know. He really cares about you; he cared enough to make a special visit here, and you insulted him."

"You have such a delicately refined sense of manners, Annie. You ought to work in protocol."

"I don't mind saying that I'm running out of patience with you. Your behavior has been absolutely disgraceful, and you're becoming an embarrassment."

"I'm not taking any of your pills anymore."

"I don't particularly care whether you do or not. It's your life and health, not mine."

"Is that a threat too? What plans do you have for my life and health?"

"I'm likely to quit on the spot. If there was anyone else to take care of you, I think I would."

"Tom and Millie would take care of me."

"Tom and Millie can't deal with you, and you know that perfectly well. I wish that I could do it."

"You have such a highly developed sense of responsibility, Annie. I'm really moved."

"I don't know if you're moved or not. I really care for you, can't you understand that? But people of your kind can't believe in caring. Everything's a matter of being bought or sold. But you can't buy feeling."

"I'm getting sick of this, Annie."

"Take your pills."

"I absolutely refuse."

"Then be damned with you," she said. "It's your life, not mine. If you want to kill yourself, you can go ahead and do so."

"No, you'll do so to me."

"Be quiet," she said. "I've never lost my temper with you yet, but you're taking me close to the line."

"I'm really moved again."

"You're a dangerous and irresponsible woman. All of you people are, I'm beginning to think. You live your lives as if you're special and better than us. Well, you're not and you'd just better remember that. You're no different from the rest of us, with all your money."

"Class tensions, Annie."

"Take these pills," she said, bringing the tray against my chin. I felt the point of it subtly digging in. "Take them right now."

"I won't submit to your poisons anymore. You'll have to do it more directly."

"The hell with you," she said, "the hell with you then." And she went to the door.

"I'm going with you," I said, getting off the bed. "I want to take a walk around outdoors. Maybe I'll even make a few phone calls."

"In your nightgown you'll walk around? It's cold out there."

"I don't think I've been out of this room in a week. I want to see something besides these walls, this damned furniture."

"I don't think that would be a very good idea," she said. "Dr. Richards feels that this should be as calm a day for you as possible, that you'd be far better off in your own room than getting yourself nervously stimulated. Who do you want to call anyway?"

"Then I *am* right," I said. "You're keeping me prisoner in here. You're locking me up."

"Get back inside."

"No," I said. "Let me out."

She put her body in the doorway, a complete obstruction. "No," she said, "you're going to listen to people who are trying to help you. Stay in there."

"I knew it. I knew it all the time."

"You'll go when I say you can go, and until that time you'll stay in there. You have to be treated like a child, since you're acting like one."

"You're keeping me prisoner! I told you. I told you you were all in on it!"

"You ridiculous woman," she said. "Get in there and go to sleep."

I pushed against her. Her body was like stone. "I'll force myself past you," I said. "I'll run to phone the police. I'll report what you're doing to me."

"You'll do nothing of the sort," she said. Her bulk was impermeable. Up until that moment of physical juxtaposition, I had never realized the massive strength of the woman, but then again she had been hired for that strength. "Now stop disgracing yourself and all the people who care for you and stay in there."

"Is that an order?"

"You can call it a pretty firm suggestion. Go on now. Get in there."

So I did. I turned from her and went back to bed. Behind me I could hear the soft closing of the door, then the implicatory click of the lock, which looked massive in the half-light streaming in, and then her footsteps going away. I went back to the bed and sat there.

Here I am then, here I am. Imprisoned in this shell of a house on the ruins of this estate, all the sounds of entrapment around me, merely waiting, waiting now for the last moments. Which cannot be far beyond nightfall. I prepared a banquet for myself in the midst of mine enemies. And now I am dining on its bitter, bitter liqueur.

2
1978 — NEW JERSEY

The history of this place is rather interesting; from all records it appears to have been used originally for the training of cheap thoroughbreds who ran at the old Empire race track and Jamaica course in New York in the 1920s. The trainer, who had used this as a vast public stable, died mysteriously in the early Depression years, apparently as the result of misleading an enraged owner to bet several thousand dollars on a horse that broke down in the backstretch. There was a very small market for such places at that time, so Daddy was able to get it cheap. Daddy was always able to get everything cheap except for some sense of his own life; that was always beyond his means, not that I want to criticize him unduly. I do not want to criticize him at all. I do not want one breath of criticism for one moment to pass these lips because everyone knows how I love and revere Daddy. So it is sufficient to say that he knew a bargain when he saw one and moved possessions in, with great plans to make it a year-round resort area for us, and eventually, when his fortunes improved, to use the facilities for a little horse-training himself, for thoroughbreds that is. He had always imagined himself at a box in Saratoga.

Unfortunately Daddy's reach exceeded his grasp, in this as in so many other details, and he was unable to make it to the lawn of Saratoga. The only horses which were stabled in the enormous barns in New Jersey or sent galloping over the training track were the broken-down jumpers and show horses stabled here for a few months on their way to the hackers. Still, even to this day, and there have been no horses here for almost a generation, the place is absolutely redolent of them; their smell still seems to waft from the stables and in the late nights I can hear them galloping, galloping. I know that this is some kind of hysteria, predicated upon my incestuous feelings for Daddy to say nothing of the symbolism of the great riderless horse, but I am only trying to tell the truth as I see or smell it. Not only the barns, but the house itself seems to reek of them; sometimes I think that if I were to fling open this door unexpectedly at a time when it was not locked against me I would see the leering head, the glowing eyeballs of a horse, pawing at the floor and glaring at me. The rooms are small, too small for people, let alone horses, but then again they are extremely patient animals, not to say long-suffering and dumb. I could sleep ringed by them, their monstrous features contorted to alertness. In the center of this net of the ruined horse, I dreamed of Empire City, or then again it might have been Monmouth at which he raced. It is so difficult to keep all these details ordered.

We let it run down after Daddy died, Jane and I. It was all our fault, we could have kept it up, we could have sold it for that matter, but we did neither. We simply let it sink slowly into the landscape of New Jersey, not to say its own wretched terrain. We let the termites and swamp have at it, and by the time we attempted the restoration it was too late for anything but the skeletal reconstruction.

It was Jane's idea to bring the estate back to what it had been in the 1940s, but like so many of Jane's ideas it lacked follow-through. A contractor was called in, and originally Jane was supposed to spend the time between her fourth and fifth marriages coming in three times a week and checking on the work.

Restoring the house seemed like a good idea, reconstructing part of the past so that we might at any time be able to go back here and recapture a kind of serenity. At least that was the way that Jane put it. It sounded very good at the time, but then all of Jane's ideas sound good at the outset, just as her marriages did. It is only after the full unfolding, the flowering of those ideas, that their failure can become visible.

For one thing there was no serenity in that past, and for another there was never any way in which we could return to it. How could we go back there? Daddy was dead, Jason was dead, Harold was dead, New Jersey was dying, the entire East Coast was turning in upon itself, slowly rotting in its poisoned history. Nicholas was dead, too. In fact, almost every person who had played a significant part in my life was dead — except Jane, who was having trouble dealing with precisely just that fact: that she was alive, that she had crossed the fifty-year line and was on the verge of being old; it had never occurred to her for a moment that she would ever have to deal with the problem of getting on in the world. She had expected to die in a spectacular fashion while still in possession of her youth.

So it was this which probably had been the real reason for her decision to reconstruct the estate. It would make her young again, she could go riding bareback over the fields in the dawn and be the child she was at six and fourteen. But Daddy was dead and I was sailing with Nicholas. She had no one to go riding with then, and no hope that when she came back to the stables, old Bill would be there to throw a rope around the horses and tell her that she was his very own Elizabeth Taylor in *National Velvet.*

None of it, none of it was there, but the damned work was half done and the estate half ready, and since we had gone that far we decided that it might as well be used. As a retreat for me. Jane, after one visit to this place when the work was done, had said that she would never spend a night here; it had been a terrible mistake and all hers, and she apologized for it, but that was her position on the matter. My feelings were not as negative. For one thing, I had not gone riding out over these fields with Daddy in the early hours, and for another it struck me from the first as an excellent place to die. Which it certainly is.

3
1963 — WASHINGTON

"You'll go with me, of course," Jason said. "This is strictly a campaign tour and I want you along."

"I don't want to go," I said. "I hate Texas and I hate being used by you. Campaign on your own. I want to go to Paris."

"And see that damned Greek again?"

"I haven't seen him in a year," I said. "That's a disgusting thing to say."

"Come on, Vivien, I'm no fool. You don't have to lie to me, I know what's going on. I can't even say I care very much, although there are nasty political implications. That man owns half his country."

"I haven't had anything to do with him."

"You don't understand," he said in his best logical, mature and restrained manner — the way in which I found him the most infuriating — not to say that I did not find him infuriating in almost all ways. "I don't care what you do, you can go from France to Barcelona to London to Martha's in a weekend as far as I'm concerned, but when I call on you to do something, you do it."

"I'm not one of your lackeys."

"You're going to Texas with me," he said. "It will just be for a weekend. I want you with me in public, at the banquets and in the motorcade. Otherwise you can do as you will. You always liked Neiman-Marcus."

"Right. I can just gather up my forty Secret Servicemen and slip into Neiman-Marcus."

"You can cooperate is what you can do. This isn't easy for either of us, by God, but you will."

"I hate the whole damned state of Texas. I hate everything that it represents. You don't have to go there either, you know that."

"I have to go everywhere. We're in the middle of a real campaign here."

"The election isn't until next year."

"We've been in a campaign since the day we were elected. Once I get past the next election we can look at this in an entirely different way, but right now we have to seize every advantage."

"That's Harold talking. I hear him in you," I said to Jason.

"That's truth."

"I'm so sick of the two of you," I said, "with your campaigns and seizing advantages and always doing the right thing and later on knowing that things will be entirely different. Why can't they be different right now? Why do you have to plan and plot everything?"

"This is getting us nowhere," he said. "This is an old argument. I want you to be there, and you're scheduled in, and that's the end of that. Now, if you don't mind, I have things to do."

"You're dismissing me, is that it?"

"Oh come on, Vivien, this is ridiculous. We're not getting anywhere when you're this way."

"I hate Texas," I said. "I hate your political career too and campaigning and everything it represents. Just once I want to have my own way."

"You've always had your own way."

"Why can't you do something for me?" I said. "Don't go to Texas."

"Ridiculous. It's all scheduled in."

"So unschedule it. Say that there's a change of plans. Does the President always have to take orders?"

"The President is the servant of the people."

"You don't believe that."

"You say a lot of things in this job you don't believe. But now and then it enables you to say something you do believe in very much and work for it. Texas is part of the price you pay for the good stuff."

"Oh, I'm so sick of it," I said. "I'm so sick of lectures in civics or political science. Can't you tell the truth just once in your life?"

"What is the truth?"

"The truth is you want to go there. You love it. And you want me to go there because it will make it even more successful from your point of view. You're not thinking of me or the country or even the second term, you're just thinking of the biggest kicks you can get and that means having me along. If you could get bigger kicks without me you'd do it that way. I want a separation," I said.

"What? What did you say?"

"I don't know," I said. "That just came out. I don't even know why I said it. I didn't mean to say it at all." Yes, I did, I thought. I never admitted to myself what I wanted until it finally came out of me. "None of this can come to any good. None of it. I see us dead. All of us. You, Harold, me. We're lost, doomed, star-crossed. Nothing can come out of this, only the emptiness of the void, the blackening of the pit…. Just forget it," I said. "I don't want to talk about it now."

"We will talk about it," he said. "We'll talk about it a great deal."

"Then face it," I said.

"Face what?"

"What?" I said. "I don't know. Life, fate, karma, call it what you will. You're trying to avoid it. Why are you?"

"What kind of a fool are you for even mentioning something like that? You must be very disturbed, Vivien, these thoughts are not the thoughts of a sane person. You have got to be a crazy person, Vivien, but I am not, and my people are not, and you're going to have to get yourself together and pull yourself out of it or very serious measures are going to have to be taken because you are seriously disturbed, seriously, do you hear me?" And he came over then and slapped me in the face.

4
1976 — PARIS

I think that Nicholas knew exactly what was going on. He *knew*, he always knew; there was a part of him which was always awake, even in intensive care, and must be awake yet.

5
1963 — WASHINGTON

The thing that I said before was not the truth, about Jason, I mean. It was a lie. He did not say those things about my being seriously disturbed and he did not slap me.

After I had said those things to Jason, he walked out of the room and we never talked about it again; perhaps we would have but perhaps we would not and because Texas was a week later we really do not know now, do we? We don't know what might have happened.

For the first time in many years I had actually reached him although in a terrible way; it might have reached him but in a way which forecast no good. After that, there was nowhere that we could go. It was all in front of us at that time: the disaster that our marriage had become, the impossibility of us ever accommodating to that marriage or ever leaving it. The shot which exploded his skull saved our marriage as time itself never would.

I must fight against the impulse to lie. If I begin to lie, then these memoirs will be absolutely worthless; they will be a mélange of the impossible and the artificial, the half or the fully true, impossible to separate, impossible to understand. And in the junkyard of all these confidences, all crushed and tumbled together, it will be impossible to separate the real from the surreal, meaning that all of it will collapse of its worthlessness. But I will not, I will not. They are all I have, I see that now, and at the moment of reeling these tales into the microphone, I found myself possessed of horror beyond even that when I saw her last night in the lights of the car; the horror of realizing that this was the last and the most precious act of my life.

Give me, give me at least this: that my life has had purpose and structure, that it has had meaning and its own kind of grace and that I do not have to lie, I do not have to lie to any of you to bring that grace forth.

6
1968 — NEW YORK

Harold wasn't like Jason. Jason would have said: "We're on the campaign trail, you're needed, come."

Harold was not that way. Harold could handle matters in an understated fashion, he could be indirect.

Harold did not say, you're needed on the campaign trail, you're scheduled in, you're coming. Harold said, "I know what kind of a strain this is on you. I wouldn't want you to think of coming. Of course your presence would be a great help, no use in denying that at all, but I couldn't possibly do it to you. It's just reliving a nightmare."

"It's reliving a nightmare for you, too."

"Ah, yes, but I have a definite sense of purpose. You do not. You do not see the true importance of this campaign."

"Yes, I do. Of course, I do."

"You do?" he said. "That's good. Then I don't have to explain to you what the stakes are and how every advantage, no matter how slight, must be taken. We're taking on the entire organization here. We've got pockets of support and we'll see them become ever wider as we start to make progress, but we have to consider the fact of what we're doing. We're coming in from the outside and no matter how much residual support we have we're going at the beginning to have to take on everyone. So of course you would help. There's no arguing that at all."

"You want me to come."

"Of course not," he said, "not if it will give you pain. You've got to think of yourself first. If anyone is entitled to be selfish, it's you."

"All right," I said, "all right. I'll come along. You let me know where I'm needed and I'll do the best I can. You are diabolical, you understand."

"No, I'm not," he said. "I am being realistic. Realism, part of it, is protecting you, isn't it? What good is this going to do any of us if it's obvious that you're just being dragged along? You have to want to come in your own heart, you've got to feel that it's right for you to be there and then everyone will see it. The other way would not work at all."

"All right," I said, "all right, but I still say you're diabolical." And so I went with him on the campaign trail, not on his plane, of course, but separately, making my own arrangements, having appearances — Harold called them *viewings* — at selected points. From Indianapolis to Omaha, from Salem, Oregon to San Francisco, to all the mysterious and terrible places of the country with primary elections. I went with him and there was not a single one where I was not waiting for the assassin's bullet, for the thin sound from far overhead which would indicate that it was all happening again, that the party, in its way, was getting back from Harold what he had dared to give them. On the platforms, in the television studios, at small meetings with the press, I went through the customary motions of elegance, sometimes beside Harold, quite often alone. But every time I came out of the studios to find them waiting for me on the sidewalk, I expected one to emerge from the rest with an aspect of purpose and say *It's all over. I'm sorry. He's dead.* At night in the hotel rooms I would dream I heard the ring of the phone, dream I had taken the phone off its stool to hear the voice say, *They got him. You'll have to plan the funeral; after all, you did such a lovely job the first time.*

And after all of this I would go on, push it away and go on, because I was not doing it for Jason. That was the way I had rationalized myself into it, that I was doing this now because I had not wanted to do Texas for Jason, maybe if I had, had shown the need to go with him, he would not have *had* to go — but for Harold, for Harold's simple and terrible need. There was nothing in his life that he had ever wanted other than to be Jason.

Edna and I would not have gotten along on the campaign trail, but Edna and I had never gotten along at all. Edna believed in Harold, while I did not; Edna was also probably aware of the fact that Harold and I had been to bed together (and imagined it to have been many times more than once), just as she knew of all of Harold's adulteries, but mine would have been the only one she could not forgive. Edna and I would have had a terrible time on the campaign trail, but fortunately she was home then, in the last stages of yet another pregnancy, and there was no way that she could have gone along without making Harold appear unsympathetic. So that source of tension was removed, although I promised myself that when Harold became President I would settle with him and with Edna in the only way that I could, give them the only gift of meaning: after the inaugural I would never set foot in the White House. I would probably never come to Washington again.

But that I withheld from Harold; I had no intention of telling him this until the time came. He would only have thought, wrongly, that I hated him. I did not hate him, I pitied him, but giving him that full knowledge probably would have destroyed him. The only way that you could hit the Kellys in the heart was to tell them that they did not reach you in the heart.

Harold, not I, raised the issue of assassination. We were in press head-quarters in Wheeling, West Virginia, a great state in Harold's memory, not so great in mine, and the press somehow had gotten the place of the conference wrong and were in the hotel across town instead of at the Democratic club; while they were being rerouted Harold and I had a few moments in the empty room, not even campaign or federal personnel around to talk.

"This would be an excellent time to do it, you know," he said. "No witnesses except for you, but then you're so used to it."

"Do what? Kill you?"

"Do we have to talk about this?"

"Why not? I know it's been in your mind from the very beginning and of course it's been in mine. It's one of the risks I had to calculate from the start, but it doesn't bother me. Do you know why?"

"You don't think it will happen?"

"It may or may not," Harold said, "but if there were logical people behind all of it they must be able to see that it wouldn't pay. Once they got away with it, but twice — never."

"You assume that it would be the same people."

"Of course," he said.

"There are a lot of lone vigilantes out there who might love to get the chance. Jason used to talk about them all the time. The night before he was killed, he did in the hotel room. Do you know that?" I reached for a glass of water.

"Do we have to talk about this?" I said. "It's hard enough for both of us, for the whole family, without being morbid."

"I don't mind facing the truth," Harold said. "I get a certain pleasure out of it to tell you the facts of the matter. Truth setting you free and all of that." He took the glass of water out of my hand, had a meditative sip, gave it back to me. "That's interesting, Jason telling you that. You never did pass it on to me, and he never talked about it with me at all. That proves what a fool he was, you understand. I have to say again as I said before, I loved him very much, but my brother understood nothing."

"He sounded very convincing."

"My brother was a romantic. He looked upon himself as some kind of focal point of history, as well as a glamorous archetype. Mailer had it right, you know; my brother was more actor than politician. He had that romantic, narcissistic streak. But if you know your American history the way Jason pretended to, you ought to understand that important political figures are never done in by vigilantes. They're done in by groups using point men who pretend to be vigilantes and they're done in for very good reasons. Just like Jason."

"All right," I said, "I'll ask you then. Why was he done in?"

He took the glass again, sipped it as if it were the purest hard liquor. I never did see Harold take alcohol, however. "I can't tell you that," he said. "I'm pretty sure that I know the answer, and I know how to deal with it, and I will, but at this point the only thing that telling you would do would be to implicate you. I want to hold it to myself; it's the one thing I've never discussed with anyone. But it will come out," he said. "Of that you can be quite sure. I'm counting on it. It's going to come out."

"And what then?"

"A lot of people are going to go to jail and a few are going to be killed."

"If that's so, why are you so sure that they wouldn't do it to you?"

"Because they wouldn't," Harold said. "They understand the way this country works as well as I do and they know that they couldn't possibly get away with it. No, all that they can do is to hope that I go away or that I get beaten, and, considering the odds as they look at them, they've got a pretty good chance. We're in a death struggle here. There's only one thing they don't understand, though, and that is that I'm going to take it to them. I'm going to win."

Looking at him, I could see that he was right. He was right, that was all; whether he or Jason had the truth on the political art of assassination, there was a force in him at that moment and all through those months which had never been in Jason who even at his best moments had seemed to be as much out of himself as in; constantly regarding his performance in terms of his own judgments. There was none of that whatsoever for Harold. He did not have to monitor his performance because he *was* his performance. I felt myself beginning to shake, and then his arm was around me, he took me against him and for once he was not ferocious, I could feel the arc of his body bend to receive me.

"This is very difficult for you, Vivien," he said gently. "Perhaps we shouldn't talk about it anymore. I'm sorry that I brought it up. It's going to be all right. It won't happen the way you fear. The bad times are over, we're going to set this country at peace with itself."

"I don't know if there's ever going to be peace for either of us, let alone the country."

"There will be."

"Why can't we just take care of ourselves and let the country go rot? What do we care about the country? What did the country ever do for

us but give us pain and murder my husband, and, Harold, I'm afraid that
they're going to murder you. I can't take it."

"All right," he said, "all right, Vivien."

"Give it up. Give up the campaign."

"Impossible. I know how you feel, but it's impossible. Besides it will
only be worse for everyone if I give it up. You think these people would
leave it at that?"

"What do you care about those people, Harold? If they're what you
say they are do you think that they're going to let you go ahead?"

"I told you they will. They have no choice."

"You call Jason the fool. I say that you are if you think they will."

"You'll see," he said and I felt him beginning to go tense against me.
Noises in the hallway, as the press found its quarry, began to beat toward
us. But not only that. It was something else tightening him the way that
he had tightened almost instantly that one afternoon we spent together
in bed. It must have been the perception that he was being touched in a
place where he had nothing to receive or feel that touch. And the lack
of that place, never perceived during all of the ordinary and extraordinary moments of his life, came upon him in shame and darkness, the pain
filtering from the other parts of him then toward the empty place that
should have been filled, could have been then a barrier against it. But
none, none, and how he got through that press conference I do not know,
but he did somehow and so did I and the press agreed that he was marvelous and that I was, as always, stunning. As if nothing had ever
changed at all.

7
1968 — CRETE

"We will need a formal contract," I said. "That is very important to
me."

"Of course," Nicholas said. "I always believed in the power of the written word. In fact, and you may not recall this, it was I who made the original suggestion for contracts a long time ago. I have no objection."

"I'm not really that kind of person, but it's the only way that there will
be peace between us. If everything is spelled out. Otherwise everyone will
always say that I married you for your money, and that is not so, but we
will begin to believe it too, and then where will we be? Where will we
be?"

"I agree with you absolutely," he said. "I will get my lawyers to work
on it immediately. It is settled then. You will marry me?"

I looked out over the railing at the Mediterranean. The owl and the
pussycat way out at sea in his beautiful pea-green boat, the waves roil-

ing around us, fifty below deck and yet the isolation so great that we could have been the only two people in this can on the sea which was exactly the impression to be sure which Nicholas wanted to give.

"Yes," I said, "I will marry you."

He put his arm around me. "I am truly grateful," he said. "I am grateful and humbled as well."

"I want my lawyers to look over the contract as well."

"If you do not trust mine — "

"It is not a matter of trust. It should be done the proper way. You are the one so insistent upon things being proper, so let's let it be so."

"Very well," he said. "Whatever you choose. I do not wish to do anything against your interests or which would hurt you." He drew me against him. "Would you kiss me?"

He was as shy as a small boy. I felt the cool, dense pressure of his lips and wondered what he would be like in bed when we had gone beyond the last contract, when all of the signatures had been notarized, when the last clearances had been undertaken. I had a pretty good idea, but there was no certainty. There was no certainty in any of it. His kiss opened up slowly and then I felt his tongue heavy, granular inside my mouth. It was not unpleasant, but the insistence into which he broke, the smell of the sea, the hard planking cutting into my hipbone as he pressed me back made the moment suddenly difficult, and he, feeling that, feeling my withdrawal, released me. He put his hands on my shoulders, held them there for a long time.

"It will be all right," he said. "I know it will be all right."

"Yes, of course it will."

"There are many difficult moments to come between us but essentially it is right. I offer you far more than sanctuary, I offer you love."

In the distance I could see the little rounded outlines of islands, brown mounds scooped against the waters, and I wondered how many women he had stood with against this railing, and what they had seen and what they were thinking. His hands were against my back and then they drifted forward, they were around my waist, and he was drawing me away from the railing.

"Never," he said, "never anyone else but you, not really. Not since that time almost ten years ago when I first met you."

"You don't have to say that. I don't need to hear you say that."

"Except that it is true. If it were not true I would not say it. I am not that way." He pointed toward the sullen little outcroppings of earth in the distance. "It is beautiful," he said. "There are many places there where you can be utterly alone, where you can bathe naked, where you can lie on the beach for hours in the sun and hear a private music and it is like you are the only person in the world. You can have that. I can give you whole worlds which only you will occupy."

"Do you think that is what I want? To be utterly alone? To be in my own world?"

"In part, yes, it is what you want. You have never had that opportunity. You have lived for others, you have been obligated to others for so very long that you are entitled to be only with yourself."

"And how about you?"

"I will be with you if you desire. Or I will not be with you as you desire. I will give to you what you want." His lips were against my neck and I felt them part, felt his tongue imprint itself there. The sensation this time was not unpleasant and I felt the beginnings of yielding. "You do not have to ask in order for me to give."

"I would not marry you if I did not want you with me."

"I understand that," he said, "I understand that." And I felt his hands against my breasts, the movement taking them there imperceptible. One instant he was holding my waist, the next my breasts, and I appreciated, not for the first time, his enormous skill. He always knew what he was doing; he had a certain, real sense of style.

"As you wish," he said and moved me from the rail just as a plume of water came over the place where I would have been. "We can have some wine if you wish," he said. "The sea is getting a little rough; I think that it would be best for us to go down."

"Yes," I said, "yes, as you wish," feeling myself quite helpless in his possession at that moment. And it was a good feeling, a feeling I had had with Jason at the beginning and then intermittently toward the end, committing myself utterly to him, a feeling of at last being able to cede responsibility for my life to someone who would know exactly what to do.

We went into the bowels of the boat together and to his cabin, a private place which I had never before seen, and in that cabin we had sex. Sex with him was in a certain way exactly as I had imagined and in another way it was entirely different. It was how I had imagined in that he was absolutely competent, completely controlled, and seemed to know exactly what he was doing at every moment, subordinating his desire to mine, concentrating with his eyes closed to some imagined rhythm of my response so that he gave to me exactly what he felt I needed at the moment that he was doing it and only at a few of those moments was he wrong. He was in control; his technique was superb and he made me his creature in that what he felt I wanted became that which I did. In this sense he gave me what I wanted and yet the sex was different.

It was different in that for one thing I found myself unable to climax, although he did everything he properly could to make that climax inevitable. It was different in that at the moment of his own long-delayed climax when I had convinced him that it did not matter, and that I wanted him to hurry, hurry, hurry toward his own finish, he collapsed upon me, his face deep into my shoulder, and I could hear for the first but not for the last time the thin and devastating sound of his tears.

8
1978 — NEW JERSEY

There is someone else in this house.

I am not imagining this. It is nothing that I have imagined. There are voices outside, and one is new. I have heard that voice before but not in months, not in several months. What they are saying I do not know. The door muffles, planks and boards and insulation of this wretched old house muffle the words, but the timbre is clear.

She is in this house. She has come inside. Annie has let her in and now the two of them are deep into discussion as to what they should do next. Whether they should wait for nightfall or whether they should do it now and be done with it. So for all I know at this moment I am in the last instants of my lifetime, and they are deciding the best way to come inside and have it done with. They may be choosing lots as to who will do it.

My money is on Annie. I would not bet against Annie. Matters have a way of working in her direction.

I could open this door and go down the hallway and find out for sure. There are only a few reasons why I am not doing this. One is that if I were to find this out for sure, the panic would be absolute and I might be unable to meet with courage what awaits me. Another reason is that I do not want to see her. If I saw her I would be unable to control myself (and the same would be true for her), and there would be an end to this immediately, an end which I am not quite ready to face.

Which leads to the third reason why I will not try the door: because it would bring this dictation to an end and I am not ready to do so. Never have I felt so close to Jason or Harold or Nicholas as I have during these last comforting hours talking into the machine. At last it is all coming clear to me at some level; this must continue, I must go on because I finally have the opportunity to understand my life. Everyone for so long has claimed to understand it and perhaps this is so but I, the center of it, never did and I am entitled to this.

So let them talk. Let them sit there and make their plans; let them calculate who will do it and how. Leave me only with these tapes.

9
1952 — WASHINGTON

"You remember me," Jason had said over the phone. "I was the Senator whom you interviewed so charmingly."

"I couldn't forget you," I said. "How could I forget you?"

I was not at all surprised that he called. I knew exactly what he was and what he was likely to do and the only surprise was that it took him three days rather than the two I had thought. But then they had had a lot of bills in committee that week, he told me. I had to stand in line.

"How could I forget you?" I repeated encouragingly, always flattering the man, as Miss Spence's had made quite clear was the proper technique for such occasions.

"I'd like to give you the opportunity to inquire some more," he said. "How about letting me pick you up at the office, say tomorrow night?"

"I won't be in the office tomorrow. I'll be out in the field."

"So you can pick me up at the Senate Office Building. Lord knows, you know where to find me by now."

Look, I wanted to say to him, this will not work out. I do not want to see you. Nothing will come of anything between us but pain and misunderstanding. It was as if I could look down the long tunnel of circumstance, could see what would come between us; listening to his voice on the phone it was as if the future itself was delivered to me in full but it was only in a single, shattering glimpse and then the curtains dropped again. The vision flicked out.

"All right," I said, "what time?"

"About five o'clock," he said, "oh make it four, the hell with it. I'll leave early for once. It doesn't make any difference anyway. There's so much bullshit in this job you wouldn't believe it. My God, don't quote me!" he said quickly. "I forgot that you're the Inquiring Photographer."

"I'm not inquiring," I said, "I'm not quoting."

I went to the Senate Office Building, and Jason was there waiting for me, and we talked for a while in his office, and then we went out to dinner and then we went back to his apartment and had sex. It was not very good the first time, but then you are never supposed to judge a relationship by the first attempts at sex. Sex has to grow between two people and find its own level, something else that they do not teach you at Miss Spence's. Although it would be much better for everyone if they did.

"I'm going to marry you," he said two days later. "You know that, don't you?"

"You seem very sure of yourself."

"You haven't said no, I noticed, so you know that it's true."

"Do you always get everything you want?"

"No," Jason said, "I do not. I rarely get what I want and that which I most want has been denied me which means that I'm the surer that I'm going to marry you because this is something I have to have."

He said this in a different tone, the words coming out of some dark level of him where his voice was slow and strained, just as it was during sex, and I believed him. I believed him at that moment. I believed him at most moments, which might have been part of the trouble. And then again it might not. They were charming, the Kellys, and they had a tendency to give others what they thought others wanted. But that touch of blarney should not conceal the fact that in many ways they did have a tendency to tell the truth. Certainly Jason did at that time. He had indeed been denied what he most wanted, and it took him almost twenty years to catch up with it on the streets of Texas.

10
1968 — NEW YORK

"I have deliberately postponed this meeting," Nicholas said. "I admit it. Carrie is a difficult and unusual woman and I do not know how you will react to one another. I want you to get along, to like one another, but I have been afraid that you will not, and that is why I have delayed and delayed this meeting of the minds. It is not easy for me." He put a hand across mine and I could feel the slight tremble. It was the first time that I had any sense of Nicholas losing control, outside of sex, of course. "My daughter is a fascinating and difficult woman," he said. "We have never truly gotten along well together, perhaps because we are too similar. She is also strong-willed."

"So am I," I said. We were in a restaurant off Fifth Avenue. Long since, it has been converted into a sleazy gift shop, but at the time it was one of the right places in New York. It had been Nicholas' idea to arrange this first meeting in public, probably because he had images of a strained confrontation. But even with that he had taken a back room in the restaurant, one of three, elegantly furnished for their most special patrons. We had met fifteen minutes before Carrie was supposed to be there, and I did not realize until that time how he really felt about his daughter and why he had put off our meeting. A fascinating and difficult person, he said, but if you can understand her I think you will like her.

"And does that matter? It is you I am marrying and living with, not her."

"Yes," he said, "yes. But it would be so much easier if you did like her, if you got along well together. It would be easier for all of us."

"I think you're making too much of this," I said, and Carrie, escorted by the headwaiter, appeared at the door of the room. Nicholas came to his feet, allowing the napkin to fall from his lap. She looked exactly as she had in the pictures although the pictures had not made clear the delicacy, the fragility of her appearance. My first impression was one of weakness, but from the way she approached her father, looked at me, took her position at the table, I saw that this was not so true; if there was any physical lack in her it had been understood early and dealt with ruthlessly. This was a girl, then in her early twenties who simply would not yield at all, not to herself, not to anyone.

"I'm pleased to meet you," she said, but I could see that she was not pleased at all and then Nicholas was on his feet, babbling, introducing us effusively, acting as I had never seen him before, deferential to the point of being frantic, the headwaiter himself looking with astonishment. "Bring me a drink," Carrie said. "You know what I want." Nicholas whispered something to him and the man went away.

The three of us sat in the room and there was a silence. "I want you to like each other," Nicholas said uncomfortably. "I want you to like one another, this is important to me."

"It doesn't matter whether we like one another or not," Carrie said. "This is a circumstance beyond our control."

"Beyond yours, perhaps," I said. "Not beyond mine."

"You will find out," she said. She looked at me openly, prolonging it to a stare. "You are as attractive as I thought you would be," she said. "The question is what you hope to gain from any of this."

"I find that a very impertinent remark."

"You are going to have to learn to deal with these remarks," she said. "You will hear a lot of them in the times to come and you cannot be protected as you think you should be."

"Protected? From what?"

"I don't think you're a martyr," Carrie said. "I am not at all taken in by your so-called legendary aspects. I think that you are a very shrewd, very calculating person who knows exactly what she is doing at all times."

"Please," Nicholas said. "This is not the purpose of our meeting. I do not wish to hear conversation of this sort."

"You certainly do, Father," Carrie said, "and that is why we were brought together. I am afraid that you too will have to learn to live with truths if you wish to survive this relationship."

The drinks came. Carrie stopped talking and looked at the two waiters with such loathing that they seemed intimidated as the staff in this place never had been before. They left quickly, little pulses of panic showing underneath their control. She held her glass and took one careful sip, then put it down. "You know my attitude on this," she said. "I have concealed nothing from my father and my father should have concealed nothing from you. I am not in favor of this."

"Who are you that your favor was asked?"

"My father probably did not tell you," she said. "I can see my attitude is a surprise to you. It would not be and this would not have been so difficult if he had been honest."

"Please," Nicholas said, putting his napkin down. "Nothing will come of this if matters are handled in this way. We all have much to learn from one another."

"Why didn't you tell her, Father?" Carrie said. "She was entitled to know. Did you not believe me? Did you think that I would come here and make this a social occasion?"

"I did what I think is best," Nicholas said. "I still feel that we can all be friends."

"That was weak of you, Father. It would have saved much difficulty if you had told her the truth."

"I don't see any point to this," I said. "If you are resigned to hating me, nothing will change things here. Maybe one of us should leave."

"I don't hate you," she said. "I understand you, which is a different thing entirely. You have your reasons and purposes just like the rest of us, but I do not happen to like them. I don't have to like them, do I?"

I put my own napkin down. "I think I am going to leave," I said. "I don't understand why you have this kind of resentment. I have no ill feelings toward you, and if you are trying to protect your father, you can be sure that he hardly needs your protection. I don't want his money. Is that the real reason for this? I have no need of his money; I have an independent income and I'm quite sure that I could triple it doing anything I wanted to do."

"But you don't want to do anything," she said, "or you would have done it already. You are doing precisely as you wish."

I stood. "This is getting us nowhere," I said. "I would have liked to have been your friend but I would settle for civility. Even that, however, you are denying me and therefore it would be best if I left."

I went to the door. She sat, hands folded in her lap, saying absolutely nothing. For a moment I thought that Nicholas would sit there too, that the two of them would be content to simply let me go and this must have shown in some hesitancy as I came near the curtains. The hesitancy disgusted me. I drove my way through and up the aisle of the restaurant, the staff looking at me, a few people at inner tables regarding me with the old, greedy interest, and I was at the revolving door before the street, the owner coming toward me, arms upraised, with an attitude of panic — when I felt Nicholas finally touch me on the shoulder and then turn me around. He was sweating.

"You must forgive her," he said. "She is only a child. She is very jealous and there were things with her mother — "

"It is not mine to forgive. There is nothing to say."

"This changes nothing as between the two of us. It could not possibly change that. Everything is as it was. I must apologize for her. She will change her ways when she realizes what we have."

"No," I said, "she will never change her ways. What she feels now she will always feel."

"That is not so, and in either case the future is imponderable. Come back to the table now."

"No," I said, "I am not going back there. I will not sit with her anymore."

"Please," he said. "For me. She will be better, I promise. Look, we are making a scene here. Many people are staring at us. In the next moment they will come from the tables and ask for autographs."

"Not in this place," I said. "People here have manners and civility and regard for others. Your daughter is very much out of place here. She would not be happy here at all."

"Please," he said. His voice was calm, but his eyes were dense and somehow wild. "Come back to the table. Do not dishonor me."

"Do not dishonor you? What is being done to me?"

"Do not make me do this," he said. "Do not make me force you. I am asking you to get back to the table. Things will be better. I have already had strong words with her."

"I don't want your money," I said. "I don't want any of it, doesn't she understand that? That isn't what I wanted at all."

"I know that very well," he said, guiding me down the aisle. I permitted myself to be led. To go out alone onto Fifth Avenue at that time of day was frightening, and who would take care of me? Who would find a cab? For just a moment the thought had come, *Well, I can call Harold and he will get me out of this*, but in the next instant was the battering realization that I would never call Harold again, that there was nothing he would be able to get me out of, not now, not ever because he was in something so deep that he could not get himself out. "You will have everything you want," he said, leading me back to the room, the curtains parted by two concerned, silent staff. She sat at the table, facing us like an ornament on display, legs crossed, holding her drink tightly.

"We are back," Nicholas said, "and there will be no more of this, do you understand me? There will be no more because I have ordered it. If she is good enough to come back despite your behavior, then she is good enough to be treated with respect."

She took a sip of the drink, shook her head, put it down. "Are you listening to me?" Nicholas said.

"I heard everything you said."

"Then apologize."

"I will not apologize," she said, "but I will not be rude either. I am willing to go on from here if you desire."

"Do not patronize me," I said. "I do not have to be patronized; I am entitled to my own dignity."

"You are entitled to what you are given," she said. She stood then, surprisingly, extended her hand. "I will never like you," she said, "and it is impossible to pretend that this circumstance will ever change. But I can tell you now for my father's sake, and for what you seem to mean to him, that I will try not to do this again. He seems to care for you and because I care for him I will do this thing. But do not misunderstand."

"You are so, so kind," I said, not taking her hand. "I am so moved by your kindness."

Nicholas came between the two of us. "I see the beginnings of some peace," he said. "I see the beginnings of the possibility of some warmth, something between the two of you. Please," he said to me, "take her hand and let us be done with this."

I stood there, thinking of all the ritual gestures which men like Nicholas had lived within all their lives; a world in which death could be given to strangers in a thousand different ways but the shaking of hands, the conferring of gifts had some mystical significance. I put my hand out to her then. It meant nothing and if it meant nothing I could do it. I felt, not the cool dry clamp which I expected but the fluttering and damp hand of a very young girl.

"All right," I said, "all right then."

"All right," Nicholas said, "all right," and began to move chairs around, rearranged the table, the three of us were sitting soon in a confidential cluster around the unlit candles. It would be nice to say that the lunch went much better after that unpromising start but it did not, it did not go much worse either. We found, Carrie and I, that he had approximately the same perceptions of Paris and the same feelings about what the expatriate colony had done to Majorca. It is even possible that we had the same opinions on Nicholas, although on these we did not hasten comparison, but on other issues there was little possibility of *rapprochement* although those issues were not forced. The *coquilles St. Jacques* were exquisite as was the *boeuf Wellington*. It was a fine restaurant that summer, but the owner got into tax trouble and fled the country; the staff took it home piece by piece, and when I last passed the site two years ago, a man with a bottle was crouched in the doorway, singing one of the campaign songs of 1960.

11
1976 — CONNECTICUT

"No," Jane said when I came back from the funeral, "it is impossible for us to live together. I feel for you as you do for me but we know it will never work. Besides, my apartment is too small. It would never work out."

Of course this was only part of the truth. The real truth is that Jane, for the third or fourth time, was involved with her ex-husband, the Count from Brooklyn with whom she could apparently neither live nor live without, and the relationship had reached a crucial and delicate stage. The Count might marry her again, but then the Count needed a lot of time to think, to explore the relationship, to see whether or not there was a chance for them in this tortured world and the Count's difficult and profound mental anguish had to be conducted in relative solitude. My moving into Jane's apartment would have brought a baggage of security agents and autograph seekers. It would have upset the ritual of their renewed affair, to say nothing of the lifestyle of the very exclusive cooperative in which Jane, with some financial difficulty, was living in sin with the Count. So I could understand that, and I could even understand her failure to attend the funeral. She had always despised Nicholas in a very quiet way, but what was not fair was her saying that she knew I merely wanted to use her.

"You have got to manage on your own, Vivien," Jane said. "In a sense you have always been taken care of, but that cannot continue. You have got to be by yourself."

"Just for a few weeks," I said, "until I get myself together more or less. The funeral was terrible, you cannot imagine the shock."

"That's crap," Jane said. If nothing else she always had an appealing directness. "It was a relief to finally be rid of him, and you're going to inherit five hundred million dollars in the bargain. The funeral was the best thing that's happened to you in years, and don't forget it, kid."

"What do you mean I was glad to get rid of him?"

"Oh nothing," she said, perhaps reacting to my tone of voice, but then again it might have been something even deeper than that. "Nothing at all. I don't want to talk about him ever again. You know that I didn't go for your sake; it was easier for you this way."

"What do you mean though I was glad to get rid of him?"

"Weren't you?" she said. "He was becoming a bore. Anyway, think of all the lovely money."

"If you weren't my sister I'd hate you."

"Don't be ridiculous. You hate me more because I'm your sister. Fortunately you love me, too."

"I'm not going to inherit five hundred million dollars. I probably won't inherit anything. You think that Carrie would let that will go uncontested?"

"Oh, I know all about the prenuptials," Jane said. "Believe me, that doesn't mean a thing. You're in a very strong position, you're his widow. The best thing for you to do, I've been thinking, would be to go to the Willows for a few months. You can have some seclusion, you can get yourself together there in a way that you couldn't in the city. Hell, we put all that money into the lousy restoration, one of us ought to get some use out of it."

"I don't want to go to the Willows."

"It's the perfect solution. You can be alone there and get some of that good New Jersey swamp air. Come on, Vivien, it's not that bad. We grew up there."

"I don't share your feeling for the place."

"Well, you should. At one time we thought it would be St. Tropez. We didn't reckon with the oil companies."

"Can't you be serious, ever?"

"I'm being very serious. You can't stay with me and it wouldn't do you any good to be in this city, and you obviously don't want to be too far from it at this time. If you don't want to be alone, hire some help, for heaven's sake. Anyone would be honored to be with you there, and with a five-hundred-million-dollar inheritance you can certainly pay well. I know some agencies, if *you* don't. We can get you some very good people."

"So I should go out to the Willows with a staff and be alone for a while. That's what you want, isn't it?"

Jane took my face between her hands.

"Very important to me, but you're just carrying over the feelings you have for others. People mostly don't give a damn, Vivien. You're old news already, the funeral was last week, and now there's some actress with an out-of-wedlock child or a custody suit. Nobody's really that interested in you, dear, even if you look at the magazine covers and think that this is the case. It simply isn't. People have their own concerns and the few of us who really care for you get mixed up in your mind with the millions who don't. I don't want to get rid of you, dear, not at all. I just think that it would be best for you to be by yourself for a while. I'll visit you and I want you to visit me too. Every weekend."

"You don't care," I said, "you simply don't care. Do you?"

"What do you mean?"

"How much do you care?" I said. "If you can turn your back on me that way. I'm appealing to you."

"You turned your back on all of us," she said. "You thought you were an extraordinary person who could live by extraordinary rules, that nothing applied to you as it did to the rest of us. Only now, at the end of it, do you come to me to appeal. You turned your back on me every step of the way, on all of us."

"I never knew how much you hated me."

"I don't hate you," she said. "Every time someone crosses you, you say they hate you. You've done that ever since you were a little girl."

"Don't you know what I've been through?"

"You did it to yourself. Actually," she said, "I don't think you've been through that very much. You've suffered but all of us suffer. You've had pain but everyone in this world has pain. You've had more attention, more money, more support than any of the rest of us. Maybe it's time for you to grow up now and go out into the world a little. This was bound to happen sooner or later. Did you think that this would go on forever?"

"I'll leave," I said, "and I'll never set foot in here again. I'll never talk to you again."

"You're overwrought so I won't take that seriously. Why do you find every disagreement an act of hatred? Have you gotten that arrogant? Are you that far away from the world? It must be the company that you keep."

"I have nothing more to say," I said. I went to the door and then I came back. "I'm going to have to sit here a while," I said. "I told the chauffeur not to be back for an hour. I can't simply stand on the street."

She smiled, and then unreasonably she began to laugh, and I could understand her laughter. It overcame me and then I found myself joining her. I was laughing with her.

"This has got to be one of the major tragedies of your life," she said. "Dismissing the chauffeur for a longer time than you wanted. The way you have to struggle to manage in this world."

And then we were laughing and crying against one another, holding each other and she said, "It's all right, it's all right." And I was crying in her arms, something I had not done in so long that I could not remember the act, crying against her.

"You don't know," I said, "you don't know what I've been through. I can't tell you, either. I can't tell anyone as long as I live, they'd never understand, you don't know, you just don't know."

"Oh yes I do," she said. "If I don't, who can, my sister, my little sister?" She was crying too. "I'll help you," she said, "I'll try to help you.

Don't you understand that I'm doing this for your own good, that you've got to stand on your own, that somehow you've got to live alone in the world? What is the point otherwise? You have got to live for yourself, Vivien, not dependent upon me or anyone. That's why all of this has happened, because you wouldn't live for yourself. You thought that it could be solved outside but it can't be. It can't."

"You're no one to talk," I said, but did not say it aloud because I was so weary. I did not want to fight with her anymore, to lose her would have been to lose everything. We held one another in her room for a while and then it was all decided, all worked out. Jane would help me hire some people to go to the Willows and I would spend three or four months there in seclusion, resting and recuperating. At the end of all this I would be able to return to the world strong and renewed to pick up all the pieces of my life. That was all I needed, a little rest. It had all been overwhelming for me, but I would have the opportunity to withdraw from the world and come back to myself, and then everything would be as it had been before except stronger and better, because I would be stronger and better. Everything worked out for the best. All a matter of fate.

I cannot blame her for hiring Annie in any case. Annie was my idea exclusively. Annie was *my* inspiration. I can exempt Jane at least from that. From nothing else, however. Nevertheless, I do not hate her for any of this.

12
1967 — BOSTON

"It was all true, wasn't it?" I said to Harold in 1967. "All of the rumors, every bit of it."

"You must have known," he said. "I'm surprised that he concealed it from you. His medical condition was a fact of record."

"I'm not talking about his medical condition. I knew all about that, but it was supposed to be under control. It never bothered him or me for the last seven years. Of course he told me about that."

"Then what are you talking about?" he said. "I don't think I understand you now."

"The other stuff."

"What other stuff?" He had that appealing little-boy trait of appearing very dense when he wanted to so that it was impossible to trap him into any revelation; information would have to be fed at him as if he were totally ignorant. "I don't follow you at all, Vivien."

"Oh damn it," I said, "stop that, Harold. If nothing else we've been honest with each other. I feel that we trust each other. You've never done to me any of the things that Jason did. Don't do it now."

"I just don't know what you're talking about," he said. "If I did, I'd
be glad to answer you, but you're going to have to come to the point and
I can't do it for you."

"Oh, for God's sake," I said. "I mean the women."

"The women?"

"All the women that he was having."

"Ah," Harold said and leaned back, put his hands behind his head,
looked up at the ceiling. "Ah, the women. The women."

"It was all true."

"Nothing in this world," Harold said, "is completely true."

13
1963 — TEXAS

In the car he could not keep his eyes off the legs of the Governor's wife.
The night before he kept talking to me about the likelihood of being as-
sassinated, speak of "death in Texas" as he would. But he was not capable of keeping his eyes off her legs. The Governor, being the kind of
man he was, probably was delighted. There was a certain honor in having your wife or lover desired by the President. Staring at her in that
covert way, his eyes squinting as if against the sun, he undoubtedly
thought that I did not notice and I let it pass, as I had all the other times,
because it made no difference, no difference.

What could I have said? He would not have changed. There was only
one time when I brought it up with him, and that so disastrous that I
knew it would never be done again. So live with it, live with the Governor's wife, the Senator's wife, the Congressman's mistress, the appointment secretary's girlfriend, the secretary for the Interior Department, the
Defense Department, the Judiciary, live with all of it and I think that I
did so with a certain amount of grace. It was part of the motivations
which were driving him: he could not let it be.

"Well, sir, Mr. President," the Governor's wife said in a very meaningful
way, "you can't say that the state of Texas doesn't love you now."

He leaned forward to acknowledge the compliment with the most delicate of touches, and surely would have had his hand on one of those
splendid legs within a moment if external circumstances had not inter-
vened. He must have died as much in the want of touch as he did in shock
and pain. Or the shock and pain might have destroyed the desire and
granted him peace: one simply does not know.

14
1978 — NEW JERSEY

Sounds at the door, a key going in. So I was quite right; they had locked me in. Just as well that I did not try to leave. Panic would have set in. Odd but I feel no such panic at this moment. I feel completely calm, in control, reserved. These last hours have helped me, also the realization that there is nothing they can do to me that I have not already done to myself.

It comes and goes, it goes and comes, and I am sure that there will be moments ahead of me right up until the very end when I will feel the terror again, but at the time I say this I feel very much in control. Part of it has to do with what I have just said, and another part has to do with knowing that I have something that none of them will ever have, something that none of them will ever get. I am Vivien Blanc Kelly Sarris.

15
1978 — NEW JERSEY

"Well," Annie said, "are you ready for some dinner now? It's close onto dinnertime it is, nearly six o'clock and you must be very hungry. What do you want?"

"I want you to go away. Tell Tom to get the car ready and Millie to pack. I want to go back to the city for the rest of the summer."

Annie said, "That is impossible, as you're well aware. You're in no condition to travel."

"Let that be a judgment left to me. I've had quite enough of southern New Jersey, so if you'll be good enough to make those arrangements I'd be most grateful."

"Dr. Richards feels that your condition is much improved and has stabilized, but that you are in no condition to travel at this time."

"Screw Dr. Richards."

"That's easy for you to say, but if you're not going to be responsible for your behavior I must be. There are people who still care very much for you whether you think so or not and are going to protect your interests regardless. I'm not going to permit you to be a fool."

"You're not going to permit me to leave this house either."

"I certainly am not. Not until Dr. Richards has approved it, and until I've gotten your sister to give permission. I am not going to permit you to do anything that will bring you harm."

"Call Jane," I said. "I want to talk to her."

"Jane can't be reached. You know that perfectly well. She'll be here in a few days. She's in Europe now."

"She must have left you a number."

"Why would she have left me a number and not you? She is in transit, dear. She should be here by the weekend."

"You're probably talking to her all the time. You're telling her everything that's going on, reporting to her. Well tell her I want to get out of here."

"I'll tell you what," Annie said. "When she comes in we can all discuss it. If she approves, if she agrees that you can leave then we'll all pack up and go together. It's not a decision I can make myself but I'm happy to leave it to her."

"You're treating me like a mental patient," I said, "keeping me a prisoner here."

"You're not a mental patient, but you came here for a rest, dear, and you're going to get it. And I must say that more and more you're beginning to act like a mental patient, Vivien. Now what do you want for dinner?"

"The last supper, eh?"

"How's that?"

"The last meal for the condemned? Do I have my choice of anything or are my selections limited? Generally they let you have anything you want."

"I don't think you're funny, Vivien."

"I'm not trying to be amusing. Where do you have her? Where are you keeping her? In another of the bedrooms? Or are you all sitting around, Tom and Millie too, discussing the situation, having a good laugh and making plans for me? I'd just like to know."

"Keep who? What are you talking about now? What kind of ravings are these?"

"You know perfectly well who I'm talking about."

"I wanted to try," Annie said, coming off her hands and knees, "I really wanted to try and be pleasant. The doctor said that I had to show understanding and that you were entitled to extraordinary consideration and I took that to heart and was going to make one last try, but this is too much, Vivien. I cannot deal with this."

"Don't get away from the issue," I said. "The trouble with you, Annie, is that you simply refuse to answer questions, you retreat into accusations. You know exactly what I'm talking about and what I mean and all I'm asking is a civil question: where is she?"

Annie looked away and finally said: "Okay, I'm going to make you what I want to make you for dinner and bring it in and then I won't talk to you anymore at all. In the morning I'll phone the doctor and tell him that I'm going to leave and then I'll talk to the agency and get a replacement. This is my final word on this."

"I heard her voice in these halls," I said, almost shouting. "I'm not delusional at all. You have to grant me that. Paranoid, maybe. You seem to think that I'm paranoid, and maybe I've overreacted a little but I haven't gone to the voices and the little men with crosses yet. I heard her. She's in this house! Now tell me, what are you doing with her? And when is she coming in?"

She went to the door. "Don't you leave me now, damn it," I said. "You're not going to do it. You're always setting up these scenes to your own convenience so that they end with you making the decision that they've gone as far as they need to go and then you walk out but this is one damned time you're not going to do it." I came off the bed, went to her and seized her by her uniform, wrenched her into the room. "Tell me the truth," I said, "you lying bitch, just once in your life, tell me the truth" and began to shake her, wrenching her back and forth, and her arms came down, breaking my grip; staggering back against the wall I saw her face and it was the face of hatred. "Don't you ever do that to me again," she said.

"You shouldn't have — "

"Don't you ever touch me," she said. "I am not your property. I know what you think of people, that you own them, but you do not own me."

"You won't tell me anything," I said, "you won't give me the truth even when I'm begging."

"Vivien," she said. "If you act like a child you will be treated like a child. Don't you ever touch me again."

"I want to know where she is. I want you to bring her into me right now or take me to the place where she is. I want to face her."

"I'll bring you your dinner, and then I'm locking you in for the night, Vivien. If you are not fit for company, then it will not be imposed upon you. You will have all night to think of what kind of person you are, what you have done to those who cared for you. Maybe by the morning you will have a little understanding."

"You can't do this to me."

"You've done it all to yourself," she said and ran her hands over her uniform, straightening. "You are never to touch me again. The next time you touch me if you are unwise enough to do it I will protect myself to the fullest extent."

"Are you threatening me?"

"I think our relationship is at an end," she said. "I have attempted to be all things to you but no more. From now on we will deal with one another very simply, as long as I stay here, which I do not think will be long. I will tell you what to do and you will do it. I will bring you your meals and your medicine and you will take it. You will make no demands upon me and I will make none upon you. That is the way you wish to be treated and that is how it will be. You will be a very lonely person."

She went out of the room and closed the door and turned the key, making no effort now to have it quiet. The click was a sharp, single abrupt sound in the room, then the sound of the swamps overwhelmed, the helpless bleating of little crickets, the dull sound of wind as it cut across the ruined grass. I lay down on the bed and it must have all come out of me then and not a moment too soon, all of the things that had happened in the last hours, days, months. And on the bed I began to weep, but the tears this time were not for myself but for poor, damned Jason, poor, damned Harold and even a little bit for the most damned of us all: that fool, that monster, that creation with no source, Nicholas.

16
1963 — WASHINGTON

"Close the coffin," I said, "I want the coffin closed."

"It isn't necessary," they said to me, "we've done an excellent job of restoration, the wounds weren't as bad as they first appeared and we have accomplished a very handsome representation. I think you will be pleased."

"I don't want to see him. I saw him in life, that's enough."

"You understand that under the traditions of our ritual," the always-helpful Cardinal said, "the coffin should remain open."

This was two hours after we had gotten off the plane in Washington. The Cardinal was waiting for us. Margaret had lapses in dealings with her sons, but her communication with the Cardinal was always excellent. He had been at the airport, and he had been beside me from then on. Margaret, he had given word, was not up to it, she simply could not face the situation now. Her prayers and tears were with me, but if I had lost a husband, if the nation had lost a great leader, then she had lost a son and maybe her loss was the most terrible. Margaret could always turn a phrase; perhaps her boys had gotten their appreciation of good speech-writing from her. "Also," the Cardinal said delicately, "if your desire, as you have expressed it again and again, is to make them see what has been done to the President, what has happened as a result of violence, then the open coffin would be the best demonstration."

"I don't care," I said. "I don't care about ritual or religion. I want to do what's right but having it open is not right. Jason had too much presence. He would not have wanted pictures taken of him dead, people to pass by and see him sleeping. There was no style in that."

"It must be your decision," the ever-helpful Cardinal said, "I can only tell you what is right according to the rituals."

"Is murder right?" I said. "Does that fit in with customs and ritual? I don't really know too much about Catholicism I'm afraid. I had a lapsed upbringing. I didn't have the wonderful advantages that were given Jason or the close relationship with you that Margaret has, but I know that Catholicism is very big on death and blood and martyrdom and slaughter, blood of the lamb and so on and the idea of sacrifice, so maybe you take pleasure in this. But I don't and I don't want an open coffin. I'm the widow here and I'm entitled to my judgments as I see fit."

"She's doing very well," Harold said to the ever-helpful Cardinal. He too had been at the airport and had been beside me since then but these were virtually the first words I had heard him say since that terrible moment when we had embraced at the ramp and he had said, *They'll pay for this, they'll pay for this.*

"Of course she's doing very well. I didn't say otherwise."

"I think that we should go along with her wishes," Harold said. "If she feels that the closed coffin is best, there should be no objection."

"I should say not," the Cardinal said. "I merely felt it my duty to explain."

"You've explained," Harold said. "The coffin will be closed," he said to me. "It will be as she desires," he said to the Cardinal. He talked very respectfully but there was something underneath it and the Cardinal seemed to back away. "Of course," he said, "whatever the family desires."

"We'd better go," Harold said. "There are cars waiting. We had better go back to the White House."

"No," I said. "I want to stay with the coffin. I want to be with Jason."

"It would be easier for you if you did not. Jason is gone," Harold said. "He is no longer in that coffin."

"All that is left of him is in there. I want to be with that."

"I won't argue with you," Harold said. He put his hands on my shoulders, turned me toward him. I could feel the shaking, then a few flashbulbs went off in the distance. Meat for the *paparazzi*, someone's Pulitzer Prize nomination in the feature category. "Are you all right?" he said. "I think you're all right. I think that you're going to be magnificent."

"I'm all right. How are you?"

"I'm in shock," Harold said, "so I'm fine. I'm completely protected. Of course, after it wears off, you have to watch out for the bad signs, but for the moment I think I'm going to be all right, and for the next few days. Do you want me to stay with you? If not, I think that I had better go to Margaret. Edna is already there."

"As you wish."

"If you want me to stay I will."

"No," I said, "it's all right."

"You ought to get out of those clothes," Harold said. He sobbed once, put his hand before his face and the moment passed, the face that came from behind the hand was as cool and bland as ever. "They're all covered with blood."

"I know that. I want it that way. I want them to see what they have done."

"But you see they don't care," he said. "They don't care at all. If anything they're proud. Seeing the blood just gives them satisfaction."

"That's what you say. I believe in blood."

"You don't disagree with the Cardinal that much, do you? You see, you have a pretty close position on the human condition. All for blood."

"They didn't want to release his body," I said. "Do you know that? They wanted to hold it for autopsy."

"I got that all over the phone. I screamed and yelled a little. I guess it helped."

"They wanted me to sign forms as if he were some common stranger who had happened to drop dead on the street. At the emergency room they even wanted identification."

"Bastards," Harold said. "Texans. They'll pay for this."

"Lawrence was all right though," I said. "He was very graceful."

"I don't give fuck for Lawrence," Harold said quietly. "Lawrence can drop dead. I'll be back with you later tonight," he said. "Right now I'll deal with Margaret, which will make things easier for you. I know you never liked her."

"It doesn't matter. It's not her fault."

"We've got to learn to like each other," Harold said. "We've got to learn to hold on, to treasure each other. Don't you see what's happened now? Really, we're all that each of us has got. We're all in this together."

He turned and walked away quickly. I had an impulse to run after him but behind me they were beginning to wheel the coffin out of the plane and my first duty, of course, was to be with it. So instead of going after Harold, I went after the coffin. Same thing.

17
1964 — NEW YORK

"This whole family is cursed," Harold said the day he resigned from the Cabinet. He said it without irony or humor, as a straightforward statement. "You made a mistake getting involved with any of us. Look at what I've done now. I've taken down half the administration with me and Lawrence still isn't satisfied. He'd make me ambassador to Spain, if he thought he could get me to take it."

"He's doing the best he can," I said. As usual I was defending Lawrence. Nineteen sixty-four was my year to defend a great number of people, all of whom were indefensible. "He's in a very difficult position."

"He's not in a difficult position at all. He's the fucking President and he's going to be re-elected no matter who runs with him and he's going to be re-elected after that too and he still isn't satisfied. He wants everything," Harold said. "He begrudges every single vote. He begrudges me breath, too. But he'll never shake Jason as long as he lives, and he knows that."

"You're too hard on him."

"You'll learn," Harold said. "You'll learn if you keep your eyes open and stay around long enough. These Texans are all the same, there's not a one of them who's worth a damn. And remember where Jason was killed."

"Please," I said, "I don't want to talk about it anymore. There's nothing more to say."

"I'm sorry I'm upsetting you with that little detail of my brother's assassination. I'll try not to upset you in the future; I'll be forward-looking."

"He was my husband, Harold."

"He was the *President*," Harold said and he put down his head on his office desk and began to cry, the whimpers of a little boy. It was not the first time that he had done this before me but he allowed it to go on longer than it usually did, perhaps thirty seconds. It was as if he measured out his moments of lapsed control the way that he measured out everything else. Very contained boys, the Kellys. I resisted the impulse to hold him; I had tried that before and he had always pushed me away as if I were interfering with his grief. His hands came down from his face and he was fine again. "Well," he said, "so much of that for now. The curse is still holding; I'm dragging down everybody in the Cabinet, you see. I think I should celebrate by spending the evening at home. Do you want to join me?"

"Edna won't be too happy to see me."

"Edna isn't happy with most things nowadays."

"You know what I mean. She damned well knows that there's something between us other than just survivorship."

"I don't follow you."

"She thinks we're fucking," I said. "You know she does."

"That's direct enough for me. I don't think she knows anything. Edna's less conscious than you might think, Vivien. She's just concerned with other things."

"Every time I'm there we have a miserable evening. It's not even her fault. I just can't make myself care."

"Your decision," he said. "God, I feel shitty. This is the shittiest I've felt since late November. Margaret said the night Jason was killed that she had always believed in the curse, but it was just something that we had to bear; we lived more hugely than others both in the great and the small and it was part of the price we had to pay. I think that she always knew what was going to happen, and some part of her might have even wanted it to happen and that is terrible but explains more than I need to know."

• • •

We strolled through his empty outer offices and down the corridor and it was at the elevators that the *paparazzi* caught us. "A statement on your resignation, sir. Any differences with the President? Would you care to say that the President's statement and your own resignation were linked in some way? What is your opinion of this, Mrs. Kelly? If Mr. Kelly were to decide to seek the Presidency independently would you back him?"

"Leave her alone," Harold said, "leave her out of this." He put his hand on my shoulder to calm me. "I have one statement and then we are leaving. Mrs. Kelly and I are old and close friends and it is unfortunate that she has to be part of this, but I think you agree that she is entitled to every consideration and should not be bothered with questions. My own resignation was an individual act made on its own grounds. I have no intentions of seeking the office of the Presidency either for this term or in the foreseeable future. The President has my complete support and I am willing to expend all efforts requested of me during the campaign. If he so desires I will place his name in nomination at the convention one month hence or I will be one of the seconders. My own plans at this time are completely unformed. I might consider seeking office in the Congress or Senate for the coming term and then again I might return to private life." The elevator doors opened with a whisk. "That is the substance of my statement, gentlemen, and I have nothing to add to it," and he guided me into the elevator and we fell away from them, all the way to the basement where he showed me the private way that led directly to his car, the chauffeur half dozing within it.

"It's all a matter of style," Harold said. "It's all a matter of handling. You have to learn that they don't take any of this seriously, they're just going through the motions but if you treat them with respect and don't let on that they know how empty and pointless their own role is, you're all right. It's only when you insult them that you can get into trouble."

He winked at me, guiding me into the car for the ride to the airport. "That was something I learned from Jason," he said. "Jason was magnificent with the press. It was one of the two things in the world he could do better than me. The other was to persuade a woman like you to marry him."

Yes, yes, all right. I guess I might as well say it. I loved him.

I loved him very much. I might have loved him as I never did Jason. *How dark my sin, darker than desire.* Roethke. Another legacy from a gentle education. Darker, darker than desire.

I loved him.

18
1969 — THE RIVIERA

For the first few months Nicholas and I were close but then I began to miss New York, to say nothing of my autonomy, and so we fell into the pattern that soon became our marriage: a week with him and then two weeks in the city, a rendezvous off the coast of Spain and then a trip to Paris, Washington and the dedication of yet another monument, then off to Montreal with Jane for a fast, anonymous weekend. I kept a careful, cryptic account, and in the third full year of our marriage found that I spent only fourteen weeks with Nicholas.

He did not seem to mind. "I want you to live in the way that makes you happiest," he had said on the day of our wedding. "I will do nothing to constrict your life, I realize that I have married not only a woman but a world figure."

Still, now and then, during the two- or three-week separations, I would find myself looking at my watch, calculating the time in the Mediterranean, wondering what he was doing at exactly that moment. Were there other women? Was there another woman? Or, outside of me was his life simply as he said: cruises and business, business and cruises? I did not know.

I do not think that I would have minded other women if there had been. It would have taken some pressure off me, diminished the sense of obligation. Only with Nicholas could I realize the good that had come out of the bad things with Jason: I was not totally responsible for meeting his sexual needs, he was able to function without me and indeed imposed upon me no sense of obligation. Nicholas was different. Now and then he told me that it was for him as it had been with no other woman and sometimes in my mind it went beyond that: he had Carrie, of course, and I had no doubt that she was his, but for a long time perhaps he had not even been able to function with anyone. Perhaps sex with me was not only the best that it had ever been for him, but, more importantly, the only sex he had had for a long time.

Carrie was not having any of it. Nicholas was able to keep our meetings to a minimum. She would shuttle on when I shuttled off, but there were occasions when he could not keep us apart. Despite her pledge in the restaurant she was not making much of an effort at all. She remained at a level of sullenness for the most part, but it was always clear that she hated me and it was not difficult, accordingly, for me soon enough to decide that I hated her.

"I know what you're doing to him," she said once to me in the Riviera house where her visit was supposed to end as mine began. It failed to do so by a day, and that meant we spent one uncomfortable night there together while Nicholas was working on some subtle, dangerous transaction involving cargo ships for Vietnam. "And I think you're killing him, that's what I think. Don't you know what this does?"

"He's never been happier. He's told me so. And he looks happy."

"I know how he looks. Don't tell me how my father looks. You're away from him two-thirds of the time or more. Don't you have any compassion for what these separations do to him? He seems to love you, God knows why, and that means he wants to be with you all the time but you seem to be happiest away from him."

"Why don't you let your father and I work these things out as we see fit?"

"Because he must be taken care of," she said fiercely. "He is my father but he is a child. He does not know what is best for him, and, except in his business, he is the world's fool. I see what you are doing to him and you're not the first but there is none he ever cared for enough to marry. You cannot go on this way."

She had become hard and beautiful in the two years since our first meeting. At twenty-one she had had the imprecise aspect of a girl who had just achieved beauty but still could not dwell comfortably within it. The two years had worked on the edges and taught her how to tenant not only her body but her soul so that she was one with herself. But the soul was deadly. It illuminated with a force which might have been stronger than grace but all the deadlier because of that. I looked at her and wondered how many men she had had and what she had done to them and then I thought, you are being very naïve, Vivien, you of all people who should know this world. This girl does not deal with men. This girl deals with no one except herself. No woman who had ever been with a man, or with another woman, who had given even the smallest part of herself necessary to the act of sex, no such woman could do so and still be like this. She was absolutely pure: the virginal holiness of Joan of Arc, except that she served different purposes.

"You stay in your part of the house and I will stay in mine," I said, "and tomorrow I will be gone and we will be able to avoid this for months."

"We will not avoid it at all. We will not avoid it for a moment, we will deal with it. Do you know how much he loves you? Do you?"

"I think so," I said. "I have a better idea of it than you do, anyway."

"Do you? You know nothing."

"I know enough," I said.

"You are killing my father," she said. "In everything you do you are killing him. And you understand nothing."

"I have had enough of you," I said. "I have not heard one kind word from you since I met you, not one. You have done nothing but try to give me the greatest amount of pain and insult and I have done nothing to deserve this. Unless," I said, "you're in love with your father in a way different from what you are *saying* and you hate me for being able to do something that you never can. Is that it?"

I should not have said it, it may be the most terrible thing that one woman can say to another but even as it came out of me I was glad. I thought that she was going to slap me and I was quite prepared for that. It was something that I had been looking for, perhaps hoping for from the outset, to have the provocation and opportunity to give to her what I wanted, what I think she needed. With that cunning which never, even up until the end, will desert her she did not do this however, she merely looked at me calmly, little white splotches carved out on her brown cheekbones.

"I did not really know, for all I said, until this moment what a fool you were," she said. "You understand nothing and never did. It is incredible. You are almost twice my age and yet you are a terrible absolute fool. I am sorry for you," she said. "Now I understand why you have lived such a tragic life. I am even sorrier for all of those with whom you have been involved.

"You will learn," she said, "you will learn and it will all be too late." And she turned and went from me and that was the last time I saw her until the funeral.

19
1976 — CRETE

"I will kill you," she said at the funeral. "You will die." Then she moved away from me. It was a magnificent day; sun high and rosy overhead, just like Texas, I must say, or the day before the night that Harold was put down.

20
1978 — NEW JERSEY

It has occurred to me, only now, which proves that Carrie may have been right, which proves that indeed I may be a fool, that all three men with whom I have been most intimately involved died in sudden, violent and terrible fashion. Does this mean that I merely have a complex kind of bad luck or could it be said as surely Carrie would say that one makes exactly the destiny which one most wants? I did not, I did not want it to be this way.

21
1978 — NEW JERSEY

Is Dr. Richards really a doctor? Or is he merely another actor like Annie? His performance is excellent, his timing impeccable, even his distraction seems calculated toward reality and yet despite his certain hand with the stethoscope and his knowledgeable talk he may not be a doctor at all but simply another hired hand to enhance, as they like to say in the theater, the illusion of reality. Could an actor use a sphygmomanometer as skillfully as he?

Could an actor chart a pulse rate with his eyes closed, dreaming in the distance of colts and geldings three and up six furlong sprints? Why not? There are many subclinical cases around which simulate all of the symptoms of lung cancer but are nothing worse than debilitating bronchitis?

But if Richards is not a doctor, other fascinating questions must be raised. If he was not a doctor, was Jason the President? Nicholas the fifth or sixth richest man in the world? Harold, a deceased Senator from the great East Coast? Me, the former First Lady and now the lady of a thousand sorrows, or merely a subclinical case of my own, enacting all of the signs of one who has had this biography but actually nothing more than a disturbed forty-nine-year-old lady rattling around the swamp house and trying to convince herself that she is the most famous woman in the world and all of her servants out to do her in?

22
1978 — NEW JERSEY

"Here's your dinner," Annie said, "and be done with it. I'll pick it up later." She put the try in front of me and then stood over it, hovering in the position of the servant. Creamed chicken on toast, carrots, something dark in a plastic glass, Jell-O: a good clinical dinner. "Are you completely satisfied?" she said. "I wouldn't want to give you anything that would give you displeasure. If you have any complaints let me know and I will convey them back to the kitchen."

"Get out of here."

"Oh, I certainly will, miss," Annie said. "I will follow your orders to the letter and I will certainly hasten to get out of here but do tell me first if everything is most satisfactory. I would not for the world want to cause you displeasure. Would you like me to take a bite of your dinner, first? Just in case it is poisoned. It is customary to have a food taster, a role which I will happily fill for you if you would desire."

"Shut up, Annie."

"Oh no," she said. "I wouldn't want the slightest doubt to cross your mind. I know how likely you feel it to be that your food is being poisoned. Here," she said, setting the tray down on the bed, taking a fork from her pocket, putting it into the creamed chicken and taking a large mouthful, chewing it slowly and then swallowing it. "I hope that's satisfactory."

"I'm not amused."

"I'm sorry, your majesty," she said, "I'm just trying to please."

"I didn't think you'd poison my food. I'd imagine that you'd have more direct and immediate methods."

"And what would they be?"

"Why should I tell you? If you don't know already I don't think I have to render assistance."

"You're a very disturbed person," Annie said, "but I don't think it's necessary to talk about this anymore. I hope the proof has been satisfactory. Or do you think I'll vomit it up in the kitchen?"

"Go away."

"I intend to."

"Leave the door open if you want to impress me. Don't keep me locked up in my room."

"I'm doing it on doctor's orders. As far as I'm concerned you can run through this house naked and call the police. But Dr. Richards says and I agree that while you're in this state it would be best for all if you were kept in your room. For your own sake."

"Does he think me suicidal?"

She looked at me wisely. "I have no intention of sharing medical information. I am a nurse and certain information passed from the doctor to me is accordingly confidential."

"He thinks me suicidal then."

"Have a good dinner," she said. "By the way, we did have a telephone call you should know about. Jane called an hour ago."

"She did? Why didn't you put me on?"

"Because she didn't wish to speak to you."

"That's impossible."

"That's what she said. She only has a message to pass on which is that she's en route from London and will be in New York in the morning and will try to get down here tomorrow or the next day. She sends you her best."

"Why didn't she want to talk to me?"

"It's an international call and she was in a hurry to get to the plane and had only a few minutes. She said she had nothing to say, just asked to give that message."

"I don't believe you."

"I don't care whether you believe me or not. We are not going back to that again."

"She would always want to speak to me."

"She didn't tonight. She merely sent her best and said that she would be seeing you soon. She asked how you were doing and I said you were doing very nicely. That's the only lie I've told today."

"You should have put me on the phone," I said. "That isn't fair. This is my house, not yours. She's my sister, she wanted to talk to me."

"No, she did not. If she had wanted to you would have been put on the line."

"Take this dinner away," I said. "It disgusts me. I don't want any of your damned food."

"Sulking isn't going to do you any good. You have to eat to keep your strength up."

"Strength for what? I don't believe you. What did you tell her when she asked to talk to me? Did you say that I was sick? Did you say I didn't want to talk to her? What kind of rotten lie did you tell?"

"No lies at all. Maybe she's as sick and tired of you as the rest of us here are. Maybe she's fed up with you already, Vivien, and wanted to be spared listening to your ravings. How do I know?"

"You are a mean and terrible person."

"You're not so wonderful yourself. You stay in this room and think about what kind of person you are that your own sister wouldn't want to talk to you."

"Take your lousy tray and your rotten food out of here."

"The hell I will," she said, "I'm paid to take care of you and feed you meals and keep your strength up and that's exactly what I'm doing. If you don't want to eat, that's your business, but you can look at the food for a while and think of what you've done to yourself. It might do you some good."

"You rotten defiant bitch."

"No more of your abuse," she said and left the room, clashing the key defiantly in the door. She gave the door a heavy kick for spite as she left and I could hear the clattering of her feet down the corridor. Heavy-footed bitch.

I sat there on the bed for quite a while, looking at the foul vapors steaming up from the soggy creamed chicken and wondering why Jane had tried to reach me. What Annie had said to put her off. Why Annie had even found it necessary to tell me of the call.

Unless there was no call and she did it merely to torture me. That too would be her style.

23
1973 — RHODES

On the beach alone I lay in my bathing suit for a while, then took off my clothing and felt an absurd playfulness seize me. I rolled on the sand like a puppy, ran into the water, came from the water to roll in the sand again, then picked my way across the thin shore, picking up strange little objects washed up by the sea, fragments of what might have been starfish, little flotsam, some sparkling stones. Into the water again and then out for a fast dry and I just stood there for a while in the sun, feeling the heat bake into me, telling myself that I was being restored, that every hour in this sun took a year off my life, or six months anyway — the odd little games that women in their forties begin to play with elements. I guess one could say that I was happy that day, at least I was less unhappy than I remember having been for a long time. Summer of 1973, that was. Nicholas was in St. Thomas that week, Carrie across the world in Rio de Janeiro with no plans or prospects for her return within the next six months; I guess my mood might have been characterized as showing a certain contentment. Beach play and sun, isolation and the dull, peaceful sound of the sea; it was all the contentment I was likely to have for the rest of my life but it was enough. It was enough. It might have been the first day in ten years that I had gone through without a single thought of Jason, of Harold.

Of course I am reconstructing this and may again be indulging in retrospective falsification. It might have been a very unhappy day for all I know, it might have been like some of the other days I spent alone on beaches, feeling the enormous bowl of sky coming down on me, feeling the water carrying me not forward but back to some mindless equivalent of death, seeping into the blood, diluting the blood but I do not think so, I think I was happy that day and I remember it correctly. For that was the day that the pictures must have been taken.

Only later did I learn of the photographer, the boat, the telescopic sight; only later with the rumors and then their appearance in one of the Italian sex magazines. My first reaction was not to believe it at all, it could not be possible. There had been the lunatic in New York following me around, assaulting me on the pavement, shoving his camera like a prick at me, but the lunatic in New York had been of a more innocent type, all that he wanted, I read somewhere, was to meet me. He had a personal affection which he was trying to show by the attention he paid, the use of his camera. But this was something infinitely worse. "Why?" I said to Nicholas when there was no possibility of lying to myself anymore, when the pictures were out and they were certainly me and the American publishers were negotiating for the rights. "Why are they allowed to do this? They can't get away with it, something like this cannot be permitted to happen."

"There is nothing to be done," Nicholas said. "Anything we do will just make things infinitely worse. We will have to make no response whatsoever."

"I want to sue them," I said. "They have no right. They can't do it to me."

"They have done it to me too, don't you understand? They have violated my privacy as well as yours. But anything we do can only increase the danger. We will give the pictures more currency than they have already. Believe me," he said, "I am familiar with situations of this type. There is nothing to do but to ignore them."

"You don't care," I said. I was distraught, I suppose that is the word; it was really the first time that I remember my control absolutely breaking. Even Texas had not done this to me, even Harold, because in both cases I had been able to go through it with a core of emotional dignity; at some basic level I was not only unassailed but drew strength from it. Looked good in black. Looked good in grief and knew so well if unwilling how to manage its artifices to intimidate. But this, my picture naked for a hundred million to wink at and run their fingers over, this was something with which I could not deal. Nor felt I had to deal. "You don't care what they have done to me."

"They have done it to both of us," he said. "You must be reasonable, however. This is the kind of thing which comes from being a public figure. There is really nothing to say other than that it is the price one pays for notoriety. It could have been worse. It could have been far worse."

"How?"

"There are ways, believe me," he said.

"You don't care," I said. It was a new perception; I had always believed up until that moment that if nothing else he cared about me passionately, that there was nothing that he would not do to protect me. It was that belief, that I had found a kind of sanctuary, which had kept me going. "It's not that nothing can be done. You just don't want to do it."

"I'm as distressed as you are. But what can be done? We cannot withdraw the pictures. We cannot make them not exist. Anything we do would simply give them more credibility, can't you understand that? You live in the public eye, you are a public figure. This is one of the penalties that you must pay."

"How would you like this?"

"Like what?"

"How would you like to be seen naked in a million magazines?"

"I do not think that anyone would be interested in looking at me naked. I do not flatter myself with that kind of attention or interest."

"Why?" I said, "why have you allowed them to do this to me? For five years they've been taking me to pieces, but this is something entirely new. I can't take this."

He shrugged. "It is out of my control," he said. "Despite your flattering evaluations, I do not control most of the world. There is nothing to be done but to live and accept."

"Do you know something?" I said. "If I didn't think otherwise, I could convince myself that you're taking pleasure in this. You want the whole world to see what a piece of ass your wife is."

"The pictures are not particularly flattering."

"That is a cruel and vicious thing to say."

"What you said was cruel and vicious. I do not care to continue this conversation," he said. "It is getting us nowhere, and I have other matters to deal with. You will feel better about this in a few days."

"Don't walk away from me now. Don't ignore this."

"Why?" he said, "why are you making these threats?"

"I will never feel about you the same way again if you walk away from this. I trusted you, I gave myself utterly to you. All that I asked in return was that you would have the same feeling. You're betraying that feeling now and you will change everything."

"I'm sorry," he said. "You have suffered many damages, I can calculate very well how much you have been hurt. There is much to your life and circumstance that I can never really feel as you do and I accept this. But on this issue you are wrong. We will talk later," he said, "when you are calmer, when we can deal with this in a better way," and then he did what I thought he would never do, he walked out of the room and left me.

Left me, left me, left me with a million images of myself naked on a beach, playing on the beach, the sun high and hot overhead, the sea cool and deep, playing there unaware of the cool, metallic probe, the hard penetration of the telescopic sights, lined up in those cross-hairs the way that Jason's head had been lined up in Texas so that his brains (and now my body!) were scattered all over the world and no way, no way ever to retrieve them.

24
1963 — NEW YORK, BOSTON, WASHINGTON

Why wasn't I killed? This was the question which came to obsess me for a time, increasingly in the months after the funeral. He could have lined me up as easily as he did Jason. It would have cost him nothing, double the fame for no more effort, and it would have been a cleaner aftermath, as there almost always is without survivors. It could only be explained by saying that he knew exactly what he was doing, but the whole premise of the explanations had been that he did not know what he was doing, an unstable young man with a disturbed emotional life and a history of failure. It provided Harold's most telling evidence, that it was obviously a well-motivated, well-planned act with almost no emotion in it.

The dreams, the dreams: the high parapet, the arching fire, the terrible pain and the little fat man who said that he did it so I would never have to come back to Texas to testify. Did it all for me and out of consideration for my feelings. If he did it all for me, then it meant — if Harold's theory was correct and everything was connected — that everything that had happened had been done for me, and I could not deal with this, could not deal with it, am falling yet. Alone and on the plain, oh my God, Jason, I did not understand why I was spared unless after all it was for you and they wanted to perpetuate your memory.

25
1953 — ARLINGTON

"*Donnez-moi, s'il vous plaît.* Is that OK?" he said, "*comment allez-vous?* I love the way you speak French; I've always been in awe of people who were bilingual. The language of love, I should say."

"It means nothing," I said. "It's just one of the outcomes of a genteel education."

"Ah," he said, "*mais oui,* but it is so exciting, *mademoiselle. Voulez-vous* to fuck with me?"

"You are an obscene man, Senator. It is a graceful language not geared to crude approaches."

"Ah," he said, "but I am not crude at all. How can a crude man be going with a bilingual lady? I love you," he said, "I do love you. You understand that, don't you?" He ran his hand over my stomach, my breasts. "I'm sure that you do. We're going to be happy together."

"Happy together?" I said, "I would rather that we be at peace."

"That too."

"I don't know," I said. "I don't know if we can ever be at peace. You are a driven man."

"Not at all," he said. "I've got everything in this bed right now that I want."

"Liar."

"All right," he said. "Children. Maybe the majority leadership some-day. My memoirs. I'd like to do a big book, really blowing the lid off this place. You have no idea how bad the United States Senate is. Nobody who doesn't live in the place possibly could. You couldn't believe it. Of course it's a wonderful institution, and I love it as much as I hate it."

"That's why you want to get out of the Senate. I know you," I said. "You're not fooling me. You want to be President."

"Ridiculous," he said. "I don't have a chance."

"You didn't say that you didn't want it, though. I noticed that."

"Why lust after what you can't have? No," he said, "I'll have an hon-orable career here, twenty-four years I think. Four terms would be about right, and then I'll be sixty and can go on an island and do those memoirs. Maybe do some teaching back at Yale; I'd like to teach gov-ernment"

"Liar," I said again, "you don't want to teach. I can't see you at any university. You want to be President." My hands drifted down to his gen-itals, I felt his erection. "See?" I said. "We just talk about it and you start to get hard. The cock never lies."

"It's not being President, it's your hand."

"My hand has been down there before. No," I said, "you might as well admit to the devil. The cock does not lie."

"All right," he said, "all right, I want to be President." He turned to-ward me, touched my breasts, wedged himself into me in a way which was already familiar. I was always ready for him. There was never a time throughout all of it, even at the very end, even when the terrible things came out, that I was not ready for him. "Is that so terrible? Is that such a terrible thing to say? I want to be President. I'd like to be Ernest Hem-ingway or Humphrey Bogart, too, but that's harmless, it doesn't mean anything." On top of me now he began to move slowly. "What the hell," he said, "they can't keep a boy from dreaming, but it just doesn't mean a damned thing and you know that."

Coupling on his bed in Virginia on that Saturday afternoon, little span-gles and splashes of sunlight coming in off-angle through the windows, hearing the sound of his murmurings building as he approached orgasm, coming apart then to lie holding hands on the bed for hours while we talked about what his life had been before and what he wanted it to be and how he could put these two parts together, me the splice, he said, me the bridge, lying throughout that long afternoon close to him in the slow passage and ritual of the blood, I think that I came as close to knowing him as I ever did, holding him, feeling him moving inside me and this is in some way a beautiful memory because it reminds me yet again that what we had between us early on was not a lie. But in other ways it is a very terrible memory indeed because it forces me to realize that we never truly got any closer than we did in those early months of knowing one another through all the soft Virginia afternoons and nights when he was thirty-five and I but twenty-three.

26
1969 — CRETE, RHODES, NEW YORK

I never knew what Nicholas' business was; it was an area of his life which he kept completely sealed off from me. Land acquisition, of course, and the movement of huge cargoes. But there were those who said that Nicholas was buying and selling *countries*, and I was in no position to agree or disagree with them, knowing nothing at all. "It's not that I'm hiding anything from you," he said one of the few times I asked him to tell me the details of his work, "it's just that it's too complicated to understand. In fact I don't understand it myself. I just sign papers that my lawyers put in front of me and try to make the best of it."

"I really do want to understand," I said. "I know that you started off in ships but that it's much more than that now. After all, a wife should know about her husband's work. I'd like to help you."

"Not necessary," he said. "There is nothing for you to understand, any more than there is for me. Business is an irrelevance anyway; at this time it runs itself. My most important duty lies with you and that is all that should be of concern."

Nonsense. Business was his life and always had been; I knew from the beginning that it meant more to him than anything, possibly more than I. I was merely a diversion. I finally came to understand this; a luxurious diversion of course and one for which he cared more than almost any other entertainment in his life, but outside of his work everything was an entertainment. That was the key point. He never deceived me on this for a moment. Of course the prenuptials carefully excluded me from every aspect of his business life. I had participation only in his personal assets and never in the corporate. So I had lied to him just as he to me. There was never any need for me to participate at all. I had no need of knowledge. Matters were entirely out of my hands.

But even so, when the story broke in Paris, I confronted him with it. I read everything about him and me that came into my hands and sent out for more. This is one aspect of my life for which there is no longer any point in secrecy: for all the fact that I claimed to ignore the press I was, at every point after Texas, fascinated with it. There was nothing about me that I could let go by; my first reaction the day after the funeral in

Washington was to seal myself away with every paper I could acquire to see exactly how the reviews had come out. Had my dress been proper, had I given the right impression, had the funeral gone with the pomp and majesty that I desired? Did my appearance come out right over television? It was a terrible weakness, wanting to know everything that was said about me everywhere, but I tended to think of it as nothing much worse than a taste for chocolates. The greed for reviews was like the greed for sweets, put it before me and I could not refuse. But it was a small vice, one carried out in private and one which, I thought, hurt no one at all. It was less dangerous than the chocolates, because it involved no medical or weight changes or diminution of my appeal. So it was quite reasonable that, in the normal state of affairs, I came across the story in one of the Paris dailies by a feature writer whose name I recognized and had always despised. He hated everything American, and that meant that he hated me, but he was a good journalist with an inventive style, some of which I could admire even in the French, and a reputation for basing his savagery upon materials which he had found through his own sources and which almost always turned out to be true.

"This story says that you're selling freighters to the North Vietnamese," I said. "Is that so?"

"All journalism is pap and nonsense."

"No," I said, "I want to know that. You won't tell me any of the things you're involved in, so I have to get them from the newspapers and that's sad but this time I want to know. It's the first thing I've ever asked you about your work."

"Don't worry yourself about my work. It is completely outside of you and of me too."

"No," I said, "I want to know. If you won't talk to me about this I'll leave the room. I won't stay with you tonight." This was the first time, too, that I had done this to him. There is something reprehensible in a woman threatening the withdrawal of sex as a way to force a man to agree with her, but I had no choice. Something more important than this conviction was driving me.

He shrugged. "Why is this of such concern to you? You know how journalists distort, how they lie, how they make the cliché that every rich man must have done something immoral in order to have achieved his position. They can see no virtue whatsoever in riches; they cannot admit that it may merely be the outcome of hard work or more talent. There have been a hundred articles of this sort. They make no difference. Ignore them."

"You still haven't answered me. Are you involved in any dealings with the North Vietnamese?"

"What does it matter to you? I hardly know what dealings I am involved in. My accountants tell me to do certain things, so I sign papers on their behalf. I have far less to do with any of this than you might think."

"I don't believe it, and you've said that to me a hundred times before. I don't want to know about your accountants. I want you to answer the question."

"Why does this disturb you so much? What do dealings with a small foreign government have to do with you and me, or for that matter even with the world itself?"

"Then it's true," I said. "This story is true."

"I don't know why you care whether it's true or false."

"That is reprehensible," I said. "How could you be my husband and do this to me?"

"Do what to you? Vivien, what are you talking about? I have never seen you like this."

"This war is reprehensible. I am the widow of an American President who has been unjustly blamed for starting this war, and the sister-in-law of another dead American who gave his life campaigning to end the war. How could you do this? Do you see the position in which you've placed me?"

"I'm utterly at a loss," Nicholas said. "I completely fail to attend to any of this so-called reasoning. What does this have to do with a simple transaction?"

"So you admit it. It's true. You did sell them arms."

"*I* didn't sell them anything. My interests might have dealt with them in the leasing of a few freighters. My interests deal with many countries and are totally apolitical."

"You can't be apolitical," I said. "You can't do something like this to me."

"This is incomprehensible. You are not a political person. This is totally out of character."

"What do you mean I'm not a political person? I'm the wife of the President."

"The President has unfortunately been dead for some years. I am as sorry for this as anyone else, but one cannot speak of him in the present tense."

I looked at him and it was as if for the first time I saw him as what he was: a short, heavy man in his middle sixties, gray on top, gray below, the unhealthy tint of his complexion somehow visible evidence of a corruption which must have been four decades old. A long time ago, before I was born or Jason, he must have been a slender, vigorous man with plans, a man who could create an empire, take a wife, conceive a daughter, live in a future as detailed as it was abstract. But he had not lived in that future for a long time. The wife was long since divorced and dead, the daughter was very possibly a monster and Nicholas lived in an eternal present where desire, if it could not be converted into immediate satisfaction, was barely worth having.

Looking at him in this way, I saw that I could have hated him, that in an entirely alternative existence, in which Jason would have lived and in which Harold would have lived, I would have loathed everything that Nicholas represented. But I had gone too far in the other direction. So had Nicholas, and calling to that person who might have hated him was like Jane calling for the little girl who had ridden beside her father in the early New Jersey mornings a thousand years ago.

There was no way in which I could reach him, make him understand what he had done, because that would have meant finding that person I might have been, and that person had been blown away, no less than Jason, in the fires of Texas. I sat down beside him on the bed, utterly without words, and looked at him numbly. There seemed absolutely nothing to say.

"If this causes you such pain," he said, "I can arrange to cease dealings with the government."

"I don't care."

"You just said you cared very much. This is possible. It will not be difficult to bring the agreement to an end. It is on a month-to-month cash basis anyway. I will do this thing for you."

"You said that you have nothing to do with your business anymore, so how can you do it for me?"

"There are ways and ways. I can intervene if I so desire."

"It is not necessary."

"You should not have said what you did then. It is either important to you or it is not."

"It does not matter."

"All war is reprehensible," Nicholas said. "This war does not differ in any degree from many others. My own countrymen have been involved in terrible wars which have inflicted far more upon them, more immediately than Vietnam has hurt Americans."

"The war is reprehensible," I said, but without conviction. The edge of passion was gone; Nicholas had shown me myself as I had never seen myself before, and the vision was not one which I found acceptable. "But we don't have to talk of it anymore."

"The war has been enormously useful for most Americans. A number of them have suffered, and of course there have been some who have died, but they are in the minority. Most of your great country has derived benefit. Your President, his cabinet, his military have achieved much. Your economy has never been stronger. There are a few dissidents who do not like the war, but that is because their own interests have been called to account and they are among the very few who stand to lose. This makes them no different from anyone else; they merely do not have the advantages. And you call this war reprehensible? If so it is only because all war, your country itself, is reprehensible and you have no right to sit in judgment of mine."

"Nor do you."

"But I am not sitting in judgment. I am merely the agent of certain transactions which are in the nature of rendering a service. I make no judgment one way or the other. I had nothing to do with causing this war on which you sit in such neat judgment, a woman who has had almost nothing to do with her homeland for many years now. Yet it is your husband who is as responsible as anyone alive for having created this war, if you care to discuss that."

"I don't think I care to sleep with you tonight."

"I have done nothing to give you offense. I have even offered to tell my interests to withdraw from a situation which seems to give you offense. I have done this for no other reason than to please you, and now when I take the trouble to point out to you the necessary hypocrisy of your own position you deal with me like a libertine. It is a fortunate thing that I love you, because you have done things to give me much dishonor."

"Jason had nothing to do with this war. He resisted it until the end. The country would never have been in the war if he had not been killed. We would have been out of it a long time ago."

"Not from any reading of the situation which I understand. No, your husband's commitment by his own testimony was to little wars all over the world in order that so-called Communists might be challenged. An uncharitable person might say that it was not Communists but the forces of revolution which he opposed. But I am not an uncharitable person, so we will let that go. What is clear is that Vietnam is the outcome of all of his policies. I do not know why I am arguing politics with you. This is absolutely ridiculous. If you do not wish to be in my bed tonight, that is your position, your affair, but why don't you simply leave? I do not care to continue this."

"He wouldn't have had Vietnam," I said, "I'm sure of that. All of this was Lawrence's doing. Jason knew it, Jason used to talk to me about the military, how they were always looking for a war, how you needed a strong President to work against them and resist them all the time or they would put you in a hundred small wars or one very big one. I'm not com-

pletely ignorant politically, you know. You may think that I'm some kind
of toy woman who you bought for an enormous price and whom you
can buy off with possessions but I'm not."

"You're not?" Nicholas said. "You're none of that? Then tell me what
you personally have done to fight this war which you say you find so reprehensible. What actions have you taken, either public or private?"

"That's not fair. I'm in a delicate position."

"You're in no position," he said, "no position at all, and you never
wanted to be, so do not speak to me of reprehensibilities. You have had
absolutely nothing to do with your country since your brother-in-law was
killed — which I want to say to you was a very regrettable act and one
which I always looked upon with horror. Your brother-in-law in many
ways was a more honorable person, had more quality, than your husband. That you who have had nothing whatsoever to do with the course
of your country, with the course of this war which you say you despise,
speaks for itself. I think you are right. I think that I do not want you in
my bed and would prefer if you go back to your own. I will be leaving
early in the morning for Paris so we will not see each other for a few
weeks."

"I couldn't," I said. "I couldn't have taken part in any of the war
protests. It would have been a total mistake, I would have been exploiting
my role."

"You have no role," Nicholas said. He yawned. "You have had no role
for many years, that was your own decision and it was the right one for
you but please spare me conversation about your obligations or your role
or your position in public life because you have none."

"I couldn't have done it."

"You're crying," he said. "Why are you crying?"

"It isn't fair. It isn't fair what you said to me. Didn't I pay? I don't think
that anyone paid a bigger price than I. You talk of caring for your country, of being an American, I gave everything to the country." I could feel
the tears beginning to come over me and it was disgusting, I despised myself, I had almost never cried. It seemed impossible that I could finally
have broken down about something as abstract as a war. "You should-
n't have said those things to me," I said. "It isn't right, it's uncaring."

"All right," he said. His body was against mine, his hands touching me,
he put my face against his and I could feel the damp of my cheeks come
against the parchment of his skin. "All right, I have hurt you. I am sorry.
There was no need, you're right; it's not my place to say what you should
or should not have done. I know how you have paid, I know the sacrifices you have made. Forgive me," he said. "We should not have had this
discussion. None of these issues have anything to do with you or me, have

anything at all to do with what is between us. We will not discuss them again. Stop crying, please. Stop crying at once. Will you forgive me?"

"I don't want to forgive you. It's not a matter of forgiveness."

"Whatever you call it," he said. "I don't care what you call it. Let us have no more of this. I will call an end to the arrangements which displease you so. I will do this for you, and we will have no more such discussions."

"Go ahead," I said, holding onto him. He was old, he was corrupt, but he was all that I had. He was what I had made for myself. "Go ahead and conduct your business. I have no right to interfere."

"I told you, I will do this for you. It involves no great sacrifice for me, and it will give you relief of a sort. We will hear no more of this."

"I'm sorry," I said. But I was not saying it to him, I was saying it to someone, to something else, my country, perhaps, or Harold's memory. "I'm sorry, I'm sorry, it just had to be that way, it couldn't be otherwise, it couldn't."

"Enough," he said. "Enough of this," and reached behind him, put out the light. He was in his evening clothes, I in my nightgown, it was the work of only a few moments for us to be naked and against one another, and there in the darkness I let him have me; I let him have at me all the myriad ways he wanted. It did not matter, he was right, I was his possession, I was everyone's possession, I had taken no responsibility for my life but had seen it refracted only through the lives of others. And now it was too late, too late for moral platitudes, too late for statements of principle, too late in fact for anything but to let him fuck me and fuck me against the dawn. Except that, as always he came fast with sheer yelping cries, the transfer of his semen, the seal of his passage, and then quickly into sleep against me. And as soon as his breathing became regular, I left his room and returned to mine and locked the door, and in the morning when I awoke he was already in Paris and it was six weeks until I saw him.

We never discussed political matters again. As far as I know, the deal with North Vietnam for freighters and munitions cargo continued, but I failed to keep up with international economic affairs or all of the devices of his empire. Therefore, I cannot be sure of this. I am sure however that he drove a very hard deal and that the North Vietnamese got good merchandise for their trouble. Nicholas was a shrewd but honorable businessman.

27
1959 — WASHINGTON

"My name is Nicholas Sarris," he had said to me when we first met. I hate you, I wanted to say, I don't want to talk to you at all; goodbye. But I did not say this, one was brought up in Miss Spence's to be polite, to always look up to the man and to never give pain when pleasure would suffice and I was nothing but Miss Spence's most willing pupil. *Je suis enchantée, énormément enchantée. Merci, Mlle. Spence. Comment vous appelez-vous? Je m'appelle Vivien. J'ai quatorze ans. Mais Papa! Où est mon papa?*

28
1978 — NEW JERSEY

I did try to eat after all. I must keep my strength up. It is important for me to keep on functioning if I am to continue these notes, which are ever more important to me. I have been literally faint all day, not only from the surrounding circumstances but from the realization that in this last week I have had very little, almost nothing to eat. I would be surprised if I weighed much more than a hundred pounds now; Richards did not comment on my weight but then Richards is almost certainly not a medical doctor. He is an actor, an impostor, who has been brought in to give the scene credibility. Weak, then, and possessed of some sense of obligation, some sense that I must try to keep myself going as long as possible, I tried to eat a little bit of the creamed chicken but gagged on it, likewise the vegetables, likewise the Jell-O. Millie is a vile cook. Only the tea was manageable, weak, cold tea choked down in huge swallows, settling like little lumps of hatred in the pit of the stomach, then to the kidneys and bladder. But I am a proper lady. I would not take this machine into the bathroom and talk while I evacuate so I am holding back. Holding back as much as possible, holding all of it in as I have for so very long in other ways.

I do not think the food is poisoned. I really did not think so when Annie brought it in. That was merely a way of showing her, finally, that I was alert to the situation. She would not be stupid enough to poison the food. That would leave traces. No, far better to die by violence and blame it all on an outsider. It is the slow, quiet, private deaths which are dangerous. The loud public ones go by very easily, Jason and Harold being evidence for this. The way to succeed in America is to do it loudly, do it as publicly and violently as possible and to never look back. Would that I had learned this a long time ago.

I am so tired. I am so wretchedly tired. With the exception of my ever-popular and useful confrontations with Annie, all of which have been faithfully reported, I have been talking into this machine constantly for the last twenty-four hours now, the little bit of tortured sleep I had last night hardly counting. Six reels have been used; I am midway on the seventh. By my own calculation then I have already dictated close to two-thirds of the allotted ninety thousand words which are given me. And yet what have I said? How much have I truly managed to give? There is no time to replay the reels, of course. That would double the time spent, and there is none to waste. But I have spot-checked here and there simply to see if the machine is functioning, and the tinny, tiny bleat of my voice disgusts me. I seem to have filled all of this with little more than whining and complaints, and this is really not what I intended at all. I wanted to give the whole truth of my life straightforwardly and without apologies but it seems that I have fallen into self-pity.

Pity I do not want. I do not deserve it. I want understanding. I feel that I am entitled to that but wonder how much is here to truly justify that understanding. What have I given but an account of disaster? It is as if I am saying that the disaster should excuse me, but this was not my intent at all, not at all, for the disaster was wholly inflicted upon me by myself. It is not circumstance but the heart which is the truest murderer. But have I truly shown that?

And there is so much still unexplained. How I hired Annie. Why I let her hire the two others, why I let her, the nurse and nominal servant, take over these premises and allowed her to make me a prisoner. Why I left the matter of hiring a doctor also to her. How, in short, I made the passage from a woman of tragedy merely in need of a long period of seclusion to one who is being kept prisoner by murderers, whose actions are adjudged insane and who at the end of it will be killed without any defense. The transition is all-important; it is this transition which I must make clear, and yet I do not know if I can. I do not know and yet somehow I must go on.

I must, as Lawrence said in a different context, I must continue, but continuance, as I could have pointed out to Lawrence, is where you can find it. And you will never, never, never, you crude, sadistic, blustering, pathetic, misguided son of a bitch, you will never fuck me.

Here's your dinner, Annie. Take it and shove it.

29
1978 — NEW JERSEY

"Well, the princess does not like her dinner, does she? How saddening."

"Get it out of here and leave me alone."

"You've got a hell of a lot of nerve. I'm sick of your treating me like trash."

"Give notice and give me the keys and leave."

"I'll do that soon enough, princess. I ought to leave you here in your own filth."

"See if I care."

"Look at you. You look awful. You haven't attempted to make yourself up in days. Aren't you ashamed of yourself?"

"You're the nurse and housekeeper, Annie. You're responsible for my appearance. If you don't like the way I look why don't you do something about it?"

"I don't have to do anything about it. Only you can make that decision. I may be a nurse but I'm not a *practical* nurse. I don't have to muck around after you."

"So let me go down the hall and take a shower."

"You have your own bathroom right here. You can do anything you want right in these rooms."

"I'd rather use the large bathroom."

"I'd rather be out of here, princess, but if I have to make the best of it, so can you or don't you want to take any responsibility anymore?"

"You give me none."

"I'll give you all you can take. Look at this. You didn't even touch your dinner. Not that I care. You can starve yourself, die of malnutrition."

"I tried some of your rotten dinner. I choked on it. Get me some real food."

"You'll take what you're given and like it."

"Annie, isn't this getting a little repetitious and boring? Just get out of here."

"I'll get out when I'm ready to get out. Don't you order me around."

"Then I won't talk to you anymore."

"You think I find your conversation so scintillating, princess?"

"Not another word."

"Go ahead, sulk. You think that that gets to me? You think that anything you can do bothers me anymore? I've got the right attitude, finally, it'll teach me for giving a damn about you. It's just a job, and a damned sweaty and disgusting one, that's all. You think that your silent treatment bothers me? Think again, princess. It's a pleasure not to hear your damned voice for once. All that I hear is insults. I haven't had a kind word out of you for days. It's a pleasure. Go on, sit there with your high cheekbones and your tight lips, maybe you think you're posing for the cover of *Paris Match*. Do you think that that means anything to me? Do you think your silent treatment is having any effect at all? You really think you're something, don't you. That's the problem with all of you people, people from your so-called class. You think you're so much better than the rest of us with your *noblesse oblige* and your fox hunting and your European shopping holidays, but you shit on the same pot as anyone and you don't know anything. You don't know anything at all. Oh, I know, you're sitting there with your tragic cheekbones and your tragic lips and your tragic expression and I'm supposed to be thinking now of all the terrible things you went through and how you suffered more than the rest of us and all the great losses you've had and what a mysterious and glamorous person you are. But let me tell you something, you don't know what tragedy is. Tragedy is rats in your apartment or your baby starving or seeing your mother die of cancer in a hospital ward somewhere in Minneapolis in a stinking slum and knowing that there's nothing that you can do for her but to watch her die and wish her the best because she's probably better off dead and out of it and is going to a better place. At least that's what you want her to believe and you tell her that, and maybe she swallows that shit. Tragedy is when you're thirty-three years old and ugly and you know that the only men you can get are men who are going to use you for an evening or a week and then dump you. Tragedy isn't riding around in limousines and going trotting off to Paris or Henri Bendel's or sitting next to your husband who just happens to be the President of the United States. And I don't give a shit if he gets his head blown off or not. You really think you're impressing me with that stare, don't you? You really think that you're looking through me and getting me all nervous and excited and upset because next to you I feel like crap, don't you? Well, you can take it and shove it, lady. You don't mean shit to me. Not one single lump of turd in a pot.

"All right, don't talk. Annie, get the tray. Annie, get the tray and get out of here. Annie, clean me up. Annie, take me for a walk. Annie, call the doctor. Annie, fix me a drink. Annie, get me my drugs. Annie this and Annie that but maybe you're beginning to learn now that you shit on the same pot as the rest of us, and you can give me all the silent haughty stares you want, they don't mean anything to me. You think they mean anything to me? Go to hell, lady. I'll be out of your life soon, and well out of it, I ought to say. I look forward to a life away from you with the greatest of pleasure, lady, let me tell you, with the greatest of pleasure.

"All right, the hell with you. The hell with you and your silent treatment and the rest of your actions. It doesn't mean anything to you. I bet you thought you'd really shake me, didn't you? You really thought that sitting there that way with your hands folded was the way to get at me, that old Annie would lose her control and start to come apart in front of you, didn't you? Well, we've learned a bit differently, haven't we? We've learned differently and the hell with you. You'll learn.

"Fuck you, princess. Fuck you."

30
1978 — NEW JERSEY

I'm glad I did it. It was just an impulse but it turned out to be the right one after all. I still have instincts. If you learn nothing else hanging around with the Kelly family you come out after a fifteen-year hitch with a highly refined and excellent set of instincts for the worst parts of human nature and how to deal with them and I certainly proved that now.

My original intention was to have nothing on tape but my own recollections, my own voice, since the most important thing at last is to get it down my own way in my own words. But deciding to keep the machine going after Annie came in, hidden under the pillow, was a brilliant stroke, I have decided. Because now the objective, historical record as they like to say is absolutely clear: now there will be evidence of exactly what kind of person she is so that it is clear that this is not in my own mind, that I am dealing with a monster and that this monster with her highly unstable mind will stop at absolutely nothing to destroy me. She wants to destroy me, and the twisted, ruined landscape of her mind as glimpsed on this tape should make that clear.

Played back a little of it just now, to make sure that the cassette had picked up what she had said and that all was as I had remembered. It did pick it up. It was as I remembered. It speaks for itself and there is nothing more that needs to be said. It is in one way a shame to blot these memoirs with the intrusion of that demented voice, that dark consciousness, but in another it is the ornament of these memoirs, because the contrast of her mind and mine should be absolute. The record will make quite clear who is to be trusted here and who is to be dismissed. It speaks, at last, for itself.

Dusk. It must be seven-thirty or eight o'clock in these lowlands now. The diminished sun casts colors through the refinery wastes, now purple in the last light. The ruined state of New Jersey shows if nothing else the attractions of corruption; the wastes here glow in a way that purity never could.

Dusk. It is my feeling that it will happen before the dawn, they will not allow the sun to rise. Surely by now the stakes of their action, the consequences of it, must be clear to them; when they began it must have been in an almost leisurely fashion as if they had all the time they needed but now they know they do not. I cannot see how they will allow another full day to pass. Carrie's words, *You are a fool. You do not know what is happening.* Annie's: *You people don't understand shit.* But neither gave me any credit for simple perception, the perception that this cannot go on much longer.

Still, there is time enough. There is time enough, four or five hours,

twenty-five to thirty thousand words of tape left. I can get everything that
needs to be said out in twenty-five to thirty thousand words. I will leave
them then with nothing at all. I will leave them empty. Everything will
be on these reels.

Well, almost everything. What I can see I have skimped on as always
is the physical aspect; it is difficult to infer from all the preceding exactly
what these people look like: what *I* look like for that matter. So much
of this seems abstract that to a large degree my memoirs and recollections
must be taken on faith. I have never been too good on physical descrip-
tions, to be quite honest; I like to feel that I live so intensely within my
own persona as to make almost irrelevant mundane exteriors. Then too,
these people are world-famous.

We are not talking about nonentities after all. Jason's face must, all these
years after his death, still be the most famous in the world, portraits adorn
more struggling households than do pictures of the Savior. Harold, too,
is not exactly unknown and about Nicholas nothing more need be said
then that he is a lot better observed than would please him if he had had
absolute control over the matter. Carrie, too, in her own way is famous
and so is Jane. We are all famous. *I* am famous. Without exaggerating,
I will only point out that not three years ago I was still ranked as the second most admired woman in the world by a cross-section of the readership of a very popular women's journal, and I would not argue with
the opinions of this readership. There is no need for me to describe how
I look. I could dwell over my cheekbones, my small, high breasts, my dap-
pled but well-formed thighs for thousands of words, but then again and
thanks to the industry of a certain photographer, those breasts and
thighs are almost as famous now as my face.

Annie and Dr. Richards, on the other hand, have not been described
and are not famous, and it might make sense to spend a little time upon
them except, except this: what is the difference? Their aspect is exactly
as it appears in my mind and they have none other. Annie to me is mon-
strously overweight and Richards effete and delicate, but testimony
from others might reveal them to be normally proportioned or the reverse
of how I describe them, and what difference would it make? Everything
is within the inner perception, this is what I want to make clear, this if
nothing else is what I have come to learn. We dwell only within the architecture of our own sensibility, architecture that in many cases has been
incompetently drafted, poorly executed, but still it is all we have, the sum
of all we have known and there is nothing to be done. Jason believed in
an objective, rational world, one which he fully perceived and, to the degree that one was in accord with his vision, one demonstrated his own
sanity. But Jason, as it is becoming increasingly clear to me now, was one

of the craziest people I have ever known, a man who would not see the world other than in strict conformity. The technical word for this is solipsist. Am I a solipsist? Is Jane? Carrie? Annie? Dr. Richards? But of course, but of course, *mais oui, mes frères*, this is what I seek to demonstrate, that all of us are solipsists, that all of us are in small pieces and painfully reconstruct the world every day only the way in which we need to see it. We reinforce our own vision, not change it, as we age. And nothing to be done, nothing to be done, the hell with how they look. It is how they *are* just as it is how I am and with what terrible justice do I see and say this: that of all the worlds we have ever thought to inhabit, the only one which we will ever see, done over and over again, is this bombed-out temple of the self.

31
1974 — NEW YORK

There is only one person who could have done it, I came to realize. One person who hated me enough, one person who knew the geography well enough, one person who had the money and the means to make it all possible.

"You did it," I said to Carrie at the opera. I had not expected to see her there. All of the continents of the world, all of the spaces of the Earth for us to occupy and it is the Metropolitan Opera House which contains us both on that October evening. She in the orchestra, I in a box, she with some Countess who must be a relative of the Count from Brooklyn, me with the conductor who had one hand in mine, another on the score. Carrie and I used the same ladies' room however, the one at the rear of the orchestra. It is simply the only ladies' room to use in that place.

Distracted, she was emerging from a cubicle, I just about to enter. She saw me first but I was the first to react. "You did it," I said to her.

"Did what?" I had never seen such hatred on another person's face before. It was not reactive, but seemed to have been implanted there so that when she saw me it merely shifted to a deeper, more personal level as if she had carried around that hatred all of her life and had, at last, found its most treasured *raison-d'être*. "What are you talking about, you bitch? What are you doing here?"

"The pictures," I said. There was no time for preliminaries. We had the intimacy of those who have hated our entire lives; like lovers we were able to pick up on conversations at the deepest level without any of the preliminaries that would only have gotten in the way of the necessary feeling. "The goddamned pictures. I knew it was you. I knew it was you all the time."

We were almost alone there. It was the intermission after the first act of *La Boheme*, which never draws a crowd since it is such a short act. The men's rooms at the Metropolitan are a different story; my conductor had left me immediately at the fall of the curtain, bent on some urgent, private contact. One woman in full evening dress gave us a puzzled look as she scuttled toward the door. The attendant, who has seen everything, and like the Bourbons remembers nothing, played dice with two quarters in her plate.

"All the time what?" she said. "Are you crazy?"

"No, but you are."

"I have to go all the way to New York to see you," she said. "I thought I was rid of you. Get out of my way, I want to go back to my seat. You're blocking my way, you bitch."

"Not so soon," I said. "It had to be you all the time and I should have known it at once. It was you who arranged for the pictures."

Understanding broke through to her and her face was filled with little reflections of light. "Ah," she said, "now I know what you're talking about. The nudie shots, is that right?"

I slapped her across her face. The attendant looked up rapidly, then looked down. Carrie put her handbag over her right arm, freeing her left and slapped me. I made no effort to block it. The two shots were clean, neatly contained, the exchange of blows could not have taken more than five seconds. If nothing else we were consummate professionals.

"You did it, you bitch," I said. "I knew it all the time."

"No," she said. "I wish I had, I wish I had been smart enough to have thought of it and lucky enough to have brought it off, but, no, I wasn't. I'm glad that someone did it, though. You looked absolutely lousy, by the way, even worse than I thought you would."

"Better than you."

"You've got lousy tits," she said matter-of-factly. She transferred her handbag back to her strong arm. "If you'll excuse me," she said, "this has been a joy meeting you here in New York and all that but I must get back to my seat now. Probably you're missed also."

"I should have known," I said. "In fact, I always did know. Just seeing you brought it all through to me. You've been out to get me from the first."

"Not that way," she said. "You do such a wonderful job of getting yourself. How you can be built like that and think you have a chance is beyond me." She put her hand to her cheek, rubbed it. Two women came in side by side, parted as they came to us, then joined after the passage and walked determinedly to a cubicle together. The attendant shrugged and let them in. "Get out of my way!" she said. "Or do I have to hit you again?"

"You'll pay for this," I said. "You'll pay or be damned. I won't let you get away with it."

"You do have a healthy dash of paranoia, don't you, darling? Don't you have an escort who is waiting for you and getting restless by this time? Or, like so many other of your escorts, is he too busy checking out the men's room to give a damn?"

I hit her again. Right-handed she hit me back, doing little damage. The attendant came from her seat. "Please, ladies," she said. "This kind of thing cannot be tolerated in a public area. I'm going to have to ask the two of you to leave."

"That's exactly what I'm trying to do," Carrie said. "You can try to talk the Queen into doing it, though. She seems to have a certain reluctance."

"You had the money," I said. "You had the photographers, the contacts. You would know where I was. And you had the hatred."

"There's only one small detail that you miss," Carrie said, "I wouldn't do it to you. I'm not that interested. You have such a wonderfully self-destructive streak that I wouldn't waste my time or my money doing something like that. Excuse me," she said and pushed by me, half-turning me around, then went to the door and was gone. The lights in the room blinked twice.

"That's the second act," the matron said. "You want to get back to your seat now, Mrs. Kelly, you don't want to miss any of it."

"I'm not Mrs. Kelly," I said. "I'm Mrs. Sarris."

"As you wish," she said. Quietly she said, "I will always think of you as Mrs. Kelly. I'm sorry to see you so upset. I want to tell you that I've always admired you."

"I'm grateful," I said. "I really am." I was, that was the ridiculous part. I felt the tears begin to come. "I'm very happy to hear you say that."

I went out of the bathroom, staggering through the carpeting, and back up through the darkened orchestra to my box seat where I found the very famous conductor coming back at exactly that time, also late, the second-act prelude playing. We exchanged one single embarrassed look as we fumbled our way back into our seats, and for the remainder of the opera we sat next to one another silent, not moving, not getting up during the intermissions, not really doing anything at all except trying to manage the passage of time as best we could. I had the feeling that something had happened to him during intermission as disastrous as what had happened to me but I damned well was not going to ask him and he, civilized gentleman of the world that he was, would certainly not ask me. It was later on that night that he said the thing about the lady of the thousand sorrows. I did not know what he meant then, but I think that he did and I am beginning to learn. I think. I think that I was a mystery to him, but I think that he was my thousand and first sorrow.

32
1968 — NEW YORK

I was in Jane's apartment when it happened, watching television, watching the end of the great campaign. Harold had sent me back to New York saying that there was nothing more that I could do for him in California, I had fought the good fight for him, and now with not an extra vote to be squeezed out, he would await the primary outcome in peace. If nothing else he had fought the good fight, and I had very likely made the difference for him. He was saying that to a number of people that week, but he was telling the truth; in an election as close as that primary, all of us with our contributions made the difference. So I went back to New York, glad to be out of it, and went to Jane because I did not want to be alone on the night when Harold either won or lost the nomination. (We knew that if he could get through in California, he would be able somehow to storm the convention; they would not be able to take it away from him then.) And we were watching television when Harold got hit.

My first thought was: This is not happening, this cannot possibly be happening. He staggered away from the podium with the same distracted expression that Jason had had when the first bullet had hit him, not pain exactly but surprise, as if he had been hit by the smallest of stings unaware. Then as he took his hand from his temple, which he had touched as if to scratch in perplexity, he looked at his fingertips, and he must have seen the blood because his expression changed, his face widened and at that moment to the sound of screams and pounding he went down, backwards, curiously graceful. Always a fine sense of style the Kellys had, mostly in their dying. He released the podium slowly, gracefully, like a man willing himself to death by water, and someone in the background shouted very distinctly, the audio pickup being excellent in that small, hot, crowded room, *No, no, it's all happening again,* and I turned to Jane then and said, "This cannot be. I do not believe any of this."

She had been reading the newspaper or dozing but now the paper had come down from her hands, at the sound of the shot she had been pulled forward intensely into the set. "Am I dreaming this?" I said to her. "For God's sake, you've got to say something to me. My God," I said, "my God, he's dying now, he's dying there."

"The audacity," she was saying quietly. It took several repetitions before I could understand what she was saying. "The audacity, the audacity of them, the nerve, I wouldn't believe this. They will stop at nothing, absolutely nothing."

And then the phone was ringing. Jane got up, lurched toward it, backing from the set, arms to her sides, staring, and I got on my knees like a cheerleader and began to pound at the floor.

"Get up, Harold," I said. "Get up, you're not hit, you're not hurt, none of this is happening. Get up, Harold. Get off the floor right now."

But he did not move, and now all of the bodies around had covered him completely. The hand-held camera was shaking the scene. "Get up, Harold," I said. I was waiting for him to appear, reconstituted, on the shoulders of the crowd but instead the scene was becoming smaller, the crowd was closing in like a compress.

"It's your mother-in-law," Jane said.

"What?"

"I said, it's your mother-in-law on the phone. She wants to talk to you."

"Oh my God," I said. "Margaret."

"The audacity," Jane said, looking at the television. "I didn't think that they would do this. It's just so raw you wouldn't think that they would do it but that just shows how stupid we've all been, how stupid and naïve. They won't stop at anything." The commentator was on now, covering the sound in the room, saying something about an assassin, a small man already under restraint.

I went to the phone. "Yes?" I said.

"It isn't true, is it Vivien?" Margaret said. "I mean, I'm watching this but it really isn't happening is it? I spoke to him fifteen minutes ago and he said that he was just going to make a small speech and go to bed. This must be the end of the speech, right?"

"Please, Margaret," I said. "Oh please — "

"I mean, this cannot possibly be happening. I just cannot take it seriously, Vivien. Now I want you to get on the phone to Los Angeles right now, you know the number, and tell Harold to stop this nonsense. Tell him that from me. I'd do it myself, but I'd only lose my temper and then he'd hang up on me the way he often does. He's very stubborn and he just refuses to listen to reason."

"Mother," I said, something I had never called her. "Oh, Mother — "

"You have to do this for me, Vivien," she said. "You have to help me here, because I am drowning. I am dying. You have got to do something to tell me that this is not going on, because in the next moment I am going to believe it and what then? What am I going to do then?"

"Please," I said, "I can't stand this. I don't believe it either. Isn't there anyone there with you?"

"Jason is here with me," she said. "Jason and Harold are very close to me at this moment. No, I'm not going crazy. Oh my God, look at the television now. They seem to have caught someone."

I watched the screen and the struggles. Jane suddenly turned it off, came to me, and took the phone away. "I want you to lie down," she said. "I want you to lie down immediately and rest. You are not to watch this anymore."

"I'm talking to Margaret."

"I will talk to Margaret," she said. "I am your sister and I will handle this as I see fit. Mrs. Kelly," she said into the phone, "I think that you should phone your doctor immediately if you are alone. You should clear your telephone in any case; people will be trying to reach you."

"Let me talk to her," I said but Jane shook her head *no* and clutched the phone. "I'm going to hang up now, Mrs. Kelly," she said. "I'm going to do this for your good and for my sister's. You've got to get some help immediately. We'll talk to you just as soon as we can," she said and hung up the phone and then took it off the hook. She turned to me. "I want you to lie down at once," she said. "Immediately. I want you to go into the bedroom and lie down."

"That's not going to do any good. Why did you shut it off? Put it on."

"No. I won't do that. Go in there and lie down. I'm going to get the doctor."

"I'm all right, Jane. Really I am. I'm not going to faint or collapse or anything like that at all. I have to see what's going on there."

"No, you don't. You have to lie down."

"Don't shield me," I said. "Why are you doing this? Why are you treating me like a child?"

"I'm doing what's best for you."

"That isn't best for me," I said, "and you know it isn't. I'm all right now. I've got to see this. Put the television on or I will."

"You're wrong," she said and put the set back on. The scene had cut away from the ballroom to the face of a commentator who was saying something about police officials already on the scene and Harold's condition unknown but apparently stable. "I want to see what's going on there," I said, "I don't want to listen to him." Jane cut to another channel and then another but several were showing movies and the others had also cut away from the ballroom. "I've got to get out there," I said. "I've got to be with him. I've got to get out there right now."

"That's why I want you to lie down and try to relax. You can't go anywhere, Vivien, until we find out what's happened."

"They've killed him," I said. "He should not have gone on this campaign. He had no right. He was warned but he wouldn't listen."

"I can't talk about this now," Jane said and began to cry. The phone rang. "I thought I took it off the hook," she said. "Goddamn it." She looked at the receiver. It was balanced precariously, just sufficient to depress the button. "Goddamn it to hell," she said again. "We just don't know what we're doing, do we? We just cannot cope." She picked up the phone. "It's the press," she said in a moment. "They want a comment from you."

"Oh my God."

"Will you get out of this room? Will you go to the bedroom and please lie down?"

"I cannot deal with this," I said. "I cannot deal with it anymore." I walked out of the living room and in a stupor went to Jane's room and lay down there on the enormous bed, drew up my knees, looked at the ceiling. "I can't deal with it," I said. Jane came in. "I got rid of them," she said, "and I ripped the fucking phone out of the fucking wall. We'll have some peace now, goddamned sons of bitches." She sat at the foot of the bed. "Please," she said, "try to relax. There is nothing you can do. There is no point in watching it. In the morning we can get you to the airport and you can go out there."

"No," I said, "I won't do that. It won't work anymore. I thought it could but it can't. No more."

"What do you mean?"

"I mean that I can't cope," I said. "I can't fight anymore." I turned toward the phone on the night-stand next to the bed, picked it up, heard the dial tone. "It still works," I said. "Pulling it out of the wall when you have an extension only means that you immobilize one phone. They can still get at you. You have to take them *all* out of the wall, individually, you understand?"

"What are you doing?"

"I'm making a phone call."

"You'll never reach anyone. You can't reach anyone there."

"I'm not calling Los Angeles," I said.

"Then where are you calling?"

"I'm calling shipboard," I said.

She looked at me and then comprehension drifted through her face. "Why?" she said.

"I want to talk to Nicholas."

She reached forward, pulling the phone from my hand. "Not now," she said. "Don't do anything now. Wait until the morning."

She was my sister; feel about her as I might, she was attuned as was no one else to the way that I thought. She knew exactly what I meant to do. "No," I said, "I want to do it now. I'm frightened, Jane."

"We're all frightened. The night of fire has begun. But calling him will change nothing."

"It will change everything," I said. "Don't you understand? I can't cope anymore. I thought that I could, but this has proven to be the end of it.

I was wrong. I can't make it anymore, Jane. Harold said they would never hurt him, but he was wrong, and if he was wrong on that, he was wrong on everything. I'm scared," I said. "Give me the phone."

"What are you going to do? Ask him to send a bodyguard?"

"I'm going to go a little further than that. I'm going to tell him that I'll marry him."

"Don't do it," she said. She held the phone tightly in her lap, hands folded around it. "I won't let you do this. You'll feel entirely differently in the morning. At least wait until the morning to see if you feel the same way."

"I'll always feel the same way."

"You have no way of knowing that. Please," she said, "don't do it."

"I know how you feel about him. I don't care. "He loves me and he can protect me. I'm so tired," I said. "I'm so frightened and I can't fight anymore. I want to be taken care of."

"I'll take care of you."

"You can't. You know you can't do that. Only he can. I'm going to marry him, Jane, if he'll have me. Give me the phone."

"No," she said. "It's the worst mistake of your life. I won't let you make it. At least wait. You're overwrought now. We don't even know Harold's condition. He may be all right; he might pull through this."

"Harold is dead," I said. "They have killed him. I know this and so do you. He has no chance at all."

"You can't tell."

"I can tell," I said. "I can tell everything. I don't want to struggle for the phone with you, Jane," I said. "Hand it over to me. Just cooperate with me, please. I can't take any more scenes with you or anyone. Harold is dead, isn't that enough?"

She took her hands from the phone and then slowly passed it over. "It's your life," she said. "I can't stop you. I won't do it. It's the worst mistake of your life. If you think he will protect you, you are wrong. You will be even more exposed. Everyone will hate you for doing this."

"Yes," I said, "they well may, I can understand that. But they won't be able to get at me, will they? That's the most important thing. I'll have sanctuary. I need sanctuary now, because they will definitely do to me what they have done to him, if they feel it necessary. They will stop at nothing." I dialed the international operator. "I may feel differently in the morning," I said to her, "and that's exactly the reason that I'm doing this now. I want to do it before I have a chance to change my mind. This is the right decision. It's the only way. I don't love him, but I could learn to care for him."

"You never will. Feeling is there or it isn't, Vivien. You will never change that."

"I'll make myself change. If I can't, he'll never know the difference. I gave the international operator his shipboard number and told her that it was an emergency. I can make sure that he never knows the difference; I can hide it all from him."

"He's no fool. Don't you think he'll know? When you call him now, at this time, don't you think that he'll make the connection himself?"

"Yes," I said, "but he doesn't care. He'll have me on any terms he can because he loves me." The international operator said it would be a few moments and she would call me back. I thanked her and hung up the phone. And that's all I said to her. That's all of it.

We sat in the room, then quiet at last, and waited for the phone to ring. Jane got up after a while and put the set back on and we listened to some interviews in the studio of political and medical experts who had been hastily reached. The medical experts said that the wound sounded serious. The political experts said that whatever the medical prognosis, it had certainly changed the direction of the campaign.

He must have known it all the time. No matter what he said to me, he was not a rationalist but a mystic. He must have known what would happen, and, like Jason, he must have sought it. I can see it. I can see it.

I can see him in the kitchen: noise, light, heat, crowds, the odor of food steaming up slowly from the crockery, the fluorescence glinting off basins. Left and right he is surrounded yet he is alone, cleaving, as always, a little space in which he is utterly removed, in which he cannot be touched. Always there was this removal, this insulation, even (or perhaps mostly) in fucking. Now he hears the voices as a thick, uneven clamor which carries him, carries him slowly out. It is a rhythm to which he is accustomed and he rides it but suddenly that rhythm breaks, there is a new sound in the clangor. He cannot identify it. He comes to a complete halt, uncomfortable with the sound. That which he cannot label has always made him uncomfortable and now he knows that something is wrong.

Something is wrong. Something is very much wrong. There is a man and the man is holding a gun. Perhaps there are two men, the one with the gun and another shielding him. It is difficult for him to know. Harold squints, trying to understand the situation. If he can only understand it, he feels, he will be able somehow to save himself yet. All that he needs to do is to comprehend, and then he will take control and the difficulty will go away. It has always been thus and so it will be again. He must understand why the man with the gun is there, why the gun is pointing at him. "Excuse me," he begins to say, raising his hand, "but if you will only be good enough now to explain yourself — "

The gun fires. Perhaps the man is not interested in explaining himself or perhaps he feels that the full and final explanation is in the gun. It is very difficult to tell with people of this sort; for one thing they are not very stable, and for another they do not have the kind of longing for control that Harold has. Harold feels the bullet penetrate the skull cavity just behind and slightly above his right temple. He knows at this moment that his life is over, that he has been killed, and yet the bullet has been only a pinprick; he feels in excellent health. His footing is steady. Perhaps this is what the afterlife is like: excellent health, the repeated perception of the moment of death. Or then again — a shrewd point for what is, after all, only a mildly lapsed case of acute Catholicism: this is purgatory and he will know the moment of penetration over and over again until it has been decided that he has paid sufficiently; then he will be admitted to the Kingdom of Heaven.

But then again maybe the man is firing blanks. Maybe he is only having an illusion of death, a humbling effect: a good scare in short. But even as he thinks this, as he sets his frame to take the one step that will spin him away from accident and into the arms of Edna (who is looking at him with concern) he feels his legs go down, then he is on his knees, and finally he is on the floor. Liquid fills his skull; it is as if a gigantic damp hand is pressed against his head. He knows at this moment that he has been hit after all, and that he is not in purgatory, not in the Kingdom of Heaven, but merely falling toward the floor in this damned kitchen. Damned kitchen, damned hotel. He knows he should have stayed out of hotels; hell he should have stayed out of the whole accursed state of California, which is in itself a form of mental illness. He is on his back now. He does not remember the moment of passage; he only knows that he is on his back. Edna leans over him, enormous, her hand, kind hand pressing his forehead. He feels the cool gathering of blood meeting the sweat in her palm. His vision comes unfocused. He knows that he is dying. He is not surprised.

He knows that it always was meant to be this way, that it could have happened in no other fashion. He needed the impact. He needed the gun.

"Do you hear me?" he says to Edna. "I needed the gun. I needed death. I needed it just this way." But she does not hear him, she is weeping and suddenly he is weeping too. Not because he is dying — that could be faced with dignity, he can well amalgamate death into the sense of his life — but because he will never be able to share this insight with her. Never be able to share this insight with anyone. Vision films and he feels passage beginning.

Pain like tears, he thinks, moving drop by drop into the vessel of memory. Like tears. Like blood.

33
1978 — NEW JERSEY

When I crouch, with my ear to the door, it is just barely possible to hear the conversations outside. They are very near, in the kitchen, and therefore with the fullest intent it is within my power to follow the dialog. Although everything, an absent cricket, a creak of the boards, my own stale respiration, can get in the way and steal the words. Still, I can manage the general outlines and I know what they are saying.

It is exactly how I apprehended. The two of them are sitting at the table in there, Carrie and Annie. Tom and Millie are not part of the conversation, although they are on the premises and from time to time, just to show their own involvement, they peek in.

They are putting together a plan. One or the other, somewhere around midnight, will come into this room and kill me, hopefully in my sleep but face to face if necessary. Then they will arrange for the four of them to drag my body to the old Coupe de Ville which Thomas keeps in the back garage, not the Caprice wagon, which is the town car, but the Cadillac, which most have never seen, and they will drive me to a swamp area near Ridgefield. Annie knows exactly the right place. Carrie is a little doubtful about Ridgefield, thinking that it is too close to the metropolitan area. She would like something a little more to the south and nearer here, so that they do not have to drive twenty miles with my body in the car. But Annie assures her that she knows this area very well, has lived a large portion of her life in southern New Jersey and can certify that Ridgefield is the tenth circle of hell; nobody other than those having urgent business with oil refineries would be in Ridgefield at all let alone this particular swamp area which has been selected.

After my body has been disposed of in a shallow culvert, they will return to the Willows. A convincing disarray will have been created in my room, all of the aspects of a disturbed mind: toothpicks, scraps of paper, articles of clothing, and crossword puzzle books, the puzzles completed incorrectly, will be strewn on the floor. In the morning they will telephone the police, stating that I seem to have disappeared overnight, and a frantic search of the premises and surrounding area has given no clues as to my whereabouts. I have been under medical care for several months for a deteriorative nervous condition, but they did not expect that I was so disoriented as to do something like this. In any case they could hardly have kept me prisoner in my room. The three of them were merely servants. By the time the call is put through, of course, Carrie will be long gone from Newark Airport, heading toward the Far West. My physician, one Leslie Richards, will be contacted and give evidence of my unhappy condition, while expressing surprise that it has taken such a dramatic turn for the worse. By this time the reports of my disappearance will have spread to the press, and nothing will be done to prevent them. Indeed, the stories will be helpful since they will spur interest in the search for the living, possibly amnesiac person and hardly for the already decomposing corpse who will be the dark lady of Ridgefield.

After a week of intensive search efforts and another two weeks of the desultory the investigation will, for all intents and purposes, be abandoned. I will take my place in history as the most celebrated disappearance of the twentieth century; indeed the circumstances of my ending will overshadow my life, to say nothing of relative nonentities like Ambrose Bierce, Amelia Earhart or the sainted Judge Crater. Only the search of mystics and seers for reports on the whereabouts of Adolf Hitler or James Dean will be truly affected by my disappearance because the Vivien Sarris business will far overwhelm these more modest souls. Two years from now it will be hard for anyone to recall exactly how I was supposed to have disappeared, by which time Annie will be living abroad on a comfortable inheritance from the estate of Nicholas Sarris and Tom and Millie will be at the other side of the world on an even more modest inheritance. Only Leslie Richards has not been quite accounted for, but they seem to think in terms of a straight cash stipend rather than a continuing income. Leslie Richards is a celebrity-fucker; what he has done he has not truly done for the money or at least he has not done it purely for the money as have Annie, Tom and Millie. A terrible disappointment to me: I thought they really cared.

All of this is being discussed in the most lucid, structured terms, being gone over carefully although in some fatigue since Annie has been under a great deal of recent strain, and Carrie has been living a lively time herself what with rental cars incognito and late night visits up the drive, her idea alone, to terrorize me. There is, in fact, only one disagreement, and it is that which could be expected: neither Annie nor Carrie wants to fire the actual shot. Each seems to think that the other should do it.

On hands and knees now at the door, talking quietly into this microphone so that everything is put down on these reels just as it happens, no time lag now, instant history, I can sympathize with their problem. In the abstract they are both murderers indeed, but it is one thing to cause the murder and another thing to actually commit it. This is what rendered Texas and Los Angeles so wondrously complex; the gap between the perpetrators and the actual assassin. Annie feels that Carrie should pull the trigger. For one thing she is enormously more motivated than Annie, who is merely hired help, doing a job, for another, she has more skill with firearms. Annie's thesis seems to be that those who arrange it should engage in the commission, and it strikes me on balance as quite a reasonable position. Carrie feels that Annie ought to do it because Annie has been hired for this job and is under orders, and her orders are to do away with me. Since she agreed when she took on the assignment to follow it through for better or for worse she has an obligation to follow it all the way through.

Annie says no and I can feel for her, but Carrie is likewise reluctant, and I can understand her position as well. Why should she soil her hands, not to say her heart, with the commission of the foul deed of murder? She is such a young lass after all and has her whole life ahead of her. Maybe in later years she would tend to regret it, and it would be unfortunate to deal with this blot on her conscience for the rest of her life; whereas Annie can manage the act within the context of a job. They each have a good case, in short, and if it were not for my most intimate involvement with the circumstances I could follow their arguments with great intellectual interest, because the whole question of the twentieth century is really being fought out in the kitchen of the Willows. Who takes responsibility for their acts? In a world where people can be reduced to abstract, wholly statistical terms to be manipulated or eliminated at will, does the question of individual motivation prevail at all? Or can one simply be an instrument of death following orders up and down the line to the point where no one at all has to take responsibility for the elimination of what, after all, are invisible figures? It is worth a good deal of discussion and can hardly be settled in one evening by two women of limited intellectual capacity and overwhelming emotional involvement, but the discussion would function as a useful start. It is unfortunate that I cannot appreciate it in a detached, intellectual fashion, because unquestionably it is there to be appreciated.

Unfortunately, however, I cannot. The situation is too imminent. That is *me* they are discussing, my body, my life, and regardless of who is eventually charged to do the deed, I am going to be the one who dies, not either of them. The nausea overwhelms me at this point. It is not precisely fear but revulsion which fills me, revulsion for the situation which step by step has led me to this impossible juxtaposition, and I find I can no longer listen. I move away from the door, clutching the recorder, and go to the bed trying to shut out the voices, the voices. Knowing that whether I can shut them away or not, they will continue to discuss as they have at every point of the evening not whether I will live but how I will die; not the uses of my life but the gift which my death will bequeath to them and through them, they think, to the world.

34
1978 — NEW JERSEY

I knew it had to come to this; I knew that she would never let me rest. She must have deduced the circumstances of Nicholas' death immediately. There is some question as to how she was able to reach Annie, but it is not much of a question. Money as they like to say talks, and sometimes it screams. The collaboration between them must have been very close; they must have been in constant communication by letter and telephone over these months working out all of the details, and how they must have laughed at me, at my ignorance and vulnerability. I made it far easier for them than they could have calculated. It was I who sealed myself off within the house, it was I who refused to come out of the bedroom for days, it was I who decided to make no trips to the village or New York, but allowed all of the household tasks to fall upon my staff. Here for a rest cure, I turned it into a sulk, and thus made their tasks even less effortful than they might have been otherwise.

It is too late to be bitter, of course. It did not have to be this way, and much of the fault is mine, but on the other hand I did it to myself without outside assistance. The question is: what am I going to do? What can I possibly do to forestall them?

I do not think that I can do anything. One has fantasies of course, flight through the windows into the village with appeals for help, confrontation scenes in the kitchen where I roar my betrayal and through sheer force of will cause them to back down, scenes of murder when somehow I find some ancient weapon which daddy stashed in one of these closets years ago behind useless possessions, seizing the rifle I come upon them and one by one blow their heads off. Of all the scenarios this is the one I like the best, although it is the most pathetic and ridiculous. Daddy was terrified of guns and would have none in the house. Any confrontation scenes in the kitchen would lead to my immediate rather than slightly delayed murder. Flight is impossible because these windows are too narrow for me to get through and in any case are barred as in a lunatic asylum. There is really nothing to be done.

I always knew, after Paris, that she would find me and attempt vengeance. What I did not calculate was her ruthless energy or her speed. I thought I had more time and instead it was much less. I did not reckon on the endless energy of the young or their dedication; I had forgotten what it was like to be twenty-five years old and rich, and at that stage of life where there seemed to be no line at all between ambition and achievement other than one's scruple. But I should have known, I should have known: it was at twenty-five that I married Jason, and only much later that I realized that what you felt at twenty-five was not necessarily the position of a lifetime. But too late, too late, too late for all of that then; one of the wonderful things about being young is the absolute rigidity of the positions one can take while believing that they come only from the state of flux.

35
1978 — NEW JERSEY

My money is on Carrie. Annie is a strong article, almost too much for the likes of me, but Carrie is something entirely unto herself. I do not think that Annie can prevail against her in a fair or even an unfair fight. When push comes to shove one can separate the truly evil from the casually malevolent, as we have found out time and again in this, the most American of centuries.

My money is on Carrie, all right. Which means that Annie will pull the trigger.

36
1975 — NEW YORK

The pictures were purchased by the widest-circulation men's magazine in America and featured on the cover. Inside there were twenty-four color pages of me playing nude on the beach, in one of them flapping a towel like a little girl at the unknown camera. The copies arrived in a plain brown wrapper from an anonymous admirer postmarked New York, who said that he had access to advance copies and was sure that I would take as great an interest in the contents as would the rest of America. Because I was staying at the Carlisle that week and had the mail delivered directly to my door, I got them immediately.

The copy was fawning. *A great lady takes her pleasure. Now we know that her outer beauty is the same as that inner strength and wisdom that she showed that terrible week in Texas; now we know that she is as spirited a creature as ever married a billionaire. All Americans always will feel that regardless of the change in circumstances she will be the first lady of their hearts.* Tit copy, they call it, the captions that high-toned men's magazines run under the pictures of naked women, a mindless babble to facilitate masturbation without guilt. It is a functional, somewhat utilitarian prose with but a single purpose. I would imagine that the assistant editors who write it consider themselves, no less than anyone, to be serious artists.

The pictures were excellent. They reproduced, needless to say, far better in the number one men's magazine than they had on European newsprint; they revealed every granule of sand on the beach. Not so many granules on me; considerately they had given me an application of the airbrush no less cunning than any of their other models. Despite the un-flattering camera angles which made it appear as if I had no breasts, a stunning canard, I looked better than I had in many years. *One can understand why a billionaire would ransom his fortune to have a woman such as this.* I think that it is at that moment, looking at those pictures, reading that text, that I began to go insane. It is from that point that I can date what might be charitably called my breakdown.

I knew that it would be impossible for me to appear on the street. Everyone would be looking through me, knowing exactly how I appeared naked, laughing at the fact that I would even bother anymore to wear clothing, let alone deceptive foundation garments. Knowing that the pictures had been printed here and there in the sleazy, sub-literate European press was one thing. Europe has a very rigid class system and none of the right people would deal with those publications on any level. But America was different. America was a single class and my own country in the bargain. Everyone read these magazines, most openly, a few in private, the very few that did not would be offered access. Seeing myself in those pages was knowing that I would be naked in a few days in every bedroom in America, that a hundred million men screwing or jerking off could close their eyes and do it to me. These were advance copies but I had virtually no lead time; already if my anonymous admirer had found them and gotten them to me in the mail they were available to subscribers. How long did I have? I had no time whatsoever. I booked passage immediately. Then I called Jane.

"Don't do anything," she said. "Just ignore them. It's a country of one-week sensations. It will all be forgotten in a month."

"Not these. And not by me. Was Jason forgotten in a month?"

"A month later they didn't even know what Jason looked like; all they had were idealistic representations. But that was death, this is sex. Sex is even cheaper in this country, Vivien. Forget it. You ought to be flattered."

"You haven't seen these pictures."

"No, I haven't and I never will. I don't think there's any need for me to see them, is there? You're making too much of this, dear. Nobody really cares."

"They'll care about these. Nicholas did it," I said. "I'm going to make him pay for this."

"That's ridiculous," she said. "I've heard you say that before, but I simply couldn't give it any credibility at all. It's not his style."

"Oh yes it is. You don't know the man. He hired the photographer and got him on one of his own boats and told him exactly where I would be. Nicholas would have been the only person in the world who knew where

I was that day. He set me up for the whole thing."

"You underestimate the capacity of the European press, their energy. Vivien, forget it. Don't get yourself into serious trouble because of this. It isn't worth destroying your marriage and you certainly will."

"How can I be married to him after this?"

"Vivien, I hope you won't take this the wrong way, but you sound distinctly paranoid. You're just not looking at this in a rational manner. What would Nicholas have to gain but his own notoriety? He wouldn't do anything that self-destructive."

"You can't judge his perversity. Besides, he had a lot to gain. Now he's shown the world exactly what piece of ass he's fucking."

"I don't want to fight with you, and I see that I can't get you to change your mind. It's your life, but I think you're making a terrible mistake."

"What can I do?"

"You can ignore it. You can ignore the whole thing and a month from now you won't remember and no one will remember what any of this was about."

"No," I said, "I don't believe that. I can't let this one go by. As long as I live I cannot forgive this one."

"Then do it," she said. "I'm tired of arguing with you. I'm tired of hysterical phone calls in the night. I'm tired of the whole business and that's no lie. If you won't listen to reason then go to hell, just don't bother me anymore with your problems. You don't know what real pain is or at least you've forgotten."

"I don't know what real *pain* is?"

"Texas was real pain. Los Angeles was real pain. What you and I have lived through together, yes. But not this and you should know that."

"Jane, I don't want to hate you. Please don't send me back there hating you. I need to have someone that I love."

"Oh, you fool," she said and she was weeping, "you fool, I *do* love you, you're probably the only person that I really have, and I just can't bear to see you acting like this. It isn't fair; you were always the strong one. I was so weak, I counted on you and you always came through. But this can't be, Vivien, please don't make me feel that you aren't the strong one anymore."

"I am," I said, "and that is why I am going to face this, because I am strong, because I will not run any longer. I think that finally I am beginning to come to terms, to have some sense of my life." And I hung up and packed the valise and called the chauffeur and within two hours was on the way to Kelly International and within three was on my way to the island. Sitting alone in first class, drinking cocktails, I had the illusion at least that no one had seen the photographs, but you could not be sure

of anything like this. They are inordinately polite in first class. If you pay
your money they make no discrimination at all between the widow of a
President and the slut who posed naked in color in the pages of the nation's largest-circulation men's magazine.

"Why did you do it?" I said to him, "why did you do it?" and I
slapped him on the face. He staggered back, his eyes small and full of
knowledge, just as I had known they would be. There was neither surprise nor hurt in his aspect, only the dismay of a man who has at last
been caught out. I threw the magazine against the wall of his hotel
room. I had tracked him to this room in Paris, one of the sleaziest hotels in which I had ever been but one which I was sure that he used to
conduct certain aspects of his business which were best kept to sleazy
corridors. "Why did you do it?" I said again, and he backed away, a
short man in his mid-sixties, heavier than me and certainly stronger,
but intimidated. Righteousness carries its own strength.

"You are not supposed to be here," he said. "I have no idea of why you
have come here now."

"Yes, you do," I said. "You have disgraced me. You have dishonored
me. You never thought of me at all. I never meant anything to you except as another possession. You are despicable," I said.

"You are terribly overwrought. I do not really know what has caused
this, but I see that you are in no condition to be dealt with at this time.
Please leave," he said. "I do not know how you found me here or what
you intended to do, but I am not prepared to deal with you now. If you
do not leave I will have to call my secretary and have you escorted from
here."

"No," I said, "that won't work anymore. I'm your wife, you're not going to get away with treating me like a messenger, like some kind of in-
terloper. You're going to have to face the truth now, that I'm more than
a possession. You thought that you could keep me in a pigeonhole but
you can't." The magazine, flapping obscenely in the little breezes that
poured through the open window, parted at the page with two shots,
front and rear, juxtaposed. "Look at what you have done," I said.
"Look at what you have done to me, and you simply do not care. You
understand nothing."

He turned, stooped, picked up the magazine, ripped out the page and
threw it against the wall. "We have discussed this before," he said, "and
I found your accusations disturbing and possibly insane but chose to disregard them, because you are, after all, my wife. But I cannot disregard
them anymore unless you stop this at once. Unless you do stop at once,
you will be in very serious trouble."

"It wasn't enough to set me up for it," I said, "you had to permit publication in my own country."

"I had nothing to do with these disgusting photographs and I certainly had nothing to do with their appearance in this foul magazine. Your accusations are those of a very disturbed woman. Please, Vivien," he said, "for the sake of all that is reasonable, I want you to leave this room. No good will come of this, it will only make things much worse to continue this."

"Not until you tell me why you did it."

"I did nothing."

"Not until I get the truth from you. I've heard enough of your lies, now I want the absolute truth. Wasn't it enough for you to have me in bed, for you to know what I looked like? Did you have the feeling that you had to show the whole world, just to prove to yourself that you could have me? Or was the only way you could have me the knowledge that a hundred million men were jerking off to me so that you could have all of that need behind you for your own come? You always had a lot of trouble coming, I know that. You had to close your eyes, really concentrate, it was like you were in agony to finish. What was really going through your mind when you were doing it? *Carrie?*" I said on an impulse, *"was that who it was?"*

He stood against the wall in frieze, his aspect changing. Then he came toward me slowly, each step deliberate, his face riven so that he looked like a different person. "Don't you ever say that to me again." He reached out, seized my wrist, twisted it hard, then brought it up behind my back. "Don't you ever say that again."

The pain was intense but I could not stop. Something drove me on like something had driven me out of the car in Texas. "Is that the truth you can't face, then?" I said. "Is that the only woman you ever wanted? You had to have something that was half yourself so that you could fuck it. You were really screwing yourself all these years then, closing your eyes and possessing a monster. Stop it," I said, "you're going to break my arm."

He brought it up harder and I felt the ligaments beginning to give, that last deadly sensation before breakage. When a little girl I had fallen out of a tree, and now I knew exactly what was going to happen again: I would vomit from the pain. But just before that instant when he would have broken my arm he let me go and stumbled away to the other side of the room. The cessation of the pain was almost as shocking as true breakage must have been, and I did not know for a moment whether he had done me damage or not. Then only in the ebbing did I see that I had been spared, the sense of release, knowing that my body, at least, had not been violated by him, even if my spirit had been ravaged. He crumpled against a far wall, his clothing in disarray, his face ruined, as if he had been violently attacked. He put a mangled hand to his mangled face, covered his eyes.

"Please go away," he said, "you have destroyed me now. Please go away."

"I want a divorce," I said. "I will never see you again."

"You cannot do this to me," he said. "Not after what I did for you. I did for you what no man has ever done for a woman in the history of a world. You cannot say that I love my daughter, knowing what I did for you."

"You destroyed me."

"No," he said, "no, I gave you life, I gave life to you for what I did. I loved you," he said, "the first time I ever saw you I loved you, I had been in love with your pictures for years. Meeting you then I knew that you were the woman who could save me but the situation was impossible: you were married to a man who was going to be the American President. Divorce was unthinkable in those circumstances, I know your country, the mores, the political consequences, divorce would have destroyed his career, and he would never have granted it to you no matter the circumstances, but I knew that you loved me too. I could see it in your eyes, your face, your manner, your aspect, how truly you loved me and would commit yourself to me only if the circumstances were different."

"You're wrong," I said. "You're wrong, I didn't love you, not then, not ever." But I could not break the flow of his conversation. He was looking away now, talking in a monotone, the words coming out slowly as if wrenched from him.

"You did love me," he said. "I knew it was true, but it was impossible. As much as we loved one another, you could not have left him. It was not permissible. So I had to follow you from a great distance, loving you, loving your eyes and face and picture and spirit and knowing that you felt the same way for me. Finally it became clear, the only way that I could have you. The only way that we could find our way toward one another in this terrible circumstance.

"He had many enemies, I knew this, I knew that his elimination could only come as a relief to more people than would find it a matter of grief. It all seemed so clear to me then. It was merely a matter of lending assistance when assistance was needed. I could do it. I was in a position where at very little risk I could make it possible for the plan to be carried out and under the circumstances how could I not?"

"What are you saying?" I said, "what are you saying to me?"

"I loved you. I might have rendered assistance otherwise, I am not saying that this would not have been possible. I had been approached before. A man in my position constantly finds himself being approached with matters of this nature, some of them quite legitimate. I might have yielded to this approach in any case. His policies were extremely defective and dangerous."

"You can't be saying this. You can't be telling me what I think you are."

"It would have been done anyway," Nicholas said. "If it had not been through my offices, it would have been through others. Do not think that one man by refusal can stand in the way of history. History onrushes. Jason would have been eliminated in any case, because he stood in its way. But an unquestioned and unique opportunity was given me and I took it. I — "

"You," I said to him, "you killed my husband. You killed Jason. You arranged his murder."

"It was not that simple," he said. He wiped a hand across his eyes. "You are always so simplistic. You Americans can understand nothing but simple causes, simple effects, you are addicted to the cheapest and easiest solutions. I did not kill Jason. He was a historical force which was obliterated; he ran against the tide of history and would be overwhelmed by other, stronger forces. I was not even the agent of his destruction, merely one who collaborated to a small extent in the deed. But if it had not been done by this group of people it would have been done by others. What you must understand," he said, "is that your husband passionately wanted to die."

"Don't tell me about my husband! How dare you say anything about him!"

"I loved you," he said. "I managed to convince myself that if it had not been I, it would have been others. But when the opportunity was given me it seemed to be a sign, a sign of our profound and real destiny."

"You are a monster," I said. "You are completely insane."

"No," he said, "I am none of that. *You* are insane to accuse me of having done something to hold you up to public ridicule and embarrassment. You are insane not to know the dimensions and reality of my love, a love for which I willingly made the most enormous sacrifices. You refused to understand anything."

I should have left the room then. It was inconceivable that I was standing there, facing him, listening to this, listening to the man who had murdered the President out of what he said was love for the President's wife. It was of such impact that it did not seem possible that I could grant the fact that the two of us were still here, having, for what would seem externally to be merely another furious marital argument and yet I found myself incapable of leaving. Part of it was absolute paralysis, I do believe this, but another part not so easy to credit is that I was fascinated: here at last I was dealing with a force so malevolent that it could literally destroy the world for what it conceived as romantic whim. I had never believed that such a thing was possible. I had never thought that he could have done something like this, not the man with whom I had slept, however intermittently, for eight years. But beneath that was a different horror: truly I could be accused of being his collaborator. To the extent that he said it was feeling for me which had driven him in this direction, to exactly that extent then I too was responsible for Jason's murder. A person less resilient, less determined than I, would have been driven quite mad by this revelation. That I was not driven mad on the spot might have indicated only that in my own way I was as monstrous as he.

"You have not heard the end of this," I said. "You have not heard the end of it. I will make a full report."

"A full report? Of what to whom?"

"I'll tell the world."

"You'll tell no one," he said. His self-possession seemed to be coming back to him, he took out a handkerchief and wiped his face carefully, not looking at me. "There is no one to report this to. Your country's investigations of Jason's murder were a joke designed merely to close the case, and it is all completely forgotten now. No one wants to reopen the investigations and no one would believe you."

"They will believe me."

"Will they?" he said, "will they believe you? If you actually succeed in attracting attention, with what will be seen as the desperate ravings of a frantic woman undone by guilt and grief, what kind of attention do you think it will be? It will only be such calculated to place you as far from public credibility as possible. Besides, your implication here is as great as mine or anyone else. No," he said, "of this I am quite sure: you will not tell anyone anything. You will make no statements."

"What do you mean? My implication is as great as yours?"

"But it is," he said, "you know it is. Do not tell me that at bedrock you did not know that the peculiar circumstances of Jason's murder were somehow tied to you. Do not tell me that you, an intelligent woman, could not have pieced all of this together if you had wanted. And furthermore, I know well that the matters between you and Jason were quite serious. If he had not been a major public figure in America, where such would have been a scandal, you would have divorced or separated. This is quite clear."

"You are wrong. You are wrong."

"No, I am not wrong," he said. He flushed and began to sweat heavily. "Now get out of my room," he said. "Get out of my life."

"You killed my husband."

"You do not understand. *I* am your husband. And now I will disown you. It will be as if we were never married. I will make such arrangements as are necessary. Get out of my room. Get out of my life." He pointed to the magazine. "And take that with you, you cheap slut. I don't want to look at your tits and cunt ever again."

I crossed over four steps and raised my hand to strike him, but he grabbed my wrist with the failing strength of a child in great pain. I could feel the flutterings of his blood, the empty stirring of the muscle system under the ruined flesh. "Do not strike me," he said. "I tell you this now you are never to strike me again."

I wanted to smash him, I wanted to smash his face open, I wanted to leave him bleeding on the floor but I could not. That impulse had been taken from me. Everything had been taken from me, I could not strike him again. Looking at him, I could see the truth of what he said, he was right. I had been his collaborator. If he had killed my husband, then I had married him, married the assassin. And who is to say that at some level I did not indeed know this, know that the richest man in the world was in love with me and that a man such as this was capable of anything, literally anything, to manifest the token of his love? No, there was no way that I was out of it, no way that I could separate myself from him. For the rest of my life or his we would be linked. I was his collaborator, his creation and to strike him then would be only to strike myself.

I took the magazine, put it into my handbag and, saying nothing more, left the room. Our parting was surprisingly matter of fact. We might have had a quarrel over sex or living arrangements, for all the drama there was to our parting. Past feeling there is only exhaustion. I understood then that in some real sense I had been feeling nothing since Texas.

37
1963 — PARIS

And it was easy to piece it together. No trouble speculating at all, I could imagine quite well how it went. If there is one thing I had learned over the years it was how matters are conducted by men like Nicholas. A telephone call here, a meeting there for dinner in an elegant restaurant, the subjects discussed only in the most tangential fashion, almost all of the conversations having to do with extraneous matters. Only a code phrase dropped in here or there so that all parties knew that they had not misunderstood one another. At this level there is nothing so scruffy as schedules, armaments, rifles, blood, death. All of it is highly abstract and well within the capacity of these men to discuss in between sips of port, little bites of excellent truffles. A spot of difficulty in the west. A planned trip to Texas.

"Yes, Texas would be an excellent place to put in the assignment. Certain people we know can take care of it. Then it is all settled," Nicholas says and signals for the waiter to bring another bottle of wine, wipes his lips with a napkin. "There is nothing more to be discussed."

"No, it is all settled. There is the question of definite arrangements but they can be placed in the hands of these parties who are highly trustworthy."

"The financial arrangements will be satisfactory," Nicholas says as the waiter uncapped the bottle. "A drawing account will be set up."

"That would be quite satisfactory."

"Timing and method can be left in the hands of these people. You are sure that they are trustworthy and efficient?"

"Oh yes. There is no question of that at all. These are people of the highest caliber. They have done work of this nature before."

"But never of such significance."

"All the more reason. The assignment will be a pleasant challenge, they will be able to bring their *modus operandi* to bear at a greater level of consequence than ever before. They will be quite honored to have that opportunity. You will be pleased with their work."

"A failure would be disastrous," Nicholas says, taking a sip of the port, letting it glide over his tongue, and then he swallows it delicately, nodding with approval to the waiter. "That is the one thing that cannot occur. A failure would raise more questions after all than could be easily resolved."

"All the more reason why there will be no failure."

"Then we can consider the issue resolved. I will set up a drawing account to which you will have access, and you will make whatever arrangements you consider necessary. I place it entirely in your hands."

"I am sure that you will be pleased with the work."

"You have no concern with the nature of the assignment? It is very important that this be discussed. If there are any scruples, now is the time to express them. I would respect you for telling me if you have any, and I will not think the less of you if you want to withdraw."

"Oh no, *monsieur*," he says, picking up his own glass of wine and draining it delicately in a single swallow. "There are no concerns. This is merely an assignment, a more lucrative and significant one than most but understood to be in that context."

"You are sure."

"I am quite sure. I am, after all, a thorough professional."

"Do you think," Nicholas says, "that there is any chance of failure? I would like to know now what circumstances confront us so that I do not have undue expectations."

"I see no chance whatsoever of failure."

"We cannot be the first who have discussed an assignment of this sort. There must be many others who have considered it or who are considering it at this moment. In what way do we differ from them?"

"In the most significant way possible, *monsieur.* We know our work, we have available magnificent resources. Therefore we will not fail."

"Yes," Nicholas says, "the resources."

His mind drifts, as it must, to the subject of money. The stipulated expenses are enormous, even larger than he thought they would be when he first decided to make the investment, and because of the nature of the assignment there can of course be no written evidence, no checks, no receipts. Everything will have to be moved in cash. This is an object of concern to him, no matter the people with whom he is dealing, since Nicholas if nothing else has acquired a reverence for the controls which can be placed upon the transfer of money. There can be here, however, no subcorporations, no governmental bonds, no fourth and fifth parties to conceal the transactions, no elegant network of receipts which will make all disbursements chargeable to a bankrupt, paper corporation. There can only be the cash itself and many millions of it. He had known that it would be expensive. He had even estimated that it might come to figures like these which could not be traceable and yet, placed against the situation as he is now he feels slight dismay. It is, after all, a great deal of money and there are no guarantees; it might fail and he will have no recourse.

"I am expecting efficiency," he says, finally. "Also, that this will be done within a short period of time. I am not prepared to disburse monies and wait months and months to find if there will be success. There must be some kind of deadline imposed."

"You can hardly request a contract."

"I am not requesting a contract," Nicholas says. "That would be ridiculous." He drains the wine glass and finds that he is slightly nauseated. The meal, excellent as it has been, has not set well with him. "We must work in an area of trust here. Still, there must be evidence that this trust has not been misplaced."

"What would you suggest?"

"Dispatch."

"It will be done," the man says. He finishes his wine expressionlessly. "There are others who are involved in this," he says, "others who also have their reasons for wishing the project to come to fruition. For that reason you are not assuming all of the expenses. This is an ongoing project, of which you will be the most significant financier, but you should not feel that it is your doing alone. In line with that, however, I will have to inform you that the initial deposit will be three million dollars."

"Three million dollars is an extraordinary amount of money. As cash it is even more extraordinary."

"I think that your resources make this a relatively insignificant sum. Which is not to say that it is a contemptible amount. Many would say that three million dollars is a considerable, heavy fortune. Still and all, it is not too much for what is demanded here. There will be an additional demand payment of three million dollars before consummation and a third payment in that amount upon successful completion of the project."

"That is nine million dollars *in toto*."

"That is what it is. You will," the man says, "permit me to pay for this excellent dinner. It is the least that I can do; I realize that these figures may be totally at variance with your own picturization."

"No," Nicholas says, "they are not. They are very credible figures. And this is my restaurant, I have an open account here and pay a statement once a year. It is impossible for you to pay for this dinner, and I would not permit it."

"Very well," the man says, "then our business is concluded. I assume that you find all of this satisfactory."

"Permit me to order another bottle of wine."

"No, I do not think so. With many apologies I think it would be best if we brought our dinner to a conclusion. I will leave, you may stay. I hope you will not find me at all impolite, but there are many good reasons why no link should be made between the two of us as I'm sure you know. Even if the security in your restaurant is absolute there is no accounting for the accidental. Discretion would be best."

"As you say," Nicholas says. "You will have one cognac with me before you leave, will you not?"

"No," the man says, "I do not think that would be wise. All that it is necessary to know now is whether or not these arrangements are satisfactory, and if we can count upon your total financial participation right through to the conclusion. Once you give your agreement, it would be very embarrassing as you can imagine for you to withdraw so I must ask for that statement of commitment now. You have not given it."

"Didn't I?"

"No. It is my business to make very precise judgments as to equivocation or lack of equivocation in what people say. Many people depend upon my judgment and it would be embarrassing for me to let them down. So I wish you to tell me now whether or not all of this is satisfactory and if so how you plan to make arrangements for the initial transfer which is due now."

"I see," Nicholas says. "I see."

He raises the napkin from his lap, leans back in the chair, again wiping his lips. He inclines his head toward the elaborate, rococo ceiling of this restaurant, then closes his eyes and allows all of the substance of the conversation to pass through the filter of himself, his own desires, his own judgment. He loves the woman, he knows that. All of his life, for all of his seeming control, his exterior which gives nothing away, he has believed deeply in the power of the impulse and the heart, also in that mystical destiny which has formed his career from the outset and turned him from an adventurous, irresponsible, mildly promising young man to one of the richest and most powerful entrepreneurs in the world. As much of the heart as cold reason has contributed to that career, he believes. He has become what he has become because he has not shut away the messages of the heart and now, as never before, he confronts them.

He raises a hand to show the man that he wishes a few moments to think, and then he considers. He is in love with the woman. She represents to him a beauty, mystery, sensuality which he has never before known and her connection to power further excites him for he senses that she is as ambivalent about that power as he is about his own circumstance. She can use it, and has, but always with a sense of revulsion; although she can deal from a position of power she has always identified with the powerless, has felt herself to be a weak person. It is this weakness of hers which excites him. He feels that he might be able to create her anew, make of her his own and most perfect testament, and in so doing discover himself as if for the first time.

For he truly does not know what he is, Nicholas thinks. He knows what he has done, the scope of his accomplishments, the dimensions of his reactions, the set of reflexes with which he confronts the world. But that is all that he takes them to be: reflexes, mere devices. At the core he does not know what he is, let alone what he might become, but through this woman, through what he can do within and for her, he might find that out and it would be something very useful for him to know before he dies. He is at this time sixty-two years old, a kind of prime, in one sense, for he feels to be at the height of his intellectual and psychological powers. But he is also a realist, and he knows that far more than two-thirds of his life is over. His father died at sixty-eight. Nicholas has no reason to think, even with all the medical facilities which are at his disposal, that he will live much longer than this. He carries his ruin in his blood; sometimes at night he awakens hearing the solemn tread of his heart and knows that it is practicing already for those anticipatory flutters which will herald the onset of his end. If he is to discover himself, then it must be soon; otherwise, like his father, he will die a man who has no idea what he is or might have been. Thinking of the pain on his father's face on his deathbed, Nicholas knows that this will undo all of his life. To have solved nothing, to have failed to unriddle oneself, is the greatest failure of all. He will have undone his life.

He remembers how she looked the first time he met her, the cast of her smile, the angle of her breasts, the tilt of her body as she leaned forward to talk to him. Perhaps it was all deception, perhaps her interest was merely politely quizzical, but then again he thinks that if she does not love him she can be taught to, he can show her those parts of himself which will make her love and she, needing that discovery, will come to him. Even if she does not love him, she can care for him and his love will bridge the gap between the two of them. He knows that he can win her. He saw that in her the very first time. She is married to a powerful Senator, but her husband no longer really loves her; that is well known and she must know it too. She lies in his arms some nights, does not lie in them others. The body does not lie, not ever. In the grave, finally, it decomposes to reveal all of its secrets great and small, but there can be knowledge on this side of the grave as well as the other.

He knows the seriousness of his plans. No American President other than the wretched McKinley has been murdered in this century, let alone in this world which has been excreted from the bowels of the Second World War. It will be a crime of the most horrid dimensions, changing everything in the consciousness of everyone alive, at the time of the murder and for generations to follow. And it will be a personal tragedy of great dimensions too. Nicholas believes in a way in the sanctity of human life, he likes to feel that he has never committed an act which will cause the death of others unless there was a clear, urgent need for it, and then it has been with a sense of mourning. He does not feel himself to be, then, a man without compassion.

But this young American President wants to die. He wants to die very badly. All of his life can be seen as a series of collisions with death, some of them nearly successful, all of them energizing him in a way which life cannot. His speeches roll with the thunder of death, his political and international concerns seem obsessed with it. As there are those — Nicholas likes to think of himself as one — who draw their power from their ability to embrace and celebrate life, so there are others, no less considerable to the history of the century, who draw an equal power from death. And this young American President is one of them. To deny him that death he seeks, an enormous death, a public death, a death which will seal him finally to his vision in a way which old age never could, would be to reverse the judgments of all history, Nicholas thinks. Besides, if he does not participate in this, other people will. It is, as his dinner guest has pointed out, in the nature of an ongoing plan.

So all of it comes together. Nicholas likes to think of himself as an organized man, as one who can fuse disparate elements into a coherent and seamless whole, who can, in short, control circumstances rather than be controlled by them. The wife can and will be his, the President must die, the plan is already now in progress. He can collaborate with history, turn it to its advantage, or he can stand aside, letting history roll on without him and forever lose his chance.

He opens his eyes, leans forward, looks at his guest who has sat there unmoving through all of this, his gaze focused and alert. He lifts up the glass of port and raises it. *"Salut,"* he says. "The money will be available tomorrow. Tell me where you wish it placed."

His guest smiles. "I knew you would feel that way," he says.

"I would feel no other," says Nicholas. He drains the glass. The wine is sweet fire.

38
1975 — NEW YORK

"Go back to him," Jane said. "Don't be a fool. He loves you, he will take care of you. And not to be forgotten is the question of the money. I hate to be cynical, but you will outlive him by twenty to forty years and can do so as one of the richest women in the world. If you leave him you will get nothing. He will arrange it that way."

"I will never go back to him," I said.

I did not tell her, of course, of Nicholas' confession. I would never tell this to anyone. It would have been so easy to have silenced her forever, brought her to shock, horror and grief that would have come close to my own by divulging that truth but I would not. I would not do this. It was inconceivable that I could tell anyone, because in a matter of this nature no one's confidence could possibly be trusted, and there was the question of my own implication. Quite simply stated, I did not know what my own position might be. Would it not be possible to find me a collaborator in the assassination? Emotions would run quite high. Aside from that, there was no judging what effect this information would have if released, and there was no way, no way at all to trust someone's confidence in this matter.

So I told Jane nothing although of everyone she was the one who I came closest to telling. "I will never go back," I simply said to her again. "I will never sleep with him again."

"Honey, you don't have to sleep with him. Half the marriages of this sort involve no sex at all, it's just a *ménage à deux* for everyone's convenience. I don't even know if he wants you sexually as much as he wants the world to *think* that he has you that way. He's a man in his late sixties, in failing health, who loves you, that's all."

"His health is fine."

"Nobody's health is fine in their late sixties," she said. "No, I will never understand your thinking here. Your thought processes are just not logical, Vivien. Consider what you're throwing away."

"I'm throwing away nothing. I'm trying to recover my life," I said to her.

"I won't abet this. I can't help you. What do you think you're going to do if you leave him?"

"I've lived more away from him than with him during all of our marriage."

"But you've always had status as his wife. I'm trying to teach you to be practical," Jane said. "You'll be in an entirely different position as his divorced wife. There isn't a great deal of sympathy for you now as it is, and there will be even less."

"I can do any one of a number of things," I said. "I always wanted to go back to newspaper work. Or I could find a job in television. I don't think that I'd have any trouble at all finding useful occupation."

"I don't think you realize what the situation is," Jane said. "You're quite insulated from your image in the American press. By and large, it is not too sympathetic."

"Are you talking about those pictures?"

She looked at me intently. "What pictures are you talking about?" she said. "I don't know any pictures."

"You know exactly what I'm talking about. Don't do this to me, Jane. Be honest."

"Oh," she said, "those. I don't think that that's of too much importance. Nobody pays any attention to stuff like that these days."

"I don't want you to mention them, ever."

"I didn't mention them, you did. Surely you're not telling me that you're concerned about that, are you? If anything that makes you appear a more sympathetic woman, being taken advantage of like that."

"I want to move in with you for a while," I said, "while I work out the circumstances. I don't want to be by myself just now."

"No," she said, "that's quite impossible. I can't have you here for a good many reasons."

"I think I'm begging you, Jane. You're my sister, why can't you help me?"

"Because I won't do anything to abet this, that's why. You're making a tragic, foolish decision. If you feel you have to do it then you must, but

I won't help you on a course of action which will ruin your life. No," she said, "I won't be able to help you at all. If you're going to do this, do it on your own."

"I never did anything on my own. No one ever let me."

"Then it's time to start."

"I can't understand this, Jane," I said. "I can't understand why you would turn your back on me this way."

"For your own good," she said. Then her expression changed. "What do I care about turning my back on you?" she said. "What is that accusation supposed to do, move me? You turned your back on me, on your family, on your country, all these years. Why do we owe you anything?"

"That was a terrible thing to say."

"It's true. All that you did, always, was look out for yourself. So now is no time to tell people that they're being selfish. You're being more selfish than any of us."

"Daddy always liked you better. I don't think he cared for me at all."

"What an odd thing to say," she said. "Daddy has been dead for twenty-nine years. Why are you bringing him up, now? That's all very childish."

"He used to take you riding. He never took me anywhere at all."

"You never liked to go riding."

"I could have liked it. He never took the time with me, he never wanted to do anything with me. He always preferred to be with you."

"The silliest thing that I ever heard," Jane said. "What does any of this have to do with the present, with what is going on now?" And then she did something odd, she reached forward and stroked my cheek gently, caressed it with her fingertips. "I never knew you cared," she said, "I never knew you cared that much. It's all right, baby. It doesn't matter."

"He always cared for you more."

"No," she said, "no he didn't, he cared for us just as much, it was simply that he felt he couldn't reach you. You wouldn't come to him. He was a shy man, he had been terribly hurt, he couldn't open up, he had to be found. I would and you wouldn't, that was all. You always made it so difficult for all of us, baby," she said, "you made us reach out for you and not all of us could." And I think I cried then. My memories of this are somewhat blurred. Perhaps it is so painful for me that I have sealed myself off from it even in retrospect, but it does seem to me that I wept and collapsed into her arms. And even if I did not do this, even if I am imagining it, it seems nevertheless to be the kind of thing that I should have done, I should have done. I wish I had done it but no way, not even in that hotel room in Texas on the last night when I could have said, "Jason I'm here, it's all right, I've always been here." But too late then to say it, too late by far, and worse yet, it might have been too late all along, from the very first years. But if I had, it might have all been different. And he with no need to go to Texas to save his career, and he with no need to look for me in all the other women, and he with no need to have his brains and blood smashed out in that terrible car, drooling essence to the floorboards as I held him only then in the way I should have held him, in life, years and years before.

39
1968 — WASHINGTON and NEW YORK

"Don't do it," I said to Harold, "don't do it. I'm terribly afraid. I don't think you should."

"What can happen to me that has not already happened?" he said, "and if they are going to do it they are more likely to if I don't make the run. This way the stakes will be too high."

"Don't do it, please," I said. "If anything happens to you, I'll die."

"No, you won't," he said, "believe me you won't. People go on. I did," he said. "I did."

I did. I did too. After a while it was very easy. The nice thing about being a national monument, the nicest thing perhaps is that there is no need for one to explain oneself. Everyone knows the interstices: the assumptions of the self are so public that everyone can fill you in. You can present them with outlines like these in a child's coloring book; the options are purely in their hands and there are no wrong answers.

I went on. The sex was a little difficult of course, not just at the beginning but throughout. How after all do you work your way around something like this? Most men are far shyer in bed than they would ever want even themselves to know, all vulnerability and openness. The cry of pain at the moment of discharge. "I just can't," he said. He was a famous author who not only won the National Book Award that year but had been invited to dinner at the White House. Myself, I had refused to set foot in the place from the moment I moved out. But that was not to say that Lawrence was not trying to be gracious. He was all for inviting writers and musicians that year, part of it trying to be like Jason, another part a simple peasant's awe. This novelist had not only been in the White House but had argued politics with Lawrence. He had lost, of course. The one thing you could not argue with Lawrence was politics. "I can't," the novelist said again and moved away from me. "This has never happened to me before."

"Don't be afraid," I said. "Don't be afraid of me."

"It isn't that."

"Sure it is," I said. I touched his shriveled groin. "I'm just a woman," I said. "I have needs and desires like everyone else. I'm built pretty much the same as most of them, I respond the same way. Don't think of Jason. Think of me."

"I'm not thinking of Jason."

"Of course you are," I said, "it's nothing to apologize for. It's not your fault. But you can get beyond it. I'm thinking of him too but that doesn't mean that I don't need you."

"You're impossible," he said. I felt a little stir of response as he touched my breast, then put his mouth against it. "You're just impossible."

"No, I'm not."

"I want you," he said, "but I feel like a shit. You can't understand that, can you? It's like taking the immortal beloved to bed. It's like the dark companion of the sonnets." His response failed and he turned from me again. "I'm sorry," he said. "I'm sorry."

Later this would turn up, changed around in one of his books so that he seduced and overcame the objections of the First Lady of the United States, a crazy and surreal scene which the critics said was among his best in a novel that was nevertheless the most self-indulgent of all; later on he would turn things around so that his novel's hero who was modeled upon him would effortlessly bring the First Lady to the first orgasm of her life. But I never held this or much else either against him; of all the categories of life, male novelists are among the most pathetic. Without their books, their lies, they would probably be unable to function outside of the walls of institutions. One must be very tolerant toward them, although it is impossible sometimes to keep one's patience. So I did not mind when this turned up in his novel in a dream version, but I minded very much when he got out of bed, stood turned away from me naked, breathing unevenly, staring through the window and then said, "I'll have to leave. It's better this way. I'll try to see you again soon and not be intimidated. I'll have to work this intimidation out on my own," he said and dressed and left, and of course I never heard from him again.

Still, a missed orgasm is not nearly as bad as a misplaced life. I would not allow myself self-pity; if I had not felt it over Jason's coffin I certainly would not because I was deprived of a fast fuck by a writer who specialized in fucking fast if at all. I merely lay there, I lay in that bed. In one way or the other I must have been in that bed for two years, and some of them could and others could not, and all of them tried, tried so earnestly hard to behave as if I was not an exceptional case. Under all those circumstances it was no surprise that when Harold came to me at last, poised and ready, that I received him. He, at least, came from the same blasted land that did I. We had endured the same cannon fire. Deep and whooping inside me, he came and came again until his semen like rivulets of blood crested deep, crested deeper, crested deeply and deeply and oh my God dying —

40
1978 — NEW JERSEY

I have gotten out of the nightgown and put on some decent clothes. If I die I am going to do so with some dignity at least. They will not be able to say that I looked shabby. Marilyn Monroe I am not; I will not enter the gates of darkness in bedclothes.

I am wearing a sweater, skirt and matching top, and with a touch of frivolity, a little pink pillbox hat which gives me a rather wistful aspect. It is a hat very similar to the one which I wore in Texas, although not the exact model, that one apparently having been discontinued. Looking at myself in the mirror I am rather pleased by my aspect, I look like a woman totally self-possessed, a woman of the world, a woman with a certain *je ne sais quoi*, and such mystery and explanation by turns could hardly fail to entice. Now, standing, walking through this room, striking a series of rather regal postures by which to admire myself in the mirror, I feel that I have reconstructed myself, I am at last the woman that I always should have been but abandoned so long in confusion.

I could not fail to intimidate them by my appearance. I am quite sure of this. If the two of them were to come in now, were to see me as I appear they would certainly be surprised, they might even be discombobulated. What has Carrie been led to expect? A sniveling little woman in a nightgown no doubt who will beg for mercy, not the proud figure who stands before this mirror, posturing, striking pose after pose that reminds me and would remind the world that I was once indeed a woman of dignity and worth. Still am. Still am.

41
1976 — PARIS

Word reached me that Nicholas had had a major heart attack and was in the intensive care ward in a hospital in Paris. My feeling was one of overwhelming relief, it was not only judgment upon him for what he had done but meant that he would, possibly, be out of my life forever. But I realized, within the first hours of receiving the reports from his New York offices, that the situation was impossible. I would have to go to him. To indicate estrangement at this serious point would only be to raise questions which would never be raised otherwise. His condition was not stable. He was in deep coma with erratic life signs and deteriorative function. The prognosis was extremely poor, and it was doubtful that he would survive the critical seventy-two hours. Under those circumstances the easy way would be to go to him. All of this was Jane's advice and for once it was reasonable. Going to him would only have been unwise if his prognosis was fair, but the prognosis was terrible. I booked passage to Orly Airport.

He had had the attack eight days after I had last seen him. Whether it was related to what had happened or not I did not know; it seemed likely. Nicholas, however, was a complex man, the body a complex organism, he might have been ready for the attack anyway. For that matter he might, as Jane had said, have been in ill health for many years; I knew of the rumors, although I had seen no indication of poor health in our own dealings. Still, he never discussed anything with me; it was quite possible that he had concealed a congenital heart condition.

My mood could be characterized as careful, reserved. I had known when I heard of the attack the greatest sensation of peace and release which I had had in years, it passed through me like cool flame, I do not think I realized until that moment how the marriage had imprisoned me. Marrying Nicholas for sanctuary, I had found only guilt. He had been a monster, but that was almost beside the point now; even if he had not been responsible for Jason's death, my own violation, the marriage itself was still monstrous. Now at last, done with it, I had some inkling of the kind of person I might become if I were only out of it. If I left him and he lived, I would never have any peace, because if he was capable of killing Jason he was certainly capable of doing the same to me in revenge. But if he died I would not have to leave him. I would be out of it. In all of these airborne considerations I did not think of Carrie, unfortunately. That turned out to be stupid, as I subsequently learned. Euphoria is not a state accompanying sound judgment, however. She was in the airport waiting room when I disembarked.

"I knew you'd be in," she said, coming over to me, accompanied by a thin man of ambiguous age who looked at me intensely and said nothing throughout. "I knew you'd be in just as soon as you got the word and it was just a matter of calling around. You are not to visit him at the hospital."

"I will do as I wish," I said.

"If you think that you will gain anything by this you are entirely wrong. My father now knows exactly what you are, and explicit instructions have been made to his lawyers. Your seeing him will change nothing. You are to return to America at once."

"I'm afraid I can't oblige you," I said.

I had, at that time, no fear of her. It was the first time in my experience that she had not intimidated me. Part of it was knowing finally the acts

which her father had committed; they were so much worse than anything
I might have done to him as to release me from any sense of guilt. Also,
I was quite sure that Carrie did not know any of this. He could not possibly have told her. Even if she had agreed with the sense of them, she
could not have given him any support. That knowledge equalized everything; previously I had always dealt with her as one who had some kind
of emotional power over me but that was entirely gone. I could tell her
something which would be utterly destructive and knowing that, I no
longer needed to.

"He's my husband," I said. "I've come here to see him."

"I'm his daughter. I refuse you access."

"You can't," I said. "Anyway, it's too late for any of this. His condition is serious, I know. It is my right to see him and I'm going to."

"Don't do it," she said. She raised a hand in warning. "Let his last moments be peaceful. He hates you so much now, let him not have to see
you."

"He is not even conscious," I said. "This is ridiculous," I said. "I am
going to get a taxi and go to the hospital. I did not even come here with
any baggage. Who is this man?" I said to her. "What part does he play
in this little comedy? What is he to you or to me?"

"Jacques is a good friend of mine. He is helping me during these difficult weeks."

"Jacques," I said, "get this bitch out of the way. Restrain this bitch and
get her out of my life so that I can go to the hospital and see my husband."

The man's little eyes seemed to glint with something like response. It
might even have been a hint of collaboration which passed between us.
He put a hand on Carrie's elbow and she shook it off. "Don't do it," she
said to me. "Just do not do it. I am warning you, the consequences will
be very serious. You owe me this one last thing: you owe me not to go
and see my father, to let him languish in peace."

"Owe you?" I said, "I owe you nothing." And I could see then that
somehow, subtly, power had indeed transferred. I had control over her.
Part of it had to do with the presence of the man she called Jacques; there
was something within him that made her very uncomfortable, I could see,
some hint of a relationship revealed which made her vulnerable. But,
more significantly, it had to be that her father, her familiar, lay unconscious and dying in a Paris hospital and with the collapse of that within
her which had been his presence, her own force had dwindled.

"I owe you nothing," I said again, "you bitch." And I slapped her
across the face. She grappled for me. I avoided her grasp, Jacques restrained her, and I walked through the terminal and to the taxi stand and

went directly to the hospital, not knowing or caring what was happening behind me. Just like Nicholas had always been.

42
1978 — NEW JERSEY

Not much more now, not much more and it will all be out. Oh still my heart, oh patient be my enemy, give me just a little more time and I will have it all done, then they can do with me what they want. I do not care, just to have it all down finally. There is so little more, I have tried to be honest, have tried to tell the story as it happened, no embroidering, nothing in my favor, just the cold, terrible, objective trap of circumstance. But I do not know if they will give me the time to be done with it. Oh, this is foolish, foolish now, I should not be wasting precious time babbling like this when every word could instead be the truth. But I am frantic, absolutely frantic, this my prayer for some little space, prayers are important too, I am entitled to them, am I not? Pater Noster, let the truth be done, our father who art in Texas hallowed be thy name thy kill be done thy shot be done on earth as it is in Texas give us this day our daily blood and forgive us our deaths as we will forgive the death of you for thine is the death and the death and the death forever and ever and ever amen.

43
1976 — PARIS

Intensive care on the sixth floor. Thank you very much. Yes, I am Mrs. Sarris. Thank you very much that is not necessary. I will find my own way. The elevator in the back? Certainly. Yes, I am Mrs. Sarris. My husband is in intensive care. Yes, I am she. Well, thank you very much. I'm always happy to hear words like that but I'm very upset of course about my husband. How is he? What is the latest condition? *Comment se porte-t-il?*

Oh, well, I am terribly sorry to hear that. He hasn't regained consciousness at all? I am sorry. You think that he has been calling me to come in his coma. I see. *Je comprends. Merci beaucoup.* I would like nevertheless to see him if I may.

Yes, I will be very careful. I would prefer to see him alone. Is there a nurse in the room? Oh I am so happy to hear that he is receiving constant care, of course, but I would prefer if the nurse wait outside while I see him. If conditions are as serious as you say, then this may be my very last moment with him and I would like to have it alone. Would you mind that? *Merci beaucoup.* Well, you learn to bear up under this kind of thing, after a while. I have had a great deal of experience, I am sorry to say.

Waiting, waiting, underneath the hot fluorescence of the antechamber. Then his private nurse came out with the angry look of one who had been displaced from a treasured nap. The third room on the left. Yes, I said, yes. Down the corridor, Daddy. Up and down all of the corridors in my nightclothes wandering through the dark, but I am a good girl, Daddy. I would never hurt you or anyone. I would never be a bad girl.

Into the room. It was the future I saw in that room: the glistening machinery pulsating away, steel and tubing, wire and aluminum, the thin hum and beep of the monitoring equipment and then at the center of all of this, almost incidental to it, the little huddled shape of a man on the bed, human flesh ridiculous in that context, uselessly attached to machinery whose pattern and symmetry it broke. The light was blue and green, little red blips coming across the cardiac monitor like the machine in Texas which they had hooked up to Jason to verify his death. Of course they had used much more primitive equipment back then. Medical science has advanced enormously in just this short period of time. The machinery here was beautiful.

Not so Nicholas. I could not have recognized him. He had shriveled, lay an inconsequential lump on that bed, wires and pipettes running in and out of all the orifices of his body, ears, nose, mouth, anus, prick, clamps on his wrists, rubber loops on his ankles. His breathing was shallow, uneven as it was during sex, but this was not the man with whom I had had sex; he looked as if he weighed eighty pounds and was a shriveled old child. His complexion under the green-blue was blue-green; I touched his forehead and it was cold. He did not move. Brain functions, for all they knew, might have been destroyed.

If it would be done, it were best that it be done quickly. I knew what had to be done now; I had worked it over in my mind through the transatlantic flight, mapping the sequence of the actions, and they were simple. Nothing to it; I had seen similar things done in Texas; I could imagine it being done in Los Angeles as well. The important wire is the one which runs from the machine to the socket in the wall; if you trace that to its source, then you apprehend everything. I did so. Daddy, I did so. His breathing broke into a stutter, he hyperventilated, seemed about to go into a bit of Cheyne-Stokes, then relented, sobbed, fell further into that dark sleep. What was he dreaming in the devastated brain? Guns and birds; the high parapet in Texas. Leave no traces. With a rubber-soled shoe put on particularly for this, I tracked the wire to the wall, gave it a single careful turn. The prongs came out slightly. Not enough. A little more of a twist. The red blips faded from the room.

The blue-green remained; his complexion still green-blue. I looked at him then for the last time. His aspect had not changed; his breathing stag-

gered on. It would take a little time. That was fine. Time was what I
needed and there would be enough.

I turned and went out of the room and down the corridor. *Merci. Merci
beaucoup.* Thank you very much indeed for giving me those few last moments with him. I appreciate it. No, I think that I will go and find a hotel for the night. As soon as I make the proper arrangements I will phone
and let you know my whereabouts and I will be back in the morning of
course. No, it is not necessary for you to book me into a hotel. I have
my chauffeur downstairs; he will help me make the necessary arrangements. *Merci, merci, bon soir.*

I took the elevator downstairs and went into the night and a taxi and
then to Orly Airfield. The next New York flight was only half an hour
hence and they had first-class accommodations remaining; my luck was
running true and well. I was in the airplane, the doors sealed and moving before it occurred to me that I had not had any last words to say to
him at the door. That was not appropriate. That was not truly my style
at all. I had had last words for everyone; I should have had them for
Nicholas, too.

But what was there to say? For once I had supplanted words with acts;
for once I had taken my life under my own direction and assumed the
responsibility for events. I should have done it a long time ago. I settled
into a thin doze, with visions not unlike those that might have seized
Nicholas in his coma, men in business suits balanced on high parapets
holding guns, the clatter of sirens, and then there was one siren which
pierced the rest, filling all of the rooms of the mind with pain, and I came
from sleep in terror thinking that the plane was falling but, no, it was
moving as if in a dream through the Atlantic night and I knew instead
what that siren had signaled.

Nicholas died at 3:36 a.m. Paris time.

44
1978 — NEW JERSEY

It was not Carrie, it was Jane. *Oh, my God, it was not Carrie it was
Jane.* I cannot talk now. I do not know what is happening to me. They
are going to come through the door again.

45
1978 — NEW JERSEY

"It was you," I said to her when she came into the room, Annie behind
her carrying an enormous hypodermic, behind Annie, Tom and Millie
staring with lustrous, interested eyes. "It was you in the kitchen with her
all the time. Oh my God," I said, "what are you going to do to me?

You've got to help me. You've got to help me, I thought that you would save me."

"You have been a very bad girl, Vivien," Jane said. She had lost weight, yet her face was puffed; she looked fifty-four years old and I am forty-nine. "You have not listened to those who have tried to help you, and you have caused a great deal of distress. I hoped that this would not happen."

Annie said, "Lie down." To Jane she said, "Please get out of the way. I am going to administer the sedative now."

"No," I said. "You must help me, Jane. You must protect me. I thought it was Carrie in the kitchen," I said. "I thought that it was she talking to Annie. Oh please," I said, breaking down at last, "please don't put the needle in me. I lied. I don't want to die."

"You are a hysterical woman," Annie said, "but we have no time for hysteria now."

Jane said, "I will make a pact with you, Vivien. If you will keep quiet now and listen to everything I say, and cooperate, I will tell Annie not to give you the needle."

"Oh my God yes," I said, "I will do anything, anything you say. I can't bear it."

"You are making a serious mistake, Mrs. Lewis," Annie said. "One which you will regret. Please allow me to administer to the patient."

"You are still following my orders," Jane said. "You are in my employ. You will listen to me." She said to me, "Do you promise? Do you promise to be quiet now and to listen? It's all of our heads if you don't."

"Oh yes," I said, "oh yes."

"Put it away," she said to Annie. "Get out of the room. I will talk to my sister now."

"No," Annie said, "I am staying."

"Again I am ordering you."

"Excuse me, Mrs. Lewis," Tom said, "but you are not in a position to issue orders at this point, and none of us are going to leave. The situation is entirely too serious for that. If you have to talk to your sister, you will do so in our presence because it is all of our necks, and we are all deeply implicated."

"That is the truth," Annie said. "You are a fool," she said. "You had better let me administer the sedative. She is highly unpredictable; she is completely uncontrollable."

"Let me do it my way," Jane said.

"I am not an object," I said, "I am a human being. I am entitled to know what has happened, what you people are doing. Why are you doing this to me? It is not my fault, everything that I did I was forced to do.

I had no alternative, you must understand that. You must understand everything by this time. Jane," I said, "are you part of them? Are you out to kill me as well? I can't accept that, I can't believe it, this is the thing I finally cannot take if it turns out that you are — "

"Oh shut up," she said, "shut up." And she hit me across the face, and I fell across the bed gasping. Tom and Millie came and propped me up, then Jane slapped me across the face again. "No," she said, "this one time you are going to face it, you are not going to get out of this so easily. If you want the truth then you are going to have to deal with it. You bitch," my sister said to me, "you stupid bitch, did you think that it would end with his death? Everything you did in your entire life you always walked away from and the terrible thing is that even now I cannot hate you. I want to hate you so much but I cannot."

46
1978 — NEW JERSEY

After they told me, they left me, and sealed the door. What they told me, I will try to talk about in just a moment, but now the question is what they are going to do with these reels. When they were done, Annie said, "She's been talking a lot into a recorder for the last day or so; I felt that it was best to let her go ahead, it would keep her occupied. Here it is," she said, and came over, moved aside the pillow and took out this machine and the microphone. "The reels are probably in the closet," she said, "the stuff she's already taped." I struggled desperately to get at her but Tom and Millie restrained me. I thought that Annie was strong but she had nothing on these people. For deceptive strength, they are unlike anyone with whom I have ever dealt. Of course deceptive strength is the key to their profession. "We'll have to listen to it of course," Annie said, "before we destroy it. Just to see how much damage has been done."

"Don't!" I screamed, and threw myself at her, but their interlocked arms held me tight. "Don't take my memoirs from me. Don't take away the truth."

"Your memoirs," Jane said. "You've been in here, you silly bitch, dictating your memoirs. We're trying to save your life and you're talking out your *memoirs?* You are the most selfish person I have ever known. No wonder you couldn't hold Jason."

"You'd better let me administer that shot now," Annie said, "before we have another struggle."

"No," Jane said. "I have a better idea. Why give her the peace of sleep? Leave her to consider what she is, what she has done. We can't afford to be sedated, why should she? Leave her here, let her think. Besides, when we have to take her away tonight, it will be easier if she isn't a dead weight."

"I still think you're a fool," Annie said mildly, "but if you want to do
it that way do it. I have nothing to say in the matter."

"I'm going to tell them to let you go," Jane said, "but if you act up in
any way you are going to get the needle."

"Please," I said, "don't take my tapes. Don't take that from me. It's all
I have."

"And what will you do with them?" Jane said, "publish for a million
dollars?"

"No, at least it will be the truth. Somewhere the truth has to be set
down."

"There is no final truth," Jane said. "There will never be any final answer. You will have to grow up and come into the world and realize that.
Let her go."

They let me go. I got off the bed, moved around the room in distracted
little circles, surprised that I could still do so. "You'll live!" Jane said.
"Where are the tapes?"

"I won't tell you."

"It doesn't matter," Annie said. "We can find them before we leave the
house. They're certainly somewhere in this room. She couldn't have taken
them too far."

"Where are you going to take me?"

"That is one of the numerous things we have to discuss," Jane said.
"You have given us quite a problem."

"I should be part of that discussion."

"You will not. We are trying to save you," she said. "We are probably
the only people in the world who can save you, and you have worked
against us at every turn. You still don't believe us, do you? You think that
we're trying to hurt you."

"Don't take my tapes. Please don't take my tapes."

"She's hysterical," Annie said. "Nothing will be accomplished by listening to this."

"Yes," Jane said, "you're right. But don't give her the hypodermic either. Just leave her here and let her think things over. She'll understand.
Maybe she'll even become reasonable."

"Whatever you say," Annie said.

"I doubt it," Tom said. "This is not a reasonable woman."

"I agree with that," Millie said.

"Nevertheless," Jane said, "we can at least try. We can give her that one
last opportunity. Anyway, it doesn't matter anymore."

"Should we take her recorder?" Annie said.

Jane shrugged. "Why bother?" she said. "We can get it later. Might as well leave it with her. Maybe she wants to dictate some final notes. We're going to destroy everything, you understand," she said. "You are talking into the wind. We cannot possibly allow any of this stuff to exist. But if you want to go ahead — "

"I have been talking into the wind all my life," I said.

And then they left me.

47
1978 — NEW JERSEY

"What did you do with her?" I said to them, "what did you do with Carrie?"

"What the hell did you think we did?" Tom said. "We had to dispose of her, that's what we did. Now we're not only your custodians, we're your goddamned hired assassins. That's what you made of us."

"I don't believe this," I said. "I saw her last night in the headlights."

"Damned right," Tom said, "damned right you saw her in the headlights. Those were my headlights. I had her blocked with the car. She was going to try to come into your room and kill you, and then when she saw that the place was patrolled she had the idea she could go the other way but she couldn't go anywhere at all."

"Then she wasn't threatening me?" I said. "She was appealing to me?"

"Could be," Tom said.

"You killed her?" I said.

"What the hell did you think that we could do?" Tom said. "Keep her prisoner? Send her back to civilization? Try to convert her? We did the necessary."

"Where is her body?" I said.

"In the swamps," Jane said, "where we used to go riding. Do you understand what you have done now? Did you really think that you could get away with this?"

"Get away with what?" I said.

"Don't play dumb, you bitch," Annie said. "Before we killed her we had to find out everything, didn't we? She told us. She was quite eager to talk as a matter of fact. She was not quite the close-mouthed little bitch that you always thought she was. Quite to the contrary. She expressed herself very freely."

"Then you see why I did it," I said. "You see why I had to do it."

"What you did was very stupid," Jane said. "It was stupid and, more to the point, it was unworkable. What did you think you were dealing with? Nicholas told her that he had told you. She already knew everything else. She knew the circumstances of his death, and she came after you."

"Then you killed her," I said. "You killed her and it's all over."

"No," Tom said, "it is not all over. It is in fact hardly beginning. Do you think a man like Nicholas Sarris would leave the matter of revenge to his twenty-five-year-old daughter? There are literally hundreds of people who are looking for you at this moment. Some of them, she said before she died, are already on the way. She made great efforts to beat them all here, and succeeded, but not, she thinks, by more than a few days. Perhaps as little as a day."

"Do you see what you have done?" Millie said. Her face was congested with fury. She was not a talkative person, Millie, but she made her contribution count. "You have probably killed all of us in addition to yourself. And we were supposed to be your protectors."

"I'm not responsible. We're dealing with monsters."

"You married one," Jane said. "You did this, not me. I came in to pick up the pieces."

"I didn't know he was — "

"Yes, you did," Jane said, "but I'll tell you something else too if you want to know, something which probably *will* come as a surprise to you. As I said, Carrie did quite a bit of talking before she died. She was quite eager to volunteer information, as a matter of fact; she seemed to have the feeling that she could convince us this way to let her live. She not only answered questions toward the end; she gave a lot of spontaneous information. You want to know what kind of man you married, bitch?"

"I know now. I found out — "

"You found out only a part of it," she said. She looked at Annie. Annie shook her head. "She doesn't want me to tell you," Jane said. "She has more compassion than I. I don't care. I want you to know. I want you to suffer, and live with this for as long as you or the rest of us have even if it's hours. He knew you were uncertain about marriage even though you kept on seeing him, and after a while he ran out of patience. Rich men find it difficult to be endlessly accommodating. So he thought that he would do something to give you a little final impetus, toward your own decision, the dance you were leading him. So he did."

"You're not telling me — "

Jane nodded. "Oh yes," she said, "oh yes indeed I am telling you *exactly* that."

She stared at me.

"He put Harold down too," she said.

48
1978 — NEW JERSEY

And here they are, here they all are back in the room as I talk into this microphone and I do not care anymore. Go ahead. Go and do what you will for here you are: Jane, Tom, Millie, Annie and the sporting Dr. Richards. How pleased to see you, Doctor, well, thank you very much for those kind words. And now they are coming closer and I see the hypodermic in Annie's hand and it moves upon me. What a surprise, what a surprise! And thank you all so very much. This is best, Richards says, this is best for now, and with sadness I understand as that great gun levels, understand that whether it bears death or life, of the thousand sorrows this is merely the first of a new millennium and Daddy, Daddy, Daddy, even you would have made no difference.

THE END

Confessions of Westchester County

BARRY N. MALZBERG

I

On Sundays, I take my pleasure in another way: I go to the amusement parks in Westchester and look at them. Jaunty Mamaroneck or New Rochelle housewives, still lithe in their sleeveless sweaters, still tender in the space between their breasts, one arm loosely draped on their husbands' wrists, ordering the poor bastards around. The husbands carry cameras or beach-bags, scuttling gracelessly to keep up with the children. The children wheel merrily in baby carriages or run shouting toward mud puddles.

"Watch it, David!" my beauties cry on fine Sundays. "Watch it, Gary, watch it, Carol, watch it, Linda! Watch the water, the grass, the dogs, the other children, yourselves. No ice cream, candy, cake, soda or trouble. Try to play nicely. Don't hurt each other. Take a picture, Harold. Be careful of the camera, Harold. Can't you hold a camera, Harold?" Etc. Harold and his brothers do not seem pleased. Rising late from his Saturday night fuck he, perhaps, had other plans for today: suburban plans of extinction and renewal, love and death. Breasts and pudenda circulate darkly through the remainder of his consciousness. Instead, he must take his family to the Playlands for closeness. One can understand his problem. For the run of men, the consequences of copulative glee are disaster, decay and death. In a generation, two or three survive copulation to emerge from it in a renewed and spiritual light, Luther being one; the remainder pay the price over and again. This is unfortunate but necessary.

Oh! Oh, God! they are beautiful, beautiful! in their sweaters, their tiny skirts, the slight pendulosity of their upper arms bulging as they press down on carriage bars, slap a whining child's face indolently. Only ten or twelve years from the sorority houses at the most, they combine the edge of youth with the first weary lushness of responsibility. Menopause lurks but at a far remove, a mere abstraction. Their breasts rise, fatten, loom against one another. If only at the play-lands they would keep their mouths shut ... but this is perhaps asking too much.

I love to watch them, hiding behind bushes or strolling free and easy on the midways, fifty cents in my pocket, a secret buzzing greedily in my brain as I watch the wheels of fortune spin. Sometimes, very carefully, I will crouch near the women's rest rooms in order to see them guide their daughters or tiny sons within. What pictures! What sounds! What spread of thighs, what unspeakable acts committed swiftly behind those bland wood panels! It is enough to drive a weaker man insane. Fortunately, living in a rectory, I have managed to cultivate some perspective.

Dominica excelsior. Panicum repens. Mort donnom est puritanica en elei-son. Kyrie, kyrie. Everything to its time and season.

Their hips move like water under their pants; their breasts, harnessed by bone into furious ascent, drive me wild. Wild! Perhaps they do the same to Gerald although in all honesty I try not to think of this poor son of a bitch. His concerns are not to be served by me.

On those fine, warm summer Sundays I am in the amusement parks seeing my beauties *en famille*, watching them cavort in the fields of their desire. On Monday—

On Monday I make my rounds.

Into their houses, through the front although sometimes the back. Milk distribution, the grocer's assistant, a policy salesman, a sewage examiner. A tax lien investigator. Welfare surveys. Public opinion. Political inquiries. A novelist adrift and seeking to touch the frenzied heart of the suburbs. An unemployed handyman. A marauder. It hardly matters. Almost anything will get me inside (unless there has been a rape-panic in the neighborhood in which case I desist one and a half days). If it does not, I go elsewhere. (Very rarely must I go elsewhere.) They are so terribly, terribly lonely, those who have not already removed Harold and placed the children, courtesy of the gleaming second husband, into an excellent boarding school. So frustrated. So bent. So doubtful. So very querulous, for all of that easy and wicked knowledge displayed coolly in pants in the park.

I take them at my own instance, creating my own circle of response. In the enclosed darkness of their rooms (the shades, I must note, are always drawn in their bedrooms, it lessens the necessity for housekeeping) I hump them like a rabbit, whispering cheer into their frantic ears, unloading my small gold again and again as I touch what Harold would think of as *his* breasts, his thighs, his buttocks, and throw my gifts richly into them. They moan and sputter; they whimper in the darkness, go off into small exhausted furies of orgasmus to make me stunned with wonder at the power of my simple organ. Nipples bursting like candlefire against my chest, small wrists scurrying like hounds on the smooth liturgical panels of my back.

Afterwards, we always talk.

We talk for my convenience and until I have completed my studies. It is during these talks that I take their confessions. Years in the rectory, courtesy of Father Hilarion, years of Hilarion's counsel and wisdom, courtesy of the rectory, have given me a superb skill and ease in this sacred task. One must understand that the role of the confessor is sublime. It connects mortality to the anchor of the eternal. They talk to me, sometimes for five or ten minutes without pause.

Always, I hear their ultimate secret.

The ultimate secret is what informs my search. "We can't make it on thirty thousand a year, honestly we can't," they whisper; or "He can't make me come anymore no matter what he does," or "Sometimes I think that I'm going crazy, I hear these voices," or "My breasts hurt so much I think I have cancer there but I'm afraid to go to a doctor and Harold cries when I tell him he can't have them for awhile," or "I never thought that it would come to this, honestly I didn't. I thought I had an interesting future, I wanted to be a writer. I'm a very sensitive person," or "Cheever was right, he told the whole truth about everything but why did he have to be so cruel?" or "Hold me, hold me, I'm so lonely, always so lonely so hold me, Luther, hold me!": these words pouring sonorously across and through my superbly shaped ears with flicker of consonant, zoom of vowels, crackle of paraphrase designed to make me crumple with wonder, expire with gratitude. It is all so different, after all, from what they have to say for themselves in the parks.

(Hilarion, when we discuss this, says that it is not, that it is the same. He adds, however, that it would take me thirty years of the most rigorous intellectual application to begin to understand this and frankly I do not have the time. I am all feeling, all response: I live on the surface. In these times the man of action is needed.)

I could weep bitterly into their cleavage when I hear them for purest love, could vault in their moment of penitence to the buried center of their multiply-occupied wombs for reverence. Precious to me: ah, precious! But I keep a close hand on myself, much as I heeded gentle Hilarion's advice years ago to reserve my seed for placement in its proper receptacle. It is not necessary to betray emotion atop my judicious benevolence, my mustachioed involvement. Too much sympathy, after all, would lead to complications.

I add their confessions to the dossier I am keeping. (Every night I bring the entries up to date: it is now ten thousand pages long, neatly typed single-space, slightly more than a page to a customer.) Then, rehearsing the rhetoric for the entries, I flee. To the next development, the next subdivision, the next suburb. Three or four times a day when the weather is fine, I spring into their little hearts, unleash their tongues and am gone.

I have done this thousands of times. Eighty thousand and thirty-three to be exact. And I am young, yet at the beginning of my powers, barely forty-five. Some day I will have all of them—an enclosed record of the suburban century as gasped through the mouths of its catchword, its center, its women—and then I will deliver unto Father Hilarion and the world the summation of these lives. The ultimate measure of their condition!

Sometimes for hours I will find myself dwelling upon this triumph: so visualized that it is almost history, the day when my memoirs will be unleashed upon the century's sea and, by inference, upon a million unsuspecting Harolds. What will they say? How will they take it? What will they make of all this Good News trumpeted from on so low? It is enough to make one question the very future of the amusement park industry.

If one takes the amusement parks seriously, that is. I do, but perhaps this is my problem and they are really having fun there.

In the meantime. In the meantime, I do my work and hold against deliverance, build my modest record into substance, insularity, and the absence of contradiction. "I need love so much," they are known to whimper. "I am such a truly sensitive person, I carry things around with me far longer than the average," they confess. "I cannot have an orgasm without thinking of the breasts of my college roommate so many years ago," they moan. "Every time he comes into me I find myself going away from him and instead I'm thinking of the children and then peanut butter sandwiches and everything breaks down," they aver. "Hold me," they predict. "Touch me, touch me," they counsel avidly. "Oh, Luther, Luther, Luther, it has never been this way for you too, has it?" and soaring, I set my pencil for the latest entry.

An interesting life. Interesting! Barring the rainy Sundays and the chill of late fall (winters I meditate). Father Hilarion, in the bargain, is there to protect my soul.

II

Hilarion feels that I am in a period of sea-change, and will one day soon emerge at a new level, free of my "obsession". He talks to God about me nightly and feeds me well when necessary. Often we converse until the little hours. He feels that he is teaching me but in actuality I have taught him almost everything he knows except the matter of confession. The confessions I have learned from him. He is known well as the best confessor in this dismal section of Brooklyn and occasionally gangland chieftains from the next county or even upstate will come down on dark days to sit in his booths. Purged, they leave the chambers humming and the contributions are handsome, handsome enough along with Hilarion's obscure errands, to keep the parish alive. No thanks to the diocese.

"Luther, I do not understand what you want; I simply do not grasp the flavor of your ambition," Hilarion says, "but nevertheless, you must soon come to some firm decision as to what you will do with your life. You are well over forty now, Luther, and it is time to make a contribution for your stay on Earth. This little obsession of yours is remarkable. It may even have some significance but it is hardly the stuff of a serious career.

"Tell me, my son, now, have you ever thought of exactly what you would like to be? It is time to extract some definition out of all of this activity, yes, my son? A surgeon, perhaps? A writer? The correspondence schools offer useful courses in machine work. Perhaps you would like to try a liberal arts foundation. But you must do something, Luther; this kind of thing simply cannot go on. There must be a point of decision."

Nevertheless, it goes on. I understand that Hilarion loves me and that his urgings are the small obeisance which he feels he must pay to certain post-technological mores in which he fundamentally disbelieves. "Someday," I tell him, "someday my study will be completed, my place in Western history will be secure and oh! how the money will pour in." He gives a wistful shake of the head, purses his lips, trying not to give this credence. "Of course I will reward the parish handsomely," I add. "It is the very least I can do, although I realize I can give you nothing personally. But not a nickel to the diocese who put you in this position."

Hilarion is my father: that is, he would be my father if permitted by the rigors of circumstance. Actually, he found me abandoned in a basket, forty and more years ago, in the midway of a travelling carnival in a Midwestern state. He was an employee of the carnival at that time although he evinced little talent for games of chance.

A handsome rosy baby I was, tucked behind the wheel of a game of names and elimination run by the gifted Hilarion. When I squalled suddenly, causing Hilarion to notice me, the pointer swung to zero and a female customer became the first contestant in history to win in this game. She was handed a pack of cigarettes, the game was closed for repairs and in due course Hilarion was given to me. (It was rumored that the manager of the carnival was my father and that my mother had placed me there in a gesture of spite but this is untrue ... untrue!) And with the subsequent approval of his Monsignor when he was ordained we returned to Brooklyn, to this very parish, which has sheltered Father Hilarion for fifty years and myself for forty-two. It is a friendly place, although a bit large and unkempt, infested with mice. Papers were ordered. Special dispensations were granted. The Pope smiled. A Mother Superior winked. I became the legal son of Father Hilarion.

Grew up, Luther did, straight and proud in the catacombs of the Mother Church (although, with Hilarion, I do not believe in religion overall and unlike him do not consider myself a Catholic). I embarked upon my mission with a sudden and swooning sense of purpose at the proper age of twenty-one and sit now, rosy as the day I was born, completing the entries for this evening.

CONFESSIONS OF WESTCHESTER COUNTY

A fine day. Fine day! Big bitch in halter top called me her "little, little boy", and added that she had been overcome for years by fantasies of whipping her husband in public, not enough to cause him permanent damage of course, but just so that the rest of the world could see what she had to put up with. "I mean, why should he have it only done his way in private?" Margaret R— of White Plains. Zoomed in and out of her with stunning force, the faithful organ complying as always to the masterful demands of its possessor and then, after a few moments of brisk conversation and reminiscence during which the aforementioned came to light, straight back to Brownsville, a nice warm shower, into the current entries and so to bed! My odyssey may be limited—indeed, it is limited—but it virtually reeks with its own satisfactions.

Tomorrow to the extraordinary Mrs. Lee about whom I have been hearing so much. At last I believe I have reached her level.

III

Stories about Mrs. Lee predominate. Although I have yet to meet her I feel already that I know her, better, perhaps than many of the thousands of ladies with whom I have taken my stately and reserved pleasure. "Oh Mrs. *Lee*," I have been told, "Mrs. Lee is something else again; I know that you find me far too easy for you, Luther, and that you really have a basic contempt because of the way that I make love so easily but Mrs. *Lee*. She would treat you differently, Luther; she doesn't put up with any nonsense at all." Apparently her reputation or its opposite has spread far beyond the corridors of her modest three-bedroom house in Rye: I have heard of her in Mamaroneck and Peekskill, in Brewster and in Scarsdale, and once a large-breasted housewife in Poughkeepsie (occasionally when I feel ambitious I journey upstate) screamed to me as she came, "Mrs. Lee! Mrs. Lee wouldn't do this for you, Luther!" This woman is of some dimension.

It is true that for some months now I have been deliberately avoiding the issue: that golden moment at which Mrs. Lee and I would at last confront one another, bared in the solemnity of her two-garage home, meeting like rabbits in the cloister of her bedroom. This is not from a fear of challenge—my whole life should be testament upon the subversion of difficulty—but rather another quality altogether.

Call it if you will a reluctance which comes from deliberately delayed sweets, something with which even a Luther can be familiar. If this woman is all that she is reputed, then a certain hard edge, a certain keenness and anticipation must irreparably dwindle within my life at the moment that I take her. Nevertheless, I can no longer put it off. Today I will

see Mrs. Lee. A small scuttling animal knocks against my loins as I drive
Hilarion's car down the quiet street and park it in front of her home
which is curiously removed from the street and hidden behind a medley
of flowers, flowers of all types and colors, bobbing in the breeze. From
an upper window up the block a form appears, retracts; my progress is
being noted. This does not afflict me with paranoia. The fact is that I am
celebrated and that my reputation, such as it is, has spread through all
of the Westchesters. No less than I have heard of Mrs. Lee, I know that
the lady has heard of Luther. So much part of the odyssey of the suburbs
am I that I was the subject of a full-page feature in the women's section
of the *Times* a bare six months ago. Of course the title was *How the
Ladies of Leisure Spend their Days at Home*, and certain "charitable activities" and "dramatic societies" were used as the metaphor for Luther-
ship; nevertheless it is perfectly understood by the *Times* reporter, to say
nothing of his subject, that *something* worthwhile must be going on upstate between the hours of nine and five, otherwise these ladies could
hardly bear the impact of their lives and would long since have savaged
these bucolic streets into little pieces of urban renewal.

Mrs. Lee! I tongue my lips, carefully incise my teeth, park the car on
the empty street and bring it to a murmuring priestly halt beneath a rather
clumsy oak which a plaque informs me is a historical monument donated
by the Daughters of Westchester in appreciation of the history which they
have been donated. Inside I flex my thighs, test my thumbs, perform certain vigorous exercises of the fingers to gird me for the task ahead. Then
I slip from the car with consummate ease and grace, not locking it behind me—there are no crimes against property in this section of Westchester—and with a light, bouncing walk, contrived out of the best parts
of myself, go up the neatly curved path flanked by children's merchandise and to the door itself. Hilarion to the contrary, I feel perfectly confident and at ease. ("You are obviously dealing with a subtle and complex woman, Luther, and perhaps it would be best not to do this,"
Hilarion has advised me; I keep him fully apprised of my progress and
plans. "Anyone of this reputation and fierce organizational capacity may
interfere with your actions. I tell you this too, Luther, not because I want
to be identified with your activities in any way, as you understand, but
only because I am looking out for your well being." We poured two more
glasses of wine and passed on then to other topics mostly involving the
poor quality of the tapers which the church has been receiving lately. The
Parish is beginning to feel the economic cataclysm as well.) With three
expert stabs I ring the doorbell and then wait until it is opened by a large,
attractive white woman who can only be Mrs. Lee herself, wearing an
elegant sleeveless dress and a simple necklace which dances fire around

the excellent expanses of her throat. Today is maid's day off, another piece of my expert planning. (Although in most of the districts I am on excellent terms with the servants.)

"Mrs. Lee?" I say. "My name is Luther Atkins. I represent the district water commission and have come to ask you certain questions about your consumption, the placement of the septic tanks and so on and so forth. Our effort is to try to reduce your tax basis while upping your assessed value." This superb ploy, which is one of my favorites, alternated with the ever-successful Book of Wonderful Things, has been selected, on the basis of all I know of Mrs. Lee, to incite her to an ecstasy of suburban property passion. "May I come in?"

She steps aside, revealing a thin exquisite sliver of entry way and beyond that the living room which is decorated in many colors. "Oh yes," she says, "Luther Atkins. I've heard of you. Many of my friends seem to know you well. Do you want to come in and make love to me?"

Although there is some precedent for this kind of abruptness (gifts like mine can hardly be kept in anonymity) I am slightly disconcerted and say, "Oh, you know then what is going on?"

"Of course I know what's going on," she says and turns, leads me unblinking through the foyer and into that splendid living room. "Really, Luther, I've been expecting you for months and months now. I thought you were never going to come. You're perfectly free to have sex with me, the children are all in school and my husband on an important call in Indiana but I can tell you in advance that you won't get a thing out of me, not a single thing. I mean, I'm not interested in having a relationship with you, I'm too involved in too many things here and anyway, from all I've heard about the way you operate, you don't go for relationships anyway."

I hear the door close behind me with a slow moan and then Mrs. Lee begins to remove her dress; she does this with consummate skill although the necklace, getting in the way as it does, creates an awkward moment and she is forced to stop at a clumsy instant to undo it and then let it slide, along with her dress, to the floor. She is a splendidly proportioned woman, her breasts still showing what must have driven fraternity leaders mad in the early 1960s and her thighs as well are quite magnificent, seeming in their stony intensity to possess strength to capture the world. I look at her with more than moderate appreciation and say, "You're very direct. I mean, I hadn't really expected—"

"Oh, stop it, Luther," she says, and opens her arms, gathers me into a strong and unyielding embrace, begins to nibble at my neck. "Come on now, Luther, don't be ridiculous; no man who's been living the way you have for all this time should be surprised at anything. Besides, I've been most curious about you; as far as I can gather you perform sex remarkably well. On the other hand," she sighs, "almost all of my friends are liars and too ignorant to know the difference between good sex and bad sex. Come here, you deceitful man you," she says and begins with extraordinary facility to strip my clothes from me: first the pants go and then the shirt, all of this while being held by her; finally I kick my shoes off with embarrassed feet and we go winding our way to a large orange couch whose pillows seem to envelop our struggling forms in a hush of mystery as we plunge our way downward. I apply myself to Mrs. Lee's large nipples, wondering, but trying not to reflect upon all of this too much as I perform my splendid tasks. Outside I hear the dim whine of cars, a gardener's rake, the sound of a siren suggesting noon. "Oh, more, more," she says. "I thought you were supposed to be so good with the breasts," and with my pride injured I spit nipples, claw at the edges of enormous boobs, ram myself again and again at the indolent wall of her thighs until slowly she parts and I guide myself into her. Her vagina grips me like a hand and expertly begins to masturbate me.

Screwing her, I decide, is like being brought to orgasm by an incredibly skillful, knowledgeable hand, a hand which has somehow externalized all the knowledge of one's own but is, miraculously, that of another, and as her little fingers claw at me, as the thumb of her clitoris bites down upon my vanished head, I squirt into her the seedlets of my desire moaning, my mouth distended over hers, seeking her lips but finding instead the bland surfaces of her shoulder. Reciprocally she has an orgasm—or something which I take to be an orgasm—in the backlash of mine, waiting until I have emptied myself into her to make her own response, and so I lean above her, regarding her with Luther's tormented, driven, soulful gaze hopefully driving her past her own blocks and queries as she spins underneath me, sighs once or twice, gulps at air and then thumps herself to satisfaction around my diminishing prick. She falls away then, seeming to flow onto the surfaces of the bed and once again I begin to work within her—the secondary orgasm is one of my minor but real feats—and just as I am on the verge of some kind of connection, my stopped-up prick beginning to unfold within her, she wrenches herself away from me, closes her thighs underneath and rolls to one side leaving me most dismayed and, I should point out, awkwardly placed upon her bed.

"Well, you're not bad, Luther," she says, "and that was very interesting, but I don't feel like anything more now if you don't mind. I mean, I'm not terribly sexually responsive and you shouldn't take it personally, I'm this way with Martin too and everybody else. Actually you're pretty good. My friends were right in saying that you knew how to have sex so don't take it personally."

"But you don't understand," I say, still straddling her, my prick from this angle having a rather lumpish and distorted aspect as well it might since what she has said has acted to further incite me and I am now quite ready for the sexual act again, or at least that simulacrum of it which according to Hilarion is as close as I can come to love, "you don't understand, I'm not finished yet. I mean, there's a certain procedure—"

"Nonsense, Luther," she says and runs her hand across my lips, "really now, I've been very nice with you and taken you seriously so far and I wouldn't want to spoil it for you now. I mean, when you come right down to it, Luther, it's pretty ridiculous, a grown man I mean, spending his days seducing suburban housewives and then trying to get them to tell him their secrets as if all of that really *mattered*. I mean, it doesn't matter at all, Luther, it isn't important, it has no significance at all and really you should have grown out of this a long time ago, not that I mean it's really my right or position to tell you how to live your life. That's your business. I've wanted to meet you for a long time though and I'm glad you finally came around just so that I have a way of comparing the way you are to what my friends say. But no more of this, Luther, it's got to end. I have to get ready for the community fund appeal meeting, it's at three o'clock and I only have two hours to dress and get over there. Maybe you think that that's trivial, Luther, but it certainly is not."

She is a difficult customer, Mrs. Lee, very much as I had been led to suspect from the various reports and intimations edging their way out from various beds and living rooms. "Oh her, Luther, you won't get a thing out of her," I had been informed by several ladies who otherwise had very little in common, "in all of Rye, New York, there's no one quite like Mrs. Lee. She was sorority president you know, even though she came from a very poor background and had to make it all on her own. Usually the sorority presidents get that way because they have relatives in the national. You may be able to get *me* to tell you everything Luther but Mrs. Lee won't." To all of these protestations I have turned a blank pan, a faintly pallid cheek, a delicately raised, exquisitely formed eyebrow. "We'll see," I have commented and closed the discussion. Naked, shuddering, expiate before me, they have been able to defend themselves only through the invocation of a Mrs. Lee who is impermeable to connections. I let them have that.

Only with Hilarion have I discussed the issue in some detail. "You had better watch this woman," he has counseled me. "I don't mean to say that I approve of your practices, Luther, because the fact is that I distinctly do not, aside from all the valuable questions of mortal sin, but nevertheless you are my son and I am entitled to have sympathy for even that of yours which I do not like. I tell you frankly that if this Mrs. Lee truly exists and is as she is represented then she may be an element of your comeuppance. I think that you are not ready yet for relationships, Luther, no matter how much success you have had with encounters."

"Nonsense," I have replied, "it's all a hoax, she's another matron like the rest of them: slightly harder, perhaps but cut out of the same material. How can she stand up against my superb devices? Why, Caroline Hawkins was the leader of the liberal democrats in her district and a believer in unlimited contraception and before I had gotten through with her she had flushed all of her birth control devices down the maid's room toilet and had admitted that in her heart Hitler had always been the founding influence of her political career. No man who so conquers Caroline Hawkins can have difficulty with the likes of Mrs. Lee!"

But here, some months after that brave but somewhat empty-headed prediction, I find myself sitting now tailor fashion before her on the bed, lacking only a flute to complete what I take to be a general picture of defeat and emasculation as she says, "Really now, Luther, stop giving me those looks. Your whole little scheme is ridiculous and if my friends won't come to their senses about this nonsense then it's high time that you met someone strong enough and practical to tell you that you're acting childishly. Where did you ever get the idea, Luther, that fucking was an open end into confession? That isn't modern, Luther, it hasn't been that way for at least twenty years, oh it must have been from that priest of yours. Don't look at me that way, Luther; if you've checked up on and heard of me, don't you think that we've done a little research on *you*? Really, Luther, we're all upward mobile here and other-directed."

Sighing, I shake my head, springing what I hope to be an artifice of sophisticated denial, world-weary disgust and say, "I'm sorry that you've so misjudged the situation."

"Oh *Luther*," she says and giggles, and her breasts give a premonitory wiggle-and-bounce (quite obscene under the circumstances since all desire has been drained most effectively from me), her nipples flaring into little open mocking cones, "Luther, really, if we know the ins and outs of the suburban school system and the secret preferences of every teacher in the elementary grades and the travel-route of very vacuum cleaner salesman in the district, don't you think we'd know something about an exotic fauna like you? Don't look so hurt, dear, you really fuck quite nicely for someone who gets absolutely no pleasure out of the act. Smooth the sheet under you, dear, that's nice. Maybe you could stay for a little while until I'm dressed and then take me to the meeting? The Impala is in the mechanic's all week, it's one of those idiotic valve jobs again, I can hardly bear it."

"I should think not," I say. "I have a very active, full life to lead and many commitments. I can't be your chauffeur."

"Oh *Luther*," she says again in that exquisitely horrid giggle. If I were not essentially a gentle and hopeful man, I could kill her on the spot. "Luther, stop sulking, it isn't worthy of you and there's really no need for it at all. You're just pouting because after we have sex I'm supposed to lie back and tell you how horrible my life is and what the hell the whole thing came to and how I wish that I didn't have to live this way, and I'm not going to *do* it, Luther; in the first place I have a very nice pleasant life, no complaints at all, and in the second you don't really think that you make sex so wonderful, do you Luther, that all I can do after I have it with you is to cave in? You don't really *think* that do you, oh I can see by your face that you do, you really do, Luther, oh it's just too much for me, just too much, who would believe it?" she asks and laughs and laughs, standing, adjusting her nudity in perfect context against the dim light coming in through the shades, and then goes into the bathroom where, leaving the door open, she steps into the shower and closes a curtain.

Presently I can hear the cheerful spatter and rush of water, the brisk busy rub of flesh against flesh while there comes contrapuntal over this the cheerful sound of a voice singing a song which was popular in the mid-fifties or during that period of my late twenties when I was still trying to divest myself of the frightening belief that popular songs had some connection to reality and that all one had to do to see life straight was to see it as a ballad. Terrible, terrible, the scent of disaster along with my mildly flavored semen seems to lurk in the air of this room. *Give me love, from the stars above* Mrs. Lee sings, and I arise from the bed myself, begin to put on my clothes in various and crazy ways, the pants rear to front, the shirt somewhat askew, all of it as quickly as possible. (I seem to be somewhat disoriented) and then, dressed at last, I open the door of the bathroom and say, "I'm leaving now."

Water sizzles cheerfully and Mrs. Lee says, "Well goodbye, Luther. It was very thoughtful of you to tell me that you were leaving."

"I didn't expect you to tell me anything. I mean the whole thing was sex, just sex. That's all I'm after, sex. You're wrong about the other thing."

"Do you want to drive me, Luther?" she says over a plop of water. "I'll be all ready to go in only about fifteen minutes; you can read some magazines or something while you're waiting."

"No," I say, "I don't want to drive you; I can't, I have a very full life to lead, thank you, and many appointments—"

"Then why did you bother saying goodbye to me at all?" Mrs. Lee says and sticks out a firm, long arm, slams the door in my face and turns up the water full force. I stand there, trying to frame a devastating conclusion to our dialogue but decide presently that there is very little to say; she seems to have had the upper hand throughout this interview and certainly has it now, and part of my superb ability (now being called into question for the first time) has been never to confuse manners with substance. Nothing more needs to be said. I leave the house as quickly as possible, slamming the front door loudly and hearing the automatic lock click; I imagine that the sound will bring to attention a virtual sorority of suburban housewives, all turned to view my conquest of Mrs. Lee, but it is really a very quiet street. Between the hours of nine and three very little goes on at all in these streets. I go to my car quickly, trying to find myself in its shadowy interior, but the first thing I see as I open the door is the parking ticket nestling cheerily under the windshield wiper, embossed in orange and blue. It seems that since I lack an authorized parking permit for these streets I am thus parked illegally and the fine is fifty dollars.

It has been a difficult morning, and for the first time in quite a while events have disconcerted me to the point where I find myself making certain basic queries in a high-pitched squealing monotone which even the parking ticket, firmly inserted between bicuspids and incisors, fails to dampen. Questions like: What am I doing here? Is it all worthwhile? Does it make any difference? Am I squandering my talents? Are there any easy answers? The questions buzz around the bottle of self like a group of discombobulated bees, and it is only with great difficulty and a lack of my usual easy grace that I am able to start the car.

She is everything I was told she was. She is everything that one could ask. Near, near, but maddeningly distant in my arms. Her body a mask, her lips a denial, her breasts an incitement, her reason a shield. Mrs. Lee! Mrs. Lee! Mrs. Lee! Slowly I drive back to the city, and it is a most lively tour indeed that I take during the trip of the familiar but half-forgotten interior.

Mrs. Lee!

IV

Hilarion does not believe in God or the existence of Christ, his only begotten son, as the manifestation of his love for man. He does not believe in the concept of Trinity either, to say nothing of the Revelations of the prophet St. John the Divine or the lesser chronicles of Matthew, Mark and Luke. He believes none of it and says that he lost his faith irrevocably at the age of twenty-five when a summer spent on the midway of a Midwestern amusement park convinced him unalterably that grace had vanished from the human spirit. If it had ever existed. Gaffed wheels, manipulated games, poisonous shills floated through his consciousness and the persona of the young Hilarion became warped, shrewd and embittered in proportion to his experience; now, thirty years later, he feels he still carries around with him a look of perpetual astonishment which set upon his features when he came to understand that only shills could win the games. Nevertheless, he has added, this restructuring of his personality has not been entirely a disadvantage; for one thing, it was in the midway that he came upon me, and then, too, he formed a vision of the human spirit which was total and complete although, possibly, a bit amorphous. It was after my discovery that Hilarion decided to become a priest.

"You see," he has said, "the point is this: it takes far more faith for a man who does not believe in God and religion to become a priest than for one who does; the latter merely enacts ritual over and over again, soothing his lower compulsions, but the former—the truly irreligious man—can be informed into holiness by what he is doing because he does not believe a word of it, *not a single word*, and yet he can overcome his revulsions to perform the rites. Show me a Godless man in the ministry and I'll show you a man of great strength. Besides," he adds, "besides, there's a small chance for belief and the universe may not be a grotesque carnival presided over by a group of shills who take the place of God in the reckoning; I could be wrong and the whole thing may have a purpose and a mystery, and think then, Luther! Think of it! Surely my passage to heaven is clear; I have enacted that which I disbelieved for so many decades and this is the purest service of all."

Hilarion, who makes perfect sense almost all of the time, tends to become a bit incoherent toward the end of monologues like this, incoherent and a little bit self-pitying as well, due largely to the amounts of sacramental wine and wafers which he tends to take in considerable quantities when explicating himself. "The point you must understand, Luther," he often says, "is that it makes no difference whether you believe or don't; it's only how you enact the devices of prayer, and the fact that the Church has been able to reckon with this for two thousand years and to use it rather than struggle against it is the key to their success, or at least one of the keys. Nothing of course can be simplistically explained, particularly a phenomenon so explicitly magnificent as the Catholic Church," and with that I have led him off burping to bed, past the sacristy itself where at almost any time of day three or four muggers can be seen praying for good luck, a prostitute or two seeking an untroublesome customer. Up the stairs sighing and into bed, the end of another long day for Hilarion as he curls up in his couch against a few handfuls of promotional leaflets which he feels encourage sleep, and then back down to the study for Luther, for a final drink or two and then rest of his own. During our dialogues, I should think, we have covered most of the major or minor issues of our time; the interesting thing is how little we have gotten from it as the sum of all this effort. Of course I cannot speak for Hilarion.

"It seems to me, Luther," he said tonight (I had told him the entirety of Mrs. Lee, no reason to cover my most dismal failures in decades and in the bargain I had been so shattered as to be unable to pick up the rest of the day. I had had certain plans for the working class district of Rye but found myself unable to function. I came home. How otherwise to explain to Hilarion why I peeped my delicate features into the sacristy at noon instead of the more conventional tea- time hour?), "it seems to me as if you have obtained nothing less than a kind of justice. As much as I sympathize with your upset, the fact is that you see to have found in Mrs. Lee an inevitability, one who would do unto you exactly as you have done to others. Also, Luther, you really didn't expect this to go on forever, did you? Surely you would come up against a lady sooner or later quite resistant to you, and you should have learned to accept the eventuality. Haven't you ever failed?"

"You don't understand," I said. "There have been numerous occasions when I have failed to, ah, sexually succeed with the ladies, but never in the cases where I have, have I encountered anything like this. This is totally outside of the run of my experience. Furthermore, I take it personally: there's no excuse for this kind of thing. I was absolutely disconcerted, Father, absolutely disconcerted. Shaken in fact. I felt as I haven't felt for twenty years, as if I had totally lost control of a situation, and all of my flounderings within it could only increase my sense of ridicule." I speak to Hilarion far more frankly, needless to say, than I do with my ladies, but there is a hint of duplicity in this as well. (I have decided that the only diary worth doing well is one which is totally honest within the limits prescribed and I have decided not to lie in these pages at all. Not to lie at all, do you hear me, dear diary? Is anyone listening to me?) I have found it necessary for years to live up to a certain kind of image which I know I have established with the good Father, and to a certain extent I feed his modest priestly fantasies much as he feeds my subtly chiselled but rather cavernous mouth. "That woman humiliated me, is what she did, Father."

"Did this ever occur to you?" he asked, and leaned back in his chair with a pleased little sigh of contentment, "that the lady has absolutely nothing to confess? That she is, as you have suggested about so many of your, urn, exploits, completely artifice, totally composed of her mannerisms and responses, and has absolutely no interior whatsoever and therefore no need to confide? This would certainly be a rewarding thought, Luther; it means that you touched bedrock."

"That's nonsense. Superficiality has nothing to do with it. They all *think* they're profound, Father; they think that they carry within themselves the virtual groanings and tortures of post-technological civilization. They think they're sensitive. Haven't you been listening to me at all during these years?"

"Of course I have, my son," he said and leaned forward, took a deep swallow from the decanter (we become progressively informal as our evenings progress) and then, reeling slightly in the chair, moved forward to a nice penitential posture, hands clasped, brow furrowed, eyes shadowed in knowledge as he addressed me. "I have listened to your every word, lo, these many years, and I don't mind saying to you as I've surely said so many times before that you've been a great comfort to me. Even though you're an immoral person, Luther, and certainly have no sense of direction and purpose, you are an interesting man doing interesting things, and by giving me a clear sense of sin you have made my path in this miserable parish much easier. Only within you do I find gradations of conduct, complexities of inference, and this is important, it cannot be denied. But the fact is, my son, and I say it to you in all sadness and affection, you take yourself far too seriously. Your insistence that what you are doing is important must be fed by an elevation of your activities far beyond their real significance. Most of these ladies are quite trivial. Now you have found one without any interior at all and you act as if this reduces you. Well perhaps it does, my boy, but not precisely in the way that you think it does. I think that I will take the midnight Mass tonight. There were actually three celebrants when I did the week before last and it strikes me as being a nice gesture. We'll have to continue this later on, perhaps tomorrow. Why don't you go upstairs, Luther, and get a good night's sleep, and in the morrow we can have a good talk about your career. I've been getting some interesting literature from a handicrafts correspondence course which really might be to your advantage; you have no *idea* what pottery is going for these days, particularly if it's ancient. Pardon me just now if you will."

And saying no more the dear old man, my adoptive father, staggered to his feet, wound his cassock close around him and made an exit of some dignity and import from the door of the study, stumbling only slightly on the threshold. I could hear him all the way down the hall, sputtering and mumbling to himself the opening lines of the Mass, and in deference to him closed the door to give him privacy and then leaned back on his couch for a long time, thinking.

There is no question but that my encounter with Mrs. Lee, in all of its highly disturbing aspects, has forced me to the kind of basic questions about my origin and destiny which rarely afflict me and which are always pointless, but on the other hand I am sure that I will, as always, prevail. Closing my eyes, I am able to fix her firmly in the mind: the weight and heft of her, the dense whiteness of her complexion, the flared cones of her nipples as they seem to open up under mild Lutheran stress; and in that darkness she is so close that I feel I can touch her, feel that I can bring out my hand and place it against the smooth resistant shell of her and penetrate to the darkest heart. I dream that I can hear her confession: she is weeping underneath me and telling of the empty vulnerability and terror of her life, but when I open my eyes, sweating in the cathedral of Hilarion's study, I understand that it was only a snatch of belief and that what I actually hear is Hilarion's high, shrieking old voice as he performs the *Benedictus Dei* for an audience of mendicants.

V

Once, not many years ago, I took a course in computer technology offered through correspondence by an institution in the Midwest whose administration building was a post office box. Done at that time during one of my random seizures of ambition when I thought that I might please Hilarion, I found the course strangely engrossing for a little while and then, somewhere between the fifth and sixth lessons, I abandoned it entirely, overcome by a flare of revulsion brighter and harder than any I had ever known before. I came to understand, working through the binary system and the question of decodes, that the correspondence school, however poorly, was giving me a portion of my future in the real to consider, and if this was the future I wanted no part of it because I could see that once you reduced everything to two numbers in multiple combinations, what you were getting was not a set of variations so much as *recitatifs* on the same theme. I could, struggling over my humble desk at midnight, get a clear picture of what awaited us: nestling in the heart of the machines we would try to conceive of the self and possibility as infinite extensions, but they would reduce always to the dit-dash of *one* and *zero*, and caught between the one and the zero we would swing forever in that damned peripety and dream that it was knowledge.

The school forecast that it could make me a skilled technician at a salary of a hundred and fifty dollars a week within three months, but I came to understand that in terms of what they were offering there would be no discrimination between the data and the programmer, and that Luther, a shy binary unit, would be coding himself into *one* and *zero* forever after. None of this, none of it gentlemen! I wrote them in a long covering letter with which I included all of the materials and my Free Tuition Refund Blank returnable at anytime before the seventh lesson, none of it at all! Luther opts for his humanity, for the speculation of infinite variety. One needs in the era of post-technology to extend the limits, broaden the possibilities rather than the reverse, and as for me, I would rather have a spot of fucking anytime than an investiture of mathematics. So goodbye gentlemen! I concluded at length and never heard from them again; since I had never paid the modest down payment for my course and was receiving billing letters daily I did not expect to. Only much later did I come to understand—did Luther, that is to say, come to under-stand—oh, only very much later did I see that the wedge of my prick was a one and that hammering into zeroes forever the whole was only another variation of the duo-decimal system and that in certain senses, therefore, I was already doomed to binary copulation and inference. But I try not to think of that too much nowadays, and when Hilarion asks me why I abandoned the computer course (he knows everything) I tell him that I decided that my creative intelligence would need at least a trio-decimal system in order to enact its fullest potential. I am not sure that he believes me, but on the other hand he manipulated a wheel of fortune once for a whole summer: with this experience behind him there is little that he should not know of the unspeakable flounderings of the human spirit, the wicked and timeless nature of dreams.

VI

On Wednesday I return to Rye. There is a new purposefulness to my stride, a new insouciance to the swash and clash of gears as I park the small car in front of the home of Mrs. Lee. I have finally settled upon an Attitude—Attitude is the key to Connection, saith Luther—and confi-dence seems to drip greenly from me as I stand before her door and at-tach myself to the huge brass knocker. The question of Mrs. Lee, I have decided, can only be resolved through attacking the question of Luther, and I have had certain epiphanies during the past few days: nothing ex-ceptional, but a Lutherian epiphany of any dimension is more explosive than those of half of mankind. After a time the door opens and a rather svelte Negress stands before me, holding in her hands a large carrot which has been skillfully half-carved; it appears to have human features. "No," she says, "we don't want none of it."

"You don't understand," I say, with what I take to be the proper win-ning frankness, "Mrs. Lee and I are good friends. I've just come to visit her."

"Mrs. Lee don't have no men friends. Just her husband. Mrs. Lee is in the city today, we ain't doing no business here."

"When will she be back?"

"I have no idea when she be back. I just come in two days a week to clean up her house and get out. I don't even live in this section, I come all the way from the city. You don't look like no friend of Mrs. Lee to me. I think that you're some kind of a phony. Come on, get out!"

She is really a rather well-built Negress, admirably constructed and in a costume which, while it parodies servility, does nothing to conceal the fullness of her breasts, lushness of thighs, etc. Also her lips are peculiarly sensual in their thinness; her eyes, bright and piercing, seem to not only apprehend but quest deeper knowledge. Dimly within I feel myself stirred. "I'm afraid you don't understand," I say, "I'm not your average hustler. I mean I really am a friend—"

"Get out," she says, and produces from behind her back a large broom, phallic in its intensity, which she now brandishes. "I got my orders. Besides, I really don't care about all you people. Far as I'm concerned, you should stay in your place."

This strange remark, non sequitur and yet wholly relevant in the context, stirs me further. I lean against the doorjamb, considering. Were I to have an adventure with the Negress it would not be the first of its kind, although as a general rule I have tried not to mix with the servant classes. My purposes are sociological rather than sensual and there is little sociology to be obtained from servitors other than the familiar dry paranoia. Nevertheless. "I suppose you wouldn't want to have sex," I say. It is rather a blunt approach, but then, what can you do with a Negress? If they appeared in the amusement parks of Mamaroneck they would only be taken for furniture; it is hard to see them as persona. "I'm just curious," I add.

"Well," she says, "not particularly. I happen to be very well fixed at the present time for that kind of thing if you don't mind. On the other hand—"

"Yes?" I say. "On the other hand?"

"On the other hand, I admit that I always found it appealing to wonder what it would be like to screw on her sheets. Right on her bed. Kind of paying her off, you understand, for calling me Melinda. Never had the opportunity, though."

"Well," I say, quite fascinated now and fully aroused, brandishing a forearm to show my gentle but superb masculinity in all of its decaying splendor, "well, the opportunity is right before you. If you're really interested, of course."

"You say you truly a friend or relation of Mrs. Lee?"

"I'm a good friend of hers. We know each other well. You just ask her about Luther."

"Well," she says, "well shit, man, I don't properly care. I mean, it's all the same to me. You ain't the most attractive man I ever been seeing, but on the other hand you got me at a good moment. Who wants to do the house, anyway? The house never needs doing. She just wants me around to show she's got a maid. Of course she's a liberal as well." She opens the door fully, admits me into Mrs. Lee's exquisite living room, and then leads me with a twitch of her buttocks up the stairs and into a large bedroom immediately off the stairway which is decorated with pictures of flowers and small insects; on a vanity dresser sits an unused incense burner, and from the ceiling hang thin but glittering shreds of crepe. "This here is her bedroom," the maid says. "She sleeps here. When they have sex I figure that she goes into his room but I never got that down straight. I'm not even sure that they *do* have sex, come to think of it, but that ain't my concern at all." She removes her shoes with quick grace, puts a hand behind her back to unloosen the belt of her apron and then, very skillfully denudes herself. She is an extremely attractive, firm-fleshed high-breasted Negress, and would be quite titillating if I thought of her in that way or was much interested in that kind of thing; the fact is however (as I am sure preceding entries have already made evident) that I am not so much interested in the mechanics of sex as in its implication, and that looking at it strictly from the viewpoint of natural phenomena I could take it, or for that matter leave it.

"Well," she says, "you want to come here or not?" and lies down on the bed, pulling up her knees to reveal a fine swatch of pudendum and then its tunnel, and with some little reluctance (after all, this is essentially a misdirection) I shed my own clothes and join her on the bed. "Hump, hump!" she shrieks as I enter her, my erection already at its fullest flourish, "hump the bastards," and we couple skillfully and completely, the first rush of my orgasm overtaking the motions of her thighs and pulling her back to a softer rhythm, and so I empty myself into her, nibbling abstractedly at one earlobe as I look at a fine portrait of a carnation on the wall above me. "Well," she says, "well that was just fine but what do you do for fucking?" and springs from the bed shaking her head, reaches for her clothes. "I don't deny, though," she says, "I don't deny that there's a certain satisfaction in it. How can she get laid staring at all that tinfoil?"

I leap from the bed and stand beside her, seized by an idea and touch her gently on the iron surfaces of her upper arm, guide her back toward the bed and sit her down with some force. For the first time she appears to have become equivocal or to have lost some control of the situation; she looks at me with wide empty eyes. "Melinda," I say, "what do you really want? What do you really think when you do something like this? and I bet you've done it many times." I might, so that the day is not a total waste you see, as well take her confession. She inserts a thumbnail into a cheek-bone, looks at me wide-eyed in the way that her savage forebears must have contemplated their human dinners not so many generations ago and says, "I don't know what you're saying. My experience in this kind of thing is very limited I want you to know."

"Oh come on, Melinda," I say, "is Melinda your real name by the way? Come on, be reasonable, I'm interested in you as a person," and she emits a high-pitched cackle which seems to mimic glee, but slides quickly and rather ominously down the scale into another quality and says rather sullenly, "I don't know what you're talking about. You better get your clothes on right swift and get out of here before I call the Rye cops and tell them that you been up here raping me; they don't take kindly to their women being assaulted.

"I did it for you; there's something very sweet about you Melinda, there really is. You aren't like the rest here even if those women just happen to be *employees*."

"Oh let's be reasonable," I say with some real pique and join her on the bed, wrestle her down to a submissive posture, and with an explosion of will begin to heave and thrust atop her in some mimicry of the gestures of sex; mimicry turns quickly into gesture, however, and I find myself suddenly passionately capable of another consummation. She senses this and tries to resist, but I am far stronger, to say nothing of motivated, and I can feel her resistance then beginning to flow out like water from underneath her. With a hitch of her limbs she admits me and I pound and pound my meat, every sliding inch of it, into her; the sensation pleasant and exotic, something like masturbation in that it is a pleasant and rather liquid joining, assurance at both ends of it. I have had poorer luck with my matrons who tend to be rather cold and tight inside and believe that fucking is little more than a contraction of the sphincter muscles. In and out I go with ease and attainment, confidence and *élan* and am soon rewarded by my own orgasm, a sensation which in sound has always reminded me of the uncapping of a cork from a bottle of cheap and explosive champagne. Shortly after this she begins to grunt and moan, throws a tongue into my ear, whispers a couple of dark Negroid threats, and then I can feel her beginning to unload against me, virtual streams and streams of African come begin to well around and down my prick and she says finally, "That's better," in a groaning sigh that is barely coherent (*thass bettuh, thass bettuh*) she says, and this time makes no move to escape me on the bed when I remove my tube from her. "That was something," she says, "you really know how to do it, don't you. You is proficient, real proficient."

"Thank you," I say to her, "you understand that I did it for you; there's something very sweet about you Melinda, there really is. You aren't like the rest of them," and as I utter these words I attain the success for which I have been recently pointing and with whose precursory signs I am so familiar. Her face crumbles and she kneads her little fists into my belly and says, "You really cared? You cared about me?" and I say "Yes I do, Melinda, of course I care. Why do you think I asked to make love to you in the first place?"

"No one does," she says, "no one at all; they just want sexin' or more likely housework and occasionally those lousy bastards downtown want a couple of dollars but no one wants me. I know there's a *me* somewhere in there to give but they ain't ever findin' it and I beginning to wonder now if it really is in there or it's just a little lost girl I'm dreaming of someday. Just a little lost girl that no one will ever find," and lets loose a perfect throaty sob, clings to me and begs me to hold her. I do, overcome by my own facility, delighted with this sudden and pleasant climax to the relationship, restored in the possession of my own abilities. I come to understand that I have lost none of the Lutherian edge—as the expensive Mrs. Lee had made me fear—but am instead in my very prime, having reduced this simpleminded Negress to sensitivity and self-consciousness within only a few swooning moments, and then against obstacles. It is quite enough to give one hope, although this particular relationship I would not care to prolong.

"They don't understand; they ain't even looking for me," Melinda whines and I pat her consolingly on a shoulder, "just for what I can provide. But when I tries to provide them with something that has part of me in them they don't want nothing. These sons of bitches won't let you live. They're all out to get you." Moved but becoming slightly bored now (I always become bored during the confessions; this is my greatest sin according to Hilarion, but once having proven that I can elicit their secrets, their secrets themselves always bore me ... if this carried over into the sexual zone I understand that I would be impotent) I shift from the bed, go toward my own wardrobe spilled tastefully in the crevices of Mrs. Lee's large bedroom.

"I know you, you're just like the rest of them," Melinda whines, "you just want what my body can provide but when it comes to the rest of it you ain't takin' nothing." I would point out gently to her that I am not particularly interested in her body either (all right, have it out and be done with it; I have a mild prejudice against Negroes ... while sympathetic to their social problems I simply cannot bear their enactment in the flesh) but the time for dialogue has already passed; I shake my head and don my clothes silently. Now more than ever I feel a compulsion to flee the Lee premises, the Lee neighborhood, the Lee suburb. I need time to reconnoiter quietly.

"And let me tell you one last thing, you," Melinda whines, having converted our relationship in her simple mind to one of uncontrollable hostility, "you think that you get somewhere with this woman, you ain't getting nowhere. You just one of hundreds man, I see them comin' in here and what they do. Talk to some of them too. Thing you think is that you is unique but you most definitely is not, only she is. And that woman hate her husband so much that she take on *anyone* to get back at him. You see what kind of trash you're sharing this bed with you think different."

Fully dressed, I nod. I thank Melinda for this valuable information and try to do so without unction. In that one glaring moment of insight I believe that I now understand Mrs. Lee for the first time, or at least am closer to understanding her than I have been previously. There are several difficult moments before I leave entirely: accusations, murmurs, threats, pleas and so on, but soon enough I am in the little car, dreaming on the freeways, passing Hot Shoppes and deer crossing signs with wild speed that seems to vault me to higher levels of perception as with one corner of my mind I frame the form that Melinda's confessions will take in my diary (I am a completist) and in the other I try to decide how the useful information about Mrs. Lee's marital status can be converted into an armory so grim and effective that before the week is out she will be weeping at my knees, telling me of her loss, her hate, her dread, the overwhelming mystery of it all, and how the enjambment of flesh against flesh is, for her, the only way of hatred.

VII

Unfortunately, however, the remainder of the week is detained by a series of confessions and it is only on the succeeding Monday that I am able to confront the extraordinary Mrs. Lee again. By "confessions" in this context I refer now to the more conventional type. Occasionally dyspepsia or urgent matters in the Midwestern Parish compel Father Hilarion to leave the rectory for some hours or days, and in these cases I perform for him the only service he has ever asked of me: I take the confessions for him. "The ritual is nothing, they can dispense with that, but if you cut them off from confessions you begin to lose the thread that holds them," Hilarion has said, and since in the confessional booth all men are equal he feels no compunction in prevailing upon me to take his role at such times. Furthermore, I can superbly mimic his voice and manner, meaning that the possibility of detection is minimal. Hilarion has taught me enough of the ritual of confession to make me feel secure during its simple processes and I have developed, through these years, an extraordinary ability to elicit not only what I take to be the facts of the confession but its significance; the penitents can, in short, utilize me on levels not only of divulgement, but implication, and all of this has led me to the understanding (abetted to some degree by the splendidly affectionate Hilarion) that I would have made a superb priest if I had ever taken any real interest in the craft. In any event, while Hilarion goes off into obscure areas of Brownsville, refreshing and renewing himself through ways and by reasons known only to him, I remain in the booths and do what I can to remove some load of guilt from mankind and transfer it to the heavens above where it more surely belongs.

In the booth I feel enclosed, protected: swaddled in those shades of darkness. It is like being in a tight bed under warm sheets with a new woman (the hint of density in the layers of skin as they connect, moan, sigh and thrust at entrance) but the confessional is private in a way that sex can never be, and I gloat within its confines, become Luther transmogrified, or at least improved. All confessions interest me, but the ones that interest me more than others are those having to do with sex, and the majority of the penitents are suffering under difficulties in precisely that area. "Oh Father, Father," they are apt to mumble to me (although occasionally they are known to shout), "Father, I desired my neighbor's wife, looked upon her breasts with lust and thought groaning of taking her to my bed." (Yes, they do talk that way, even in Brownsville. Some whiff of the ancient litany or Papal unction overtakes them when they enter these confines and they conspire with me to Talk Elegant.) "Father, Father, my wife turned from me the other night and although I was full of desire she would not have me. So I masturbated." "Father, I desired the handyman." "Father, I desired a priest."

To all of these plaintive admissions I cheerfully request names, dates, specifics, places and so on, forcing the penitents to a precision of tone they have possibly never before achieved and then the two of us, collaborating on the question, so to speak, go into the issue from various angles, trying to understand not only the origin of the sin but its consequences. "You must understand," I like to tell them, "that I can grant you absolution, there's no problem at all with that, but I'm not entirely sure that I speak for God Himself. You could very well go from here singing in release and find out forty or fifty years from now that you'll be spending a long, long time in purgatory simply because your old priest missed his instructions. Better to look for salvation through inspection: why did you desire your neighbor's wife? Do you understand what might happen if you went to bed with her? Do you truly love her?" And so on and so forth until at last the small throbbing heart of purpose is revealed in every confession: they are not sure. They do not know why this is so. They are not sure what will happen to them. They are lazy, fearful. They are afraid, Father. They are afraid.

Madness. Madness! In this parish there is a proportion of illegitimate pregnancy, prostitution and disease to be found nowhere else in the civilized world (other than, perhaps, in Mamaroneck, let us always except Mamaroneck): derelicts and scavengers prowl by God's own daylight seeking goods or the lives of passersby; a large lot outside this church is populated by a small vigorous family of Gypsies who sup upon the contents of garbage bags tossed from the tenements, and for a change in diet assault passersby; within three square blocks of this church it is possible, yes inevitable, to find oneself set upon by nervous men and women offering to buy or sell things of all dimensions and consequences, yet once they walk into this church they seem to part not only from the streets but from every sense of them; they seem to feel that a certain elegance of rhetoric is required along with a certain refinement of moral feelings, and shades and inferences are invoked here that would be nowhere else. It is absolutely astonishing. Even granting, by Hilarion's estimate, that something less than one twentieth of one percent of the parish has ever set foot within this church in their lives, it is still not to be easily explained.

Nevertheless, Luther struggles on. They are interesting, these confessions; not as interesting as the other type because, although they are no more dreary, they lack a certain sense of irony which the nice Westchester housewives are occasionally able to invoke during their most difficult hours. The solemnity, the terrible, terrible solemnity of it! and yet these people live such terrible lives, their poverty is so real, their fear so explicit, their future so damned, their possibilities so vanquished that there is simply little Entertainment Value to emerge from all of this ... whereas in Westchester I love to hear their little sufferings and complaints: the juxtaposition of affluence and suffering is so luscious! The irony so complete! That is why I doubt that I would be happy as a priest. A certain sense of irony is lacking.

Nevertheless, and as they say, horses for courses: I do my best for Hilarion just as so many years ago he did his foundling best for me. How the diapers and formulae must have confused him! Nevertheless the dear man struggled on, only to be rewarded by one who so mocks everything that he has made himself live by as to be little more than a perpetual warning against indiscriminate adoption. (Use a reliable social agency and get a child you can Live With.) On Friday, a low-voiced man, obviously middle-aged and somewhat ill, came in for early confessions and told me that he had looked upon my son (that is to say, Hilarion's son) with desire. "I want to touch him, Father. I look upon his body with passion. His elbows send me into fits of need. He is only my age but he looks so much younger. I know this is terrible, I feel as if I am violating not only him but you."

"In the first place, he is not my son," I pointed out with admirable poise and a resumption of my striking ability to conduct myself with dignity under even the least tasteful of circumstances, "he's my adopted son."

"Yes. I meant to say that, Father. I realize that priests don't have children. It was a silly thing for me to say."

"No it wasn't, and stop apologizing. You really must learn to have more confidence in yourself, that's the first step. Of course priests may have children. They cannot have children after their ordination, that's all. The rules of celibacy are not *ex post facto*. There are many outstanding fathers of splendid children in the priesthood who have abandoned their wives and families to devote themselves to Christ and His Teachings."

"Yes, I understand that, Father. I know it was very stupid of me. I don't know too much about the ritual but I try to believe."

"How can you believe if you know nothing! It's like saying that you're in love even though you don't know the person at all."

"Well I am so in love," he said rather sullenly and rattled the curtains. I thought I could see the dim, premonitory outline of a fist. "And anyway, I don't know how they got to the moon or any of that stuff but when I saw it on television I believed it. I mean, I knew that they were on the moon. I don't have to know how to get there to see it."

"It could all have been done in a studio," I pointed out to him with some asperity. The question of the moon flights interests me but is, unhappily, irrelevant to these documents and must be discarded. (I will say that I have never understood the simple and human urge to confession as well as I did when the robots began their slow dance upon the surface of the Moon. What history! What artifice! What torment! ... and nothing we had ever known capable of subsuming this.) "But I don't want to discuss this now. You were talking about my adoptive son, Luther."

"Luther," the penitent agreed eagerly, "that's right, his name is Luther. Once he helped me get to my feet when I had a small seizure after Mass and the touch of his hands was so gentle upon me. Anyway, I can't get him out of my mind."

In a flash, I realized who the disgusting little man was. It was a landlord, one of the two or three in the district who actually come to collect their own rents and who can be seen on their property. I had seen him come trembling through the district toward Vespers, fleeing the curses of tenants; I had seen him crawl into the service entrance of his building very late at night so that he could, undetected, set the heat on low. I could also remember helping him at Mass that morning. Overcome by a *Deus in Excelsio* he had fallen to his knees in a locked position and might, for all I knew, have remained there yet had I not come to assist him and get his disgusting little frame from the building. A most asymmetrical man, and into the bargain one whose flatly atrocious old buildings, painted in tones of pink and green, lent an even more depressing aspect to the district than would otherwise have been possible.

"You must be strong," I said as thoughts like these and others skittered through my mind. "You must be brave. You must purge yourself of these unclean thoughts and live simply. Try hot baths."

"I know that Father. I know that I wouldn't do anything. It's just a desire, you see? I know I'm strong enough."

"You'd better be."

"I'd better be? Don't I get any forgiveness though, Father? I mean, I didn't ask to have these thoughts. Anyway, I have not committed an act of sadamical since I was fifteen years old and that was when I was drunk."

"Sodomy."

"Sodomite. I meant sodomite. I'm a married man, Father, and I have children of my own. What do you think I must think of myself when something like this goes through my mind? What would my wife say?"

"You'd better get a good hold of yourself," I said, "that's all. You'd just better learn that certain parts of life, like four-fifths of it, are not even to be considered; they are not even the proper stuff of dreams and you had better put that stuff completely out of your disgusting mind. You'd better not make any moves toward my son or you'll find yourself excommunicated and without the faintest possibility of remission."

"Father, that's not the reason a man should do something. That isn't the way a priest should talk either. I mean, no one ever—"

"Try hot baths," I said, "try fasting and prayer. Try a little self-discipline and a little self-respect. Get a good hold of yourself. I don't want to hear about this anymore."

"No grace, Father?"

"I'll think about it. I can't decide yet. My son is very precious to me. I think of him exactly as I would were he my own. I cannot lightly put aside the gross attacks you have made upon him."

"But Father, I never did anything. I mean I only thought—"

"I'll consider it," I said. "Confession over."

I left the booth quickly, shoulders hunched, not knowing or caring if there were any behind him. Nor without the booth. The things that I must undergo in pursuit of my knowledge are one thing—and I know that they are self-imposed—but this is distinctly another. It is the kind of hideous event-without-causation that I must have represented so many times to the women, not excluding the hapless Melinda who oddly I find myself remembering during the confessions. I know that if ever were a homosexual attack to be made upon me, Melinda would do what she could in defense.

On Sunday, Hilarion returned beaming and full of stories of new sources tapped in the diocese. As usual he refused further explication but stated that the Monsignor's intransigence had proven to be the best thing that had ever happened to him and the church.

"I've been able to meet the people," he said, "to get out and around and to understand the nature of the people here, the condition of their drives, the quality of their ambitions, the strain of their hopes. The energy, Luther! The sheer untapped energy here! You could not possibly imagine it. If they turned to religiosity half the energy that they put into the profane you would see the absolute reconstitution of the temple here. Or something equally wonderful. It's a shame that people with such potential have utilized so little of it." He mumbled something to himself (Hilarion is something of a compulsive and many of his statements are entirely private) and sank into a chair, wiping his face. "On the other hand," he said, "the trouble is that most of them do, in one fashion or another, believe in God unquestioningly, and this also is a kind of waste. There has hardly been a beginning made, Luther, the whole situation here has barely been tapped! By the way," he said, leaning forward with some intensity and looking at me straight on with a wise and solemn look, "by the way, I am beginning to hear some interesting reports about you circulating, there seem to be more and more people, Luther who, uh, sense your activities and tend to think them a bit strange and sooner or later we'll have to have a good long talk about this and many other things and try to take stock. There seems to be a feeling of general distrust about you Luther; people are not so open as they were a year ago on the question of your conduct. That's the wonderful thing, the truly hopeful thing about getting out in the air and making these little expeditions, one begins to understand the people as one never could otherwise. God bless the Monsignor for being so intransigent."

"Everything was all right here."

"Everything all right? Good. Excellent! I am sorry to impose upon you every so often in this way, Luther, but the only link to the Church for so many of these people is the confessional booth; they might lose all interest if shop were closed up for even a day or so. I do hope that I didn't, ah, interfere with your plans and progress upstate."

"That was something I wanted to talk to you about, Father. A certain Negress—"

"Negress, eh? Well that sounds interesting, Luther, something of a new thing for you, but of course there's no shortage of them in the diocese.

No shortage at all. We will have to talk this out and soon, Luther, talk it out at great length; I miss our nightly discussions but I am afraid," and Hilarion stifled a delicate, sacramental yawn, "I am terribly afraid that I'm awfully tired right now and could hardly concentrate. The effort, you know, the sacrifice. Everything as usual, however, eh? No crises, no unusual confessions and so on?"

"Adams said that he wanted to violate me."

"How's that?"

"Frank Adams, the landlord. You must know him. I took his confession on Thursday. It seems that he's desired me for months and months but never had the courage to speak his heart until now. I told him that I'd think about it."

"Adams? Oh *Adams*, now I know who you're talking about. You mean that wretched little man who goes around in a gray suit all the time and collects the rents in person. Desires you, does he, Luther? *Desires* you! Sodomic wishes of course. Desires you? Oh my, Luther," Hilarion said and covered his mouth again, his shoulders shaking, "oh my, I don't mean to be impolite to you, my one and only dear adopted son, but I am so terribly tired now and it just struck me as funny. Desire you? How could any man desire *you*, Luther?" Hilarion asked, and with something of a belch stood and staggered his way toward his quarters. Somewhere midway toward the door the belch turned into a whoop and a snigger which I must say disconcerted me enormously, but I let the moment pass and sat quietly in my chair until the shuffle of Hilarion's feet departed along the corridor and the closing bang of the door signalled that the evening was truly over.

Hilarion is a remarkable man and indeed I owe a great deal to him, almost everything, in fact. Nevertheless he can be at times, quite irritating. For some reason even now, some hours later, the sound of his last remark sticks in my mind, moving uneasily toward my stomach, scuttling lively in the lower intestines as I sit shrunken into quandary and try to understand what is going on.

Desire me? How could I not be desired? One can understand the evil of carnal knowledge from a member of one's own sex. Nevertheless, and finally, why should the desire toward me be unlikely?

Somehow, this all fits in with Mrs. Lee. I do not quite understand it yet but I am sure that I will, and strangely this does not fill me with anticipation so much as gloom. All must come together in the end, the prophet saith ... but must it come together so soon? So soon? So soon?

What they confess are the same as the confessions of my housewives, and what they both confess can be seen scribbled on the sidewalks in this neighborhood. I must remember that. It is interesting. This must be made part of the record. There is no difference. The differences are created only by the diocese which, in any event, refuses to meet its reasonable obligations.

VIII

To Mrs. Lee again on a warm, hazy Monday morning. Having missed my usual Sunday excursion (Hilarion returned very late that evening) my mood is somewhat sour, but tends to brighten as the Peugeot creaks merrily up the Palisades Interstate Parkway, and then is fully reconstituted as I soar grandiloquently over the Tappan Zee Bridge and toward the New England Thruway, path to my delights. (Question if you will why I take such a circuitous route from Brownsville to Rye. Question why one must pay a double toll and extra mileage in order to make this transversal, and one will understand the answer. This is not a journey made for smooth transitions that I can make it so easily day after day fills me with guilt. Therefore I impose penalties upon myself. In my highly individualized fashion, I am an extremely moral man.) By the thruway itself my mood is all gaiety, gaiety and small bubbles of song inching their way through my still smooth throat as I take the Peugeot up to the last remnant of speed (fifty-five or on a cloudy day fifty-eight) and try to remember the lyrics of all the songs I ever loved. Living in a rectory and thus being forced to play the portable radio on low through my adolescence means that my opportunities were somewhat limited, nevertheless, I have been able to put together a splendid if limited repertoire, composed largely of the hits of the vocal quartets of the fifties and early sixties. The Four Coins. The Four Tops. The Four Lads and the Four Preps. The Four Freshmen and The Four Miracles. *Twenty six miles across the sea my one sin in life is loving you/for you and I have a destiny/three coins in the fountain/with love forever and ever true/Santa Catalina is awaiting for me/which one will the fountain bless/Santa Catalina the island of/if I stop loving you my heart will be untrue. Make it mine make it mine. Put a light in your window; in the window of your heart. Just step right up and meet the little white cloud that cried, crying in the chapel.* My mood is reconstituted. Reconstituted!

Reconstituted! that is to say. On the seat next to me lies a bouquet of splendid proportions; modelled upon my best recollection of the decorations in the bedroom of Mrs. Lee it is a parody of such facility that it could only be taken for admiration. The bouquet has cost me fifteen dollars and eighty-five cents (with tax), the largest single expenditure I have ever invested in a mission, and knowing this fills me with a kind of virtue; I certainly cannot be accused of not taking Mrs. Lee with sufficient seriousness. Throughout the morning I have carefully plotted my approach, and now I am sure that I have it under control. With the lunacy of an old horseplayer returning for the first time in years to the scene of his disasters, I am convinced that there is absolutely no way I can lose. I even fondle my wallet for the bulge of prophylactics in my childish glee. Some of them do not take their pills until very late in the day, and a little Luther, grandson of Hilarion, is one complication which I sincerely wish to avoid.

I drive into Rye singing the earlier works of one Elvis Presley, alternating them with some of the more romantic ballads of a group called The Platters which has subsequently, with most of the diocese, passed on into history. Small children scatter respectfully before the tootling advance of the Peugeot, it occurs to me only then with an overwhelming apprehension of my idiocy that today is a holiday and that the children of Mrs. Lee are almost certainly at home. Schools have been dismissed in honor of one of the anniversaries of war, or perhaps it is peace, it is hard to say, having kept up only poorly with my history, but those are indisputably children which I see involved in their childish games as I drive the street of the Lees and park incautiously in front of the house itself, which retains its hushed aspect. I must be mad. There must be something profoundly destructive about me. Nevertheless, what could the Lee children do if they saw me, or I them? I would hardly know them.

Sighing, balancing the bouquet (heavily slanted toward carnations and chrysanthemums which are more reasonable in this season, but with a sprinkling of ivy and roses) I wander up the path toward the house exactly as the Peugeot must have wandered up the block, and ring the doorbell hopefully a few times, already enmeshed in my strategy of retreat. If the door is answered by a child I will become a flower salesman in the act of retrieving his goods; if the door is answered by Melinda I will spring upon her an allergy, if not the bouquet. If the door is answered by Mrs. Lee *avec* child, I will question her about the demographic possibilities of anti-Semitism. But it is opened by Mrs. Lee alone, wearing a nightgown of the thinnest and most striking material through which, if I cared to peer intently, I could probably see the enlarged nipples of her breasts. "Oh," she says, "it's you. I've been wondering when you'd be dragging yourself back again; you're a little bit later than I thought. Well, you might as well come in; there's no point in staying outside and scandalizing everybody. I hope those flowers aren't for me, I hate flowers and anyway the only ones I'm not allergic to are the artificial. Maybe you can just throw them into the garbage can in the hall on the way in if you will, that way I won't have to fumigate the place in a couple of hours."

It is not (let us face it) an auspicious beginning, but on the other hand

I am inside the house and Mrs. Lee appears to be alone. At a gesture of her forefinger I throw the flowers with some violence into an ornate wastebasket, then, under her piercing and intelligent gaze, I stomp them into shreds with a clever foot, causing veritable puffs of greenery to float through the anteroom. In response she seizes me by the wrist and guides me into her living room which has somehow changed decor since the last time and now appears to be done in Early Brown or perhaps Late Blue with a large photographic painting on the near wall of a couple of pigs copulating. "The artist stinks but he has a reputation," she confides, "and besides that, Harold thinks that it's amusing. It's practically the only kind of thing that titillates him nowadays, so I leave him alone."

She takes my wrist with some confidentiality, places me on the couch, and with a lovely kind of reverse soaring sits beside me. "You're just fortunate that Katherine is off my hands today," she says, "they have a special school which only meets on days when the regular school is out and it's been a lifesaver. Of course there are days when even the special school is out, like Christmas, but they're trying to start a school to meet on those days too. The only problem is what they'd do with the staff for the rest of the year, but they'd better do something." I agree that they'd better do something. "Melinda told me you were here last week," she says; "that was really quite stupid of you. I thought that our relationship was made most clear the first time. That there were to be no repeats. Normally my impulse would be to lock the door on you, Luther, but after Wednesday when I realized that you had come all the way out just to see me again I became kind of touched, don't ask me why, and I decided that I'd see you this one last time. Did you have sex with Melinda?"

"What's that?"

"It's a perfectly simple question, Luther; you don't have to look at me like that. You wouldn't be the first one, you know; Melinda's very free with herself. Sometimes I think that one of the reasons I've tolerated her for so long is that I envy her ability to do exactly what she wants to do, although all those men hanging around at odd hours makes for questions. She said some very nice things about you, Luther."

"Well, I'm very pleased. I mean, I don't quite know what to say."

"So say nothing, Luther. Honestly, you don't have to talk about everything all the time. That's one of your problems, Luther, you try to put labels on everything. I suppose that you came up because you wanted to have sex with me again, right?"

The simple directness of this query, rather than disconcerting me, tends to snap me back into a kind of perspective; it reminds me once again that I am a serious man embarked upon serious purposes, and that after all most things are a matter of relativity. "I suppose so," I said. "I mean you're really an attractive woman—"

"Oh Luther, spare me that nonsense, will you? You see the point is that I don't like to cheat on Harold too many times with the same man. I mean I admit that I do cheat on him because you've seen it, but I have this rule that I try never to have sex with the same man twice. That way it doesn't get complicated. Anyway, I think that Harold would understand if I ever talked to him about it that it's not really disloyalty, it's just a question of those long afternoons. Ordinarily, I wouldn't see you again, Luther, but I was touched that you came all the way up here twice."

"Well," I say, "it's my pleasure. I mean you don't have to if you don't want to." A small worm of excitement begins to work its busy way through my intestines; for reasons that I still cannot quite label, I understand that I am on the verge of some kind of qualified success. How to explain it? But perhaps the penitential aroma, the possession of the confidant, has been coming off me in even waves this morning and has brought the difficult Mrs. Lee into some realization of my gifts. It is not easy to say, but at this moment I can sense her loins opening, feel the dribble of passion that expires from them, and at some dim reach of the consciousness it seems that I can even hear her talking in the aftermath: the tinny, tiny sound of her voice telling me then everything which I want to know. All illusion, of course. "On the other hand I'd kind of like to."

"What if Katherine had been home? I mean, you had no way of knowing that she went to a special school. What was I supposed to do then?"

I shrug. "I didn't even know it was a holiday," I explain. "I'm sure we could have worked out something."

"Oh well, Luther," she says with a shake of the head and stands, motions me with a crook of her finger to follow her, and we go once again into her exquisite bedroom which seems little the worse for the wear which Melinda's efforts and mine have inflicted, "oh well, I suppose that it's all the same thing and anyway a lot of my friends said you'd never come back anyway, just the way you never came back to any of them. I knew you would, though. I told them that I was sure you'd come back because you hadn't gotten anything out of me yet. I was right, wasn't I, Luther?"

"You told your friends about this already?"

"Well for heaven's sake, Luther, what do you think? Who else do I have to talk to? Anyway, we're all very close." She winks at me, performs an intricate gesture of forefinger and hair which in women has never failed to move me, and then, shaking the hair out of her eyes, divests herself once again of all her clothing. The already-familiar Lee body springs from its various crevices and beckons to me, the damp lushness of her breasts particularly notable on this fine Monday morning. I feel slightly bored with her already—it is very difficult for me to sustain interest in a woman a second time—but hasten to comply and, at the first touch of flesh, feel my own arousal; her body is moist and warm, heat seeming to come from its various apertures, and feeling linked to her I fall slowly atop her toward the bed, immediately ready for penetration. "Oh that's wonderful Luther," she says, "your body feels so good on mine. Let's do it fast today, let's do it just like dogs. Did you ever see dogs fuck, Luther?" and without waiting for a response parts and turns from me, hoists up her knees, exposes her fair flower of a vagina and indicates that I should settle amidst her buttocks which even in proportionate terms are quite huge. I clamber aboard gracefully, reaching my hands around to snatch and tug at her opening breasts, and then, with no forethought, I begin to work at her.

I understand that in certain senses this may be my Last Chance with Mrs. Lee, and I do everything I can to avail myself of the opportunity. Through some sliver of knowledge gained through the long testing weekend I try not so much to overcome her with sex as merely to use my organs to raise her to her own responses; settling the placid tube of me within her walls I wait there, allowing her to generate her own motion, her own responses, and slowly, after a fashion, she does, the walls of her cunt turning into a slow, even viscosity as she envelops and pounds, and I begin to work on her nipples then with a certain Lutherian swiftness, patting and squeezing them alternately, trying to duplicate that pattern of dependence and betrayal which they have always known (I have some rather strange ideas about sexuality but in the long run most of them tend to stand up) and she begins to groan her high strange whimpering groan, muttering something to me through closed lips that is indistinguishable except that it sounds vaguely like the lyrics of the very popular songs which I have been singing this morning. *Which one will they bless?* Mrs. Lee seems to query, and I allow the full unsheathed grandeur of my prick to rise within her in support; she slowly kneels upon it, the full weight of her now down onto the singing bone, and she begins to sway back and forth evenly. I feel the old uncautious rising, urge myself to hold back, and am able to contain my own necessity while letting her ride out her own cycle; still working on her breasts, I find myself seized by an idea and begin to talk to her.

"Think of swimming pools," I say, "think of split-level developments. Think of duplexes. Think of guided tours of Morocco. Think of necklaces." She begins to whimper eagerly, a small girlish sound emerging from the cords of her neck, and I say, "Think of furs, rich furs swaddling you as you move down the ramps of descended jets, the flicker of pho-

tography haloing your face. Think of the Hamptons. Think of two summer homes." "*Two* summer homes," she says, "two of them." "Yes," I
say, "one of them on the ocean and one with a swimming pool," and it
is at this precise moment that Mrs. Lee begins to come. I can tell, can tell
not only from the sudden unfolding of her petals but an accelerated, one
could say, a greater density of rhythm within, and she falls back against
me, the slick full surfaces of her back pressing into my chest; I hold onto
her with forty-five years of acquired strength and knowledge while she
unloads herself like a man panting and groaning against me. "Uh," she
says, "uh, ah, eh! Furs, swimming pools! Jewelry!" and it is the high wistful bleat of her little come-stricken voice that sends me off as well, and
I pour into her virtual streams of Luther's gift, delivered from the deepest part of him and into the darkest well of herself, clinging and bang-
ing into her in a frenzy while the colors of the flowers seem to change
before my eyes. Growling I bite a shoulder, pinch a nipple to softness, and
she moves off into another orgasm, somewhat quieter than the first but
none the less enthusiastic, more feeling in it, more pain as well, and then
her face tears around (how she does not break her neck is beyond me)
and we begin to kiss, heavily, hotly, wetly, mouth to mouth and tongue
to tongue, and her little mouth working deep into mine seems to be frantically busy, talking, talking inexhaustibly, divulging secrets which only
my tongue can know.

It is strange and satisfying to fuck Mrs. Lee in the quiet of a suburban
morning deep in the recesses of her house: it is a consummation which
Hilarion would never understand or appreciate, but nevertheless there
it is, and as she whips her body around toward me, still holding my ag-
onized and distended prick, whipping herself furiously into me, I begin
to understand once again the appeal of these women. Truly, there is nothing like them upon the face of the earth. No obsession can be totally misplaced which has objects like these; the sheer *misdirection* of so much of
it. The energy! The possibilities! We groan like animals in a heated cage
and finally spring apart, fall together again, muddle on the bed. Her
breath fades from racking gasps to a deep even inhalation and she runs
a finger over my lips with something approaching affection. "You really
are good," she says. "They weren't wrong. You're everything that you're
supposed to be. I'm very surprised."

"I try," I say, less flattered by the comment than dismayed. How
could she possibly not have known this the first time?

"Oh Luther," she says, "Luther, I just can't stand this anymore."

Instantly I am alert. My sensibility seems to shift downward several levels, or perhaps it is merely upward that it shifts, it is difficult to say, but
there is a kind of attunement now, a refined alertness which I have felt

so many times before that I understand it all too well. My breath quickens, I quickly do some deep secret flexion exercises in order that my respiration will be unknown to her. "Yes?" I say, "yes."

"Oh Luther, I don't want to talk about it. I mean I know that this is what you're waiting for, that I should confess my soul now or tell you secrets. That's what you do with everybody and I just can't stand being part of a pattern. I'm different."

"It isn't that way at all," I assure her, "You're very much yourself. Please feel free to talk to me."

"You do it to all of them. I know what's going on."

"I want you to consider me your friend," I say. "It isn't a question of seduction. Closeness is the truth of it."

"I don't understand what you're saying."

"Don't try to understand," I point out, squeezing a breast until the rosy flush of it overcomes the whiteness and I think that I can see the network of her veins within, "just follow your heart." It is unfortunate that I have to operate within a context of this nature, but one must take one's accomplishments where one can find them.

"I just don't want to be another one, Luther. Another one of your, uh, conquests."

"Never," I say, "never, Mrs. Lee."

"Call me Wanda."

"Wanda," I say, "Wanda Lee."

There is a long silence. I decide not to disturb it, but content myself with eying the ceiling and thinking long deep thoughts of restraint. I decide in order to comfort myself that if the bitch, after a suitable time, does not come clean, I will kill her. She cannot put me through what she has already without some kind of a return.

"Well," she says, "it's Harold. I hate him."

"Harold? Oh Harold. Your husband."

"Of course he's my husband. I thought you knew everything about all of your women."

"You are a mystery," I say. "You are a mystery."

"I have the feeling that any moment Katherine is going to come in from school and see us here. She always wants something to eat when she comes home from school and the bitch comes right in to see me wherever I am. She's an impossible child."

"She won't come home from school. You told me, she goes all day. It isn't even noon."

"She might get sick. She's always getting colds or indigestion. Actually I can't stand her either. She's just like Harold in so many ways. She has all of his selfishness and stupidity but she's so much *younger* ... I try to do what I can for her but the child doesn't have a chance."

"Tell me about Harold," I say. "You were talking about Harold."

"I hate him. I just hate him, Luther. He's ruined my whole life. All he does is work in that goddamned stockbrokerage office in the city and I don't even know what he's *doing* anymore. The son of a bitch is gone at eight and back home at nine and he expects me to be ready as soon as he comes in to give him dinner and take an interest and put the child to bed and then have sex with him. Then he goes to sleep, I don't know what the hell he's doing down there. He says that it's too technical."

"Have you ever tried to talk to him?"

"I can't talk to him. There's nothing to say. He has no sensitivity, no understanding. Anyway, the market is falling now, I understand, and he can't bear to talk about business. He's ruined me," she says, "he's ruined me. I hate him so much—"

"Yes?" I say, "yes, go on?"

There has, perhaps, been a shade too much eagerness in the way I have delivered this line; either that or the conversation has been thrust into angles and currents with which she does not choose to deal. In any event, her very pores seem to contract and then she is sliding away, sliding away from me, retreating to her corner of the bed. "Of course," she says, "I was wrong. I shouldn't have started talking about it. How can you understand? Besides, I'm just another entry in your diary. I bet you keep a diary, you son of a bitch. All you people do."

"No," I say, sitting and leaning a confident arm across her shoulders, drawing her against me with what I take to be ease and a kind of secure force. It is like an extension of the confessional booth except that here sex has entered into it. "Feel free," I say. "It's hard to get these things out. But necessary. Keep on talking."

"He's ruined me," she says after a pause. "I was a lovely sensitive girl. You don't have to believe that, take a look at my yearbook sometimes. We were supposed to make our lives together. Now I find myself on this hideous street surrounded by these hideous people and I'm bored to death. He didn't make me a life, that son of a bitch. He took me away from a life. I could have been a writer. I got all A's on my compositions."

"It's a common problem," I say, adding hastily, "I mean, you run into that general pattern a great deal. Of course most people aren't as sensitive—"

"Oh Luther," she cries and falls against me, her teeth biting into my shoulder in what I take to be a shriek, the panels of her body sliding maddeningly against mine, "oh Luther, I just hate him so much! If I had the guts I'd kill him! I'd poison him or something. He's got plenty of life insurance. Of course I wouldn't because I just don't have the guts. But I want to! He deserves to die! I wish he were dead."

It is there. There at last and a slow, heaving sigh overtakes me; gently I turn it into a skillful belch while I feel relaxation overtaking me, relaxation and ease, contentment and release. The confession. The confession of Mrs. Lee. It is there before me and never had I realized until now how sweet the wanting could be if the goal were attained. I suppress a mad impulse to get dressed on the instant and flee, enter all of it in my diary while still fresh, but this, of course, can certainly do me no good at all, and sighing I sink further into the bed. She runs a hand over my marvelously flat stomach, entwines my faintly iridescent and handsome pubic hair, runs a palm over my cheekbone. "Oh," she says, "I just feel so silly and stupid now. Like I've been used. I've made such a fool of myself."

"No you haven't," I assure her. "You've spoken from your soul and that's the important thing. The central, the basic, the meaningful. You've opened yourself up. You've confessed and performed the purgative function. Don't you feel better?"

"You think that I'm just like all the others. A silly, stupid, selfish woman who has no control of herself. Oh I just feel so useless, Luther."

"No I don't," I counsel her, but in truth I am becoming suddenly and terribly weary of all this and only wish that I could leave, "it isn't like that at all. Of course I have an appointment—"

"You don't think that I'm like the rest of them? I mean, you think I'm something special?"

"Of course I do," I say. "Don't you know that?"

"You care for me, Luther? I mean, in your way. You really care for me and think that I'm different?"

"Yes," I say, "yes I do."

"Would you prove it?"

"Prove it?"

"Prove it, Luther. Would you *prove* that I mean something to you? That I'm different?"

"I don't understand," I say. "I don't understand."

"I think you do. Luther, if I mean anything to you at all, would you do me a favor? I mean it's all the same to you, Luther, you're just something of a drifter and it's obvious you're not very well connected and don't have too much you have to worry about. It would be so easy for you, no one would ever know and it could never be traced back."

"What's that?" I say as her fingers now take the full pulse of my half-erect prick, cupping and squeezing it gently as she looks at it with something approaching reverence. Although I am handsomely endowed, no woman has ever looked at my genitals in the way that Mrs. Lee—Wanda

Lee—does right now.

"And I'd cooperate and tell you everything and help you set up and prepare because I know all his habits and we can even work out an alibi if you need it and everything. I mean really, Luther, it would just be the simplest thing, the simplest thing imaginable—"

"What is it?" I say, "come on now, out with it. What *is* it?" This is not the technique to be recommended in the box, but on the other hand it is becoming increasingly clear to me that what I have been taking within the last few moments is certainly no confession.

"I want you to kill him, Luther," she says. "I want you to kill Harold. It would be so easy for you and they'd never trace it back and it would solve everything. I want to and I know exactly how, only I haven't got the will. You must do it for me, Luther, you owe it to me."

"Owe it to you?"

"Well of course you owe it to me, Luther. You seduced me, didn't you? You have to show a little consideration for my feelings here too. I mean, you just can't manipulate a woman the way you've manipulated me without giving something of yourself in return."

"Kill him?"

"There's nothing to it, Luther. I've thought the whole thing through a thousand times. It's really very simple, there's nothing to it at all. I'll tell you exactly what to do and everything. It's just a matter of following my instructions."

"But don't you understand?" I say, and a certain high plaintive note extrudes at this instant without which I could cheerfully live, but on the other hand the circumstances are unusual and it is at least explicable. "Don't you understand, Mrs. Lee, I've never killed anyone before!"

"Wanda to you," she says, "and there's always a first time for everything."

IX

Although I am a frequent reader of the crime magazines, murder is not one of my interests. The appeal of the crime magazines to me has always been their bloodlessness; they have managed to make murder as clean as the housekeeping magazines have made sex, and although there is a corpse generally in view it tends to be a sanitary old corpse, killed painlessly and with no emission of bodily fluids, pulled offstage as hastily as possible in order that the more amusing revelation of the story may now proceed.

When I was in my writing period, some years ago, I attempted to publish in the crime magazines a whole series of short stories which were always returned with the notation, "I'm afraid this is too grisly for our readers" or "I'm really afraid that this is too political for our readers" or "I'm afraid that this one is really a little bit too bloody for our readers" or "we try to discourage stories which use blunt weapons for the commission of crimes" or "child-murderers are one of our absolute taboos." At first I thought that I had somehow missed the premise of the crime story or confused my admittedly inept style with one of high inference, but soon enough I came to understand that while these magazines were very interested in stories which *utilized* murder, they hardly wanted them to be *about* the act. Murder, which is a rather discomfiting phenomenon, could be best handled within these magazines by the kind of minimization which turned it into an odd and bizarre inconvenience. I could imagine their audience (composed in the main of aged people who were really not so well off as they used to be) reading the stories and wondering where was the sting or the victory of the grave? Certainly the question of murder as depicted in these stories, the portrayal of death, was only a slight inconvenience, less important or calamitous than a missed pension check. (I abandoned my writing career when I decided that in these chaotic times the act of writing in and of itself was irrelevant and only the man of action could play a meaningful role. When I understood subsequently that I could unify action *and* rhetoric to produce this superb and revelatory diary my ecstasy knew no bounds. I was able to utilize my talents without apologizing for them!)

Perhaps it was the crime magazines or only some errant streak of compassion discovered at the critical age of forty that turned me against murder as an activity capable of dealing with most human problems. Certainly it was not Hilarion who would do so; Hilarion and his beloved Catholicism alike foster a clean, brutal apocalyptic streak which can neatly embrace the phenomenon without dropping a bead at Vespers. Dedicated to the act of generation, I decided that I could not in any way come to terms with its opposite: Luther would be the sanctuary of life and repudiate all those dedicated to its extinction. It was the very least gesture I could make, or so I felt, to my harmless, vulnerable, desperate ladies who were, in other obscure ways, being murdered far more effectively than I ever could, every day of their lives.

For these reasons, it can be made clear that I left the home of Wanda Lee in a very somber and reflective mood.

Our interview had not terminated where I have left off in the last section, but rather continued for a significant period of time additional, a period during which she had instructed me in great detail on her husband's movements, her husband's predilections, her husband's convolutions, with a kind of cold precision which astonished me: certainly if the pathetic Harold had known as much about her daily activities as she did about his a stop would have been put to this kind of thing a long time ago. Throughout it was the chilling matter-of-factness of her *recitatif* which so moved me; she did not repeat her request for me to murder her husband, having taken for granted, apparently, the fact that I would. Her emphasis was all upon details, movements, policies, procedures. At the end of this she placed in my left hand (since I am moderately ambi-dextrous) the most delicate of lady's revolvers, and bade me go upon my holy rounds. It turned out that she had picked it up on her own in one of those savage Southern states four years ago, in the hope that she might someday be able to use it. Only after several unsuccessful attempts to kill the poor man in his sleep in his separate bedroom had she realized that she was of too gentle a nature to do it.

"It needs to be done, believe me Luther," she said, "and I think that Harold would agree with this himself because you can't imagine how many times he's come home from that terrible office and said to me that he knows he'd be better off dead. He really wants to die, Luther; there's a lot of guilt mixed in with his cruelty and that's why I can't hate the man. I want to do him a favor. I want to give him this gift of death. But I just don't quite have the strength. Thank God that you do, Luther," she said and sent me on my way, my thoughtful way to the Peugeot, the revolver clutched madly to my ribs and seeming to emit a high-pitched squeak which could only have been some amplification of my contained but hys-teric reactions. Halfway down the steps I believe that I met the missing Katherine herself, an appallingly self-contained child of nine or ten in bangs, who went by me without a look of recognition, singing an abysmal popular song to herself. (I have never been particularly attrac-tive to children, I do not know why. Hilarion informs me that I was a beautiful infant, and certainly in public school I seem to recall the req-uisite number of crushes. Perhaps they sense my conduct and disapprove of it, although knowing the children who come from these suburbs, I do not see how they could disapprove of anything.)

I clambered into the Peugeot, started it with much awkwardness and clashing of gears, and commenced my brisk drive into the city, without music this time and with only a good deal of recollection to keep me lively on the way. Before I had left, just after the Donation of the Revolver, Mrs. Lee had granted me a final and truly rousing siege of copulation, whether to seal a pact or encourage me to agreement I do not know. Finding the standard efforts only half-effective, she fellated me skillfully on her knees, looking over the broad reaches of my chest and into my eyes with an unusual piercing and soulful expression as I groaned and grunted, heaved a load of revelation into her mouth. Said load she drank down swiftly, with graceful little clawing gestures around her cheeks, and then smiled at me. "You see what I'll do for you, Luther," she pointed out. "I'll do almost anything for you. I mean, our relationship is just truly beginning now. Think of the fun we'll have when poor Harold is gone. I get every cent of the insurance money except for the little escrow left for Katherine, and we can travel all over the world. I'll put her in boarding school."

Throughout almost all of this I had maintained a cool and deferential silence, not refusing her horrid request point-blank, but not, to my mind, rendering her any encouragement either. Certainly the vicious woman had absolutely no basis on which to make her final remark as she bade me to the door with a tongue-kiss of striking force and facility. "So you'll do it tomorrow," she said, "I think that this is the best thing. I think you're quite right in wanting to get it over with as soon as possible, Luther; it's kind of a horrid thing even though it's for the best, and best to get it out of the way as soon as possible. You can come up here the day after tomorrow and we'll talk all about it then. I'd ask you to come up right after you do it but I think it would be best if I made the bridge meeting tomorrow, that way fifteen of my friends will know that I've been up here with them, and I think that this would be the best, Luther, because there's just so much insurance that I'll be getting. No one will ever suspect you, of course, and anyway if you slip in exactly at eleven as I told you to, no one will even see you. I'm so glad that you've decided to do this, Luther: it really takes a load off my mind."

The revolver, cool when first handed to me, cool in my hand during fellation, cool as I passed the frightening little Katherine, seemed to moisten, to heat as I drove. By the time that I had reached the Henry Hudson Parkway the temperature around my ribs was almost a hundred and I was forced to pull the car into an access road and gasping, remove the dreadful little weapon from its hiding place. I carefully wiped it, shrouded it in a handkerchief and put it on the seat beside me, half-tucked into my buttocks so that no passing police car could possibly suspect my activities. Then, sweating lightly, I continued the drive home, arriving at the rectory shortly after three o'clock, a little earlier than my usual homecoming. I put the car into the garage and went inside to find Hilarion in his study, reading a letter with his lips moving heavily and shaking his head repeatedly. His garb seemed slightly disarranged and a fine layer of sweat, not totally ascribable to the weather, covered his large dense brow.

"Oh hello, Luther," he said, "I'm glad for once that you're home early. The most amazing thing has happened. Simply amazing!" He stood and began to tremble his way around the study, patting books into place, absently using the backs of his hands to wipe grime from the desk-top. With a sudden clarity of vision I could see that Hilarion was getting old and this truly distressed me; the clergy should not subscribe to the simple laws of mortality which contain the rest of us. "I got a letter from the Bishop," Hilarion said, and waved it in front of me, something typed in uneven, smudged lines on a badly creased sheet of paper, "and he's closing the Church as of the first of next month. He says that we no longer have any function to serve. No function to serve, Luther!"

"Let me see it," I said and took the letter. Written in the Bishop's customarily obfuscatory rhetoric, but managing to squeeze in the point into the penultimate line, it was indisputably authentic. "I don't know what to say," I said, and gave the letter back. "This place has been my home for forty-four years."

"And mine for longer than that, Luther! He says that I can go into a retreat and that I've earned the privilege of rest. Retreat, Luther! What am I going to do in a retreat?"

"I don't know," I said. "I don't know what I'd do either."

"He doesn't even have the courtesy to offer me another pastorate, he just says that he thinks the purposes of the Church and myself would both be served by this act. Did you ever hear of anything like that, Luther? And just when things were going so well, too! I raised over a thousand dollars on my travels last week! A thousand dollars! We would have had new candles in the offertory for the first time in a year."

"It's very sad," I said, and indeed as the significance of this news started to pass through me I began to feel severely shaken. Hilarion in a retreat? I had dim visions of living somewhere in a pair of furnished rooms in the neighborhood, moving my weary frame from one cubicle to the next while sounds of old liturgies went through my bald, graying head. And no more confessions! "I suppose we'd have to split up," I said. "I mean, I don't really want to go to a retreat right now."

"Nor do I, Luther! How can they do this to me? I mean, I know that I've never been a religious man, not particularly, but I've tried to make up in ritual what I lacked in feeling, and I've done everything I can to serve the needs of the community. Now he writes that there's no community left anymore. What does he think the purpose of the Church is, to pick its domiciles? This didn't even come from Rome; I know that the silly old bastard did it on his own hook. He just doesn't like this Church, he never has. He thinks that it takes down the whole image of the diocese. That's why he would never give us any money."

"I don't know," I said, "I don't know what to say. I've had a rather shocking experience today myself, and I can't think properly, this woman—"

"Oh, don't tell me about your women, Luther!" Hilarion said nastily.

"I'm sick and tired of your activities if you want to know the truth. I'd just about reached the point when this letter came that I was going to throw you out of here. I love you, Luther, don't misunderstand me, but I don't think you have any future, and even though you take confessions nicely you're no asset to the Church. I don't want to hear about your women! Can't you see what he's done to me? The beginning of the month! That means I've got ten days to pack and get out like a common pauper. Aha!" Hilarion said with a sudden mad change of expression, his face twitching, and as I watched his features crumble into the softer and yet somehow more menacing posture of insanity I realized that due to recent events he had probably lost his mind. "Aha! that explains everything. Now I understand. Why didn't this occur to me before? He's sold the whole property for a pretty penny, that's what he's done, I'm sure of it. Turned the whole thing over to an urban redevelopment corporation or one of those middle-income projects. That explains it! Oh the greed, the monstrosity of it! Look at me, Luther, I've devoted fifty-three years of a mostly wretched and deprived existence to building on this rock, and this is the kind of thing they do to me! Don't bother me with your problems now, you idiot lout, and stop staring at me, can't you see that we're dealing with something fundamental?" And Hilarion fled from his study, clutching the letter to his chest in an oddly grieving position looking something like a Madonna with Paper he disappeared into the eaves of the Church, possibly to pray. I went upstairs to my humble rooms to think this and many things over.

I lay on the bed for quite a while with the door locked, holding the revolver in both hands, and then I levelled an experimental shot or two at the ceiling, hitting target in a fine shower of plaster which came down and covered me like soot. The Church is so muffled and enclosed that the shots would, of course, attract no attention whatsoever (I am told that the same is true of Harold's offices). Then I arose from the bed, putting the gun neatly under the pillow, and going to the drawer opened my manuscript box. For a long time I looked at the fruit of twenty years of research; stacks and stacks of pages, millions of words of rhetoric, the rhetoric pounding and waving on, sometimes hysterical, sometimes logical, sometimes credible, usually not, and in all this time it had been read by no one, no one except Luther, not a single soul, all of it buried in the upstairs room of an obscure parish in a dying section of Brooklyn.

Nothing. It had come to nothing. I began to understand that now. Hilarion had put in fifty-three years and was now going to a retreat; I had put in forty-four and was on the verge of a furnished set of rooms. It had come to nothing, the whole sum of it was nothing, and as I looked at the pages I began to understand for the very first time that I really could not

write very well at all, and that the majority of the entries were unintel-
ligible, even to me.

I thought of Mrs. Lee and I thought of Rye and I thought of Harold,
and then a dim vision of space overcame me: space and foreign lands and
strange saucy natives chattering in their idiosyncratic tongue, luxury hotels and room service, souvenirs and customs, castles and palaces. Then
I went back to bed and laid my head on the pillow, the outlines of the
gun seeming to cling warmly to me without interference from the silk and
stuffing. The heat was pleasant now, although somewhat enveloping.

After a time I heard pounding on the door which might have been Hilarion come in to abuse me further (or to ask forgiveness), but it meant
so little that I ignored it and after a while it went away. Eventually I went
away too, into the deepest and most searching of sleeps, and when I
awakened it was five in the morning, not a sound in the parish, not a
sound inside, all of the world silence, and in that silence I arose and
dressed, checked certain information in the telephone books and then,
taking the keys to the Peugeot, I was on my way. I did not pack; there
was so little to worry about except the manuscript, and I never wanted
to see the manuscript again.

X

It is ten-thirty and I sit uneasily in the coffee shop of the Holliman Building on lower Broadway. The coffee shop has one of those audacious and
idiot names which are supposed to provide charm: it is called *The Last
Kettle* or some other one of those whimsical names which so many dull
restaurants patronized by office workers seem to accrue. Maybe it is
called the *Foc'sle Fiend*, or perhaps it is the *Palatial Paradise*, then again,
for all I know I might be thinking of the *Nautical Neighborhood Nook*.

My state of mind, unsteady in the beginning, has been further exacer-
bated by several cups of hot coffee which I have been drinking steadily
here for some hours, surrounded by newspapers and these very notes
which I try to keep up to date. Whatever the name is, the decor of this
coffee shop is obviously one of the sea; the walls are plastered with
chipped and peeling old paintings of fish, and attached to a ship's rope
dangling from the ceiling is an embalmed sailor ... or it looks something
like an embalmed sailor; perhaps it is merely a mannequin. The figure
has on the uniform of a rear-admiral in the United States Navy and wears
a monocle. Its features have been tilted into a grotesque smile, and the
index finger of the right hand is lifted in a signal which perhaps is to indicate that the fleet is full steam ahead. The waitresses here—two of them,
both over fifty—are dressed in dirty blue uniforms decorated with por-

traits of ships, and the menu, which I have been reading off and on for some hours to pass the time, lists items like "saucy scallops" and "seascape shrimp" and "chicken of the sea-licken-tuna-fish" and "a cuppa hot joe." The food, I can comfortably attest, is vile, and most of the few customers who have eaten in the place over this long breakfast hour have come away from their yo-ho-ho eggs or pastoral pancakes with faintly nauseated expressions which become ever-grimmer as they take the check, confront it, and stagger wearily to the cash register to pay their bill. It is not the kind of place which I would want to get into the habit of frequenting, and I am reasonably confident that when I leave it within a (hopefully) few moments I will never come here again. But one thing can at least be said for this staff: they detest their jobs and location so thoroughly that they have virtually no eyes whatsoever for the patrons. It has cost me thus far only eighty or ninety cents to frequent it for the past four hours, and I am quite sure that were I to bring bedding and a night-light with me I could spend a long summer's afternoon for little more than this price. Not that I would particularly recommend this as a hotel location; the customers seem particularly eager to leave when they do, and were I possessed of their options, I am sure that I would be as well.

It is into this shop, the *Foc'sle Fiend*, that I am informed Harold Lee comes at ten to eleven every weekday morning to purchase one coffee and danish for a take-out order, a late breakfast for Harold or a very early lunch, depending upon the state of the market and his own digestion. Harold picks up his orders himself because none of the brokers in the agency has a secretary to do this kind of job, and Harold, who resents tipping above and beyond the necessary cost, does not care to use the delivery service of the *Foc'sle Fiend* itself. In this way he is able to obtain not only a break from his morning's duties but to save twenty-five cents, which is a dollar twenty-five a week, sixty-five dollars a year thus, or approximately one-tenth of Katherine's yearly tuition at the special school which meets on the days when the regular school does not. I do not deprecate this. A penny saved is a penny well-meant as anyone involved for many years with the peculiarities of collection-plates would testify.

Harold's habits have been carefully mapped and observed by his wife for many years, precisely for an exigency such as this. While she assures me that she has absolutely no idea what Harold's job is or how he works, she is utterly familiar with the logistics and gymnastics of his calling, and since his existence tends to be highly routinized in the first place, she has been able to brief me with admirable precision and economy. Harold will leave the *Foc'sle Fiend* at approximately eleven with his coffee and danish and return not to the large office containing the communal ticker tape where he performs the early morning tasks, but instead to his small private cubicle. Once there he will lock the door and perform the customer-relations segment of his day, which has to do with contacting his accounts and telling them the drift of the market, placing his orders, and so on. Until two o'clock he will remain in this office, from which he will then saunter to have a late lunch. However, he will not be leaving at two o'-clock today.

The private cubicle is distinguished, as are all the private cubicles in Harold's offices, by the fact that it has two entrances, front and rear. The rear, something of a service entrance for confidential clients or secret messengers, can be reached directly by the rear stairway to Harold's office, and is always kept unlocked. This is particularly convenient since the front entrance is always locked by the newly-danished Harold before he begins his morning tasks. For this and various other reasons, his absence, or one should say non-appearance back in the communal room, should not be noted until well past three o'clock. By that time, of course, I should long since be on my way singing through the leafy glades of the Palisades Interstate Parkway.

It is all very precise, very carefully maneuvered and astutely planned, the kind of work one would instinctively expect from the likes of Mrs. Lee; but a certain restlessness has now overcome me, particularly in the area of the elbows and knees, which joints have been essentially immobile for the past three hours. I have been in the *Foc'sle Fiend* since slightly before eight o'clock this morning since Mrs. Lee has advised me of the possible irregularity of Harold's schedule. Occasionally he will go down for his danish as early as ten fifteen, and at least once during the past twelve years he has appeared for it at a quarter of eight, having been cajoled by a state of post-marital fucking into a coital depression which he took for hunger. Exactly how Mrs. Lee has compiled this astonishing array of facts is beyond me, along with her taste for eventualities, but I thoroughly agree with her that if something is worth doing at all it is most certainly worth doing right and so, as the Oldest Living Resident (or so I feel) of the *Foc'sle Fiend*, I have cooperated with the staff to give it some aspect of bustle for over a hundred and eight minutes. Even with the solace of these entries mounting before me, I succumb to fatigue.

Eventually, however, and as close to ten of eleven as human frailty will permit, a large, fat, shy, brown browed man appears in the entrance of the *Fiend* and then moves doubtfully forward, his fine wide shoes seeming to shuffle rather than stamp over the floor, his large hands rhythmically grasping and ungrasping the set of corporate reports he holds. Behind his prescription-lensed sunglasses wise eyes blink, his little nose twitches testing the air of the *Fiend*, his wedding ring catching the fluorescence. I know that this is Harold but in order that there not be the slightest shade of confusion or embarrassment (Wanda could hardly collect if I killed the wrong man) I note that he is wearing the yellow striped suit which Wanda has promised to send him to work within this morning. The suit is tight fitting, shows a gleaming expanse of shielded crotch, waves like a buttercup before my battered eyes in the dim light of the Fiend. Beyond question, it is Harold.

I shift in my seat, subtly, imperceptibly, folding my notes unto myself, likewise the coffee cup, the pencil, my glasses, etc., which have been comfortably scattered about in the booth for so long that I have had the feeling of establishing a domicile. My attention upon Harold is total, complete. He is not only the man I am going to murder—which is reason enough to show some interest in him—he is the man who has been fornicating with Wanda Lee for lo, these many years and on that basis alone he would be fascinating. Has his fornication ennobled him? Has the possession of those massive breasts brought to that high brow of his a certain febrile knowledge? Does the clamping reminiscence of Wanda's great thighs bring to his eyes a twinkle of circumspection, a *moue* of knowledge?

None of it. None of it at all. The fact is that Harold is no different from all my other Harolds in the play-land; he is distinguished by nothing except the beaten look around his features and a certain clammy lack of distinction which enables him, even in the peculiar confines of the *Foc'sle Fiend*, to be unnoticeable. Indeed, he does not seem fully-formed; seems to be in some embryonic, unachieved state, wavers within my gaze as I stare at him. If I looked away it is possible that I might lose him. Yet Wanda Lee assures me that a scant seventeen years ago he was rushing chairman of his very important fraternity at Cornell University and made the final decision as to whether or not given initiates were allowed to participate in Hell Week.

Harold! Harold! He orders a cup of light coffee and a pineapple danish, signs a chit for the cost (a house charge account, courtesy of the *Fiend* for its regular customers, and it has no others, one dollar and five cents including the tax) and looking neither forward nor backward saunters from the enclosure, only a slight stagger to his gait suggesting that the market may have been on a slight downward course this morning. I follow him easily, bringing to the task all the skill accumulated through twenty years of experience in my trade, allowing my tread to mesh with the floor, my canter to the ceiling, the slight sway of my arms to the rhythm of the embalmed sailor. Outside the air-conditioned enclosure the accumulated heat of the day sags into me like a basketball and I double

up grunting, frantically re-acclimating myself as Harold goes into an elevator and presses the button for his floor which is, of course, seventeen.
I cannot accompany him; this would be too obvious (and would involve
the question of receptionists), but I am localized for time.

Now I must climb sixteen flights of stairs. Were not the contractor of
the building foundation a man who believed in witches, it would be seventeen. I exchange a brief, careful look of loathing with the aged elevator starter and then dart into a service staircase and am gone. The only
moment of possible difficulty, Wanda assured me, would be at this instant, but since the service staircase door is open and the starter is blind,
my situation can be said to be very much under control.

Jamming my memoranda into various pockets, moving my hand into
a right front pocket to check the presence of that beauty, her gun, I take
the first six flights two steps at a time, soaring, vaulting, feeling a kind
of exuberance overtake me in the sense of release after three hours in the
Fiend. After these six flights, however, all has faded into dull intimations
of mortality and it is a much older, much more cautious and informed
Luther who slowly plods the next five flights. At the twelfth floor I decide that whatever the nature of my activities as to my cerebral and sexual areas, they have been ill-preparation for the rigors of the Physical Life,
and by the fourteenth flight I have grim thoughts about the mission for
the first time since late last evening when everything became so chillingly
clear. By the fifteenth flight I realize that all has been a misdirection and
that it is nothing so much as fear and loathing which have taken me to
this course, but then there remains only one more flight, and by that time
rage has supplanted everything. I must kill Harold for forcing me to do
this. Wanda remains an open question.

I open the service door slowly to find that I am at the far end of a long
corridor of small offices, these offices emitting murmurs of music and fluorescence, two fat brokers at the end discussing the grievous failure of
Sonatox as I slowly close the door and wait them out. Some minutes later
the Sonatox problem has been solved, but Leatherette remains an open
question which they discuss vigorously and with many gestures. I put my
hand on the gun, remove it and aim carefully down the hall (better a
sheep than a lamb of God, saith I, and there were no witnesses) but at
this moment the problem of Leatherette is tumultuously solved by the
ringing of what seems to be a lunch bell and they disappear. I come into
the corridor drenched and panting, hold the gun in my pocket and carefully count down four offices on the left, then bear sharp right, and seizing a promised doorknob, whisk into Harold's office. He is sitting in deep
concentration over what appears to be an annual report and does not
hear my entrance until I slam the door vigorously to confront him. When

CONFESSIONS OF WESTCHESTER COUNTY

he does acknowledge me, it is almost matter-of-fact.

"Oh," he says mildly, "if you're looking for lunch it's in the cafeteria down the hall. You can have a snack or a full meal. You're the new man, I suppose. Pardon me for not going in to say hello to you this morning but there are just so many new men every day and it's hard to pay your respects. How are you?"

I remove the gun from my pocket and show it to him. Now that at last I have completed the horrid preparations: the *Fiend*, the staircase, the Leatherette company, the aspect of the mild, beaten Harold as he indicates with a shrug of shoulders and tip of palms that he does not care to eat lunch at the present time; now that I have, as I say, transcended these preliminaries, I am overcome by nothing so profound as a desire to do the task and to get out. Murder can only be anticlimactic after what I have undergone this morning. The *Fiend's* coffee churns unevenly in my stomach and seems to be heading toward the vicinity of the bowels; at the last instant, however, it flips upward (this is why the *Fiend* has become known throughout the building as a distinguished and unforgettable stop) and forces me into a belch. The belch makes the gun rather shake and for an instant I feel in danger of losing control of the situation.

"I don't understand," Harold says. "I don't know what you're doing."

I remove a handkerchief from a pocket (dislodging a page of my memoranda; it falls to the floor, blows in the air-conditioner breeze, but I will not pick it up, no matter) and wipe the *Fiend's* spoils off my lips. "I'm afraid you will," I say, "I've come to kill you."

"Come to kill me?"

"Well yes," I say. "I'm your wife's lover. We've worked the whole thing out, the two of us, and because of the insurance and the things you've done to her life and so on and so forth, you've really got to die. Don't take it personally, you're just the victim here."

"You've come to kill me, huh? You and Wanda worked this out?" His expression is beneficent, mild; his hands idly play with a stack of papers as he speaks. The air conditioner blows gentle, refreshing air into the room. In another context the mood would be reserved, almost pastoral, certainly confidential. "I suppose I couldn't try to take the gun away from you."

"Certainly not," I say, another snatch of the *Fiend's* coffee moving upwards and making me rather burble, "you wouldn't want to try that at all. As a matter of fact, I'm going to shoot you now. I wish we could talk and so on, but that would only make things worse."

"Of course," he said, "you've got to keep it depersonalized. I can understand that." He sighs, his body relaxes, his head seems to loll to one side. "I don't give a shit," he says, "I've been dead for about ten years. Just go ahead, kill me."

"I will."

"I really mean it," Harold says, "You know this isn't deathbed rhetoric or like that, it isn't bravado either, I really don't mind. This has been due for a long long time. It's all gone to pieces in the last few years and I'm tired, so tired, and the goddamned market seems to recover but every time it gets back to 700 on the Dow it all goes to pieces again, so you watch it and think that if the market improves you'll improve, but that doesn't work out either and the whole damned thing is worthless. The sex hasn't been that good either, come to think of it, and I just never have a minute to myself. Who needs the car? I thought the car would be something nice to have but it's just the same old shit. Come on, shoot me will you, or is it the same old bluff? I mean, I couldn't stand to go through this whole damned thing and find that it was just another one of those goddamned office pranks. Shoot me, man, get it over with! There's nothing to be afraid of. Wanda's no bargain by the way."

I shrug and shoot him. The bullet enters cleanly above his left temple and his body arches to receive it much as a woman might to receive a phallus, then sighs and relaxes. He plunges to the floor clumsily, elbows pulling over the chair behind him, and as the chair topples atop his damaged skull with a clatter there comes to light in his eyes for the first time the violence and horror I had expected. Now his face is suffused with rage, his hands clench, he pounds the floor and screams a terrible scream as he tries to get at my ankle, and I dart away in fear, but then I understand that it is only rigor mortis or advance rigor mortis and that Harold is dead. He rolls over neatly on his back, exposing his vanquished features to me, and one eye emits a horrid wink. His mouth flutters and he seems on the point of saying something; his features gather to a point, arch to alertness at the importance of the message he is about to deliver, and despite myself I clamber to the floor and put an ear against his body so that I can hear him better. He rises, rises against me, chokes, starts to say something and then he breathes out his last breath and dies, leaving me without a speck of information for all my trouble.

It occurs to me only at that moment, and with a thrust of dismay, that not until now had I realized that Harold too might have had something to confess.

That in fact all of the Harolds might have had something to confess, and those confessions none the less vital than any of the wives'.

But it is too late now for anything of that sort. My researches—at least my more conventional researches—are finished. The rectory is being closed down and Hilarion will go into a seminary for monks. The church will be supplanted by a high-rise. Luther will be supplanted by a generation of mendicants with more original requests. The Peugeot will fall before the onslaught of the New American Compacts. Nauseated, terrified, stricken by something more horrible than what I have known before (or maybe I am only thinking of the *Fiend*'s coffee) I snatch my discarded memoranda from the floor and I run. Out the door, down the corridor, down sixteen flights, past the lewd blind eyes of the starter and into the parking lot where, after an infuriating five-minute wait while the Peugeot is reconstructed in the upstairs region, I leap into my transportation and am gone. All the way up the West Side Highway Harold's mouth follows me, opening and closing to its last confession, but by the time I have reached the Bridge I feel considerably better, and at one of the parking areas of the Palisades Interstate I jam the car to a halt, leap from it with my memoranda, thrust all of the pages into little balls of incoherence and throw my words from a cliff, my words drifting and swaying into the mindless, heaving river. The river takes them gratefully, and much lightened I return to my car. By noon even the *Fiend*'s coffee has turned to grace inside and my belches are like small flashes of sunlight, spattering on the Wanda-bound windshield of the little car.

XI

The first thing she wants to know when I come up the path is whether I have done it and the second is the whereabouts of the gun. "Harold gave that to me," she says; "it was my purchase but he paid for it. He said that I was very precious to him and deserved to be protected at all times. I know that that gun is going to make me always cry," and then she does indeed break into easy, moist tears whose prolificacy and dimension overwhelm me with their apparent seriousness, and continues for some time while I twist my hands over the object and finally hand it to her barrel first. She takes it in a swooping gesture (and for one idiot instant I feel that she is going to aim it at me) and then drops it into the pocket of the voluminous housedress she is wearing.

(Oh the horror of it! It is difficult even now to apprehend that moment at which the gun darted in the air; during that stricken instant I thought that I saw all of it and it shook my bucolic frame right down to the soles: she had planned everything, and by murdering me would then remove the one dangerous scrap of Lutherian evidence. I could see all of it, the clarity, the closeness, the sheer acuity of it all, and set to trembling, but the gun twinkled away. So much for apprehensions. So much for paranoia.)

"I certainly will save that gun," she says in a level voice, and wipes her

eyes with an air of finished business. "Is he really dead, Luther?" she asks.
"Did you really kill him?"

"Yes," I say, and add a very convincing portrayal of the death of Harold
Lee, holding back only the moment of disastrous near-revelation before
the climax, and of course the issue of the *Fiend*'s coffee which even now
percolates within me as from some distant shore. "But I don't think that
he felt much pain."

"I hope not," she says absently. "It *was* Harold, wasn't it? I mean, you
didn't kill anyone else by mistake?"

"No," I say, and then feel impelled to add to my description of the death
a description of Harold In Life, one which apparently jibes with her own
recollections of the subject. "Well," she says with a sigh, "I guess that it
really *was* Harold. It really was him that you killed. Thank you very
much, Luther. I really appreciate it. Even though of course I'll miss him."

"I didn't want to do it," I say. "You understand that, don't you?" I remove a handkerchief from an inner pocket, mop my own rather distended brow, and sink down upon the couch, the cushions feeling thin
and vaguely protective. "As a matter of fact, I wasn't going to do it at
all until something came up last evening."

"Oh," she says, "oh well, that's very interesting. Of course. It's so awfully *good* of you, Luther, to come by and take that load off my mind,
but I don't know how quite to put this, I'm afraid that you can't stay. I
mean, I want you to stay and so on, but Katherine is due home from
school in a very few moments and then I'm supposed to have Mrs. Lowe
in for tea at four-thirty. It's important, don't you think, that everything
be carried on today just as if it were normal; I can't let on a thing. Luther,
I can't tell you how much I appreciate your time and your trouble, and
of course when things get straightened out I want you and Katherine to
meet in some nice way, but today just isn't the day. I'd make love to you
and so on but I'm sure you understand. Maybe next Monday. No, Monday is the hairdresser and by then I'll probably have to be sitting down
with the lawyers. Assuming the funeral is Sunday. Yes, Sunday will be
the funeral and Monday the hairdresser and the lawyers and then Tuesday I'll have to get packed for a little trip. Maybe I can put off the hairdresser on Monday because I'll certainly be going to him before the funeral which means I'll be going on Saturday. Then I'll have to go away
for at least a week to get myself in order again. The best thing I think for
you to do, Luther, is to leave me your full address and telephone number and I'll be in touch with you just as soon as I get back from my trip.
Strange that his office hasn't phoned yet, to inform me. But then he stays
alone in that little cubicle until three or four in the afternoons sometimes,
so he might not be discovered until late. You don't really mind, do you,

Luther? It's just that my mind is running away with me now and I have to make plans. It's very upsetting for me after all these years to lose Harold."

"It was the diocese," I say, "the diocese closed down the church. They're putting Hilarion in a retreat."

"Are they? That's interesting. What's a retreat? Luther, I love you and I really appreciate everything, but you'll have to go."

"What was my future?" I ask. "As far as I can see it would just be a series of furnished rooms. I hadn't realized how central Hilarion and the church were to me. When I understood—"

"Maybe I better call *his* number. That would be reasonable, I often call to say hello. Let's see, if I just ask to speak to him and they get no answer on the switchboard, someone will go in to check him."

"I had to do something, don't you see?" I said. "Just once I had to establish some concrete act—"

"And then they'll send one of the secretaries in and she'll find out and probably start screaming. I'll have to break down over the phone."

"Because there's been nothing, nothing, the whole thing has only been a question of meaningless acts, repeated over and over until—"

"Luther, I can't really concentrate when you keep on babbling like that. It all sounds fascinating and I'd like to find out all sorts of things about your life and so on, but can't you see that this isn't the proper time and place? Later; there'll be time for that later. So when they tell me, I'll have to be terribly calm and say I don't believe it."

"And an emptiness, the basic, searching emptiness: what was I trying to prove? What did I want to extract from them that the penitential box had not given me over and over again? Or did I merely want to prove that all the world is a confessional and—"

"Luther, I can't listen to any more of this. There isn't *time*. Katherine will be coming soon. Luther dear, I'm awfully sorry but you'll have to leave now. I'll give you a call in just a little while, soon's I get back to the city, believe me," and so saying Mrs. Lee seized me by a limp elbow, hauled me flopping to my feet, and dragged me to the door as I swam in her arms like a fish. My mood, which had verged at this time upon the sheerest disassociation, was nevertheless one of the completest clarity, and I had the feeling that I could see the two of us as if at some far distance: here, down the tube, in this dwindled diamond of a living room is a large, sensual woman with white arms wearing a housedress slightly too large for her; in her arms she carries a thin man with mustaches and overstuffed pockets which appear to contain packets of prose. The man is talking, facing the woman, pouring confidences into her ear, but it does not seem as if the woman is listening; rather she is concentrating on the task of tugging him vigorously toward the door. The man protests, seems to back away, pulls back an arm to try to make a point in gesture, but the woman is remorseless or at least certain and recapturing the arm she intensifies her efforts to take the man to the door. He resists again; then, suddenly, at something she has said, this resistance seems to go out of him. No longer fishlike, he drapes himself like a cloth over her frame as with some difficulty she supports him and opens the door. Breezes rustle in and the rich brown hair of the man waves almost giddily; he bends his face to insert a long tongue in the woman's ear and say something, and she submits for an instant, then straightens and with a final push she gets him out the door and then, leaving heavily upon it, almost panting, she lifts the chain and bolts it. Now alone in the living room she wanders in circles, touching a finger to her tongue, thinking, or possibly it is only walking, but the vigor in her gestures is purposeful and this is, even to the distant observer, clearly a woman who knows what she is doing. Or thinks that she knows what she is doing, there being no substantive difference.

The man? The man goes slowly down the walkway shaking his head. A battered old car intercepts his stumbling gait at a certain point (he walks straight into it) and he looks at it without recognition for a moment, then tongues his own lips, reaches into a pocket, extracts keys and walks over to the driver's side. He opens the door. He closes the door. The car begins to move. The car containing the man drives down the quiet block, its right directional light flashing, and at the corner it turns and it is only then that the observer loses the thread of it, his vision being interrupted by something which seems to be tears. Obviously he has been straining his eye for too long at this strangely-shaped periscope, and the severe strain has become an irritant. Weeping, the observer extracts a handkerchief to moisten and soothe his eye and at that instant the scene goes blank: blank in the grayness of dreams, and the swimming fix seems to be lost forever, circling lost in a myriad of constellations and phenomena, dead planets and violated stars.

XII

I enter the rectory, and instantly sense desertion. I have lived with Hilarion for too long not to know what has happened: he has dealt with the situation in his own way, made his own obscure preparations. It is quite empty; all of his possessions are gone. The church is locked and bolted, but somehow one miserable penitent has managed to get by the bars (or perhaps was locked within, it is impossible to tell with these people) and hands clasped, deep in meditation, seems to be unaware of a situation which might otherwise end only in starvation and death. I decide not to deal with this for the time being and instead go to the modest study where Hilarion and I have spent so many fruitful hours. On the desk, as I expect, lies a sealed envelope addressed to me. I open it and read Hilarion's last statement.

(I point out in all fairness that I have always despised the epistolary technique, which seems to me to be nothing more than a device exploited by weak authors to escape the narrative mechanics of dialogue, scene, characterization and so on which would otherwise defy them—the construction of a novel without furniture, so to speak. For this reason I have always sedulously avoided it in my own journals, although the letters which the ladies have written me are myriad and would of themselves compose a fine appendix.... But I felt that a document of the importance ascribed to this journal should not seek the epistolary answer to complex problems. All this to one side, I *do* have a problem here: Hilarion wrote me a final letter and I read it. What am I supposed to do? paraphrase Hilarion? This would hardly be fair to my adoptive father who wrote a superb if rather cracked prose. Skip over it? But Hilarion's influence upon my life has been prime and no completist can ignore this significant statement. Try to dramatize it with props, perhaps an auditor or two to whom I can read the letter while occupying myself with cigarettes, ashtrays, table legs, rugs and so on? But there was no one except the inexplicable penitent, and it might have taken hours to open up the church if the keys were not readily available. No, no: I stood and I read the letter. This is not dramatic but it substitutes for the bellows of drama the infinitely sweeter music of the truth and it is the truth which I am seeking in these final notes. Truth! The truth! Sweet, sweet reason!)

Dear Luther:

I really cannot stand this anymore and have decided to deal with the situation in my own way. I have no plans but will make some. Eventually you may hear. You stole my Peugeot, you son of a bitch, so I have to bus myself out of here like any common spic in the precinct, you denied me even that last dignity. You will note that in this extremity a certain unction has vanished from my rhetoric; I feel free, as if for the first time, to truly speak my mind. Of course I am a prejudiced man. I never said otherwise. Still, prejudice need not be a failure of the heart.

You stole my Peugeot, Luther; that was not very kind of you. As far as I can gather from the secretary (the Bishop, inevitably, now refuses to speak to me, the poisonous, rank, greedy old fool) the Church will be in the hands of the assessors by Thursday next or some three days, time enough for you to make your arrangements and get out but not time enough, alas, for old Hilarion who would only regard these three days as a Trinity of destruction and might during those seventy-two hours of transition do something quite rash with himself, even mortify the old flesh. You are young however, Luther, and with the spring and speed of youth will be able to make adjustments so fluid that they will seem to you to be elastic, will inform the whole world you regard with the imminence of unchanging possibility. One can envy you.

Nevertheless you stole my Peugeot. I would not need it at the destination I envision but this was still not very nice of you. You always left the gas tank empty, Luther, and abused the transmission so greatly that no less than three new clutches have been installed within a period of two years. I shielded you from all of this, feeling the benign protectiveness of the father (even unnatural father) toward the son, but you have caused me much trouble and inconvenience and should be advised.

Some final words:

I have been into your memoirs rather thoroughly over these past years as you might have expected, feeling it my mild liberty as the one who succored and protected you to see what you were up to. Furthermore, I had the distinct feeling reading these pages that they were written for my eyes alone and that I occupied a role no less important than you in the commission of your activities: I was the auditor and through that became the Collaborator. The Collaborator was the one for whom you performed all of your acts; without his presence they would have been unnecessary.

I have kept to myself about your activities except for certain mild advisements and protestations, but now that it is too late I really must tell you, Luther, that you have laughably misinterpreted the policy and function of the confession booth from the day you began. Untrained as a priest, you nevertheless found the artifice of the confessional fascinating and in your clumsy, unpriestly way, attempted to give it some focus in your own life. But you got it all wrong. Instead of becoming a confessor, you have become a manipulator. It was as if I were to venture into these dangerous and filthy streets, club strangers over the head and drag them unconscious back to the church where for several hours I told them in the confessional context how failed they were. I would be confusing the confession with the limitation, Luther, and so have you. And now, in the person of Mrs. Lee, it seems that you have begun to pay the piper, Luther; it would stand to reason inevitably that if you sought out people to bludgeon through the framework of confessions you would sooner or later meet one who knew your secrets ... and would use them to destroy you. From an abstract point of view, this is a consummation as deserved as it was evident.

Nevertheless you remain my son, attached to me by mystery and coincidence, years of shared pain and everything which we have known together. I cannot disengage myself from you totally; I still have feelings. You are a vile person, Luther, but you are inestimably my own, my own creation, my own construction loosed upon the world, and pity and terror must intermingle. Do not listen to this woman. Do not do her bidding. I have nothing against the commission of crimes since, as you know, I do not believe in mortal sin (or in almost anything else) but the sheer inconvenience which would afflict your life as this life would be monstrous and would obliterate your still interesting potential. Do not do this woman's bidding. She has ideas for you, Luther. It will not end there. There is a whole network of obligation and involvement with women that you do not, despite your vast experience, at all understand. There is no end to their demands. This is the principal reason why I decided upon the priestly vocation I now confess (it is time for all confessions); I feared and detested women but did not wish to be accused, in any way, of entertaining homosexual desires. Therefore I took on the frock.

This is already too long, Luther. I must bid you farewell. Do not get into vagrant affairs. Abandon the route of confessions: you will learn nothing because these people have nothing to confess. Get a good job. Make something of yourself. Be inner-directed. Guide yourself in your own best terms. These and other banalities are all that I can now give you; I am a very old man. Give the Peugeot a grease and oil change immediately and at every five hundred mile interval thereafter. I give it to you, my small and panting treasure, the only thing which I have ever truly owned.

Your Father

Touched I sit over the letter in the gloom of the study for a long time, folding and refolding it, considering the creases, looking at the words which with repetition seem to lose their sense and take on only the aspect of Hilarion's high, rather whining voice. Finally, carefully, I shred the letter into various shards and pieces and inflame it with a match, drop it into the empty wastebasket where it expires along with a couple of extra sugar packets from the *Fiend* which, with the *Fiend's* matches, I have extracted from my coat pocket. A black burning husk of oxidized sugar remains in a ring around the basket; it smells something terrible. The acrid

odor reignites for me the slight odor of Harold's flesh as fragments of it
decomposed before me on his carpet, and I feel a heave of nausea, stand
quickly, rub my hands together briskly, try to feign action and interest.
After a time I decide upon a simple task which will keep me ordered; I
go into the church to clear out the penitent. The keys remain in Hilarion's upper right desk drawer and I draw the bolt carefully, then walk into
the church with a purposeful air. The penitent, who seems to have fallen
asleep, twitches into awakedness when he hears my footsteps and looks
at me with large and shallow eyes, rubbing his fists together. It is Adams.

"Oh Luther," he says, "oh Luther, I just came in here to pray hours ago
and I must have fallen asleep. Luther, Luther—"

"The church is closed," I say. "You must leave."

"Oh Luther," he says, and raises a hand to touch me. The sudden awak-
ening has apparently left him without sufficient time to make the transition into reality from his disgusting fantasies and something approaching love shines in his eyes. "I'd just like to stay and pray a bit,"
he says as I back away from him.

"I don't think you understand. I said the church was closed. Permanently. The diocese has closed it. You must leave now, Mr. Adams."

"Luther," he says, weaving in his seat, "Luther, I've always loved you.
I am an ugly old man but—"

"None of that," I say with as much briskness as I can cajole and, shuddering with revulsion, seize him by a shoulder, put an assisting hand near
his foul old thigh and force him into an erect posture, then carry him chattering out of the church. "I'm drunk, Luther," he says, "you must know
that I'm very drunk," and "I just wanted to pray, Luther," and "I know
it's impossible but if we could work something out," and so on and so
forth until with one mighty heave I pitch his repellent, shivering old frame
down the steps where he falls clattering into a despondent position on
the sidewalk. "That wasn't necessary, Luther," he mumbles, "I only
wanted to tell you something."

"It's too late," I say. "The church is closed. I'm afraid that there can
be no more prayers or confessions in the district. You'll have to take your
business to Fort Greene," and slam the door on him and go into the al-
leys of the church muttering to myself as well, sounding surprisingly like
Mr. Adams as I find myself saying, "Take your business to Fort Greene,
take it to the Williamsburgh district, take it to Flatbush Avenue. Go to
Gowanus, Red Hook, Bensonhurst, all the eaves of the city, but there will
be no more confessions in Brownsville. No more, no more," I sing and
lock all the doors and retire to my room *avec* some confusion to make
my Last Stand.

XIII

Two weeks elapse, two uneventful weeks during which I neither hear from Mrs. Lee nor am confronted by grim-faced workmen come to reconstruct the church. I have decided to stay here as long as possible; the end surely confronts me but there are certain virtues in postponement, and also, I tell myself that I have plans. I bring my memoirs (slightly disheveled by Hilarion's last reading) up to date; I read newspapers; I keep the doors barricaded except for deliveries from the neighborhood grocery.

Two days after Hilarion's departure, the brief notice which I have been waiting for appears on the obituary page of the *New York Times*, my favorite newspaper of all times. Harold Lee, a stockbroker, found dead in his office. Thirty-five years old. Apparent suicide although no weapon can be found. Police rule however that suicide the only explanation. Services to be held at. At the hour of. Survivors are his wife Wanda and a daughter, Katherine. No flowers. Contributions to the publicity department of the American Stock Exchange, an organization to whose cause the decedent was deeply devoted.

I think of going to the funeral, decide not to. It is listed, in any event, as private. On the morning of Harold's burial I awake with a sharp pain in my right side which I feel to be a heart attack, but it quickly passes and I understand that it is only metaphysics. More time elapses. I read my memoirs over and over again, conclude that the style is juvenile, the events described embryonic, and that in no way have I reached my potential as a man and Confessor. Oddly this cheers me.

I come out late at night to pay my accounts in the grocery store. Hilarion left three one-hundred-dollar bills intact in the emergency fund in his study. My own modest bank account, sustained through the years by Hilarion's contributions and small thefts from the collections is well over one thousand dollars. There is plenty of money. Enough for the time needed. Money has never been one of my prime concerns.

On Tuesday, a week after Hilarion's exit, the phone rings. Sometimes I answer it, often I do not; but I conclude that this may be Wanda, freshly expiated and back in the city. It turns out, however, to be the Bishop. He wants to know Hilarion's whereabouts. He also wants to know what I am doing in the Church. Excavating, he advises, will begin a week from Monday on the site of a new two-hundred-story office building, part of the general attempt to upgrade the neighborhood and improve its visibility. I tell him that I do not know where Hilarion has gone.

"That's impossible," he says. "We have his retreat all prepared for him."

They have been waiting for some days."

"I don't think that he wants to go to a retreat."

"That's insane. Besides, that's the orders clear through Rome. What are you doing there, Luther?"

"I'm holding out," I say.

"I don't understand you."

"I'm staying here. I protest the closing of this Church. I bear witness to the corruption of the diocese."

"Now now, Luther, there's no point in being bitter. Your father always spoke highly of you," the Bishop says, gently if irrelevantly. "I can understand how you feel but there's nothing to be done."

"I'll go to the newspapers. I'll see the city marshals. I'll write a letter to Rome."

"You don't understand," the Bishop says softly, "it's all fixed. You'll just make a spectacle of yourself, Luther."

"This is my Church."

"Of course it's your Church. It's my Church too. It's everybody's Church, even the heathen and the uninitiated; the Church exists for all of us. The Church is a great enveloping spirit. Its physical manifestations mean nothing at all, Luther. You will have the Church wherever you go."

"I won't take it," I say, "I don't believe that stuff. I'll write letters to all of the editors. They'll publish my letters in all of the dailies. I'll tell the buildings department. You won't get away with this."

"Oh Luther, Luther," the Bishop says gently, with infinite weariness and a kind of solace coming out of his voice as well; a solace which frighteningly I want to respond to, "Luther, you don't understand, the whole thing is fixed. Everything. There's nothing you can do, Luther, but you've got to stop taking this so seriously. In the next couple of days you'll really have to get out."

"I won't go."

"Perhaps you can go to the retreat we prepared for Hilarion. The monks and nuns will be happy to see you. It's a pastoral atmosphere, Luther, and you can get a lot of thinking done. I don't think we'd let your lack of conversion stand in the way."

"I don't want to go on retreat."

"Ah well, Luther," the Bishop says with a giggle, "ah well, if that's the way you feel you must respond. Most assuredly, my son, you are going to have to do something. Don't make me take different action."

"I'm staying."

"Goodbye my son," the Bishop says gently, and the phone hangs up into a silence as pure and timeless as glass. Since then I have not heard from him. I keep all the doors firmly locked during the day and peer from

the windows. Once two discouraged civil servants came to the back entrance and rattled around for a while but they seemed to lose interest
when I began to drop stones on them, and ran. I do not believe that the
serious efforts have yet commenced and by the time they do I hope to
be well out of here. I quite agree with the Bishop about the overall hope-
lessness of my position.

From time to time, penitents come around, up the front stairs, and pull
at the doors beseechingly. The sign that I put up on the first day—THE
CHURCH IS CLOSED PERMANENTLY, PLEASE PRAY IN AN-
OTHER MINISTRY—does not seem to have discouraged many of
them. Possibly they cannot read, or possibly they cannot understand that
the Church, which has been on this site for one-hundred-eighteen years,
has been taken away from them. They will stand, sometimes for hours,
hammering at the doors, and then I can hear the thin sound of their
prayers wafting heavenward. Perhaps they feel that prayers in the vicinity of a Church are better than the more conventional bedroom kind. I
let them pray in that fashion; it does not disconcert me but I could do
with a little more privacy. Now and then they leave coins on the steps,
which coins, if not stolen by passers-by, I retrieve in the hours of the night
and add to the emergency fund. There is no point in waste, it disgusts
me.

I had not realized that there was such religious fervor in the parish.
While quantitatively it does not seem to afflict a large cross-section of people, qualitatively it can be said to inhabit the few as it never tenanted the
many, and if this fervor could have been broken up and distributed in
more modest lots to the population, there is a chance that things might
have been entirely different here.

Of course this is all pointless random speculation and means nothing;
it is merely taking the place of my more direct memoirs which have fallen
into disuse and failure and already reek from abandonment. But what
pleasure I took in them! What the sum of them meant to me! Ah, ashes,
ashes, vanity, vanity.

Time passes. I fall into a vaguely malnutritive state, nibble onions, look
at the phone. Throughout all of this it never occurs to me to call Mrs.
Lee. A certain relationship has seemingly been established. Nevertheless,
I can understand that I hate her for not having called, and know that I
will want to have a further look at this sometime.

Friday, nearly two weeks after Hilarion's departure, the phone rings.
It could be the buildings department, but it is Mrs. Lee. "Luther?" she
says, "Luther?"

"Yes," I say, "it's me."

"Luther, how *are* you? I meant to call you the instant we got back from

Portugal, Katherine and I, but we had a whole big meeting with the lawyers on Wednesday and then yesterday Katherine got a strep throat and I had to put her in the special school for illnesses. I haven't had a free moment until now. How are you, Luther?"

"I'm all right," I say. "My father has left me."

"Your father? Oh, you mean that priest! I'm sorry to hear that, Luther."

"It was necessary. It doesn't mean anything."

"Luther, he left me everything. Can you imagine that? He didn't even give Katherine a trust or anything. And he had an extra hundred thousand dollars in insurance policies which he had never told me about. He took it out four years ago on my birthday as a secret present to me. And he had a savings account for fifteen thousand dollars, probably for special gifts, which he had never told me about either even though somehow he had gotten my signature and made it a joint. I got everything, Luther! Oh, he was just the dearest man," she says and begins to snuffle. "On the other hand I don't want to be a hypocrite or anything and I know that wherever he is, he's happier now. Did everything, uh, work out all right for you, Luther?"

"It was okay," I say, taking an onion from the manuscript box before me and peeling it skillfully with a thumbnail (one can acquire a certain facility if one has been doing something like this for four days). "I mean, there were no complications."

"It went down as a suicide, you know. Harold didn't have an enemy in the world and there was simply no motive. They closed the case right away."

"I'm glad," I said.

"I didn't really mean to make you leave so fast that day, Luther, but you can understand the things I had on my mind."

"Oh, that's all right," I say. "I think I understand that. Don't worry about a thing."

"It was really awfully nice of you, Luther. You did a beautiful job. He was such a dear man and cared for me so much, but you did a beautiful job and I appreciate that part too."

"Don't worry about it," I said, with sudden understanding. "I didn't do it for you. I did it for myself."

"Excuse me?"

"Nothing," I said. "Maybe I even did it a little bit for him too, come to think of it. That doesn't matter."

There is a thick uneven pause for a couple of beats, and then Mrs. Lee says in a slightly changed voice, higher-pitched, more childish, "do you want to see me today, Luther?"

"I was hoping you'd ask that."

"Why don't you come up this afternoon? About two o'clock, say. I'll be able to make myself ready for you by then."

"All right," I say. "I'll try to make it by that time. I have certain minor problems around the rectory which might delay me but I'll do my best."

"Luther?"

"What's that?"

"Luther, do you think that you could come by bus or rent a car? Anything but that little Renault. They might recognize it. I mean, I think that it would be better for the two of us—"

"It's a Peugeot," I say.

"They're both French, aren't they?"

"I'll rent a car, Mrs. Lee," I say and before the conversation can deflect itself into further complication, I hang up on her. Sitting there in a massive unfulfilled silence, I realize that this is really a pretty poor return on a call that I have been awaiting for a fortnight, but on the other hand— ah, on the other hand!—the call has at least given me a sense of purpose and now I can go on and lead my life as I choose.

I leave the church, carefully boarding it up behind me and leaving only one imperceptible keyhole through which entrance might be gained. I then start the Peugeot for the first time in two weeks—the motor rasps a little but the car is sound, the car has more of a sense of destiny than I do, and begins after a while to draw breath in a series of rumbles—and drive it down the dangerous decayed streets of Brownsville until I find an appropriate spot littered with whiskey bottles underneath a lamppost, and here I leave the car, remove the keys and license plates and walk rapidly away. A group of drinkers on the near corner eye me and the car with equal interest, decide that the car is more accessible in daylight and amble off in that direction. I continue my stride, not feeling fear, knowing that my identification as the son of Father Hilarion has always brought me passage in this district. At the nearest kiosk I take the subway into Flatbush, and at Flatbush I rent a car, and it is that car—a splendid Continental with fins and a bathroom behind the back seat—that I drive up toward Mrs. Lee.

I feel that I have earned the right to be direct. I take the East River Drive, the Triborough Bridge, and the New England Thruway to Rye. I need no longer slink over from the west like an unwelcome invader; I may come through the front door. I have paid my dues to Rye in a very elaborate way but nevertheless I have paid them and I feel no compunction in taking this direct route.

The car has a stereo with an interesting assortment of selections from the mid-sixties hit parade as well as an uncut recording of *King Lear* as

done by the Royal London Company in Paris in 1956. It is *Lear* to which
I listen as I roar down the New England Thruway, the old king's rant-
ing and rhetoric curiously comforting as I wind the car up to ninety-five
miles an hour and consume utterly all things within my path.
Never never never never never.
Kill kill kill kill kill kill.
Sa sa sa.

XIV

I bring the Continental, now huffing ungently (something has happened
to the bearings) and spilling oil, to the front of Mrs. Lee's home and cut
the engine. One has the feeling of reconstituting the past or perhaps
merely extending it in certain simplistic ways; in any event, it is with a
profound feeling of *déjà vu* that I wander up the path at what I hope to
be an indolent, handyman's shamble and put my hand on the knocker.
Despite the absence of Harold, the lawn remains clean, bright, well-kept;
the house has a freshly-washed look. It seems that nothing about his life
so improved his domicile as his leaving of it. Mrs. Lee opens the door,
wearing tennis shorts and a sweater of much tightness; through it, her
newly-widowed breasts spring with the indulgence and coyness of large
lambs staggering through a meadow. "Luther!" she says, "you're early."
"I'm sorry," I say. "I told you I had certain logistical problems with the
rectory. Never mind that, but I thought you'd understand."
"But it's one o'clock! You're a full hour before time! I just came back
from playing tennis and haven't had a chance to shower or look presentable or anything. Well, do come in; it looks very bad with you just
standing there on the steps. Luther, I said, come in," and I am ushered
into the home while the door clatters vigorously behind me. Everything
looks very well, neatly ordered and in place, and on the couch in the living room sits a large black wreath from which dangles a greeting card.
"Harold's associates," she says, "they wanted to remember him in some
way. I think it's terribly depressing but it was brought up by special messenger just a couple of hours ago and I have no idea where to put it. I
don't want to throw it out just yet."
"It looks very well."
"Well listen, Luther, there's no point to this. Why don't you just have
a seat and I'll take a shower and get presentable and then we can really
visit? It would have been much more convenient if you had waited until two—"
"They had a businessman's special with the Continental. You take it
out at noon and return it at six and that way you save seven dollars and

ninety-five cents. But you have to take it out; they have people on the roads spying to make sure that you actually drive their cars and once I started driving I had no place else to go."

"Well, it all sounds very tortuous to *me*," she says and seizes my palms, looks at me intently. "You're not looking too well, Luther," she points out, "you've lost a lot of weight and your face looks preoccupied. You aren't, uh, starting to have guilt feelings or anything—?"

"No," I say and almost laugh, "nothing like that. I told you, I did it for me."

"Because one thing I wouldn't like, Luther, I wouldn't like it at all, would be you starting to feel guilty and deciding that you have to talk to the police. It wouldn't matter to *me*, Luther, because you'd be just a harmless little man who I never heard of in my whole life and who was making up psychotic stories, but it would be very bad for you and that would make me sorry. You aren't thinking of doing anything like that at *all*, are you? You'd probably get the death penalty, Luther, and I'd be very sympathetic and very sorry but I'm sure you understand why I wouldn't be able to do a thing for you. I couldn't even visit you or anything like that."

"I told you," I say, with the beginnings of exasperation beginning to inform my mild tones, "I don't have any feelings like that at all. I'm not guilty and I'm not upset and I'm not unhappy and I wish you'd stop this."

"Oh, I'm so terribly glad, Luther!" she says, and coming over to me, gives me a moist, delicate kiss which lasts for some instants, breaking into something fluid and open for a moment and then retreating as her mouth closes like a butterfly's wings and she backs away from me. "I wanted you to say that. I wanted to know that I could trust you, Luther. And I think that Harold would have wanted it that way too; there was this thing about him, he couldn't stand to see anyone suffer, even a little child."

"That's very nice," I say and sink into the couch, feeling the smooth film of the leatherette covering me and simulating nonchalance I remove an onion from my pocket and delicately begin to peel off its various layers, putting them into my mouth. She looks at me with some horror, then shakes her head and goes to the door. "Look, Luther," she says, "just let me go and wash up a little bit and I'll be right back, is that okay? I don't know what you're doing there but you've picked up some kind of a disgusting habit. Watch the couch and don't spill any of those things."

"It's an onion," I say. "Actually, they're quite tasty. I've been eating them quite a bit within the last week. They're nourishing and they fill the stomach quite comfortably."

"Oh," she says without any interest, and leaves the room. I sit more deeply on the couch, try to make myself comfortable, try to concentrate on the onion (a new eccentricity for me, this vegetable, but the flavoring is most pungent and satisfying when I bite down sharply and the intimation of tears it brings to the crinkles of my handsome eyes is also pleasant; the vanished Harold would have appreciated the gesture) and my own place within the larger scheme of things. The decor of the living room has changed subtly since I have been there last; the coloring seems to be somewhat more sober, but on the other hand all vestiges of the hapless Harold have vanished. The pipe rack is gone; his photograph which had been discreetly tacked to a wall underneath a nude painting is gone (strange how I only noticed it in its absence); the carpeting is somehow lusher and more full. It has become a perfectly proper room for contemplation or confession, but it is somehow not quite as comfortable as it might once have been. I run my hand over the wreath, noting that it is artificial, and listen to the cheerful sounds of singing and rushing water from some distant eave of the house which signify that Mrs. Lee is making her preparations for me. Memoirs crackle in my pocket. I sit stiffly so that the paper bulges will not be noticeable. On a sudden impulse, I pick up the phone (green-and-white, shaped like the head of a child, pushbutton dialing; they do things better up here) and dial the number of the Bishop which I incidentally know by heart. I get his secretary and eventually the Monsignor, and with the Monsignor my efforts almost come to an end, but somehow I am able to convince him that my business is urgent and the Bishop turns up within his eyesight, back suddenly from a trip to Philadelphia. "Hello, Luther," he says, "have you got any good news for me?"

"I thought you should know that I took the confessions for years. In Hilarion's absence. He would charge me to go into the confessional box and do the expiation. I was better at it than he was."

"There's some precedent for that," the Bishop says judiciously. "You'd be truly surprised, Luther, at what is in some of the confessional boxes nowadays. This whole question of anonymity has led to some very strange alternatives, strange byways indeed. I wouldn't worry about it."

"I delivered remission and grace even though unqualified. Sometimes I forgave terrible crimes for a small contribution."

"It happens," the Bishop sighs. "Our time on Earth is limited. Our time afterwards is not. We must do what we can for one another in the brief time that we are here, but otherwise try not to worry about any of this too much. I am sure that it will work out for the best, Luther. Do you wish me to grant you forgiveness; is that why you called? I would like to see you out of the Church, they are going to start blasting on Monday."

"No," I say, "that wasn't why I called at all. I just thought that you might be interested in that kind of thing but it's only an incidental. The real reason I called was to tell you that I'll never leave. Never. I'm neatly holed in there and I have no intention of ever leaving."

"That's an unwise and imperious decision, Luther."

"I have plenty of supplies and strong locks and an utter command of the grounds. You'd have to take the area by force and I want to tell you right now that I could be armed if I chose to be."

"That's all very unfortunate, Luther. We don't contemplate the use of force. There are other methods. Nevertheless, I think that you will regret this action."

"I won't leave!" I find myself saying loudly, the onion adding a dim overcast of pathos to this announcement. "Don't you understand that? I'll never, never leave!"

"Oh yes, you will," the Bishop says. "You most certainly will leave, Luther; you'll leave any time we choose to make you go and that time simply hasn't come yet. If necessary we'll just go ahead and excavate the premises without your removal. Eminent domain."

"Monstrous!" I shouted, "you're all monstrous!"

"That's a matter of opinion, Luther. I'm afraid that you don't understand the situation, still. The church property has been sold. There's no point in your talking to me at all, Luther. I have nothing to do with this now."

"Then why do you say *we?*"

"Well," the Bishop says quietly, "we do retain a small interest in the forthcoming construction, of course. Just the seller's edge so to speak; it isn't a controlling amount. But it's enough, Luther, it's quite enough and now I really must get about my little tasks," and laughs grimly and hangs up the phone with a clatter which reverberates in my ear some seventy miles to the east in a way to make the very spurs and bones tremble most lively. I find that I am clenching and unclenching my palms, which means that the onion has made quite a mess not only on my hands but on the couch, and in fear and fury I throw the noxious vegetable viciously out of an open window and see it bounce in the late Harold's garden. I then get to my feet and begin to pace, mumbling; I do not know precisely what is on my mind, but whatever it is it does not seem to forecast immediate solution, and I note with the ironic detachment of the distant observer that the very Lutheran frame seems to have come undone; it is trembling most alarmingly at the sprockets and in various crevices. Mrs. Lee enters and notes all of this with some interest; she is wearing a brassiere and panties which show the well-known expanse of her flesh to some advantage, and she comes up behind the distrait object or subject and puts her arms around his stomach, squeezes gently. "You were on the telephone before," she said. "Who with?"

"How do you know?"

"Oh, I wasn't listening in, silly. I'm not that kind of person. It was just that I wanted to make a phone call of my own to someone and I had to wait until you were finished. We should have gotten two numbers but Harold always objected, may his soul rest. Who was that man you were talking with, Luther? I just listened in for a second before I put the receiver right down." She drops a palm to my groin, inverts it, cups and massages my genitals which wearily spring to response and almost without my knowledge begin to quiver.

"Oh, no one really," I say, "just the Bishop."

"Bishop? Oh, I understand, you mean a Roman Catholic Bishop, not a chess piece or a movie actor. That's right. Is something wrong with your priest, that Father Hilarity?"

"Hilarion."

"I mean Hilarion," she says, and opens my zipper, puts a nimble hand in, takes out the wad of my cock and begins to prod it absently. "I *said* Hilarion; really, Luther, you've got to stop being so edgy. We could have a very nice afternoon if you would just relax and stop behaving as if things were abnormal. I'm *interested* in you, but if you don't want to talk—"

"Hilarion went away," I said, "he disappeared. They're closing down the Church. They sold it for a development."

"Oh really," she says in a little girl's voice, running her forefinger over the tip of my penis, which oozes somewhat for her, although above the waist I seem anesthetized; there is absolutely no situation comparable to this in my difficult history, "well, isn't that interesting? Of course the Church is something of an anachronism as you know, and I guess it's hard to keep it going in those difficult sections. Do you like this?" she says and parts my pants fully, drops them with my underpants to a bunch around my knees and then flexes her thighs, gathers me within them and begins skillfully to move up and down against me while she works on my genitals two-handed. "I thought this is something you might like."

"Oh, it's all right," I say. There really is no proper response and so I do then what I must do, what is required in the circumstances: I turn and put my body against hers (fortunately she releases her genitalic grasp as I am doing this, otherwise I might have been garroted in a very unusual fashion) and put my hands on the panes of her back which feel like window shutters, part her brassiere and then press her against me in a rather precarious grip which is not abetted by the groping hold her ankles and calves retain behind my legs. "Do you like that?" she says. "Is this what you were dreaming of doing, Luther? Go on, go on, you can do anything that you like. I know that Harold would have wanted me to come back to myself just as soon as possible after the terrible tragedy and I know that if he were able to see what was going on now he would approve. He was almost impotent for five years, you know."

"Oh," I say, without much interest. Harold's impotence seems to be at a particularly great range from me now because in truth I am tangling with my own, coming during this last speech of hers to the astonished realization that things are not quite working as they should be: that to the contrary, my sportive genitalia have gone quite suddenly and completely limp as I turned to face her. Now I seem to be thrusting against her thighs and belly nothing but a large rag of some dimension and uselessness which flops irregularly as it mimics the gestures of copulation. I search for her lips; she provides them indolently. I drop my hands to her breasts and cup them with some force, then apply pressure, hoping that I can drive myself into some kind of connection through the very pain I am bringing the breasts, but a warning tap from her finger on my elbow indicates that this is not to be continued, and I drop them, return to more standard procedures. We groan our way to the couch, mumbling and shaking our heads, collapse on it, huddle together, and as I crouch over her she removes my shirt, I kick off my pants; I then fall atop her and attempt to copulate, but in no more than three fast pumps I know that it is quite hopeless. It seems that I have been rendered impotent by certain atmospheric phenomena, or maybe it is only the events of the last fortnight, it is hard to say, and for all the difference that it makes, it might as well be sonic disturbances from the moon.

It has never happened to me before—not, at least, since I reached the age of sexual reason some quarter-of-a-century ago, and for years I had found myself thinking idly about impotence, wondering what drove men into it and how, in particular, they dealt with it when it developed. Did they apologize? Ignore it? Subvert it? Plead fatigue? Or did they merely show the emblem of their loss to making their shame prideful, turning, with an easy laugh, the conversation and activities to other matters? I have thought of this, as I say, in a rather idle manner, never expecting it to have any application or relevance to the producer of those thoughts, but now all of this dim speculation seems to have finally come to some use; as I bang and thrust against the ample and cooperative Mrs. Lee it occurs to me with the kind of dread certainty with which nausea turns into the heaves that I am not going to be able to reach a climax. Not today, certainly not today, and now something interesting happens to me: that which I have previously desired becomes repulsive; that which I have looked upon (to quote from Scripture) with lust now becomes as rotten to me as the core of the doomed apple, and I spin from her, gasping (quite taken by the sensations, but not in any pleasant way), and reel over to the far corner of the room where I stand against the wall for a moment, trying to regain control of myself. It has all been quite harrowing, there is no question about this, even though, at this extremity, my native courtesy still demands that I try to put the best front on things.

"A little indigestion," I say, "a spot of salmon, perhaps that I had on the road," and then, with talk of indigestion, comes back to me for the first time in days the true odor and aroma of the *Fiend's* coffee, the way it felt settling heavily against my esophagus as I performed the act of remission upon the damned Harold, and at that moment, only at that moment, *at that moment, ladies and gentlemen,* (consider if you will how long your respondent had taken to have this kind of response! Surely his forbearance, to say nothing of his will, is to be commended!) I feel myself go out of control. "A bathroom," I gasp, "or perhaps a sink," and without waiting for response dart toward the door of the Westchester living room in search of a Westchester comfort station turning right in a black bolt at the kitchen, I open what I took to be an entry door into a Westchester bathroom and vomit a pure stream of Lutherian essence into one of the largest and dankest service closets in all of Rye, New York. Oh the sturm! the drang! the pity and terror of it! as I douse one of the late Harold's warm overcoats with my deepest comments upon the nature of his destiny, the anxious hands of Mrs. Lee upon my shoulders barely felt, the anxious Lee knee pressed against my vitals unnecessary in this extremity—and now I have a confession: yes, Luther too has a confession (having not confessed enough already it seems); Luther has something to say if he may take the podium for a moment, ladies and gentlemen. He is taking the stand now: hear Luther as he comes weaving and staggering to his modest lectern (dyed a rich olive brown through atmospheric changes and careful polishing by the staff); here is Luther's confession, yes, yes, so be it! I put into the act of vomiting all of the misplaced energy which should have been mine in sex, and never was orgasm so violent, never was love so consuming, never was penetration so satisfying as that purest load of *Fiend*-colored bile which I put into the service closet on that warm Monday afternoon. Pity me certainly, gentlemen! But consider also the nature of your own satisfactions, the sense of your own coupling: of all those myriad twitchings and groans which you know as love, how many have truly moved you? And if in some you could be engaged by an experience which would make you heave your load, whatever it might be, from the deepest part of you, would you derogate it because it came from the stomach rather than the prostate? And to what consequence, gentlemen, to what consequence? Love can be known—I can tell you this from the heart—in a service closet in Westchester no less meaningfully than in that county's large and ill-lighted bedrooms shuddering with flies and heat on a long Sunday afternoon.

XV

Granting that the preceding has been an epiphany, life, nevertheless, must go on. My next recollection is of the hands of Mrs. Lee, weaving their rather indolent and wonderful way across my supine form; her voice humming; the Lee arms flickering as she brings me back to consciousness with the aid of small droplets of water which she takes and sprinkles generously on me from a bowl. I groan variously and open my eyes, flicker back into a kind of focus; she looks at me with a strange, full glance (her eyes not so much full of tears as something else) and says, "Luther, are you better now? Luther, I was worried about you; Luther, do you think you're going to be all right? I was so concerned."

"I think so," I say. "I'm really truly sorry—"

"Don't be sorry, don't be sorry," she says, and I see that she has once again donned what I have called the dressing-gown-with-flowers, the flowers seemingly in a post-pollinative state now, with more of a profusion of insects. I was wrong, it is a different gown, with more of a beetle- than floral-motif although the garden in which it takes place appears to be the same. "Don't be sorry, Luther. I want to apologize; I've had no understanding. You've been under such a terrible strain for these past couple of weeks and I never thought of *you*, never thought of what you must have been through and how you must feel. I was terribly selfish, Luther, and I won't be that way again. I'm getting back to myself now and I'm really a very considerate person. No, Luther, don't move, don't even *think* of moving, just get some more blood into your head," she says, rubbing her hands over that abused organ with a certain proficiency. "Just rest, Luther, just rest, come back to yourself; I need you, Luther, really I do, it's just that we've been so broken up about poor Harold that I haven't been able to think, but I'm really quite considerate. Are you better, Luther? Are you feeling any better now? Don't talk, that's not necessary, just nod your head up or down."

"I'm all right," I say, rather astounded by this outpouring of concern, but discomfited as well; from the little I have been able to learn of the ethos of Westchester over the past couple of decades, vomiting into the closet of the hostess is not the best or most venturesome way to extend a relationship, "really, I'm feeling much better, in fact—"

"Don't talk, Luther. I told you not to talk. Just nod your head. It's important that you rest now, you poor broken thing, rest and try to come back to yourself. Would you like a drink?"

"No," I say, "really I don't need a drink, in fact I'm feeling so much better now," I say reaching for her, feeling the amplitude of her arms through the housedress with my suddenly re-sensitized palms, "in fact, I'm feeling so much better, Mrs. Lee, that what I'd like to do is—"

"Oh, no, *no*," she says with a rather roguish wink, disengaging herself and moving at sufficient distance to take a large wet towel from behind her and wipe my dry brow, "oh no, Luther, I'm glad that you're feeling so much better and perhaps there'll be plenty of time for that later, but right now all I want you to do is to recover your strength and rest and come back to yourself. I pushed you too hard—"

"Oh no," I say, "no, no, no, *you're* the one who doesn't understand," and sit only slightly lightheaded on the couch, feeling a slight division in my pants which is caused by the largest erection I have had in my thirty-five years of sexual existence: a monstrous, glowing erection which sends small flickers into the disparate halves and causes me to quite moan as I reach for her, "no, you don't understand, Mrs. Lee; what's happened—"

"Don't try to do too much, Luther, you're still convalescing," she says dryly, and with a skillfully proficient gesture grasps my erection and with a squeezing gesture Does Something To It (I am sorry that I cannot be more specific, or perhaps the word is "medical," about this, but I am turning out these notes under increasingly great pressure; the pace of events is accelerating, to say nothing of the decomposition of that modest individual, your correspondent) which causes it to go down, clawing in agony, inside my clothing. I feel for a moment that it has virtually vanished within my body, but a quick, frantic clasp at the spot where last seen reassures me that the genitals are basically intact if somewhat worried. "I'm sorry about that, Luther," she says, "that was something I had to do with Harold every so often when he began to get ridiculous, which he often did on weekends, poor man. I hated to do that to you, but really, Luther, there is no time. Don't worry, everything comes back to normal in about two days."

"Two days?"

"It was always two days for Harold but probably it'll be less for you, you're so much more vigorous. I had a roommate in college who was in the School of Nursing and she taught this to all of us at the sorority. You'd be surprised how handy it would come in, Luther; boys would simply drive you crazy. Of course it isn't the kind of thing that I like to do anymore."

"Oh," I say, "I'm delighted to hear that."

"Oh, stop that, there's no need for you to act injured and innocent with me," she says, and abandoning her efforts at being a Sister of Mercy, goes to the orange chair in the corner and puts her face in her hands, "not after I just lost my husband and after everything that *you* had to do with it. You made me a widow, Luther, and don't you ever forget that."

"Oh, Lord," I say, sitting up again and staggering, this time feetward, to establish a tottering relationship with the floor. In the next seconds I go rapidly through all of the gestures which are otherwise associated with long convalescence: weakness succeeded by despair, and then growing strength, assurance, and finally a kind of winsome and petulant manner as reestablishing my stride I go over to her and pat her on the cheek, saying, "I really do think that I'm going to go now. Enough is enough."

"Go now," she says, "are you crazy, Luther? Of course you're not going to go now, you're going to meet Mrs. Wilson. You knew perfectly well that you were going to see Mrs. Wilson today. What kind of courtesy are you showing? If you don't have any manners—"

"I don't know, Mrs. Lee," I say, "I don't know what's going on."

"Wanda," she says automatically. Now she is no longer crying; instead she is sitting alertly on the chair, palms flatly to the knees, looking at me with a piercing and winning gaze. "Always Wanda to you. And we really shouldn't fight so much, Luther, not after what we've shared together and what we can offer one another. Mrs. Wilson is a friend of mine and I want the two of you to meet. I'm sure that I told you she was coming over at three this afternoon. I don't know how it could have slipped my mind. I'm always so organized. Anyway, she's coming over at three to meet you, and it's five of now, and you were passed out on that couch for nearly an hour, so don't blame *me*. Don't blame *me* for your moods. But I really think you'll like her, she's a very nice person. My closet friend. I think that the two of you should meet."

"I don't want to meet her," I say. "Can't you understand, I don't want to meet anyone? My whole life has changed—"

"Oh, don't be embarrassed about that," she says, running her hands over the print of her dress, bringing some of the beetles to alertness and stinging life as she folds creases carefully. "I know all about your past life, Luther; didn't I discuss all that the first time we met? Whatever you did in the past is all over. I'm quite sure that you never met her, but even if you did it wouldn't change my feelings about you. I can't be jealous over something that happened in the past, can I?"

"You're missing the point," I say, but actually I am not so sure that she has missed the point as that I have missed the entire thread. Things seem to have lurched entirely out of control, I should say out of any intellectual grasp whatsoever, and I feel that there is only one act left to me which would unite the situation and my role in a satisfactory way. I storm toward the door, and it is possible that I would actually open it and exit therefrom into a new and wonderful life (although I have not the faintest idea where I would go or what I would do; my career in the ministry, I suspect, is quite wrecked, and as for the other business, a certain charm has gone out of it since I met Mrs. Lee) but instead the bell rings and, fluttering demonically, Mrs. Lee goes to answer it. She brushes me out of the way as if I were one of simple Harold's portfolios and admits through the door a woman who seems to be a strange copy of her, except that this woman has a rich chestnut complexion in all the places where Wanda is white, and her sweater, coming alarmingly around an otherwise unclothed upper section, reveals an expanse of breast that from all physical evidence would seem to be all nipple. I wish that I could say that this excited me, but detumescence seems to be the new Key to the Day; my prick stirs uneasily within its cove and is then silent. *That's it, Jack, I quit*, it seems to whisper to me, and indeed how can it be blamed? For thirty years it has served me beautifully; how have I served it? What have I ever put back to it one-tenth so precious as what it provided?

"Luther, this is Verna," Mrs. Lee says, "Verna Wilson, my dearest friend. I did so much want to get the two of you together. Let me just rush into the kitchen and see if everything is all prepared. We'll have some tea, or would you like a drink, Luther? Pardon me I'll just be a second," and she leaves us in a sweeping glide which in its sheer efficiency and dramatic removal well rivals her detumescing grasp of a few moments ago. Doors slam somewhere in the intestines of the house, a rush of water spews. "Sit down," Mrs. Wilson says. "So you're Luther."

"Yes," I say. She is really quite a striking woman, although there is something about the flatness of her belly, thrust of breasts, tilt of jaw, line of mouth, which is quite threatening. I can see how certain men in certain situations might become afraid of women like these. "Not that that means anything," I say in a pitiful attempt at what I take to be defiance. "And if you don't like it that's too bad," I add in a siege of insanity, "take it or leave it."

"Take it or leave it," she says, getting on the couch and with an imperious thrust motioning me to sit in the chair which, unwillingly, I do; it has a faint oozing warmth from Mrs. Lee's thighs and buttocks, although not quite of such a quality that I would like to be immersed in it forever. "Well, she said you were rather foolish and to tell you the truth that's what I gather from all my friends. That you're a foolish, foolish man. But I frankly don't believe a word of it because I have a feeling, Luther, that you have resource."

"Resource?"

"Resource! Quality! A hard inner surface which belies this outer stupidity and incompetence. In any event, Wanda has never steered me wrong and this would be the poorest time for her to do so. Look, boy," she says, leaning forward and looking at me with a faint merry appraising light glowing deep in her rich eyes the color of her complexion. "As you see, I'm a woman of very few words. I try to come straight to the point. I hope you appreciate that. Now, what I want you to do is the same thing for me as what you did for Wanda and I'll pay you well."

"Excuse me?"

"Oh, come on," she says and leans back, smoothes her knees in a gesture very close to that of Mrs. Lee except that she seems to be right into the crevices of the skin itself and not nearly so interested in artifice. "We really don't have any time, boy! No time, no time! The whole world is crumbling underneath us, our children are biding their time and plan to eat us alive; there really must be something under the *manneria commedia*. You did a beautiful job for Wanda, clean and discreet and high time too, and now I want you to do the same thing for me. I want you to kill my husband. I'd do it myself, you see, but it would be impossible for me to get past all the security and the guards and so on and go into his office and do it without there being too many witnesses. He's a bank president and they've had a lot of robberies there recently so now even relatives have to sign in and so on. It's not that I don't have the courage. I know that that was Wanda's problem but it isn't mine. It's just security."

"I guess you have the courage," I say.

"Of course I have the courage," she says, "I'll even pay you for your services; that's something which I feel I should do. I'm a woman who tries to meet all of her obligations and be responsible. I'll give you five thousand dollars when the double-indemnity comes in. How's that for generosity?"

"I don't think you understand," I say. "I'm really not a murderer. I did this thing for Wanda for very special reasons but I didn't think—"

"Nonsense!" she bellows and hits her knee a ringing slap which makes mine tremble at the consideration of what the impact might have done. "If you do it once, you can do it a thousand times. Once a murderer, always a fiend. Come on, be reasonable. I don't even have to discuss this with you, you know, but I'm being courteous and giving you the benefit of the doubt. But you're definitely going to do it. Wanda says you do excellent work. Besides, I can't stand him anymore, I've paid all my dues. The hell with him."

Mrs. Lee enters from the side door carrying a tray of cookies and humming a little song, drops the cookies on the table before me, says that she hopes that we are getting along nicely together just as she would want two good friends to do and goes through the doors. Mrs. Wilson follows her with a meditative look saying something about how the bitch has been impossible since she got her options re-opened and then turns back to me with an expression subtly heightened and refined, a cold arch of one eyebrow quite thrilling me (I have had a very painful and disruptive afternoon, my emotional barriers are quite destroyed) and takes a cookie to eat meditatively. "Come on, Luther," she says, "take one, they're perfectly good, and anyway I don't have too much time to waste."

"Thank you," I say, much as if she has provided the cookies (well, then, perhaps she has) and take a fine chocolate construction, all brittle and well-molded to the sight but turning out to have a rather limpid ooze between the teeth. "I don't think that I can do it," I say, feeling in a haze of chocolate that it might be possible to come to some kind of understanding with Mrs. Wilson.

"Don't be ridiculous," she says, "we've settled all that already. Wanda has said some very good things about you. I want you to know that she's very pleased with your work. Don't worry about what she says to you; she's a difficult woman and gives praise grudgingly."

"How would I do it?" I say. "In the first place, it's impossible. You talk about the security—"

She leans back and laughs richly, looking at me through narrowing eyes, and says, "Luther, that's *your* problem. Five thousand dollars is a very generous settlement; you don't think that I'd do this kind of thing for nothing, do you? Use some ingenuity!"

"The security—"

"The security should be no problem for a man of your gifts," Mrs. Wilson says and takes another cookie, flipping it into her mouth back-handedly and looking at me with an odd kind of concentration. "You'll be able to figure that all out. Now, I don't have time to waste, I have an appointment with my ear specialist downtown. You could be a most attractive man, you know, if you combed your hair in a different way and got rid of that mustache. That mustache does you no good at all, it takes away all dignity."

"It does not," I say rather angrily, "the mustache lends me balance, a certain flair—"

"It also makes you too conspicuous and like an eighteen-year-old boy trying to be mature," she says. "Well, that's neither here nor there, Luther, I don't have the time to give grooming advice to you." She opens her handbag, removes a small card on which a large amount of data has been neatly written in small green ink and hands it to me. "This is all the information you'll need. On the front is his name and business address and so on and on the back are some suggestions. I think that you should do it tomorrow, Luther, or by the very latest Wednesday; after Wednesday new premiums are due on one of the minor policies and we might get into a question of lapsing. I have no intention of paying out that money if it won't be necessary."

I take the card from her, it has a cold ingratiating slickness in my palm and put it, without reading, into my upper coat pocket. "I think you've got me wrong," I say, "I'm not really a mass-murderer."

"Oh, Luther," says Mrs. Lee, re-entering through one of the doors, "Luther, don't always act so *suspicious*. I didn't tell Mrs. Wilson that you were anything of the kind; in fact I happen to think that you're a very nice man. It's just that I'm so *proud* of what you were able to do for me that I wanted you to help one of my friends. Is everything settled? I knew that the two of you would get along so well together. Any cookies, anyone? I have lots more."

"No, thank you, Wanda," Mrs. Wilson says, standing to her full height which is perhaps five-feet-eight in heels and a very imposing woman she is too—although the darkness of her complexion takes on the aspect of illness in some sudden tricks of light and her mouth is a bit elongated. "I have to keep an appointment now. I do hope that you'll do it tomorrow," she says to me, "the sooner the better I think. And also he's been so unhappy lately, the earlier he's out of his misery the more of a favor you'd do him. Give me a call when you're finished, please— you'll find my phone number right on the back of the card along with the other information *and don't lose that card*—and we'll arrange to get together if you want. Actually, I think it would be better though if we don't have any contact; I'll get your address from Wanda and just mail you a check as soon as the settlement comes. Don't get impatient though, these insurance companies can take months to settle, even on a silly double-indemnity that's open and shut." She goes to the door, bestows upon the two of us a sharp farewell nod and goes out into the street, showering us momentarily with the light of day which quite jumbles my features and makes me start. Finding my feet with difficulty, I begin to pace the floor quite restlessly, the card jabbing an edge into my thigh from the jacket pocket in which it has taken refuge.

"She's a lovely person, isn't she? I'm so glad that you could get together. Is everything worked out now?" Wanda asks and takes me gently by an elbow, leads me to the door. "I'm so glad that you were able to work things out, she's a nice lady and she has the most terrible marriage, it isn't fair. I do wish that you could stay longer but Katherine will be coming home again and I have all kinds of silly appointments to keep so we'll have to do it later, maybe next week. She's kind of forceful, isn't she? She gets right straight to the point. I wish that I could talk like her but some-

how they taught me when I was young that it wasn't ladylike and I missed
out on the whole thing. Come on, Luther," she says, taking my elbow
and guiding me.

Her touch, for some reason, quite incites me, my demoniac erection,
despite her medical recommendations, re-asserted and I turn toward her,
putting my hands on her shoulders, feeling veritable surges of excitement
seeming to illumine me and I put my hand on her buttocks, my cheek
against hers and, feeling stripped of rhetoric for the moment (perhaps for
all time although I should doubt it), find myself only saying, "Sex. Sex.
I want sex."

"Oh, come now," she says with a giggle and escorts me toward the
door, "come now, you really must go."

"I want sex."

"Oh, no you don't, Luther," she says with a clear, terrible peal of mer-
riment as she opens the door and thrusts me out into the sun. "Oh, no
you don't. In the first place you only think you do, you wouldn't be able
to function—"

"Yes, I could. Yes, I could."

"And in the second place," she says, expelling me with a moan, causing me to fairly stumble down the driveway, "in the second place, you're
not really interested in sex, you never were. It was something else and
now you've got it. You know perfectly well that sex was only a substi-
tute for something else. Don't be ridiculous, Luther, don't you know what
you are by now?"

And slams the door and bolts it behind her. I am standing on the pavement, I am moving toward the Continental, I am inside the Continental, sounds of machinery down the street, steering wheel hot in my hands,
Mrs. Wilson's card a needlepoint of sensation sticking me in my thigh as
I start the car and wend my way westward, toward the New England
thruway and home. I do not know what I am quite yet, but Mrs. Lee
might take pleasure in the knowledge that I concede I am getting close.

XVI

So I commence my career as a fiend.

When I return to the rectory I see a few discouraged-looking workmen
playing wearily with surveyor's rule and tape measure; a guard in brown
costume stands in front of the main entrance twitching his old hands in
fugue or St. Vitus dance and playing with a large misshapen pipe. It is
evident that the Bishop has taken what he feels to be strong and determined action but at an understanding of how pitiful are the forces
which he is able to unleash, a smile of the purest wickedness crosses my

handsome face (I am really rather an ungenerous man and recent events have tended to make me even colder) and I park the car two or three blocks away in front of a liquor store and wander back on foot. It is a matter of the greatest simplicity and ease to achieve entrance into Hilarion's study through a foothold on the small shrubs outside his office in the rear and once within I find that the premises themselves are undisturbed (as well they might be considering the security precautions I have taken). I go into my own quarters and remove Mrs. Wilson's card from my pocket.

Now that I have decided to help Mrs. Wilson—for I have so decided for reasons that might as well remain obscure; she *is* a most imposing woman—it would seem that the best way would be the quickest and so I regard the card with almost fervid interest trying to extract from it not only the details of the pre-decedent's station but information as to his disposition. Harold (yes, Harold) is indeed the president of a large downtown bank specializing in loans to charitable institutions (I am familiar with it; Hilarion petitioned them unsuccessfully half a decade ago. Already I have motive, aha!), he is five-feet-seven-and-a-half inches in height, weighs one hundred and sixty-three pounds and is distinguished by the constant use of sunglasses and an exceedingly trim waist—which said waist he achieved by the constant use of an exercise machine. He naps in his office between eleven and eleven-thirty in the mornings and then drinks heavily until two in the afternoon. Having achieved the presidency of this important bank at the minimal age of thirty-eight he is reacting perhaps to both pressure and guilt. All of this information and more Mrs. Wilson has been able to squeeze onto this one small card and the triumph of cursive script is abetted by the facility and spareness of her rhetoric; she has not only provided information about the pre-decedent but has as well made a certain opinion manifest as clear in the final line of her jottings which is, *get rid of him for God's sake I can't stand it anymore!* This touching plea, the first visible evidence of emotion I have ever gained from Mrs. Wilson, moves me into an excess of determination. I decide that I will not fail her. What has been put before me I did not ask for but if the cup will not pass, etc. I come to understand in those brief moments in my quarters that Mrs. Lee has been more accurate about me than ever she could know; it was not sex, after all, that I was pursuing during all of my sunny afternoons in Scarsdale but was indeed something else, something dimly perceived as if behind a thin wall, something whose lurking reality would only touch me at odd moments … such as during or shortly after my conversations with Hilarion. While embracing my housewives I was embracing something else, something softer and yet more resilient than ever they could be and I know at this moment that if I thought about it, tried to understand what I really wanted, I could know ... but I do not know, not yet. There will be time enough for this later. Right now, I have decided to become a fiend, and Fiendship is an occupation whose demands cannot be tossed off lightly.

I wander humming through the rectory, slamming doors and touching objects—mild obsessive-compulsion but controlled well within the outer ranges—and when I come to Hilarion's modest bedroom I know what I am looking for; I open his wardrobe door and finding it therein remove it. Hilarion's clothes are there, an armory of clerical and sports garb which now in his absence brings back to me warm and poignant memories of the man: his little foibles, his little traits, the rather endearing odor which would trail delicately from him on hot days in the summer. I go into the bathroom with the priest's garb and for the first time in my life don the vestments of the faith, admiring myself then from many angles. I look properly priestly. There is no question about this.

I am so moved by my appearance in fact that I wander into the church itself, turn on all the lights and electrify the organ and therein, while I pick out small liturgies on the keys (without vibrato) I conduct a high requiem mass. It is the first service I have ever conducted and I am properly pleased with myself; almost without knowing, the ascents and elements of liturgy have infiltrated their way into my subconscious and it is a most satisfactory service I conduct; I chant the offertory and I chant the resolution, I chant the *Agnus* and I chant the *Dei*; my voice takes on the full groaning tones which had been Hilarion's specialty and when the service is finally over—having taken an hour or more—I sit at the organ, my fingers hanging loosely on the keys, quite touched, even taken by myself, my capacity, my history, my potential, my memory. There is no question but that the priestly is another calling which I have missed but this loss disturbs me less than some of the others; I can, after all, reconstitute liturgy as I never could electrical wiring. I turn the vibrato up to full and pick out with one finger all of the famous tunes of the fifties which inspired me and which I have loved: *Blue Suede Shoes* and *Delicado* and *Heartbreak Hotel* and *Crying in the Chapel* and then I curl myself into the smallest of fetal balls and soothe myself to sleep over the still-humming organ, the wickering and whine of the motor carrying me further out into a kind of consummation of which I have never dreamed, and that is the way I sleep the rest of the day and the night through. I have not been sleeping well during this period and there is a lot of sleep to catch up with. Besides, there is really very little to do until the morning and I suspect that the sleep I am getting is likely to be the last of its type that I will get for a long, long time.

Who has ever known the comfort of sleep as I did that night? The lush-

ness of dreams, the silvery filaments of recollection as, winding tighter
and tighter around me, they carry me out to some dim and unknown
shore where the birds still congregate in the first flames of sunlight, the
whisper of fish in the distance as they inspect with mindless interest that
most secret of all our origins.

XVII

In the morning, I return to the *Fiend*. Somehow, it has become tied up
with my enterprise; I feel incapable of killing satisfactorily without the
hot rancid fire of their coffee neatly complementing the outer disturbances. The decor has been slightly changed over the past couple of
weeks, the prevailing mode now somehow less nautical than scientific.
In place of the embalmed sailor hangs a replica of a crippled spaceship,
spinning wildly in orbit, *Us International* brushed in red over its silvery
dented surfaces. From the mock windows the face of a trapped astronaut
appears to peer wildly. Underneath, the coffee urns and menus have sim-
ilarly been decorated with emblems of the Age of Space; I gather that the
Fiend, no less than the rest of us, is celebrating the successful return of
a trio of mechanics whose craft broke down into sections while on the
latest investigation of the Moon. It is very thoughtful of the *Fiend* to celebrate American technology, courage, and unselfishness in this way and
I feel that I can do no less than they for the cause of spatial exploration;
accordingly I order from the menu two space station doughnuts (shaped
I am told like orbiting capsules) and a glass of that very synthetic juice
which was carried along to the Moon by the mechanics on this latest disastrous mission. The doughnuts land within me heavily, dangerously and
begin to churn like a capsule filtering out of orbit; the juice inspires me
into high golden belches which seem to vault me to a new perspective.
All that remains is the necessity to have a pint of the *Fiend's* very own
coffee which I drink with appreciation, feeling the muddling effects as it
moves shallowly within me, reflecting that the *Fiend's* coffee is so perfect an accompaniment to murder that I would tell the manager himself
if there were a manager in sight and if this temperate endorsement
would be guaranteed to assist their business. I do not think, however, that
the *Fiend* can make a case for its services on that basis; too, how would
the manager take the news? "The murdering priest says that our coffee
is the best?" There is no way in which certain endorsements can be put
to work.

It is a strange experience wearing priestly garb in public; it has been,
in all ways, a strange morning. I begin to understand how the very nature of the vestments could create a long, subtle psychosis which would

lead to polarization and dissociative facts; certainly Hilarion's abrupt resignation from the world and its goods becomes explicable in terms of the
experiences of the morning. On the street I have been looked at more and
with greater intensity than I have ever known in my life; while it remains
true that the majority of pedestrians in this city are oblivious to all but
their own neurasthenia the fact is that one out of every four or five has
favored me with long sidewise looks; some of the looks have been surprisingly hostile, others filled with loathing, a satisfying proportion have
been admiring and one or two (although, alas, from young men) have
been outrightly sensual—mouths open and dilating, fists twitching, it
seemed that they wanted to touch the priestly garbs themselves to draw
power from it or perhaps the reverse and as I proceeded on my new and
stately way, taking the subway into Manhattan, a strange and insane
benevolence began to fill my person. I could feel a smile of sheer madness beginning to filter its way across my benign features and my hands
seemed to acquire a strange sensitivity as if they were cupping the brows
of penitents; in the subway I found myself enjambed against a large sweating woman who wiped fluid from her arms and, turning to me, said that
she thanked me for the wonderful work that I had done, there were too
few like me in the world and she wanted me to know, on behalf of everyone, that we were appreciated. "But you don't understand, madam," the
Murdering Priest said in a tender lisp (not wanting to give any indication of my identity I had shaved my mustache in the morning and reminded myself that I had a palate difficulty to alter my speech), "you
don't underthtand, I have been in a monathtery for thome theventeen
yearth and have only taken thith thpecial trip out on religiouth
buthineth." "Oh, that's perfectly all right," she said, "all of the good men
are in monasteries anyway and the important thing is that you're here.
Do you know I've never spoken to a priest in my whole life? I've always
wanted, wanted so terribly much to do so but I wasn't born of that faith
and I've found them so forbidding, but it's just a wonderful thing that
we're sitting next to each other on the subway this morning and I want
you to know that I appreciate your work."

"No thankth netherthary, madam," the Murdering Priest said quietly
but the woman had apparently been overcome by my charm—or only
the faint Hilarion-odor which came dimly from the robes like the flut-
ter of distant birds—and seizing my left wrist in a fierce clumsy grasp she
kissed my hand and then fled at the Jay Street station before I had a
chance to properly come to terms with this gesture in the only way I could
have seen fit which might have been to strike her a heavy blow. The other
passengers in the car looked at me with curiosity and longing and I came
to understand that they did not think the woman to be insane nor the

Murdering Priest to be at all strange in his actions; to the contrary, the tableau had moved them and I distinctly sensed weeping in the car to say nothing of moans and murmurs. Is this what Hilarion had to put up with? The car rocked through the tunnel without further incident and I fled at the first stop in Manhattan—which happens to be the very one above which nestles the offices of the large bank in which Harold Wilson (that second and most doomed of the Harold Wilsons) arranges the financial affairs of his dependents—then up two blocks and over three for some of the *Fiend*'s very own and here I sit, gathering strength. I have decided to go into the bank at 9:45, a proper hour it would seem to me, to arrange a loan or confer death. I have done the best I can in once again securing the Church but as I fled down the street, the keys in my hand, I heard the sound of workmen (or maybe it was the Bishop and Monsignor) cackling and I am not sure that things will be intact when I return home. On the other hand, I realize that this kind of thing cannot go on forever. My living situation, strictly speaking, has not been quite tenable since Hilarion left and is now rocking into disorder.

I arise from the seat bumpily (I have taken the services of one of the *Fiend*'s tables, located near the rear of the establishment and toward the kitchen; a wonderful sequence of odors assault me every time the door is opened and also I have an excellent view of decor and customers) and take the check in my hand, having decided that there is really no point in further delay and, in any event, a penny of time saved would be an hour of time earned. (Also and I might as well come straight to the point in these notes: I know that my time in this role may well be limited and I certainly would find no advantage in being other than strictly truthful.... It is a pleasure at last to be truthful: I can recommend the truth highly; I am rather looking forward to the prospect of murder. Murder is unquestionably a light narcotic, neither as interesting nor as binding as cigarettes but possessing, if you will, a certain baroque charm of its own. Who is not to say that it is any less sacramental, any less an act of grace than a caress?) As I move toward the counter with a certain familiar clumsiness of gait to pay the bill, I am intercepted by a rather large and beautifully constructed girl of twenty-five or so, wearing clothes of a rather alarming cut and pulchritude. (Dress like a priest and think like a priest. Huddled within these thick dank robes and their darkness I can understand how priestly celibacy would be easy to carry off, even for the young, and always with a certain flair). Her breasts jiggle, her arms tremble, her eyes widen, her nose dilates and she retains me in the walkway to the cash register with an alarming embrace of much force, I can feel her virtually squeezing the reverential breath out of me and then her arms part and she leans against me, her warmth steaming through the thin layers of her dress. (But none of this is sexual. My sex drive has vanished. It has something to do with Mrs. Lee and almost everything to do with this damned *costume* which, I believe the Pope blesses before it hangs in any priestly closet.) She says, "Father! Oh, Father."

I almost point out that I am not her father until reason overcomes panic and I understand the situation. "Please," I say, "please, Miss, I'm on my way to a blessing now and—"

"Oh, Father," she says and begins crying, "Father, I know that you're on the way to do wonderful things, you're always doing wonderful things but I had to stop you. I have to take one moment of your time, Father, I can't stand it anymore. Father, I'm so evil, Father, I've sinned so greatly, Father, I want to confess to you! I must make my confession! Is that the way you say it? I'm not a Catholic but I want to learn."

"I'm afraid you don't understand," I say, looking around sidewise in what even a heathen would take as an expression of despair, but no one is coming to help me; indeed, the few customers and personnel of the *Fiend* are leaning over counters and tables regarding us with something midway between interest and pity: is this the kind of thing that goes on in the *Fiend* every day?, "I mean, I'd like to help you my dear but—"

"Then you *must* help me, Father," she says huskily, putting a limpid hand on my wrist and drawing me in nearer; she is really a disconcertingly pretty girl, one of the prettiest of her type I have ever seen (although I do not, normally speaking, make a virtue of women in a lower age or socioeconomic bracket than my familiar lovelies) but a certain strange insane certainty lights her features, seeming to draw them together into a burning knit of concentration and accusation and I wonder if I of all people have come into disconcerting contact with a religious fanatic. "I know all about the Catholic religion, my friends and all tell me that stuff and it says that a priest is always there to hear people and always there to help them and you can talk to a priest anytime about anything, it's kind of sacred. You must talk to me, Father, I can't stand it anymore, I feel like I'm coming apart," and then she puts her head into my stomach, skillfully butts me backward so that I fall gasping into one of the *Fiend's* finest hardwood seats and kneels at my feet and seizes my hands. "I know I can trust you, Father," she says, "you have such a wise and kind face and you look just like the most wonderful sort of priest. Father, I feel like my whole life is coming apart, I have sinned, I have—"

And it is at that point—pretty damned late in life, one of you gentleman in the gallery might suggest, pretty damned late for even Luther but better late, the prophet St. Matthew suggested, better late than never— that I decide that I have had quite enough of this. I stand rapidly and furiously, pulling my garments into position with such ferocity and aplomb that she recoils as if I had struck her, then backs away from me as I move toward her threateningly, a forefinger raised. "Now you listen to me, young lady," I say, "you listen to me and get this perfectly clear ... confessions are finished. There are no more confessions, young lady, I want to hear none of them anymore, not from you, not from penitents, not even from myself. I want to simulate control, simplicity, even if this life is mad and irretrievably out of control I will act as if it is not. It is all over! There will be no confessions! There will be no more vulnerability and misery and questioning! There will be an end to all of this because I will it so and that is the way it must be! My suggestion to you, if you feel your problem is really urgent, is that you take it up with an obstetrical advisor or policeman or perhaps solicit strange men on the street for sexual purposes because I will have none of it. Repudiation! Kindliness! Decency!" I shout at her in tones so loud that the very walls of the *Fiend* seem to shake and, brushing past her, I stride toward the desk and slam my check down before the cashier, demanding to know exactly what I am owed. She looks at it and then up at me and says that as a courtesy of the house and as a matter of long policy due to the policies of the late owner, no charge is ever made to members of the clergy in costume. This blandishment combined with the shocking information that the *Fiend* had or has an owner (it is impossible to believe that an institution of this sort could actually be *planned* by anyone) leaves me quite stunned and the girl coming up behind to tug shyly on my robes and ask me one last time if I will hear her out thrusts me past some final barrier of madness. "No confessions, no confessions!" your correspondent giggles wildly. "None, none, the grave would be better than listening to any of this shit anymore; how much of this do you think someone can take, I've been listening to this crap all my life and it doesn't change a goddamned *thing!*" and with these words the humble undersigned (who even as he transcribes this is still wearing his vestments but more of that presently, at least they are warm) ran full tilt through the door of the *Fiend* (be grateful that the safety glass had been removed by an errant car a couple of weeks ago and had not yet been replaced) and into the streets of lower Broadway from which he made rapid scuttling exit toward the famous Bank of His Choice. Behind him, your correspondent seemed to hear words, sounds, pleas, admissions but none of this interested him anymore; he had a more direct sense of his destiny than could ever be yielded by pedestrians with pointless secrets. Your correspondent ran up Broadway, past Centre and, turning right at Wall, began to recover his aplomb; by the time he had managed Rector (get that) he was almost back to himself and at Church Street he was fully reconstituted. I looked at the bank in which Harold worked, pacing back and forth before it quickly like a

Priest in Search Of a Business Arrangement and then, wiping all thoughts
of the girl, the *Fiend* (but not the *Fiend's* menu) from mind, I walked
briskly into the main entrance and told the first guard I could see that I
had come to take the confession of Harold Wilson.

My plan, as conceived to me some twelve hours ago, seemed perfectly
sane if a little bit mad; I would gain entrance in Hilarion's garb—as I
never could in my own—and proceed with dispatch to accomplish the
necessary, pausing on the way out only to remove the clerical garb and
don a large false beard which I carried in the left rear pocket. Inside the
bank, however, things appeared neither that comfortable nor easy; apparently the imminent reconversion of Harold Wilson necessitated one
phone call or three and I stood there, sweating lightly from the crown
of my scalp to the balls of my feet. Some minutes elapsing, I cursed myself several times for not having had the simple foresight to understand
security. The guard, an old man wearing two guns strapped on opposite
sides of his body, returned presently to say that he had spoken to Mr. Wilson's secretary finally and she had spoken to Mr. Wilson who said that
he didn't really know any priests but if it wasn't a collection I was wel-
come to come up and chat with him. "You're not going around for any
of those Homes, are you?" he asked and I assured him that I was not,
that I was indeed the implacable enemy of whole generations of orphan
boys who had been compelled to maintain their Homes without any help
from this quarter. Then, feeling a marvelous reconstitution of body if not
soul, strode into an elevator and pressed the button to the 23rd floor with
a flourish. The elevator in due time deposited me (being stuck between
the 19th and 20th floors for only two minutes during which time I and
the starter had a soothing conversation dealing with the buildings department in general and the power departments in particular until an errant cable reassembled somewhere and the machine moved me heavenward again with a swoosh) and I came into a large, glassy area, told the
receptionist (a striking double of the *Fiend's* penitent but with a contained
face and very assured eyes) that I was Harold's priest and just a little bit
later the receptionist herself ushered me past an anteroom and into the
office of the president himself from which corner Harold, a small man
with trembling hands regarded me. "This is highly irregular," he said
when the door closed, "I mean I usually don't service requests of this kind
but you got me curious, I must say, and I had a few moments to spare.
You said you were here to take my confession?" He ran a hand over his
spotted tie (fauns and angels gallivanting on a background of musical notation, small coffee stains in the front) and leaned back in his chair, gaz-
ing at the ceiling. I would have taken him for five feet four, not the five

feet seven and a half which his wife had stated but then again Mrs. Wilson had had to put up with quite a bit from the fiend and it was possible that she had genuinely believed him to be larger than he was.

"I'm not really a priest," I say, removing the gun from my pocket and cupping it to be concealed in my right hand as I faced him. Dispatch is once again the order of the day it would seem, the important thing about a satisfying murder (I am already something of a connoisseur) is to get it over with and enjoy the afterglow. "The whole thing was a ruse. In fact, I'm here to kill you." I show him the gun which fairly twinkles under the sickish bankly glare and then put an experimental shell into the ceiling to assure me that it works. (It would be embarrassing if it does not. Only then does it occur to me to hope that the office is soundproofed. It turned out to be.)

He jumps and twitches, removes a large red handkerchief with which he wipes his forehead and says, "Oh, my God. I always knew that it would happen. I always knew that it would end this way. I can't believe you're not a priest."

"I'm not," I say, and lift my robes to show him my underclothing; a gay, multicolored sport shirt and a pair of simple khaki pants, Luther's escape garb. "After I kill you I plan to run downstairs, dropping these robes on the way and then make my escape undetected. I happened to have the clothing around, that's all."

"That bitch. That bitch put you up to it. I know she did."

"Which one?"

"Ah, God," Harold says, "ah, God, I can't stand it anymore. There's really no future in it. The hell with it," he says and makes a mad agile leap over the desk, reaching for my gun, so I shoot him once in the temple and then twice in the heart, polish him off in the stomach for good luck (some vague sense of delicacy makes me unable to aim below the waist) and then watch him as he arches in flight, slams the floor birdlike at my feet and then looks up at me with a strange gaze. "Oh, Father," he says, "Father—"

"I'm not a priest."

"*Father*," he says and uses a ruined wrist to beckon me near. I kneel on the floor next to him since I take this to be something in the Line of a Last Request and I am apt to be all the clergy that the unfortunate Harold will get. "Father, Father," he says and murmurs into my ear, cocking his bleeding head from the floor, "Father, I want to confess. I want to make my confession now, I have sinned grievously—"

"Oh, no," I said, "oh, no, there will be none of that at all," and point the gun again. I do believe that I would shoot him but this act of inconsideration is deemed unnecessary because Harold, like his predecessor, expires at my feet in a moan of blood and I understand that there will be no need for a further confession on this day. His eyes show a strange knowledgeable glaze, they seem to be looking outward or inward at great distance, his body rolls on the floor, in some premature rigor-mortis as I stand, put the gun away and briskly leave by a side door. "He's perfectly all right," I say to his secretary who looks at me without interest, "I didn't take a confession but we had a very useful meeting," and then your faithful old correspondent bolted his way into the corridor, past roomfuls of clattering, chattering secretaries and assistants, out the front door and there to a halted elevator (what daring!) where with enormous *élan vital* he waited, simulating nonchalance until the doors closed on him and two unsuccessful applicants for loans and down the three of us whooshed, suspended in space as the day we were conceived: three petitioners, only one of them successful and at the exit I bade the starter a cheerful goodbye, left by the front door, stopped in the light of full Broadway to remove my vestments which I chucked cheerfully into an ashcan ("I think he's one of those modern priests, he's abandoning the calling," a woman said to her companion) and then, did I ever bolt! Did I run! What clatter of feet, chatter of mad song, twinkle of finger, flash of foot as I hied myself to the nearest kiosk, waited calmly on line until it was time to buy a token and then, dashing past the turnstile, just managing a departing uptown express. In the aisles I hummed, strutted, murmured little songs to myself, an excess of cheer and good feeling so great that it virtually lit up the car with fellowship. And when a blind beggar wheeled his way through I added to his modest gains a sparkling silver quarter of my own, glistening as a teardrop, ruddy as a cleric, feeling his blessing illumine all the walls of my being and racing uptown, how good I felt! How good it was! How simple the world seemed in the aftermath of direct action.

Unhappily I had gone the wrong way and had to turn around at Grand Central to take the train the other way. By that time my mood had much abated and by the time the train passed the stop for the late Harold's bank a sheer film of remorse seemed to cut me off from the rest of the passengers, making the ride far less merry than it might have otherwise been.

Not remorse for the murder (I have been perfectly honest throughout: I have become a fiend). Remorse that I did not take his confession. His was the second confession I had refused that day and by all indications, would have been the more interesting.

XVIII

No one is at the rectory when I return. A lopsided sign saying MEN AT WORK, CONDEMNED PREMISES reminds me that my housing situation is complex but the locks are unjammed and the church a great arena of quiet. I quickly doff my costume, shower briskly and then, stark naked, a cleansed murderer, go to the phone to call Mrs. Wilson. She seems only minimally pleased to hear from me and it takes several seconds before she is even clear who I am.

"Luther?" she says, "Martin Luther?"

"No," I say, "not that one. This is Luther. *Luther.*"

"Luther who?"

"Mrs. Lee's friend," I say desperately. In the background I hear voices, a merry jumble of dishes, singing, shouts and laughter. It all sounds very much like the *Fiend* must on a summer lunch hour although the *Fiend's* customers surely would not greet their food with merry cries.

"Oh," she says, "*that* Luther. Yes? What is it? I can't really talk now, we're having guests over and—"

"I just thought you'd like to know I did it."

"Did what?" she says vaguely. "I'm not quite following you, you've got to be more specific—"

"Harold," I said desperately, "to Harold. I *did* it. Remember?"

"Oh!" she says, "oh! Harold. That business. You did it, did you? Already?"

"You said you wanted it done as soon as possible."

"Oh, did I? That's right, I did. I said that Wednesday would be all right too. So you did it now, right? That means I'll have to miss the party tonight."

"I did it," I say. "Aren't you going to thank me?"

"Oh. Oh, of course. Thank you, Luther. You caught me a little by surprise, I hadn't heard anything from the bank yet and I assumed that they would call me first. Maybe they think he's in meditation or something. Well, that's awfully good of you. Thank you so much."

"What?"

"I said thank you so much, what am I supposed to say, Luther? I thought that our basis was clearly established on this thing yesterday, you'll be taken care of when the insurance comes and not a moment before. I have no money to give you."

"It wasn't money," I say, "I didn't call you about the money."

"Well, you called me to say that you did it, I said thank you very much and really, Luther, I can't talk anymore I have half a hundred ladies here, we're having a social and I just can't spare any more time. I've got to get organized. And now, when they call me to tell me what you did the whole afternoon's going to be ruined. You could have waited a day you know."

"You said—"

"I know what I said but you didn't have to take me so seriously, you could have shown a little initiative, a little common sense and handled the situation with some control. For heaven's sake, Luther, I can't do *everything* for you. I can't talk anymore, I'm sorry. Here come my friends," she says and hangs up, leaving me speaking into miles and miles of disconnected wire which seems to focus into a whirring buzz directly into my ear. I put down the phone and wander into Hilarion's study, looking for some reading matter. The thing is that now that I have decided what my career will be, there seems little else useful to do. Also Mrs. Wilson's lack of appreciation has disconcerted me. I am almost grateful when the phone rings. Although it is impossible, perhaps it will be Mrs. Lee with a different view on the subject.

Instead, however, it is the Bishop who this time makes the call directly. "I see you're still there," he says, "I had hoped you'd be out by now."

"Not quite," I say. "I do have plans."

"Plans are always good," the Bishop says. "The trouble is that too many of us live our lives in an excess of planning. Luther, I'm giving you fair warning; we're going to commence excavation of the premises at three tomorrow morning. Without fail. We have a special permit from the buildings department."

"You lied," I say. "All of you lied. You said that confession was good for the soul and was equivalent to self-realization but you didn't see that it was merely levels of self-deceit. How can you gain confessions from people who have nothing inside?"

"That's an interesting point, Luther, but I really can't discuss theology, not now. I'm too much of an administrator these days although I do look forward to the contemplative life at some future date. The excavation will begin promptly at three a.m. and we are going to use dynamite."

"There's nothing inside them. Nothing at all. Just self-pity which can hardly be converted into anything else."

"It's unfortunate that we have to level the church, it's a fine old structure and there's a lot of nice architecture in it. Nevertheless, it's easiest and most efficient to simply get it out of the way. Are you listening, Luther?"

"It's all a lie."

"Are you referring to the dynamite or the church, Luther? If you're referring to the church you've got an interesting metaphysical speculation there which we'll really have to take up one of these days but if you're talking about the dynamite, that's another thing. It is most definitely real, Luther. It has to be done."

"You want me out, don't you?"

"Not so much anymore, not so much, Luther. On the other hand, fair warning is fair warning. The structure will begin to topple before dawn. It should be quite a mess if you're not out of there by then, son."

"Just like Apocalypse, is that right?"

"Oh, Luther," the Bishop says with a merry little cackle, "Luther, I think I'm beginning to understand your trouble now and really, my lad, it's too pitiful and sad. You take the whole thing so seriously. Maybe that's the reason you never took up the calling in the first place."

"You don't understand. I have plans—"

"If you hadn't taken it with such high seriousness you might have made an excellent priest. Oh, by the way, we found your Father Hilarion. I thought you'd like to know."

"Where is he? How is he?"

"Well, I'm afraid that that would become absurdly metaphysical again, Luther. We found Father Hilarion—or rather the state police found him—in a small ravine off exit fifteen of the New York State Thruway, about five miles east of Suffern. He's dead, Luther. I should point out that there was a most beatific expression upon his face and there was no evidence to indicate foul play. The police theory is that he was hitchhiking, was left off on the road by a car taking that exit, was unable to get another ride for some hours, despaired of his life and took some sleeping tablets. It's a theory with which I'm inclined to agree."

"That's terrible," I say, "that's tragic." I find that there is nothing more to say and for a few moments the Bishop and I exist in an almost amicable silence, dim clicking and whirs from the far reach of the telephone keyboard keeping us together. I search myself for some feeling but there really is very little; Father Hilarion is part of the whole pattern of culpability I have discovered and any man who would commit suicide because he is unable to get a ride should probably seek a rental-car agency. This is not the most generous of attitudes but on the other hand, there has been a Lutherian personality-switch recently and it is difficult to know what the younger or older Hilarion would have had to say.

"Well, it's one of those things," the Bishop says, not without remorse. "The whole parish has been a disaster for more years than you could remember and I simply couldn't go with it anymore. He really wasn't a very good priest, Luther, there were certain things in his background which really wrecked him. But why go into that now? I do hope you'll be out of here tonight, my son, otherwise, things could get most difficult. I know that Hilarion would have wanted you to leave."

"You lied," I say, "you all lied."

"Well, in a way that's true enough," the Bishop says cheerfully, "but after you consider the alternatives to lying for a while, Luther, you may begin to feel a lot more generous about the whole issue. If you have a chance to drop in and talk sometime in the future, do so. I'd be delighted to meet with you. But not for the next three weeks, please, I have important business to finish and then I'm taking a little flying trip."

"I don't understand," I say, "I simply don't understand," and on that it seems like as good a time to terminate the conversation as any so I hang up, thrust my assassin's hands into pockets and go for a last ruminative walk through the old sacristy, stopping at all those points which were Hilarion's favorite haunts, going into his study for a last look around, finally going to the altar and lighting for him a cautious last candle which flickers but refuses to stay on cue. I understand that I have no feeling whatsoever inside and that I am really looking for an attitude which will carry me through but no attitude seems satisfactory: it is hardly appropriate to cry for Hilarion (who for all I know misappropriated me from the great destiny that surely would have been mine had I been allowed to take my chances on the midway) but not to laugh for him either; no man I knew had a greater fear of death as manifested in an excessive attention to the minor details of life and he can hardly have been in optimum mental condition in order to have exited from life so meaninglessly but dramatically. Perhaps if my own hands had not been so compromised by recent activities, if I had not worn and discarded his very robes to commit my grotesque acts, I could generate more feeling than I now have but under the circumstances I feel that I am doing very well indeed to squeeze out a couple of rancid tears before the altar (but more in frustration for the candle than loss of Hilarion). Meanwhile there is the question of dynamite and ultimate destination, questions far more pressing than Hilarion's true reasons for his penultimate insanity. I give up the candle as a hopeless *causa*, mumble a few Latinisms and leave the church forever, returning to my rooms where I begin to pack. It is just the basics I take: toothbrush, mustache cup, changes of clothing, the revolver, a single Concordance and so on. I pack with growing facility and industry, my hands showing more skill than they ever have; in these humble actions (murder is a wonderful physical conditioner; it obviously tones up all of the motor skills) and since I am finally doing something well I decide to dedicate the very act of packing to Hilarion but already his simple, humble features are receding in memory and I am not sure what he looks like, cannot fixate him to pay proper respect and so must settle for the sense of his odor which I imagine to be enfolding me. In his odor I swoop and glide, sing *Hosanna in Excelsis* as I drop multicolored shirts into a valise, whisper simple rosaries to the ceiling and it is the closest I have gotten yet to Paying My Respects but in the middle of this charming if rather solitary scene the phone rings, quite jarring my mood and I pick it up unthinkingly, ready to tell the Buildings Department that if they dynamite me I will most certainly dynamite them back. Instead, however, it is Mrs. Lee, who comes across more warmly than she has so far.

"Luther," she says, "how are you?"

"Tired," I say, "and making other plans. They found Hilarion dead on the New York State Thruway."

"Oh, really? I'm so terribly sorry. You really admired him, didn't you?"

"No, I didn't really care for him at all I just discovered. But it was shocking."

"Of course it was. Luther? I heard from Mrs. Wilson just a little while ago about what you did and I wanted to tell you that I thought you were wonderful. I didn't misjudge you. You're a very courageous, warm, giving man, Luther, and I think that it was a wonderful thing that you did. Mrs. Wilson was just thrilled—"

"She didn't sound thrilled. She was goddamned arrogant and snide," I say, releasing the first vent of anger I have ever expressed toward my lovelies and how long it has been in coming! But the provocation, I do believe it has been demonstrated, is extreme.

"Oh, that's just her way, you shouldn't take her seriously. She has a tough exterior because she's just a little girl inside and so frightened; besides, you interrupted her right in the middle of a bridge meeting and she didn't know just what to say. But she was so happy, Luther! The bank called just a few minutes after you did and said that he had shot himself to death in cold blood and it was the most horrifying thing they had ever seen. The police had already come and gone and the doctor and everything. There isn't even going to be an investigation this time, isn't that something! You must have done a wonderful job."

"It was all right," I say, a prideful glow, despite all of my problems, enveloping me. "One gets more professional as one goes along of course."

"Well, of course. That stands to reason. Anyway, she was just delighted and she wanted me to call and thank you for her again because she's all tied up now with her psychiatrist and with relatives and so on and won't be able to talk for a while. Luther? Do you want to come over tomorrow?"

"What for?"

"Oh, for nothing," she says, rather coyly. "I mean, hope you're not mad at me or anything similar."

"Mad? At you?"

"It just had to be done. You're a charming man in so many ways but you don't have a sense of *situation*. Luther? Are you there?"

"I'm still there."

"Could you come over tomorrow morning at say nine or ten? Katherine will be out and I don't think that I'll have anything doing with the lawyers all day. I'd really like to see you."

"Katherine," I say. "What is this about Katherine? Why don't I ever meet her?"

"Do you want to?"

"Not particularly."

"Then why ask?"

"Oh, I don't know," I say, "I can't really answer that. I just feel that I'm in fairly close contact with your family now and I ought to meet all its members."

"You're cute, Luther," she says. "You play at one thing but you're really another, do you know that? You're something entirely different from what you think you are."

"No I'm not."

"Oh, yes you are, Luther. Now, will you come over tomorrow morning? I do want to see you and talk to you about a few things."

"I don't want any money. I didn't do it for money."

"I wasn't even thinking of offering you any. Now stop being silly and I'll look for you at nine tomorrow."

"The church. They're dynamiting the church."

"So they're dynamiting the church. I'm awfully sorry to hear about that and about your father but you really can't come over tonight. I mean, I'd love to have you and so on but it would look terribly suspicious and anyway I'm still in deep mourning. It hasn't even been probated yet."

"All right," I say. "Listen, all right. I hear you. I understand. I'll be over tomorrow, tomorrow at nine o'clock," and hang up before I can hear anything else because what has come over me is the dreadful feeling that if the conversation goes on even ten seconds more she will say something to me with which I simply cannot deal, something which will go far beyond my slender and humble means of coping and I know that I will not be able to take this. There is no way that I can come to terms, on this day, with one more revelation.

I finish packing. I put my notes in last of all and secure the valise. I clean out Hilarion's study in a neat series of brown paper bags which I put into the large garbage can which he had christened the *Magdalene* and left outside of the vestry for contributions or anything else. (This had been one of Hilarion's more inventive touches.) I check the kitchen, the dining room, the study, the two bedrooms one last time to make sure that everything is in order, inscribing it upon my brain in the same way that Harold's blood was inscribed upon my habit a few short hours ago. Everything seems to be in order. It is a pretty pallid, washed-out place for one which has absorbed so many of my energies for so many years, to say nothing of the sentiment involved.

I go to the door, take one last look back and then, going into the kitchen for the last time, I turn all the jets on the stove up to full after first having shut off the pilot lights. I then close the door to the kitchen, close the outer hallway door, close the outer door proper and go briskly down the walk, noting the drunks, the dope peddlers, the old ladies with shopping bags, etc., one last sentimental glance at the old neighborhood for Luther before he moves briskly to his Peugeot.

When the dynamite comes into contact with the sacrament which Luther has left, there is likely to be no old neighborhood at all. So Luther hopes. So Luther surmises, so Luther prognosticates, so Luther dreams as he moves toward his father's old car in the first twilight of a summer evening in Brownsville circa 1970 and if his gait is a bit unsteady, his step a little short, his posture a little ungainly, his steps a little reeling, let us, for God's sake, accept that in the spirit offered and let us, just this once, and for the next few moments, try to leave the poor bastard alone. He is getting old. He is getting older. Soon he would have been forty-six, four years short of fifty. Senescence and death would soon overtake him. Have pity. Have mercy. Leave him alone, see him rise slowly as the dusk takes him.

XIX

I spend the night in one of those "residential hotels" for which this area is so famed, sheltered between a Puerto Rican family of twelve who are living in the two rooms to my left and an eighty-five-year-old woman on the right who is occupying one. The Puerto Ricans become murderous toward midnight and begin to threaten one another, in perfect English, with knives and bullets, but the old lady has problems too: it seems that her water simply refuses to come to a boil for her tea and she devotes long hours (it seems like hours) to solemn fits of weeping. "It won't boil, it won't boil," she sobs, "and I so much wanted a spot of tea for me cold." The thoughtful lack of sound-proofing in the hotel enables me to pick up her complaint with stunning accuracy and it comes through in a rich English accent fortified by seeming alcoholism, "An old lady is entitled to her spot of *tigh*," the woman murmurs, "why won't this farkin' water bile for my Sparta *tigh*; the buns is gettin' all coold, oh love, please

boil the farkin' water for me," and so on and so forth until, long after
the time when the Puerto Ricans have all killed themselves and gone to
bed she remains murmuring over her tea which is still not at a drinkable
state, murmuring over her pot which is still useless. "Don't make no
farkin' sense," the woman says and, wrenching myself out of bed, I find
myself for the first time in weeks in exaggerated agreement with something. It does indeed make no sense: it is three in the morning (dynamite
hour the Lutherian souvenir watch from the midway shyly informs
him), lights are down all over the city and yet the farkin' water still will
not bile and, muttering and screaming softly to myself, I lurch from the
room and throw my body heavily against the adjoining door until small
scuffles and muttering within convince me that I have established some
kind of contact.

"Who is that?" deponent within saith and correspondent says, "I'm
here to bile your farkin' *water*," and the door is pulled open suddenly
to reveal an old, old lady, translucent in all the skin and veins, wearing
dark glasses and holding a movie magazine. "Crazy," she says, "what
kind of lunatics," and I say, "Madam, I just heard about the water and
I wanted to *bile* it for ye," and she says, "If I wanted bilin' I woulda asked
ye, I'm just talkin' to me cat," and with a strength unknown in all the
history of my dealing with old ladies she puts her small arms directly
against correspondent's faithful chest and pushes him from the room with
such force that he stumbles into the hallway and is reeling back into his
own premises before he quite knows what has happened to him.

"I don't understand this, I don't understand this," I moan but at least
there is no more dialogue with the water that night; instead the complaint
seems to shift against certain Hollywood celebrities, all of whom the lady
thinks to be "whores" and "slatterns" and the acts and possibilities of
one Tuesday Weld (who is Tuesday Weld?) quite possess her from the
hours of three forty-five to five; it seems that Tuesday Weld has not only
sullied her heritage but gone to bed with cats and dogs in the process and
this quite incites the old lady—if not to the degree that the pot has. It is
five o'clock finally when Tuesday Weld, along with some of her more
bizarre partners, passes dimly into recollection and stentorian sobs from
the adjoining cubicle indicate that faithful correspondent's roommate has
gone to sleep. At five-fifteen however, the Puerto Ricans begin to stir, quite
disconcerted, it seems, at the fact that those with whom they are sharing the room are still alive, and a lively dialogue begins.

It is at this point that I hastily redeem what clothing I have placed in
the closets and hastily leave the St. Withers Lounge & Custom Hotel in
downtown Brooklyn, not even waiting for the elevator (which would
probably not be functioning at this hour anyway) but instead clamber-

ing down seven flights and past the desk clerk who asks, "Did ye have a good sleep, laddy?" I tell him that I think I did not and the clerk then asks if that is the case why the fucks is I leaving daddy-o or something to this effect but by that time I am in the street, next to my humble Peugeot which is quite itself except for a missing hood, a smashed windshield and an obscenity painted in green over the left rear tire. I decide that this is all for the best (Hilarion would certainly have willed it to me but only as damaged goods) and get into it panting, toss my goods into the back seat and drive rapidly in the direction of upstate.

Halfway toward Atlantic Avenue I have a thought and cut out of my way, go up and down filthy gray avenues and corridors, through traffic lights and over the inert corpses of animals and arrive, at approximately six a.m., at the site of the church. For some moments I feel peculiarly disoriented; I know by all circumstances of direction and street sign that I am indubitably at my alma mater and yet the street has a subtly different aspect: where the church had hurled its humble outline into space there is only a large vacant lot dotted with rubble, shining with glass, through which the forms of errant animals seem to move, sniffing to the dawn. It takes me some minutes before the truth of it—your faithful correspondent is truly not very bright but consider the unusual strain! the turmoil! the march of history!—percolates inward; this is St. Bellow itself— or what was left of it—lying before me, the dynamite having worked with its usual superb efficiency or at any rate, not having entirely misfired. Seen in this way the church has more of a curiously religious aspect than I have ever otherwise noted; plaster figurines of saints can be distinguished, prayer books and scrolls, a cross or two and some ceremonial dress, even a few keys from the organ can all be discerned in the gathering sunlight and although it is almost certainly a hallucination or some kind of religious frenzy, I believe that I can vaguely hear the *Agnus Dei* being pumped from the background. Perversely, I wonder how Hilarion would have taken this and the revelation comes upon me almost blinding in that dawn: he would have liked it very much. It would have confirmed everything that he understood about the Church. He might not have had his thruway disaster if he knew that this sight was coming.

And it is at that moment too that I fully understand how Hilarion's last moments must have been: he stands on the thruway surrounded by heat and density, the whine and wicker of machinery passing him so close that his ankles fill and seem to wander in the sudden wind. Behind him flies scamper, a muskrat in the meadow, a hint of pall over a mountain but it is not the desiccation which fixates him but only the road: the road containing thousands of cars, the road which carries these cars, groaning with speed and repression toward him. He feels at this moment as if he were the last man on the Earth and that man is pinned between machinery and loss, speed and emptiness, waste and darkness, unable to find any accommodation between himself or between these qualities and as he raises a hesitant thumb yet again—he has been here for many hours now—he begins to understand that he will never get another ride on this road because the cars feel that he is part of the scenery. He is simply another element of the road, provided by the great thruway authority which in its beneficence donates reflectors, restrooms, snack bars and guard rails for its patrons, stinging crashes and the threat of terror; all of this the authority has provided and now they provide something else: that archaicism, a pedestrian. No one will ever stop for him because they are not sure that he exists. Hilarion understands this. He understands it as he has known nothing else in his life, even the Latin-isms of the Mass or the empty passion of the Divine. He thinks of snakes now, the massive twisting snake of the heavens, come past Adam's heel to some real meat and it is at this moment that casually, almost briskly, he steps into the road and is hit by a 1961 green Cadillac convertible, registration #3Y72151, driven by Mrs. Laurence K. Jenkins of Saratoga Springs, New York. And as Mrs. Jenkins screams, as Laurence Jenkins, age 64, screams, as Dorothy Jenkins, their daughter, aged 38, screams, as Grandmother Jenkins, 98, screams, Hilarion's body moves with terrible grace and clarity in the air, ascending, vaulting, flying, passing the guard rail at a hundred and ten and smashes soundless into the valley at an angle that causes limbs and appendages to fly, moving in solemn and careful procession toward the sun. Only a limpid Concordance, opened to the seven lesser sins, flapping wearily on the ground, would attest to the identity of the decedent.

XX

Despite all of this, I find myself whistling in the morning as I drive to the Lee residence. Two hours' restless sleep in a service area on the thruway have helped, so has a generous portion of the Winter Wonderland pancakes served up by the thruway concession, a splendid glittering residence which is rivalled only by the *Fiend* in decor and quality of the food. The service area is several miles north of the New England Thruway exit, compelling me to double around and return, during which return trip I am given a ticket by a dour state patrolman for driving a car without any hood and with an obscenity painted on one of the rear tires. I explain that I am related to the famous Hilarion who died in one of the most recent and exciting thruway disasters but this does not seem to move him. He belches unhappily. Perhaps thruway cops live in their service areas and take of no foods unprepared by the Winter Wonderland. This would go a long way toward explaining many things. I tear the ticket into shreds and pitch it singing out the window as soon as the patrolman's car has overtaken and passed me; I have no intention of continuing a life in which a traffic ticket will be of any consequence whatsoever; to be concerned with traffic tickets is to make some apprehension of the future in terms of Point Systems but I do not think that my prospects, strictly speaking, are quite so limited. I leave the Peugeot in gear and hobble up the steps of the Lee residence—due to the many hours I have been spending in the Peugeot recently, a bit of lower back syndrome has once again extruded as it never did during copulation—and knock confidently, smile at Melinda when she opens the door and brush magnificently past her. "Where's Mrs. Lee?" I say.

"She coming, she coming," she says. "Haven't seen you in a while."

"I been busy."

"You want to see me again?"

I look at her, admire the sheen of her color, the mystery of her flesh and say, "No, I don't think I do. It's nothing personal of course, but things have gotten complicated."

"I figured," she said. "That's probably for the best; I ain't got no use for you neither. She firin' me you know. Today's my last day. No severance or nothing. She says she's got other plans."

"That's too bad."

"She probably gonna fire you too so no sense acting so superior."

"You don't understand," I say, "our relationship is entirely different. It's more complicated."

"Complicated," she says, "the only thing you folks talk about is complication but I don't think you understand how simpleminded you are." And seizing a broom, walks away, leaving me to my thoughts which are neither long nor broad because Mrs. Lee enters immediately, stage right, and bestows upon me a light forehead-kiss. The whole thing has been so precisely stage-managed that I have the feeling for an instant that I am staggering through a very bad play, but knowing all about the sophistries of dissociative reaction I push this from my mind. "How are you, Luther?" she says. "Right on time."

"I try."

"Were you glad to see Melinda again? I'm letting her go you know but I held her over just for one more day so that you could meet her again. I thought that it would be nice if you could say goodbye."

"It means nothing. It meant nothing."

"Of *course* it meant nothing, Luther, that's precisely the point. I just want you to *know* that it meant nothing so that you don't get all sentimentally tied up and so on. Your whole old life was a fraud, you understand that now, don't you?"

"Oh, I suppose so," I say, "you've certainly given me some insights into it. But it was kind of fun."

"No, it wasn't. It was sick."

"It was sick but it was kind of fun. It's possible to have the two of them together you know."

"No, it isn't. If it's sick it's not any fun at all. You may think it's fun but that's because you're lying to yourself. Inside all you want to do is to get rid of the sickness."

"It was fun," I say with a curious insistence. "It *was*."

"No it wasn't and it wasn't fun for anyone else."

"It had its uses," I say, "and it was *so* fun. It had everything that a lot of things don't. I'm not saying that it was good or that I could go back to it but it was fun."

"No it wasn't, it wasn't at all."

"Yes it was," I say, overcome by a curious stubbornness and we look at each other for a moment; her head rises and I see hatred in her eyes and I begin to understand that Mrs. Lee's behavior toward me throughout has not been totally composed of altruism. In fact it is quite a bit more than that I sense; I gasp, reel and turn around, lose my balance instead and fall into the familiar-but-hideous couch and in an instant she is over to me, cradling my head in her arms. "Oh, forgive me, Luther," she says, "forgive me. I didn't mean to fight. It's just that I want you so badly to be happy."

"All right. All right."

"And that's why I sometimes get stubborn but I don't mean to be, Luther, now just relax and please don't get sick again because I don't think that I could stand it and Melinda absolutely refused to ever do a cleanup job like that again. I'm sorry for saying that your old life was sick, if you say it wasn't then maybe it wasn't, but—"

"It was sick. It was sick but it was fun."

"All right, it was fun, it was fun, Luther, just relax now, take it easy, take it easy, baby," and draws me into her breasts. I feel their warmth and closeness although with no particular lunge of sexuality and she rubs the back of my neck and talks to me meaninglessly for a time about buys and skies and flies, finally pushing me away gently and saying, "Do you feel better now?"

"I'm all right."

"Because I really want to talk to you but if you're still not feeling well and you want to rest a bit—"

"No," I say, "I'm all right. I'm out of the rectory."

"Hmm? Hah? Oh, you mean that church, that horrible place where you live with that priest of yours. The one who you told me was killed. Well, that's probably all for the best; that isn't a very nice place for any normal man to live who's interested in women."

"I don't quite know where to go, though."

"Oh, well," she says vaguely, "we can work something out. There are lots of very nice rooming houses all through the area and I'm sure that you can find something although Rye is zoned out of rooming houses and I don't want you staying here. You feel well enough to talk?"

"I'm all right," I say, grunting, heaving myself up on the couch, "of course I didn't think that I was coming up here just to talk."

"Well, what did you think, Luther?" she says and laughs and then her expression changes and she crumbles and says, "Look, look, I didn't mean to hurt you, it's just that with what I've been going through I just won't be interested in sex for a while. You can't understand that, being a man, but women are more sensitive, more delicate, they have more complicated emotional equipment—"

"It wasn't just sex."

"Subtler glands and on top of that they think of things other than sex while having sex; there's no way that a man can understand that. No, Luther, that can't be for a while, of course in time these things will smooth out and then who knows? Besides, I'm surprised at you, being interested in sex. What I did should have taken care of you—"

"I said it wasn't just sex."

"No, we have to talk, Luther." She goes to a corner of the living room, fishes in a chair for something, comes out with a piece of paper and carries it slowly toward me. "This is what I wanted to talk about, Luther."

"That paper?"

"Yes."

"Well, what is it?"

Suddenly shy, even demure, she clasps it behind her back and says, "Well, it's kind of special. I don't quite know how to put it." She smiles again, winks, blushes slightly; I begin to see how she must have looked to the Alpha Beta Rho chapter freshman in, say, 1955 and it is a disconcerting sensation even though I am not that chairman. (Harold, however, was, I suspect.) "Well," she says, "you see, I have lots of friends."

"I don't."

"Well, you're a solitary man. My dearest friend is Mrs. Wilson of course and I just had to tell her first of the wonderful thing you did for me. We've known each other for five years and we're really terribly close. But I have lots of other friends too, some of them were over the day you called and—"

"What is it?" your old correspondent asked, feeling in the place above his upper lip where once his splendid mustache had rested. Had the mustache been the key to his power and its elimination the end of it? It was something to think about. Hilarion would have drawn thundering parallels to Samson although this silly allegory otherwise embodied everything which he found to be repellent about religion. "What is it?"

"Well," she says, "well, all right, I'll come right to the point, I don't know how to put this so I'll be direct." For the first time, Mrs. Lee is slightly off her pace but there is no way that your correspondent can take advantage of this since your correspondent—oh cursed prognostication!—already senses the drift and is so stunned that he can only gulp fish-like as she proceeds.

"Well, Luther," she says, handing me the paper, "I have a lot of friends, this isn't all of them but it's fifteen. My fifteen next closest. All of them were so thrilled at what you did for me and Mrs. Wilson and how you were able to save our lives and give us a second chance and so on that they all want you to do the same thing for them. And what's more important, Luther, *I* want you to do it. They deserve the same chance that we had; just because I was fortunate enough to meet you first doesn't mean that I should be the *only* one favored. I tell you, they're all entitled. They have a right to it! Anyway, this paper has all the information, the names of the husbands and the addresses where they work and special comments about their habits and so on and all you have to do is just to go right down the line and check them off. It shouldn't take you more than a week to do all of them and we'd really appreciate it being a fast job so that we can get the alibis prepared and out of the way. You *will* do it! I can tell by your face! You're starting to smile. Oh, that's wonderful of you, I knew that you would but some of my friends said they didn't have any faith in you and you were probably just another inefficient suburban handyman. We'll show them, won't we?"

"Sure I'll do it," I say, taking the paper from her, folding it neatly and putting it in my breast pocket. "That's what you want me to do, isn't it?"

"Of course it is. I mean, you should want to do it too, it should be for *yourself*—"

"That's not what I asked. I asked if you wanted me to do it."

"I would really appreciate it, Luther. It would mean a great deal to me if you would."

"Are they paying you anything?"

"Me? Oh, just a little percentage of the insurance. Nothing really. I'll negotiate for you, Luther. I think that five hundred dollars apiece is about right. That's almost ten thousand dollars if you take care of all of the names here and of course with the five from Mrs. Wilson you'll have enough to really make a start in life! You'll have a nice place to live and you'll even be able to get a nice car."

"I'm not in this for the money, you understand," I say. "I mean, no one would possibly get into this for the money."

"I know that, Luther, and I know that you really got into it for me," she says and sidles close, rubs her head against my shoulder, trails her fingers in my neck, even places the most delicate of kisses against my cheek, "I know that, dear, and I'm very moved by it but you can't exist just for one person forever, you've got to go beyond that and begin to act for yourself. They're suffering, Luther, all of them suffering so terribly—"

"I didn't do it for you either. Not completely."

"Nevertheless," she says, putting her hand in my pocket and running it sensuously over the paper therein, "nevertheless, it has to be done. You understand that, don't you? I mean, this kind of thing simply can't go on. It's got to come to an end."

"I'll do it," I say, "you know I'll do it."

"That's wonderful of you. I know that we'll always appreciate—"

"But it isn't for the reasons you think it is," I say rather obscurely, moving away from her. She lets me go and I scuttle backwards into a wall, then weave and wander forwards, "It's for something else."

"Whatever you say, dear,"

"Do you want me to get started now?"

"Oh, I leave that up to you. It should be done fairly soon, I think. If all of this happens fast it'll just look like a terrible fiend is killing all the husbands and there will be sympathy—"

"I'm not a fiend," I say, "I'm not."

"I didn't say you *were*. I only said—"

"No," I say, "I take that back. I am a fiend. But it's more complicated than you think it is. The whole thing is complicated. If it weren't like this it would only get fouled up in another way."

"Don't be so pessimistic, Luther, it isn't that bad."

"Do you need me for anything else? Or should I just go on my way now and do what has to be done?"

"Well," she says, adjusting her dress and looking out the window, "I always love to see you, you know that but—"

"You want me to go now."

"Katherine and I will be taking a little trip. My doctor thinks that it be best if I get away from all this for a month or so. We'll probably be leaving tomorrow or the next day. But when we're home you can call me anytime and we'll get together. I think we're going to go to Europe but I'm not sure about that. There's so much to be done. I've never had a chance to get involved with life, to really see things."

"All right," I say, going to the door and standing there, looking at her. From this distance she is simply a woman, nothing else, a little more sensual than most of her age but nothing remarkable. In the park I would give her three glances but never a fourth; in my bed I would make pictures behind my eyes of her for only a few moments before turning on to other pastimes. Nevertheless, she has had a stunning effect upon me far beyond her resources; I know I will have to consider this. "Goodbye," I say.

"You're not mad at me or anything are you? I mean, I don't want to seem abrupt."

"No," I say, "that's all right."

Melinda re-enters as if on cue, wearing a coat and carrying a small valise in her left hand. "You supposed to give me a ride to the station," she says. "She told me that."

"Yes, Luther, would you? This is Melinda's last day and she's leaving early. I'd really appreciate it if you'd take her to the station or something," and Mrs. Lee then bestows upon me a horrid and fulsome wink. I understand that she is giving Melinda to me as it were, as some indication of my station and although I wish I could appreciate this, the fact is that I cannot. "Just to the station," I say. Melinda comes to me, we stand in a curiously formal pause at the door for a minute and then Melinda opens it behind me and the two of us go out into the day. Mrs. Lee comes to the door, stands there, waves our way down the walk and my last glance at her is a very satisfying one. I know that I will remember her that way forever; framed in the door she has the curious archaic look of a Restoration painting (or maybe I am thinking of mid-Victorian)—her features suffused with light, her eyes dark and knowledgeable—and I wave back to her tenderly, entertaining a feeling for her at a distance that I never could in the real and then assist Melinda into the hood-less Peugeot, check to see that the list is still in my pocket and then go on to the driver's side.

"You want to go anywhere?" she says and settles back on the seat.

I look back at her with only the slightest sensual interest and say, "I do. I have many places to go. But I'm going to drop you right off at the station. That part of my life is finished, do you understand that?"

"If you say so," she says and giggles and wipes moisture from her forehead and we go off toward the train station where I leave her without another word, knowing as I drive away that she is looking at me but not returning that fixating gaze which if only given a chance, I understand, would pin me to the spot, fluttering like an insect, against the mumble of the train come from the East to spirit me away.

XXI

I become, then, fully *engagé*.

At this point, things seem to go slightly out of focus and it is difficult to recapitulate the events of the next few hours or days with that cold, hard precision which has characterized these notes to date. I believe that I can be forgiven this: I am under a great deal of emotional strain and in the bargain chronology, organization, structure, stenographic resource, no longer interest me. Who cares about order? Who needs progression? What the hell is the difference: it all comes down in the end to lovely slaughter, appalling murder, screams against the wall.

Slaughter! Murder! My recollections become a chiaroscuro of montage and the montage always involves Harold: Harold is looking at me groaning, pain coming from his fishlike eyes, Harold is lying on the floor flopping like a landed shark, Harold is backing from me, a terrible knowledge coming into his dull face and saying "No, no, no," Harold holds onto me as he slips to the floor groaning, Harold hurls himself at me but—

Harold! Harold! Referring only intermittently to the slip of paper in order that I may be localized for time, place and person, I go about my cheerless task immediately and with a kind of efficiency which I have never otherwise demonstrated, even in the Playlands, even in the bedrooms of western New England. I perform my tasks methodically in an orgy of slaughter, moving from one office to the next, doing it in anterooms, even in a restaurant or two (but never in the *Fiend*: Harold takes his lunches usually at some elevation) and then making my stumbling graceless exit, gun smoking, eyes burning, bullets popping. Waitresses scatter for me, likewise receptionists, secretaries, editorial assistants, chambermaids, prostitutes and so on. If I had discovered the simple levelling effect of the gun upon women (and men too, alas) years ago I would not have been driven to subterfuge. Murder!

—Harold looks at me, chest heaving and says, "Why did you do it? I was just beginning to get somewhere in my profession and now you make me feel that the MBA was worthless. I could have saved the money and gone right to work—"

—Harold embraces me in death grip and says, "I couldn't stand it you know, I couldn't take any of this much longer, you've really done me a favor—"

—Harold hugs himself, shrinking on the floor and says, "Oh, son of a bitch, I let the double-indemnity lapse."

—Harold flees at great speed in the restaurant, dodging waiters and dishes, screaming, but I catch him with a good shot in his glowing scalp and he falls heavily amidst a stack of the *fruit du jour*, groaning; grapefruits and melons sag and run oozing down his head. "I knew I shouldn't have come to one of these places," he said, "I should have stayed with luncheonettes. For that matter, I was never so happy as when I carried a brown paper bag."

—Harold looks at me moistly, weeping. "You poor bastard," he says, "she put you up to it. You must really take her seriously to have gone this far. I pity you," he says, "I truly pity you."

—"Well, that's the end of the college education," Harold says and expires, flopping on the table of the board room. "They'll have to either go to work or attend a municipal university."

—Dying, Harold motions for me to come nearer to him; I lean over and he touches my cheek in a gesture as delicate as any I have ever known. "I wanted to touch someone," he says, "I haven't touched someone for years."

And so on and so forth, an active and busy day which I later understand to be labelled in the newspapers as the *Rampage of the Century* although they simply did not understand that I merely do my work by my own lights and hope for the best. In that arena, surrounded by Harold, I do what I must, shooting and maiming and killing until finally all of the lights go out and when I come back to myself I am in the darkness of a cell somewhere and only the tapping of a guard's feet in the distance indicate that on its own terms, the world is still willing to deal with me.

XXII

Because of course they do catch me, catch me fleeing up Park Place with the very smoke of murder still coming crisply from my weapon. Ten of them, fifty of them: patrol cars, sirens, an ocean of the deepest blue surround me, pin me against a wall, talk to me soothingly as they break my wrist and take the gun, then put me into an embrace as tight as ropes and hustle me into an enclosure. "You're a fiend, do you know that?" one of them says to me. "You're crazy. You're crazy."

"By whose lights?" I say but they whisk me away from there and into another place with many lights and bluish carpentry (my recollections become blurred) and there we talk for a while, "Why?" they say, taking my fingerprints and shining a light with tender concern into my eyes at a distance of three inches. "Why did you do it? Why?" and I feel the poignancy of their confusion, the true sadness of their puzzlement and do not answer "It is a mystery," which would be my inclination. I say only, "Because the whole thing had to be cleaned out." "Cleaned out?" they say, "cleaned out for what?" "Why not?" I say, thinking of Hilarion's conundrums and eventually they leave me alone after having me sign a large number of papers in the presence of a well-dressed man who says that he is my "lawyer" and he will "save" me. I am then taken upstairs many flights and put into this very fine cell from which I can contemplate all of the city or at least that part of the city which falls within my modest purview. Now and then a clanging below indicates that some kind of routine is being observed: I concentrate rather on the doings on the streets below which are always interesting, overlooking as this window does, a small park which seems to be full of all kinds of people possessed of the most unusual energy. "To clean the whole thing out," I mumble now and then to remind myself that I remain rational (at the root) and that I had my reasons. "I mean, it had to be cleaned out," I explicate, "I mean, this kind of thing just can't go on and on without any comment at all." I wonder if I am trying to make a confession but decide that if so there is certainly no one who could take it, not at the level which I want to enact anyway.

"To clean it all out," your correspondent mumbles, "and to restore the freshness of desire. Desire, redemption, possibility and hope!" And so on. Dinner is apparently served from the *Fiend* itself and I sip coffee and eat biscuits meditatively, wondering if the decor in that restaurant changes weekly or whether they simply respond to important public events as they see fit.

Now they are having a rally on the green. With marvelous perception, with focused vision, I can see them. Women, surrounded by a large throng of confused or admiring men, are parading in a circle on the grass. They carry signs and shout. The shouts filter dimly up to me and I cannot quite catch the words but the signs are explicit: GIVE US OUR RIGHTS, GIVE US CONTROL OF OUR BODIES, CHAUVINIST MALE STALLIONS, UP THE OPPRESSORS, FREE ABORTIONS, EQUAL EMPLOYABILITY, and so on. Curses wind their way up here although they do not retain their original form. "Luck!" they seem to be shrieking, "luck the ball! Luck pen! Bastard oppressive mine! Luck, luck, luck!"

Luck I murmur, and return to my dinner, now stale but still tasty. Power to the people! I find myself saying. Control of their bodies! Freedom and unity! Sexism deplored! These slogans give me comfort—because I agree in principle with everything that they are saying—and in due course they woo me into sleep; I lie sprawled on the floor casually dreaming while the cars on Hilarion's Thruway rise in their power to dismember me, limbs floating from their windows like sausages, the sound of feminine laughter in the breeze as the cars then dwindle toward all the Winter Wonderlands of the night, dreams, death, and the first of all the caresses of Knowledge. Known again and again *kyrie eleison* and for all the Harolds, the Revolution.

THE END

After the Fall

BARRY N. MALZBERG

Two novels of course but bound as one and it could be argued that they are a single novel: the hidden surge of darkness, the bleak and destructive machinery of our country's history and function are anatomized in these two works which prowl through the wreckage to roughly the same outcome. That outcome is the assertion that the decor, the tumble and distraction, the sheer complexity of technology and wealth of misdirection can keep that buried life at bay but only for a while. Eventually it overwhelms. Hilarion's religious counsel cannot suppress the outrage of his adopted son. All of the subterranean ugliness and intricate conspiracy holding *Lady of a Thousand Sorrows* in place can, at last, no longer repel the truth. "My God, they have killed my husband!... "I am not going to change this dress... I want them to see what they have done to him." The oath in the plane. The blood and roses.

Confessions was written in 1970, it is still an early novel, my twenty-fifth or so but an outcome of that early and illusory sense of command which sustains the illusions of the still formative novelist. *Lady*, written only six years (and about 40 novels) further on is representative of a different constituency, it is a very late novel. Clearly at the end of a long passage through obsession which had driven the writer into a wall, it is a novel of culmination masked as explanation. It induces at least a psychic nausea when I take a look at it. *Confessions* at least leaves the possibility that an outraged and outrageous screw conducted in the terrain of Cheever's country might at least suggest an agenda for rebellion. *Lady of a Thousand Sorrows* offers no such illusion. The Republic may still stand but it is empty of all but desire and desire untethered is another form of apocalypse.

There is this about *Lady*: it seems page by page to possess a horrid plausibility. Dean Koontz and I were close friends four decades ago and he read the manuscript. "You read this and it all seems crazy, unbelievable, but what came over me is the feeling *that it could have been exactly this way*. He was referring to the overheard conversation in which step-by-step the conspiracy is laid out (in a restaurant!) and then detonated. "Thinking that this is all crazy is about the only defense you have against that plausibility" Dean did not add but I am going to attribute the line to my old lost friend anyway, because what the hell, that is what he meant and if he did not mean it, well the *Lady of a Thousand Sorrows* did not mean to be in an affair which overturned the world and destroyed the polity. The review in *Publisher's Weekly* was murderous. Those who have or will read this new edition over four decades later and have some historical grasp on the year 1968 will know why. I should have known this would happen. My editor at the Playboy Press probably did, being in full retreat from the work before the advance check had cleared. Great editors learn early to bury their mistakes. Editors who do not know this become adjunct professors or go back for Master of Business Administration degrees.

Confessions is about another kind of ruination. My protagonist here is almost jolly in his gloom (a familiar Cheever characteriological construct and this novel was meant to be a pastiche of that placidly terrifying writer) and as the adopted son of Hilarion is not unfamiliar with hilarity. The inception of this novel afforded me an experience I have never duplicated: at Rye Playland in January of 1970 with my wife and four-year-old daughter, seated on the Boardwalk, staring at a shabby ferris wheel in the distance, my mind was taken over by an alien very much like Hal Clement's adolescent fellow in *Needle*, the alien in this case being this novel in its entirety. Characters, plot, key scenes, the bedroom dialogues, the line Harold speaks just before he is shot ("I've been dead for years already!") all were there in an instant, blinding flash as the cartoonists like to caption. The final scene—the feminists' furious demonstration in the streets surrounding Harold's jail cell—was there in the strictest frieze, the cries, the angst, the rebellion, the ladies' stricken, divided souls. All I had to do was write it. Mozart—I hasten to note early and often that I am no Mozart—referred to some of his compositions as having emerged "like taking dictation." That is how *Confessions* went. (*Underlay* too. But that was a different horse.)

Confessions, like its successor, met a quick and horrid death. The Olympia Press was rapidly spiraling down the toilet of Girodiasian Kharma by that time and it would be only a few years before a bankrupt and wholly chastened Maurice was scuttling back to France where over the next decade and a half the comic and tragic odyssey drew a few laughs from a near-empty gallery. The novel was probably the least erotic (let alone pornographic) work which the Olympia Press ever published with the arguable exception of *Lolita* which certainly was campaigning in races far above the $3500 maiden claimers in which Hilarion's offspring was forced to run. I think it is pretty good, quite remarkable in fact for that 32-year-old fat kid who later in the year was to produce *Un-*

derlay but my ideal reader, the person I most wanted to see the book certainly never saw it and would have quailed if it had shown, unbidden, in his mail. Still, I think that if he had been bribed into reading John Cheever would not have minded much. As posthumous catalogues have revealed, Cheever had nothing against outrage or transgression (as long as it could be kept out of Ossining). The author of "The Jewels of the Cabots" or "The Death of Justina" would have gotten the joke.

I got the joke too, kind of, and persisted in writing science fiction, then more science fiction, then the criminous novels with Pronzini which failed at their intended bestsellerdom but unlike the two novels at issue were able to stay out of the deadly undercurrents. Undercurrents and rip tides for these two but Stark House, a lifeguard unborn in the 70s and possibly too late now is bravely attempting rescue. Somewhere in these novels is the true and final explanation of how we have gotten ourselves into the mortal hell we now know as the "Republic" and if I can find it I will be glad to share. That is the novelist's unwanted, unneeded, too often contemptible mission.

New Jersey: December 2017

BARRY N. MALZBERG BIBLIOGRAPHY

FICTION (as either Barry or
Barry N. Malzberg)

Oracle of the Thousand Hands
(1968)
Screen (1968)
Confessions of Westchester
County (1970)
The Spread (1971)
In My Parents' Bedroom (1971)
The Falling Astronauts (1971)
Everything Happened to Susan
(1972)
The Masochist (1972)
Horizontal Woman (1972;
reprinted as The Social Worker,
1973)
Overlay (1972)
Revelations (1972)
Herovit's World (1973)
In the Enclosure (1973)
The Men Inside (1973)
Phase IV (1973; novelization
based on a story & screenplay
by Mayo Simon)
The Day of the Burning (1974)
The Tactics of Conquest (1974)
Underlay (1974)
Beyond Apollo (1974)
The Destruction of the Temple
(1974)
Guernica Night (1974)
On a Planet Alien (1974)
Out from Ganymede (1974;
stories)
The Sodom and Gomorrah
Business (1974)
The Best of Barry N. Malzberg
(1975; stories)

The Many Worlds of Barry
Malzberg (1975; stories)
Galaxies (1975)
The Gamesman (1975)
Down Here in the Dream
Quarter (1976; stories)
Scop (1976)
The Last Transaction (1977)
Chorale (1978)
Malzberg at Large (1979; stories)
The Man Who Loved the
Midnight Lady (1980; stories)
The Cross of Fire (1982)
The Remaking of Sigmund Freud
(1985)
In the Stone House (2000;
stories)
Shiva and Other Stories (2001;
stories)
The Passage of the Light: The
Recursive Science Fiction of
Barry N. Malzberg (2004; ed.
by Tony Lewis & Mike
Resnick; stories)
The Very Best of Barry N.
Malzberg (2013; stories)

With Bill Pronzini

The Running of the Beasts
(1976)
Acts of Mercy (1977)
Prose Bowl (1980)
Night Screams (1981)
Problems Solved (2003; stories)
On Account of Darkness and
Other SF Stories (2004; stories)

As Mike Barry

Lone Wolf series:
Night Raider (1973)
Bay Prowler (1973)
Boston Avenger (1973)
Desert Stalker (1974)
Havana Hit (1974)
Chicago Slaughter (1974)
Peruvian Nightmare (1974)
Los Angeles Holocaust (1974)
Miami Marauder (1974)
Harlem Showdown (1975)
Detroit Massacre (1975)
Phoenix Inferno (1975)
The Killing Run (1975)
Philadelphia Blow-Up (1975)

As Francine di Natale

The Circle (1969)

As Claudine Dumas

The Confessions of a Parisian
  Chambermaid (1969)

As Mel Johnson/M. L. Johnson

Love Doll (1967; with The Sex
  Pros by Orrie Hitt)
I, Lesbian (1968)
Just Ask (1968; with Playgirl by
  Lou Craig)
Instant Sex (1968)
Chained (1968; with Master of
  Women by March Hastings &
  Love Captive by Dallas Mayo)
Kiss and Run (1968)

Nympho Nurse (1969; with
  Young and Eager by Jim
  Conroy & Quickie by Gene
  Evans)
The Sadist (1969)
The Box (1969)
Do It To Me (1969)
Born to Give (1969; with Swap
  Club by Greg Hamilton &
  Wild in Bed by Dirk Malloy)
Campus Doll (1969; with High
  School Stud by Robert Hadley)
A Way With All Maidens (1969)

As Howard Lee

Kung Fu #1: The Way of the
  Tiger, the Sign of the Dragon

As Lee W. Mason

Lady of a Thousand Sorrows
  (1977)

As K. M. O'Donnell

Empty People (1969)
The Final War and Other
  Fantasies (1969; stories)
Dwellers of the Deep (1970)
Gather at the Hall of the Planets
  (1971)
In the Pocket and Other S-F
  Stories (1971; stories)
Universe Day (1971; stories)

As Elliot B. Reston

The Womanizer (1972)

As Gerrold Watkins

Art of the Fugue (1970)
A Bed of Money (1970)
Giving It Away (1970)
A Satyr's Romance (1970)
Southern Comfort (1972)

NON-FICTION/ESSAYS

The Engines of the Night:
   Science Fiction in the Eighties
   (1982; essays)
Breakfast in the Ruins (2007;
   essays: expansion of Engines of
   the Night)
The Business of Science Fiction:
   Two Insiders Discuss Writing
   and Publishing (2010; with
   Mike Resnick)

EDITED ANTHOLOGIES

Final Stage (1974; with Edward
   L. Ferman)
Arena (1976; with Edward L.
   Ferman)
Graven Images (1977; with
   Edward L. Ferman)

Dark Sins, Dark Dreams (1978;
   with Bill Pronzini)
The End of Summer: SF in the
   Fifties (1979; with Bill
   Pronzini)
Shared Tomorrows: Science
   Fiction in Collaboration (1979;
   with Bill Pronzini)
Neglected Visions (1979; with
   Martin H. Greenberg & Joseph
   D. Olander)
Bug-Eyed Monsters (1980; with
   Bill Pronzini)
The Science Fiction of Mark
   Clifton (1980; with Martin H.
   Greenberg)
The Arbor House Treasury of
   Horror & the Supernatural
   (1981; with Bill Pronzini &
   Martin H. Greenberg)
The Science Fiction of Kris
   Neville (1984; with Martin H.
   Greenberg)
Uncollected Stars (1986; with
   Piers Anthony, Martin H.
   Greenberg & Charles G.
   Waugh)
The Best Time Travel Stories of
   All Time (2003)